THE
GAME

SCOTT KERSHAW

ONE PLACE. MANY STORIES

HQ
An imprint of HarperCollins*Publishers* Ltd
1 London Bridge Street
London SE1 9GF

www.harpercollins.co.uk

HarperCollins*Publishers*
Macken House, 39/40 Mayor Street Upper,
Dublin 1, D01 C9W8, Ireland

This edition 2023

1
First published in Great Britain by
HQ, an imprint of HarperCollins*Publishers* Ltd 2022

Copyright © Scott Kershaw 2022

Scott Kershaw asserts the moral right to be identified as the author of this work. A catalogue record for this book is available from the British Library.

ISBN: 9780008531621

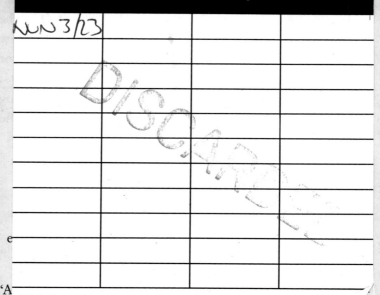

d intrigue
nale'

'Chilling and original... with an explosive
ending you'll never see coming'
Stephanie DeCarolis

'A cracking concept with a killer sting in the tale'
Lizzie Fry

Scott Kershaw lives in Lincolnshire, in a Victorian cottage that was formerly ruled by mice. He likes the crackle of vinyl, the smell of paperbacks, the taste of a stiff drink and the view from a front-row barrier. He's getting too old and heavy for crowd-surfing, but that rarely stops him from trying. His first real love was cinema. His beagle, Darwin, is the one true king of dogs. As a child, Scott believed in monsters. Sometimes he still does. *The Game* is his debut thriller.

For my family

LEVEL ONE

1

PLAYER ONE

Just past sunrise, pallid light pours in freely through a broken window onto every parent's worst nightmare: the bed is empty, the child gone.

Maggie Dawson is standing in the bedroom doorway paralysed, trying to process the scene. Her eyes go from the tousled bedsheets to the shattered window, to her little boy's blanket on the fire escape outside. Her legs are heavy, lungs too small. She drops his breakfast, Pop-Tarts falling, and when air finally returns she can barely scream his name.

'Jackson!'

The room is so cold there is frost on the carpet. Maggie stumbles forward, bare feet treading glass, and then hesitates at the window, too terrified to look, her thoughts a siren, a wailing litany:

He fell, oh Jesus Christ he fell, he's down there on the ground, sometime in the night, he fell, he's hurt, he's dead, he fell, he's—

Outside is the wrought-iron fire escape, one of those zig-zagging staircases you see on mid-rise apartment buildings all across the States. Maggie lives on the highest floor, five storeys up; even the fresh snowfall wouldn't have done much to cushion a fall. She wants to close her eyes, to turn away, but she has to see. Through the cracks between her fingers she glances down, holding her breath.

No Jackson. No tracks in the snow. Nothing.

Just his Spider-Man blanket caught up on the handrail, the fabric frozen stiff as if he wet it in the night.

Has he run away from her? Would he do that? Last night's forecast was for twenty below freezing. A grown man couldn't cross the city in that, let alone a boy. *Her* boy. Her son.

She focuses on the window: shards on the floor, broken inwards. A heavy gust might have done that, or something to do with ice; fluctuations in temperature? She has to get her head together. This is Saint Paul, for Christ's sake. The land of Minnesota Nice. It isn't Mexico or Venezuela or Brazil. Children don't just vanish here. Do they?

Her palms slap the pockets of her flannel dressing gown and come up empty. Sprinting back through the flat, she finds her phone charging beside the sofa where she woke up only minutes ago. There's something onscreen: a text message. Without pausing to read it, she dials.

'911, what's the address of the emergency?'

'My son! My son is gone! I-I think—' The words are heavy. Choking. Impossible. 'Somebody took him! Somebody took my boy!'

The voice on dispatch is firm, trained. 'Can you give me the address?'

'Apartment 13, Laurel Flats, Western Avenue North.'

4

'OK.' The clicking of keys. 'A car is on the way. How old is your son?'

'Eight. I went into the room and he's just … He's just *gone*!'

'What's your name?'

'M-Maggie. Margaret Dawson.'

'How old are you, Maggie?'

'Twenty-four. No, twenty-five.'

'Are you alone?'

'Yes.'

'Is the apartment secure?'

'The window in his room, it looks as if it's been broken from outside.'

The rest of this conversation is hurried and indistinct. Did she see anything? No. Did she hear anything? No. The woman tells Maggie not to touch anything. She tells her to wait.

Help is coming.

Maggie hangs up and tries to steady her lungs. Breathe. She looks around the living room. An empty Southern Comfort bottle by the sofa. It was only half full to begin with, but it paints a lousy picture. The roach of a single joint is lying like a dead bug inside the bottle. Just enough to help her sleep, she'd told herself. Enough to pass out on the couch and sleep through anything. God, she wishes she could wake up from this nightmare.

She snatches up the bottle, the last of the weed, the papers and the lighter, and stuffs them all into a grocery bag. Then she bursts out of her apartment and drops the bag into the chute at the end of the fifth-floor corridor. From somewhere far below, she hears the contents crunch. Her head is light. Turning back, she sees slick, bloody footprints leading from the front door. The glass in her feet. 'Fuck!'

Tears finally come as she hurries back inside for paper towels. All she needs now is for the cops to find her mopping up blood by the rubbish chute. Way to go, Maggie. Who ever said you were irresponsible? She checks her phone before making it to the kitchenette, to see how many minutes have passed.

Only now does she pay attention to the notification onscreen.

She opens the text message, stopping dead, and reads. It isn't long, but it takes her a while, as if the words are composed of another language altogether. They aren't. Concise, clear, cutting, their simplicity is chilling. She gets to the end and starts again. Twice.

There's a photograph attached. She downloads the image. It's hard to take in.

She drops to her knees. She is surely having a heart attack.

*

Moments later, the phone is back against her ear.

This time it's a man. '911, what's the address of the emergency?'

'I-I just called about my son,' she croaks. 'He's—'

'What's the address?'

'Western Avenue North.'

'Western North …' Tapping keys. A casual sniff. 'Are you Maggie?'

'Yes.'

'You reported your child missing?'

'Y-yes, but—'

'Officers are on the way, they should be there in—'

'I found him!' She says it so fast it sounds like a scream.

'You found your son?'

'Yes.' She can't quite believe what she's saying. If she hangs up now, the help will arrive. There'll be sirens. Uniforms. Guns. But they'd never find Jackson alive. The message she just read was simple. The photograph speaks for itself. The rules are clear.

'He was hiding,' she hears herself whisper. 'A prank.'

'It says here that you reported a broken window on the premises.'

'I panicked. It's open, that's all. The room was cold. So cold …'

For a while, the man is silent. Silence is bad. In her mind, Maggie can already hear this atrocity being played back on the evening news.

'OK, Maggie,' he says. 'You sound as if you're in shock. I'm going to let our officers proceed as planned, and—'

'No!' She's close to hysterics. 'Can't you hear what I'm telling you? He's fine! I don't need them here!'

'Ma'am.' Just like that, the tone has somehow changed. 'I need you to remain calm and stay right where you are. The officers are only two minutes away. If you need any—'

She hangs up. Her thumb does it for her, her body working faster than her brain.

Two minutes away. Two minutes. She needs to move. *Now*.

One more glance at the image on her phone – the photograph of her boy – is enough to get her going.

She yanks a pair of red high-tops onto her feet, bursts out of her apartment and hurtles past the bloody footprints and down the staircase through the belly of the building.

One minute.

She runs out into the snow in her dressing gown and underwear, with nothing but her phone in her hand. Her son has been taken, the police are almost here, and yet Maggie Dawson is fleeing the scene.

It's a little past eight o'clock on a January morning.

The Game has just begun.

2

PLAYER TWO

Brett Palmer feels like he's the only black man in the arena; it's a strange, discomforting sensation that he hasn't felt for a long time, this impression of being the odd one out, or simply odd, and he can't seem to shake it.

He mentions this to Craig as they manoeuvre through the packed concourse and Craig laughs out loud. It's easy for Craig to laugh; he weighs over two hundred pounds and his skin is winter white; he voted to Make America Great Again; also, he's already half-cut from the shots in Hooters, the drinks that Brett was plying him with.

No, not plying. Presenting. Birthday shots. Jägermeister and tequila. All the bad stuff.

Craig looks good in his oversized jersey; anyone can see that. It's mostly blue, the home colours, and filled out at the shoulders. Brett feels skinny in his. Weedy, as they used to say in high school. He's over six feet tall and high school was a long, long time ago, but he can almost feel the bottom of his jersey skirting the knees of his jeans. It's all in his head, he knows that, just like this acute sense of his own blackness, yet he can't drop these weird vibes. This is supposed to be their night, but he's feeling edgy and out of place.

'Lighten up, dipshit,' Craig says. 'You used to love hockey.'

'Still do. I'm just saying, look around; it's a white guys' game.'

'You know what they call that, don't you?' Craig is carrying one of those oversized foam fingers, and he jabs it up into Brett's face. 'Racial stereotyping. What're you going to do when you and Kelly *finally* get around to having some of them cute mixed-race babies? Hold each kid up to a colour chart before you assign it a fucking basketball or hockey stick?'

Brett catches the foam finger and aims it back at Craig. 'Why don't you sit on this?'

Craig laughs again. 'I bet you'd like to see that, wouldn't you sweetheart?'

'In your dreams.'

They approach the nearest kiosk on the concourse and, with the hand that isn't wrapped in novelty foam, Craig reaches for his wallet.

Brett catches his arm. 'These are on me.'

'Get out of here. You covered the tickets.'

'So?' Brett slaps his own plastic onto the counter. 'What's the point in working if a guy can't spoil his best pal for his fortieth?'

'Whoa there!' Craig clears his throat and winks to the young woman behind the bar. 'You'll have to excuse my buddy here. What he meant to say was *thirtieth*.'

She returns a timid smile. All the ladies smile for Craig. As far as Brett remembers, they always have.

The cheapest beers are cans of Miller Lite at eleven dollars apiece. Brett orders six, as many as they can carry between them, and tries not to flinch when the girl swipes his Mastercard. Ordinarily, he's very conservative with spending, and his mind automatically tallies the figures in his head. On top of these tickets, which were close to four hundred for the pair, and the wings at Hooters, this is turning into one of the most expensive nights of his life. For this reason alone, he keeps on telling himself, he mustn't back out when the time comes. His stomach is in knots.

All he can do now is wait for the moment to present itself and hope that he'll know what to say when it does.

Tonight, what he has to do, has been decades in waiting.

Their seats are high up in the 200s, overlooking the enormity of Madison Square Garden, and the atmosphere is electric. They only just manage to fit the beers in the area beneath their folding chairs, and Brett almost knees the head of the guy in front, but the squeeze is worth it for the view. The smell of the ice is fresh, its chill almost sobering. Blue spotlights move across its pristine surface to a soundtrack of riotous masculinity – AC/DC, Rage Against the Machine, White Zombie – and then it's on to the city's anthems, twenty thousand voices bellowing along to 'Theme from New York, New York' and Billy Joel's 'New York State of Mind'. It really is breathtaking.

'God damn!' Craig slaps Brett on the back with a hand like a shovel. 'Rangers versus Devils at the motherfucking Garden! How long we been talking about this?'

'Long time, pal.'

'Forever! You're a hell of a guy, Brett, you know that? I don't say it enough, but you really are.'

'Ah, I don't know …' Brett shrugs it off, but he's smiling

from ear to ear. He takes his phone from his pocket. There's a message from Kelly telling him to behave and have fun. A joke, of course; as if he's ever misbehaved in his life, never mind the nine years they've been living together. Instead of replying, he takes a photograph of the rink, uploads it to Facebook and checks into the game. He tags Craig Wilson, which sends an alert to Craig's phone.

Craig sees the update and sniffs. 'Ah shit. There goes any chance of me taking a sick day on Monday. Working on my fortieth birthday, man. Good fucking deal. I never thought they'd make us work the holiday, even if it is only Martin Luther King Day.'

Brett's smile, which he already suspects might be the last genuine smile of the night, fades a little. 'You've got tomorrow to shake the hangover. Besides, Kirk is likely to can your ass if you miss another shift.'

'Kirk can suck it. I'm about ready to bury that faggot.'

Brett says nothing.

The lights dim, a fresh chant of 'Let's Go, Rangers!' fades away, and the guest of honour is introduced for the ceremonial first puck. It's a woman in a wheelchair, a decorated veteran – the announcer tells them – of three tours with the United States Marine Corps.

'Oh, man.' Brett follows the audience's lead and hauls himself onto his feet. 'I hate this part.'

'Poor bitch squatted on a landmine,' Craig mutters, careful not to be overheard by those nearest. 'Use your legs while you've got them.'

'I know, I know, it just … It makes me feel awkward, that's all.'

'Awkward? It's called serving your country, dipshit. Fighting for our right to drink these brewskis. Somehow I don't see *you* leading the charge at Fallujah anytime soon.'

'Hey,' Brett whispers, 'I've seen combat! You're talking to the guy who stood up to Trent Nolan in eighth grade, remember?'

'I remember having to drag you out from under a linebacker's size twelves before he put you in traction, if that's what you mean.'

Brett grins, but the gesture has lost all warmth. 'That'll be the last fight I ever get into.'

'Oh yeah?' Craig raises his eyebrows. 'We don't always get the luxury of choice, bud.'

The veteran starts to sing, lyrics broadcast over the arena in neon, and Craig holds the foam finger to his chest and nails every word.

'*Oh, say can you see, by the dawn's early light, what so proudly we hailed, at the twilight's last gleaming?*'

Brett mimes along, his thoughts turning over the conversation ahead. He knows he's in for a bittersweet night. Finally, the time has come. His heart feels close to breaking.

One way or another, with every passing moment, the end of their thirty-year friendship is drawing nearer, and Craig is none the wiser.

Brett reaches down for another beer as all the good Americans return to their seats.

They roar as one, the entire stadium, and in a flurry of lethal blades the players descend onto the ice below.

3

PLAYER THREE

Sarah Mulligan doesn't realise how long she's been sitting in the bathroom until she checks the time and feels her heart crawl up into her throat.

That can't be right. The clock onscreen says it's almost half past five.

'Shit.'

She jumps to her feet, uprights the lid of the toilet upon which she has been sitting, and then dashes out of the bathroom and down the staircase.

The children are in the living room, precisely where she left them. Archie is babbling away in his bouncer, reaching for the crinkly thingamajig that dangles from the overhanging toy bar. Hannah is napping on the carpet, surrounded by Duplo and dolls like the scattered debris of some fantastic nail bomb. *The Little Mermaid* has finished and returned to the DVD menu. An instrumental segment of 'Part of Your World' cycles on a loop.

Sarah dumps the iPad she's been carrying onto the cluttered coffee table and heads for the kitchen, where this evening's chips are still raw white potatoes in the cupboard. She fires the deep-fat fryer, grabs the speed-peeler from the cutlery drawer and gets to work.

She's rushing, being careless; four frenzied strokes into the first potato, the peeler slips through starch and takes off the very tip of her ring finger.

'*Shit!*' She feels the warmth escape her face. The potato goes rolling like a head from a guillotine. She launches the peeler and clutches the finger almost tight enough to break it. She tastes tears and loathes herself for it.

Stupid cow. Idiot. The sharp, searing pain is astounding.

Then she hears it: blood hitting the tiles below with an impossibly heavy *drip*.

That's all it takes. The kitchen cabinets dissolve to grey and her legs go out from under her. She falls backwards against the washing machine, winded.

For a short while – twenty seconds, maybe more – there is nothing but calm, comatose grey. The sound of rain on faraway windows. Peace. Then she sees the cherubic face of her tiny daughter looking down at her through fog. Hannah's eyes are glassy, and her bottom lip is quivering.

'Mummy poorly?'

'Yeah.' Sarah swallows as she heaves herself into a sitting position. 'Mummy poorly.'

Hannah fumes, storms across the kitchen like a true red-headed little madam and smacks the fallen potato where it lies in a jacket of dog hairs. 'Naughty taties! Naughty taties!'

Sarah can't help but smile. She takes a deep breath and reluctantly surveys the damage. A millimetre sliced from her fingertip, maybe less. Four droplets of blood on the floor. That's about the sum of it, but she still feels close to vomiting.

As it turns out, the rush was all for nothing. Outside, the garden gate clangs.

'Daddy!' Hannah is already off like a firework down the hallway. 'Daddy! Daddy! Yay!'

'Yay,' Sarah grumbles, trying to haul herself up off the floor. Her back hurts from the fall and her knees are perpetually weak. She's gained more than forty pounds since the wedding three years ago; baby weight the babies have so kindly left behind.

The front door opens, and Neil Mulligan trudges into the house and wipes his boots. Sarah hears him scoop Hannah up for a kiss. Then she hears the momentary pause as he surveys the living room on passing. Tonight's inspection is greeted with the familiar husky sigh.

He comes to the kitchen doorway in his overalls with their daughter hanging from his neck, watching his wife struggle to get back onto her feet.

'What have you done now?' he asks.

'Just an accident,' she says, finally upright and brushing dog hairs from her trousers. 'There was blood and, you know …'

Her husband's flat eyes move across the tiny spatters on the tiles. 'For Christ's sake, Sarah, you're thirty-seven years old.' She's thirty-six, but Neil has a habit of rounding up when he's aiming to belittle. 'What if something happened to one of the kids? Would you fall on your arse then?'

Hannah, with one arm still wrapped around his neck, points accusingly. 'It was naughty tatie, Daddy!'

'No,' Neil says. 'Mummy just needs to be more careful, doesn't she? Tell her she's a naughty mummy.'

Hannah giggles, redirecting her point in her mother's direction. 'Naughty mummy! Naughty mummy!'

This hurts so much more than the throbbing in Sarah's hand. 'Thanks for that,' she says.

Neil lowers Hannah to her own wobbly feet and turns to the potatoes on the worktop. 'Don't tell me that's my tea.'

Had she expected anything more? Not really, no. Not for a long time. Still, she tries a weak smile on for size. 'I thought we could get a chippy tonight.'

Neil glowers. He's a large man, doorman-bald, also unrecognisable from their wedding in every conceivable way. 'We just did the big shop two days ago!'

'I know, I lost track of time and—'

'You're not seriously going to stand there and give me that not enough hours in the day crap when I've been on my knees laying flooring since eight o'clock this morning, are you?'

She bites her lip, shrugging one shoulder.

Neil shakes his head, droplets of rain reflecting light like the world's most miserable disco ball. 'I don't ask for a lot, Sarah. I just want to come home to a tidy house with tea on the table, and you can't even manage that. Did you even bother to get off your arse at any point to walk the frigging—' He stalls, frowning down at his feet as if he's expecting to see something there.

Sarah's stomach lurches as she realises what's missing from this picture.

Her husband storms past her, into the cramped utility area at the rear of the kitchen, and he throws open the back door. Within seconds, Duke, their massive German shepherd, comes charging in out of the downpour, soaked from nose to tail and slimy with mud from digging up the flowerbeds. The dog shakes black over the entire kitchen, which causes Hannah to bounce up and down, laughing and shrieking at the top of her lungs. In response, from the living room, Archie begins to wail. Suddenly, it's a mad house.

'For God's sake!' Neil shouts, holding the dog at a distance with one boot. 'How long has he been out there?'

'Just a few minutes,' she lies, watching in horror as paws paint the tiles.

'It's absolutely chucking it down!'

She opens her mouth. A fiery disobedience from deep inside would like to remind him that this is Salford, Greater Manchester, one of the wettest parts of England. She catches her tongue. This isn't the postcode's fault. She forgot about the dog, plain and simple. That's on her.

'The fryer's hot,' she says, scrambling for a tea towel. 'Let me sort this out, and then I'll—'

'Forget it. I'm off to the chippy, *again*. Get this cleaned up before I get back, if you can manage that much.'

He marches through the house, cursing under his breath, and slams the front door hard enough to send a framed picture crashing off the hallway wall.

It's a photograph from their honeymoon in Benidorm. Sarah sighs.

The dog is now having an excellent time rolling on the tiles, spreading its own filth like a mop in reverse, while Archie is still bawling in the living room and Hannah is staring up at her mother with huge, wary eyes.

Fighting the ache in her knees, Sarah gets down to her daughter's level and puts a hand under her chin. She stares at her for a moment. 'All for you, my miracle. You make it all worthwhile.'

Hannah doesn't understand – she's still not three years old – but she kisses her mother's poorly finger and smiles. As always, that makes things a little better.

4

PLAYER FOUR

Noah Durand has never been anywhere quite like this before. He's acting as if it's nothing out of the ordinary, but he's wearing a suit jacket for the first time since his father's funeral, and he's pretty sure it shows.

This hotel, Shangri-La, is in the most prestigious neighbourhood in Paris. It was built in 1896 as the home of Prince Roland Bonaparte. Noah was raised in a *banlieue* many miles from here, a Parisian suburb for citizens of Maghrebi origin. A glorified slum. Sofia, the goddess on his right arm and, somehow, his fiancée, doesn't know this about him.

Sofia is Estonian, and after living here for just one year her French is still limited, so the concierge is speaking English, their mutual second language. The concierge is a short, moustached man named Pascal. He gestures to the walls of this magnificent room, which are adorned from floor to ceiling with brass detail, but his eyes rarely move away from the incredible length of Sofia's body. Noah can't help but feel bitter about this, though he isn't exactly surprised. He still wakes up every morning in disbelief.

'This room we call *Le Grand Salon*,' Pascal tells them. 'Decorated in a classic Louis Fourteenth style, the architectural detailing is all original, with motifs specific to the Bonaparte family. Note the imperial crowns, bees and lion heads. The crystal chandeliers are also original, as is the marble fireplace. In this space in 1907, Princess Marie Bonaparte herself was engaged to the Prince of Greece and Denmark. For the banquet, our capacity here is a hundred and twenty guests.' He pauses, eyes flicking to Noah. 'Where is your ceremony being held?'

'St Joseph's,' Noah replies.

'Ah!' Pascal claps his hands together. '*Église Catholique anglophone Saint Joseph?* Perfect! That is only five, maybe ten minutes from here.'

'Yes, that's why we came.'

'And you have come to the right place.' Pascal leads them into the larger *Le Salon Roland Bonaparte*, the former stables of the Prince. 'If you are hoping to have a dancing party, then this is the room you need. It holds up to two hundred guests and has the finest entertainment technology concealed within its original features.'

'It's very beautiful,' Sofia says. Her English, unlike her French, is very good, though she speaks it with a strange mix of Eastern European and North American accents, despite never crossing the Atlantic. This is because, she once told Noah, whatever English she didn't learn in school, she simply mimicked from sitcoms such as *Friends* and *The Simpsons*. She's several inches taller than Noah, with sharp, striking features and almost luminescent green eyes. 'Truly stunning.'

'Yes,' Pascal agrees, eyeing the shape of her long black coat. 'Then, of course, we have Le Terrace Eiffel. Please …'

He beckons the young couple forward and, like a magician revealing his greatest trick, opens double doors that lead out onto the terrace.

Sofia is first through, breaking away from Noah's arm. She hits the winter air and stops still, clasping both hands over her mouth. 'Oh my God.'

Noah follows and halts alongside her. 'Wow.'

He's lived in this city all his life, but he's never seen the tower from this angle; it almost looks as if it was built solely for the viewing pleasure of the people on this balcony. He wonders whether he could hit it by throwing the water glass he's carrying and bets that he probably could. He turns to Sofia, preparing to share the joke, and sees she is close to weeping.

His stomach sinks as he realises that, for his bride-to-be, nowhere else will ever match up to this.

Pascal shows them to a table on the terrace, where brochures are already waiting by the glow of a patio heater.

'First,' he says when everybody is comfortable, 'we have the Emerald Package. This includes five canapés per guest and champagne on arrival, your own personal menu designed by our two Michelin-starred chefs, wine on the tables, another glass of champagne for the toasts as well as the wedding cake, flowers and stationery. For the Bonaparte room, this would also include the dance floor and podium.'

'OK.' Noah swallows hard and takes a huge breath before the plunge. 'The price?'

Pascal leans forward, unclipping a silver pen from his lapel, and circles a number on the nearest paper. 'Three hundred and five per guest, including taxes.'

A soft noise escapes Sofia's throat.

Apparently unaware, Pascal continues. 'The Jade Package, however, is our most popular. It includes everything from the Emerald, as well as a deluxe suite for your wedding night and an open bar. This price is four hundred and fifteen per guest, including taxes. Do you have any idea of numbers?'

Sofia flaps her mouth open and shut, open and shut. Noah sees that she's going red and quickly answers for her. 'We haven't finished our list yet, but something like seventy, depending on Sofia's family and friends making it here.'

'Very good!'

Sofia has discreetly taken her phone out of her clutch bag. She keeps the screen turned away from the concierge, but Noah can just make it out. With the calculator, she multiplies both prices by seventy guests. She runs each sum twice, as if the phone has made a mistake.

Recognising the silence, Pascal joins his fingertips in a crude imitation of the landmark behind him. 'Of course, I expect that you will want to go home and discuss this.'

Sofia nods sadly, glancing to the tower. It's a fleeting, infinitesimal movement, but Noah catches it. The dulling of her eyes. The realisation that, once this meeting is finished, she will never have this view again.

'I don't think we need to go anywhere,' he hears himself say.

Pascal raises his eyebrows. 'No?'

Noah shakes his head. 'Let's work out the deposit on this Jade Package.'

Sofia's immaculate complexion whitens. 'You're serious?'

Noah shrugs as if he's the coolest guy in the world. 'What do you say?'

She doesn't say a thing. She bursts into tears and throws her exquisite warmth around him.

Pascal leaps to his feet, beaming. '*Magnifique!* This calls for champagne, yes?'

'Why not?' Noah laughs over her shoulder, holding her tight, feeling dizzy.

Pascal goes off to fetch champagne and the contract. Sofia corrects her eyeliner and then hauls Noah to the edge of the terrace for a selfie with the tower between them.

He tries not to look so light-headed, because he knows this could be on Instagram within the hour. Sofia is currently averaging thirty thousand likes per post; if only she earned one euro per like, then this photo alone would almost pay for their wedding. She takes around twenty snaps with slightly altered poses – some with Noah, most on her own – before kissing him softly over and over again.

She's the best thing he has ever tasted. His heart almost hurts.

'You're fucking crazy!' she whispers.

'*Moi?* A little. It's only money.'

This makes her frown. 'It is *never only money*, Noah.'

He leans close, catching a tail of brown hair from behind her left ear, and breathes her in like a drug. 'I want this to be right. The woman of my dreams deserves the wedding of her dreams, and I'd do anything for you, Sofia.'

She presses her forehead against his, knowing that he truly means it.

He'll do anything for her, and he'll do anything to keep her. Anything.

5

PLAYER FIVE

Linda Malone should've clocked off at seven, but it's almost nine by the time she's dealt with the trio of backpackers in departures.

After eight hours of screening a continuous herd through archway metal detectors, the last thing she needed was for these three delinquents with their red, puffy eyes to come shuffling down the queue towards her, reeking of cannabis. They must've decided to get a head start on their trip to Amsterdam, and it has ultimately cost them their flight.

What did they think would happen? Who tries to board a plane stoned?

It's times like these that Linda is thankful her own daughter has always been such a level-headed girl; Alyssa would never do anything so stupid.

Linda manages to unload the bewildered backpackers onto the relevant officers, and then she can finally get out of the terminal. Despite her security uniform – a black stab vest over a white shirt – she has to show her ID pass to access the staff car park. She sometimes smiles to whichever colleague is working the exit. Tonight, she doesn't. She's not in the mood.

Luton Airport isn't huge – in fact, its size means it is technically an aerodrome – but it's always so busy, and Linda crawls through traffic on the exit route, silently fuming. It was crap like this that made her leave the old career behind. All that good old-fashioned family time missed out on because of work. Nights wasted. Years lost. This job was supposed to be different, but this is the fourth night this week she's got out late.

Through the BMW's Bluetooth she tries to call Alyssa to see if she has already eaten. The call won't connect, which further sours Linda's mood. The signal this close to the airport is always rubbish, and her pay-as-you-go phone is ridiculously dated. She decides to pick up some frozen fare just in case, because there'll be nothing much in the house. It'd be easier to grab a takeaway, of course, but Alyssa is seventeen and Linda can't keep up with her diets and mood swings; the last time Linda came home with an unplanned bucket of chicken, it had ended in a two-day sulk. Teenagers.

Linda stops at the Express Food and Wine on Lyneham Road. She does this almost every evening. It's a cramped, unremarkable shop run by a polite Bangladeshi family. There are hundreds more shops like it in Luton; this one just happens to be a few blocks away from the airport.

She takes two frozen lasagnes from the chest freezer with the sliding doors, couples these with the cheapest bottle of red on the shelf, and pays Ajay, the shopkeeper, in cash.

She's already back in her car outside, about to start the engine with her purchases on the passenger seat, when the hooded figure appears some way off along the pavement.

He's a scrawny man. She can see that much by the way his dark clothes hang from his frame in drapes.

As he walks, he's checking the street in both directions. Suspicious. Somehow, he doesn't seem to have spotted Linda in the shadow of her car's interior. He's bouncing a little, like a boxer psyching himself up outside the ring. There's something in his right hand, something that catches the yellow glow of the nearest streetlight. It's a knife. Great.

Linda watches in silence as the man barges into the shop, almost taking the door off its hinges. At first, her heart rate barely quickens. For as long as she can remember, she's been trained for this sort of thing. She dials 999 and reports the armed robbery without fanfare, then hangs up and fingers the key in the ignition.

It's been a long day. Too long. She doesn't need this. She's fifty-one years old, for God's sake. It's not her place to get involved. Alyssa is waiting at home. Think about Alyssa.

Overhead, a plane ascends from the single runway at the airport, lights blinking, engine roaring. It rattles the car. There's nobody else on the dark street, and nothing in the windows of the surrounding houses except for muted lights behind drawn curtains, the soft strobing of televisions. Linda remains behind her steering wheel.

There's a cash machine embedded in the shop's outer wall, which leaves only a narrow strip of window overlooking the counter, but she can see the story well enough from here. The hooded man has overturned the display case full of scratch cards. It looks as if he's still holding the knife with one hand while he stuffs entire rolls of scratch cards into his holdall. The shopkeeper, Ajay, appears to be unharmed. That's good. The till is wide open, empty by now. Ajay is hastily throwing packets of cigarettes into the hooded man's bag.

Linda shakes her head. Cigarettes are more expensive than ever. Fifty packets might make this idiot another few hundred quid, but he's wasting precious minutes. They are less than a mile from the airport. The sirens will be here soon. This has nothing to do with her.

Go home to Alyssa. Cook supper. Catch up on the soaps. Be a mum.

She examines the bottle she just purchased. Like every wine in the Express, it's sealed with a screw top. She opens it and takes a mouthful. Malt vinegars have tasted better. The nerves are stirring now, a million jolts of electricity crackling beneath her skin. She's starting to feel sick in a thrilling sort of way.

Looking back to the shop, it seems like the thief is finishing up. He's zipping the holdall.

No flashing lights though.

He's going to get away with it. Linda stamps one shoe in the footwell: *he is going to get away*.

'Sod it,' she says, screwing the lid back onto the bottle.

She climbs out of her car, quietly closing the door behind her, and carries the wine by the neck at her side.

A crash from inside the shop. Linda can't be sure, but it sounds like the man has just toppled the centre aisle on his way out. With her empty palm, she presses the thickness of her stab vest to make sure it's still there. She can almost feel her pulse pressing back now, which is surely impossible, but she isn't scared. She's too excited to be scared.

The door to the Express Food and Wine opens inwards. The bell jingles pleasantly.

The thief comes bursting out, headfirst into the arc of Linda's double-handed, cricket bat swing. The bottle explodes on impact. The guy hits the pavement, hard. Linda kicks his knife away as cheap vino runs into the gutter.

It's another few seconds before the car comes around the corner, siren flashing.

The first officer to jump out of the car is pulling a bright yellow Taser. 'You!' he screams. 'Stay where you are!'

Linda checks her watch. 'Six minutes,' she says calmly. 'What took you so long?'

The officer hesitates. Squints. He holsters his Taser, shaking his head. 'For Christ's sake, Malone. What have you done?'

She looks down at the hooded heap and shrugs.

Above them, another plane roars into the darkness.

6

PLAYER ONE

Maggie Dawson makes it fewer than twenty paces before the cops show up on Western Ave.

The cops she called after realising her little boy, Jackson, was missing.

The cops she desperately needs to lose, if that harrowing, anonymous text message is to be believed.

And why shouldn't she believe it? Her boy is gone. That's a fact. Some psychopath has taken him, and she's been sent a single photograph in return, with instructions.

Not just instructions. Rules. That's what they called them. Rules, like this is all some sort of a—

She dives into a snowbank behind a parked Dodge and peers back towards her building on the opposite side of the gritted road. Her bare legs are freezing. The tiny splinters of glass from the broken window are now screaming in her feet. She's also starting to feel stupid.

What if this *is* some kind of a sadistic hoax?

Shaun and Caroline, Jackson's legal guardians, have never wanted Maggie back in the boy's life. Not really. Maggie knows this, in spite of what they say. Why would they? To them, Maggie will always be the brat who put her baby, her own child, on the market. She was looking to sell, and they were looking to buy. Supply and demand. They covered her expenses, and so much more, and the two households went their separate ways. Everybody won. For a while. But when Maggie came knocking eight years later – a grown woman now – they agreed to let her have Jackson for one weekend out of every month. This was on a trial basis.

Now Maggie can't help but wonder: how far would they go to get her out of the picture for good? To prove her negligence once and for all?

Not this far. Never. This is really happening.

The patrol car is a hefty Ford with a bull bar on the front. Two officers emerge from it, big guys in dark coats over blue cotton shirts. They're both armed, of course. Wearing shades. It's shortly after eight o'clock and pale sunlight on snow is blinding.

This is her chance. All Maggie has to do now is stand up from behind this car and be seen. She's a distraught blonde in a dressing gown and sneakers. She's hot, according to most, and she's white; she hates to think that way, but it just might count for something. She can tell the cops everything, show them the message and the photograph, and they will help. They're trained for this. She needs to forget about these so-called rules.

She swallows, scanning the empty windows of the surrounding buildings.

Is she really being watched? Unlikely. The road is totally bare. It's Martin Luther King Day, so the schools are closed, the nearby families enjoying an easy morning. That writer, Scott

Fitzgerald, was born on the next block. It's a nice neighbour-hood. Quiet. Safe.

Get on your feet, Maggie. Yell. Scream. Just stand!

She's almost upright when her tornado of thoughts goes back to that terrible story from the news a few years ago. Some woman in neighbouring Minneapolis called 911 to report a rape and somehow ended up being shot dead by the first responder. It's a random thought, but it's enough to drag Maggie back into the snow. More and more often, it seems, there are stories like that. Cops with itchy trigger fingers. She needs to think this through. Her eyes go back to those blank windows reflecting dead winter light. That feeling of being watched is real.

She jumps at the sound of her building's buzzer and peeks around the Dodge. One of the officers has his finger on the button at the entrance. No answer, obviously.

Cop Two, meanwhile, is walking the perimeter of the build-ing. He reaches the bottom of the fire escape and pauses, looking up. 'Hey, Stan! Get over here.'

Cop One, Stan, is the shorter of the two. Maggie watches him take great big moon-strides to land in his partner's footprints.

Footprints.

She stares back along her own path. Sure enough, a frantic trail leads from the front doorsteps of the building to this very spot. She needs to move. Forwards or backwards? Her heart is hammering. This is hell.

The cops talk between themselves.

'Up there. What's that look like to you, Stan?'

'Flag, maybe. I don't see no stars though. Red and blue. Could be Red Sox?'

'In Saint Paul? I don't think so. If you had kids at home, you'd know those colours anywhere.'

'How's that?'

'Spider-Man. Looks like a blanket to me. Comforter, maybe.'

'The sort of thing an eight-year-old boy might have, you mean?'

'Exactly.'

A moment of quiet. 'We'd better try one of the neighbours.'

By the time Maggie hears the buzzer again, she's already moving on all fours. Her hands are pink and numb. She scrambles from the shadow of the Dodge to a neighbouring Toyota, then on to a Honda Civic, and then she's out of cover and running free. Fleeing again. She sprints north, fighting sharp pains in both feet, crunching over salt in the middle of the road. This is the most exposed part of the street, but the pavements on both sides will be deadly with ice.

The cops never see her go.

At the end of the block is Selby Avenue, one of the neighbourhood's main drags. There's a coffee shop, Nina's, on the left-hand corner. It's open. Maggie halts. She's on first-name terms with every barista here. She could pretend to have locked herself out of her apartment in her dressing gown. Ask to borrow Cindy's coat, maybe. And then what? She catches sight of her own reflection in the café window and recoils. This is the first time she's been outside without makeup in a decade. Cindy wouldn't recognise her. She hardly recognises herself.

Directly across Selby is the YWCA. Behind that, the headquarters of County Intervention for Domestic Abuse. Maggie isn't sure how either charity works. Could she walk in and ask for a pair of jeans? She'd probably break down before she managed a single word.

A car comes rushing along Selby. Maggie just stands, petrified and stupid. It passes, splattering freezing, dirty slush onto her naked legs, and the obese driver honks his horn appreciatively at her, a semi-nude blonde. Maggie stares after him, aghast. Her little boy is missing, and this prick is as happy as a pig in shit. She has to get off the street. She feels close to collapsing.

There's a narrow alleyway behind Nina's. Maggie retreats to the shadows of the ice there, crouches down onto her haunches and sobs. Images are coming fast, and each only adds to her agony.

Jackson, her boy, lost somewhere in the cold and dark of last night.

Broken. Undressed. Dead.

She leans forward and vomits. The taste is Southern Comfort, extra sour.

Who would do this? Who *could* do this? One man? More?

She'll go back to the police. She has to, or else she's doing whatever sick bastard sent her that text message a favour. Her fear buys the kidnapper time, but the truth is that the internet is one gigantic trail of breadcrumbs, isn't it? Cell phones are like fingerprints. State Patrol could read that message and have him – and she's sure it is a *him* – locked up within the hour. The feds even faster still.

And if they find out about the weed in Maggie's system then she'll probably lose her access altogether. This breaks her heart, but it's a small price to pay for Jackson's safety.

Her mind flies back to the message, and her heartbreak momentarily gives way to something else, something fierce.

A mother's love. She has failed that boy too many times already; is she going to fail him now?

No.

Whoever is responsible for this is going to pay.

This is the United States of America, after all.

Maggie can always get a gun.

She takes out her phone and, crouching in the cold, reads through the rules one more time.

7

PLAYER TWO

Brett groans and reaches for the bedside table. Through blurred, gluey eyes he checks the time on his phone. Almost eleven. No messages. He slams the phone facedown and groans again. Then whimpers. His skull is out of shape. The light through the blinds is all wrong. He can hear his own pulse and the volume is unbearable.

He rolls out of bed, crawls for the bathroom in his Rangers jersey and throws up. It takes four goes to get down to the dry heaves. He passed out with his contact lenses in, and it takes him a few minutes to prise them off his stubborn, puffy eyeballs.

Today is going to be a write-off. So long, Sunday. Better luck next week.

He finds Kelly sitting at their breakfast bar. She's leaning over a spreadsheet on her iPad with a latte fresh from the machine. She takes one look at him and bursts out laughing.

'Laugh it up,' Brett mumbles, venturing into the refrigerator for the orange juice, which he necks straight from the carton.

'Poor baby!' Kelly slinks over, throws her arms around his waist and moves in for a kiss.

Brett jerks his face away. 'You don't want to do that.'

'No?' She playfully gags and releases him. 'Then I'll pass. Who won the game?'

Brett hesitates, stumped. 'Rangers.' He isn't really sure. He doesn't remember much from after the second period.

'I bet Craig went typically crazy. Was he a handful?'

Brett shrugs stiffly and has another drink.

Kelly is intelligent, ambitious and occasionally hilarious. She's also sexy. He accepts this as fact. She's naturally curvy with wavy brown hair and thick, porno-secretary glasses. Men and women alike will stare at her enormous chest on the subway, uninterested in the backache it causes her. Teenagers have often yelled 'cougar' from the safety of the opposite platforms, which she despises; she says it's another way of calling her old. She's always telling Brett that he's handsome, but he doesn't feel it. Ever. Especially now, since he's approaching forty and hasn't gone to the gym in seven months. Kelly is the second woman he's ever slept with.

Brett takes a deep, shaky breath. 'Look, about last night. I was drunk. Really drunk, and you know what it does to me …'

'Hey, don't worry about it. I was probably too tired anyway.' She smiles sympathetically, which makes him feel worse. 'You'll just have to stay sober and make it up to me tonight, won't you?'

A thin, empty laugh. 'I think I can manage that.'

'Oh yeah?' She takes a long sip of her coffee, eyes burning into his body like sunlight through a magnifying glass. 'Don't make promises you can't keep, big man.'

He smiles and turns to the window. It looks cold outside. His smile fades.

He remembers coming back to Brooklyn in the Uber. The driver was listening to some pounding techno, and by the time they'd come off the bridge, Brett was feeling nauseated and the night was spinning around him. He remembers getting into bed. Rebuffing Kelly. So why can't he remember the hours before? There's a gulf of blackness, and somewhere in that bottomless void, it all went wrong. The dreaded conversation happened, he told Craig the truth, but it exists only like a memory of a memory now, retention of emotions instead of actual words.

He clicks his jaw and feels a dull pain under his left eye.

Did Craig *punch* him? Is that how it all ended?

Not like that. Please, not like that.

He's still gazing out towards Prospect Park when his view blurs with sudden heat. There's a pain in his chest, something he'd forgotten could hurt so much. It's loneliness and shame.

'Oh no …' Kelly is at his shoulder, stroking his back. 'Is it really that bad?'

He laughs and scrubs his tears away with the heel of one hand. 'Can't bounce back like I used to, I guess.'

'You need to get yourself on the couch with some Netflix. I went out this morning and got you all the essentials. Milkshake, bacon, aspirin, Pedialyte.'

'You did?' He sniffs like a boy with a scraped knee. 'You're too good to me.'

'And you're just feeling sorry for yourself. Go on, lie down. I'll fix you some breakfast.'

God, she's good. Perfect really. As he shuffles through to the sofa, Brett looks around at the home they've built together, their nest of trinkets, picture frames and memories. Their brownstone is beautiful, one of the most sought-after properties in

Brooklyn. It's a duplex, of course, but the neighbours are no trouble. Kelly is a big data scientist dealing with recruitment for the likes of Microsoft and Amazon. It sounds boring to Brett, but she enjoys it, and her salary has allowed him to work on his own career. Six months ago, he managed to get Craig a position at his place, but Craig doesn't share his enthusiasm for the job.

Brett wraps himself up in a couple of throws and decides to finally start *The Crown*, though he doesn't really watch five straight minutes of it. He's half-wishing he could remember what happened last night, and half-hoping he never will. He spends the day drifting in and out of sickly sleep. Usually, on a Sunday in particular, Craig is an almost constant presence through WhatsApp, either commentating on whatever sport he happens to be watching or sending short, sick videos that range from bizarre, stomach-churning pornography to footage of fatal workplace accidents or violent cartel executions. Today, Brett's phone stays silent. He can't help but feel abandoned. He checks his outgoing text messages and sees that there's nothing to Craig, which is one small blessing. Ordinarily he's a nightmare for drunk dialling.

He's still suffering at seven o'clock in the evening when Kelly, who is now curled up beside him, begins to walk the fingers of her right hand higher and higher up his thigh. Her eyes remain on the television, but Brett can feel the heat radiating from her flesh as she reaches the opening in his loose underwear. He clears his throat, mumbles something about needing the bathroom and goes. On his way back to the sofa, he manages to stomach his first beer. It's laborious going, but over the next couple of hours he drinks another five.

Kelly watches, but she never says a word. She's good like that. Always has been.

Perfect really.

Later, Brett falls asleep as soon as his head touches his pillow.

The next day is Monday. Craig doesn't show up to work.

8

PLAYER THREE

Sarah is up at half past five on Tuesday morning, humming tunelessly beneath her breath, soothing Archie in the dark.

He's getting heavier every day, and her knees moan under the strain. In one hand she's holding her phone and scrolling through Facebook. Nothing much posted since she fell asleep six hours ago. The iPhone's screen illuminates the Disney plaster wrapped over the end of her ring finger. Cinderella looks smug.

Hannah wakes up a few minutes later and waddles from her bedroom to the gate at the top of the stairs, yawning. The man of the house snores. Sarah takes the children down and switches on the lamps. January mornings are bitter, and she has to turn on the water now if it's ever going to be hot enough for Neil's shower. They'll be getting a combi boiler any day now. They've been saying so for years.

She opens the back door to let the dog out, tightening her gown against the chill, and waits for him to stop sniffing and empty his bladder onto the frosty, overgrown lawn. With Duke back inside, she prepares Archie's first bottle while Hannah groans around her feet because CBeebies doesn't start broadcasting until six. Sarah kisses her daughter's head, and patiently shows her the clock face. When the hands come to a vertical line, she tells her for the hundredth time, then her programmes will be on. Explaining this to a toddler is useless. Hannah wants everything now.

A little over an hour later, Sarah hears her husband heading for the bathroom overhead in a trail of grunts and morning farts. Once he's showered and dressed, he sits in the living room with the kids while Sarah sorts his toast. She brings it through and regards him with silent envy. He always gets the babies at their cutest. Even the dog curls up at his feet.

The sun doesn't rise until half past seven, at which time Neil kisses the kids and leaves for the day. Sarah can't recall the last time he kissed *her* goodbye. She isn't particularly bothered. How things can change in just a couple of years.

Once he's gone, the second act of the familiar morning cycle begins.

There's already a sink full of dishes to clean and a carpet of fur to vacuum. The house smells like wet dog mixed with haddock and chips, despite the papers going straight into the outside bin, and it's a good job Archie can't get himself around yet because Hannah alone is a hurricane. Sarah potters while the children stare at the television, but her fingers are already twitching like those of any addict. She's grinding her teeth. Her eyes keep drifting to the iPad on the coffee table.

By eleven o'clock, Duke needs to be walked. He's a big dog and he gets restless without exercise, but just getting both kids ready and out of the front door is a mission in itself. Besides, they're already drifting off into their first nap of the day. Sarah adores her children, of course, but their naps provide her only respite, and that isn't something she's going to sacrifice in a hurry. She locks Duke out in the back garden where he can run in circles for five or ten minutes. It isn't raining, and the ground seems dry enough. Nothing to worry about.

She pours herself a cup of tea and collapses onto the sofa with the iPad on her lap. She unlocks it with her passcode, has another compulsive check of Facebook, and then it's on to business. She cracks her knuckles, opens her browser and checks today's schedule.

There are four ninety-ball games starting within the next five minutes. She buys twenty tickets for each game, which comes to a total of two pounds. Small change, but this is just a warm-up. Since she began playing online bingo a year ago, she has accumulated a profit close to £9,000 in her account. This is her secret. This is her game.

To the right-hand side of the webpage, always open beside her tickets, is the chatroom. The players vary throughout the hours of the day, but she can always rely on a few names. She says good morning to Jill, Mandy, Sue, Mo and Jen, and they return the greeting, wish her good luck, and then resume talking about last night's *EastEnders*. Did Sarah catch it? No, she was too busy bathing the dog.

These strangers are probably the closest things Sarah has to friends, and yet she has never seen their faces. They could be anywhere. They could be anyone. As a teenager she'd had too many friends to count. After that, what happened? The years went fast, and her friends went faster. More to the point, her friends had children, and she did not.

At some moment in her twenties, Sarah's social outings

changed from boozy nights out with the girls to jelly and ice-cream birthday parties for the girls' many children.

Soon enough, even those invitations stopped arriving altogether.

Poor old Sarah, she used to imagine them saying, *the last thing she'll want is to come to Freddie's party, what with all those kids around. Poor old Sarah, you hear she lost another? And another? How devastating. How sad.*

Her eyes move now from the screen down to Hannah, who is napping in her usual spot on the carpet. Hannah, the first of two miracles Neil Mulligan brought into her life, when her life had surely reached its darkest period. Sarah watches her breathe, watches her dream, this incredible living machinery that started out one-part mother, one-part father, and every day becomes more of her own unique person. Sarah still loves her husband – it might not be the flowers-and-poems love little girls dream of, but it's a shade of love all the same – and for giving her these kids she will love him forever more.

She's indebted to him, and it's a debt she's glad to bear.

Moments before the bingo begins, an alert informs her that all card sales are now closed. The four games she's playing are arranged in tabs across the top of the screen, and she cycles between them as the computer's simulated caller begins flashing numbers at a pace of one every second. Because of this, each game can last no longer than ninety seconds, though they each end when their respective winning ticket reaches Full House.

Sarah loses the first four games and sips her tea moodily. Over the next few rounds, she wins a couple of lines, but it takes forty-five minutes to get her first Full House of the day.

'Bingo!' She fist-pumps the air, and then swiftly slams a hand over her mouth. Hannah has shifted slightly, but the outburst was masked by the ambient volume of the television. Sarah takes a deep breath. She's on for another winning streak, she can already feel it, and her adrenaline is pumping. Nothing gets her going like this; honestly, it's better than sex. She slips out of the room, carries the iPad up to the bathroom, shuts the door and perches on the toilet with the lid closed.

This is her favourite place to come and sit. It's the only room in which she gets any real privacy anymore, a den where Hannah will not follow or question, but time has a habit of slipping away from her. Because of this, and in light of what happened yesterday, she sets an alarm on the iPad. Twenty minutes. The children are unlikely to wake up before then, and the front and back doors are both locked. Everything is fine. Everything's cool.

But twenty minutes seem to pass in five, the alarm goes off as planned, and it takes three snoozes before Sarah finally relents to the incessant chiming, bids a *BBS* to the rest of the ladies and leaves her games. Her account is up another twenty pounds. She hates to abandon a winning streak, but it's not the end of the world. She can probably squeeze in another half an hour this afternoon, once she has finished walking—

Duke.

On her feet, she runs down the stairs, praying to God that he hasn't got himself into another mess like yesterday. That's the last thing she needs. She charges past the living room, throws the iPad onto the kitchen worktop and opens the back door.

Sure enough, Duke is at the very back of the garden, snout buried deep in the damn flowerbed; the garden is a jungle, but she can see his shaggy hindquarters sticking up from winter weeds.

'Duke! Get your arse *out* of there!'

The dog ignores her. She leans outside, socked feet still inside the house, gripping onto the doorframe.

'Right! It looks like he wants another ...' She holds off before dropping the dreaded word. '*Bath*!'

The dog doesn't move. Not an inch.

This stirs the first uneasiness within Sarah. Ever since Duke was a puppy the size of her hand, that word has never failed to incite a response, an *immediate* response, and it isn't just the fact that he's ignoring her that is so oddly disquieting. It's his silence. The utter silence of the outside world, in fact, and the dog's total stillness, as if she has opened the door onto a snapshot, a freezeframe, a glimpse of a universe paused.

All of a sudden, something seems very, very wrong.

Sarah runs her tongue across her lips and finds them dry.

'... Duke?'

She says his name three more times before she realises the dog is dead.

9

PLAYER FOUR

Noah is sitting on the ledge, blowing smoke out into the crisp evening. He's cooling off, entirely naked in the open window, but that doesn't matter much because the view only looks out onto the brick wall of the neighbouring building.

He turns to Sofia and watches her stretch like a feline on the bedsheets. Even flushed and sweaty, she looks incredible. Noah is wondering, as always, if she was faking. It's hard to stay confident in her presence. Noah knows he's nothing special. He has his French father's surname and ashen skin, coupled with his mother's dark Moroccan eyes and black hair. The combination makes him look like a vampire, eternally trapped in moody youth. He's thirty-one, but he looks about twenty-five, which happens to be Sofia's age.

Sofia, like so many others, came to Paris to work on her modelling career. Noah met her at an event in a nightclub almost a year ago, and he promised her the world.

Their rented bedsit is not the world.

Paris is divided into twenty urban boroughs, or *arrondissements*, which are referred to by number. Noah and Sofia live in the easternmost part of the 18th, La Chapelle, a neighbour-hood more commonly known as Little Jaffna because of its large proportion of Tamil refugees. If Noah were to starfish widthways across his mattress, he could probably touch every wall of their room at once. Their kitchenette is a camping stove in a cupboard. They wash their pots in the bathroom, which is only just big enough for them to both stand in.

Sofia doesn't seem to mind. She says she is happy, but no matter how many times she says it, Noah finds it impossible to believe. He tells her he has savings inherited from his parents, which are tied up between various banks in some slow bureau-cratic procedure. His parents left him nothing. Sofia never asks for the money, nor does she ever call him out on his bullshit, and yet he hears the same old lies coming out of his mouth as if telling them frequently enough might make them true.

He tears his eyes away from her body, but there's nowhere else to go. Where there once hung Noah's collection of vintage cinema posters, the walls are now plastered with photographs from the last autumn–winter fashion week: Sofia in Chanel, Dior, Louis Vuitton and Lacroix. She's building a respectable portfolio. Unfortunately, working for the exposure doesn't bring much money to the table.

She rolls onto her belly, catching lamplight across her der-rière, and scrolls through Instagram on her phone. 'You should start getting ready, *mon chéri*,' she says. 'It's almost time.'

Noah sighs, '*Oui*,' and flicks his roll-up into the dark. He closes the window, which has to be slammed because the wooden frame is old and bloated, and the sirens of the city are barely muted.

Since booking their €30,000 wedding eight days ago, the

thought of going back out to work has nested butterflies in Noah's gut. Diseased butterflies with razor wings. As he takes his uniform down from the hanger, he has to remind himself why he's doing this. It's all for her.

He's half-dressed when Sofia, now cloaked in a bedsheet, follows him into the cramped bathroom. She wraps her slender arms around him from behind so that, in the mirror, he can watch as she fastens the buttons of his shirt, concealing his hairy, bony chest, and then she slips the staff lanyard around his neck.

From over his shoulder, her reflection smiles. 'Look at my handsome man.'

He does, and he tries not to look too devastated. The shirt is short-sleeved, black, with the Hard Rock Café logo embroidered on both arms. The lanyard is modelled after a guitar strap and boasts the three lapel pins he has earned over ten months of service: a plectrum, a Rickenbacker guitar and the Eiffel Tower. His teeth are slightly stained by nicotine. His stubble grows relentlessly patchy. He is, to put it bluntly, no model.

'What do you see in me?' he asks, surprising himself.

She runs her fingers through the curls on his head and answers without hesitating. 'I see my fiancé. My future. My hero.'

'Hero?' Noah repeats it, but from his mouth it sounds all wrong. 'I don't think so.'

'I do. Paris is a dangerous city for a foreign girl. Even a year ago, I don't think I realised this. Not really. Not until I see the women on the corners at night. I was –' she pauses, only briefly, for the English word '– naïve. Romantic. You have given me a home. You make my career possible. You *are* my hero.'

He grumbles, unconvinced. 'You're going out tonight?'

'*Oui*.' Still playing with his hair. 'I'm meeting Gabriel to plan the next shoot.'

'Gabriel.' Noah spots the flinch in his own reflection. 'These agents are like bats, Sofia. They only come out after dark.'

'You know Gabriel.' She shrugs. 'He's always so busy.'

Noah nods. Yes, he knows Gabriel. Him, and men just like him. 'Where are you meeting?'

'Harry's. I'll be back before you finish work.'

'Harry's Bar?' He pauses. 'It might be difficult to concentrate on work, no?'

Instead of answering, she uses both hands to turn him around and kisses him softly on the mouth. 'I love you, Monsieur Durant. Only you. Don't forget that.'

In his stomach, the butterflies are fighting. 'I love you too.'

'I know.' She backs away as far as the room will allow, which is about half a step, lifts her arm and sniffs with a teasing expression. 'Now go! I need to shower. I'm beginning to smell like a Frenchman.'

'*Sacré bleu!*' He kisses her again. 'Go on. I'll call you after work.'

He edges out of the bathroom so that Sofia can squeeze into the shower cubicle and he closes the door behind him. He steps into his shoes, ties his laces and waits for the water to come rattling through the old pipes. He chooses his longest, most nondescript winter coat. The black one with the hood. A criminal's coat if ever there was one.

Then, when he's confident that Sofia is soaped up and unlikely to burst back into the room, he reaches for the air-conditioning unit mounted above the front door. The air-con hasn't worked since they moved in. He unclips the dusty grill, bending it out far enough to squeeze his hand through, and retrieves the small cloth bag from inside.

The Hard Rock Café is on Boulevard Montmartre. It takes thirty minutes to get there on the Metro. But Noah has no intention of using the Metro this evening.

Last week, he quit his job at the Hard Rock Café. He did it without flourish, and he kept it a secret.

He returns the grill of the air-conditioner to its original position and checks the floor below for fallen dust.

Then, as Sofia begins to sing in sweet Estonian beyond the wall, he slips the bag with the gun into his coat pocket and leaves for another long night of work.

10

PLAYER FIVE

Linda Malone takes a new bottle down from the shelf at the Express Food and Wine, to replace the one she broke only minutes ago against the skull of an armed robber.

She leaves a five-pound note on the counter alongside the empty till, opens the bottle and swigs a couple of mouthfuls. This one is white. Room temperature, but it still tastes better than the red in the gutter. Her hands are shaking. Delayed reactions. It was always the same. She steps over spilled tins of ravioli and broken Pot Noodles and leaves the shop.

Outside, the residents of Lyneham Road have all emerged like moths to the flashing lights. There's an ambulance here now, along with a second police car. The thief is in the back of the ambulance, bleeding into gauze. Not good. The shopkeeper is giving his statement.

The officer who had been first on the scene, the one with the Taser, is now leaning with one shoulder by the cash machine, notebook and pencil in hand. He's a neat thirty-year-old named Chris Hudson, a man Linda remembers being much chubbier back when they worked in the same building.

'He'll need stitches,' he tells her as she steps outside. 'Right now, that's our best-case scenario.'

'He should've looked where he was going,' she says. 'Idiot ran straight into me.'

'You think any solicitor's going to believe that, Ma'am?'

She frowns, more weary than annoyed. 'I'm nobody's Ma'am, Hudson. Not anymore.'

'No.' Hudson looks her up and down. 'Couldn't stay out of a uniform though.'

'Airport security. Not exactly the front line.'

'And yet here you are. Still looks good on you, by the way. The uniform.'

Linda feels the briefest of flushes and glances to the closed door beside her. Hudson is either lying or just plain stupid. The woman reflected in the glass is tired and worn, her blonde hair turning grey along the parting. She's splashed in burgundy; it almost looks like blood, and maybe it is.

'He came at me with a knife,' she says. 'You ought to mention that when his solicitor tries to play a hand.'

''Course.' Hudson clears his throat and raps his pencil against the cover of his notebook. 'Still, you might want to give a statement. Just in case.'

She shakes her head. 'The shopkeeper, Ajay, will give you more than enough to get your charge. He keeps a camera over the till. He's always seemed decent.'

'And what about you?'

She fishes the car keys from her pocket. 'Think I'm going to make the most of this civilian life. Play the role of anonymous bystander for a change. The sort I never could stand.'

Hudson manages a sombre smile, but his eyes move

pointedly from the bottle in her trembling hand to her BMW parked across the road. 'Are you going to be all right getting home?'

'It's only two minutes from here,' she says.

'You wouldn't prefer it if I called Richard for you? Let him know what happened?'

A sharp pain – *wham* – right in her chest. 'No.' Linda tries, and fails, to keep her voice from dulling. 'Richard won't be there.'

'Oh.' Hudson glances away, colouring slightly. 'Sorry.'

'Don't be. That water's been under the bridge for a long time now.'

An awkward silence. Hudson sighs. 'All the same, I'm going to have to ask for your address and phone number. You know how it is.'

'Yes,' she says. 'I know how it is.'

She leaves calmly, and she keeps her temper until she's driven two blocks from the scene and is flying through the quiet residential roads at almost double the speed limit.

'That's a great idea, Hudson,' she barks to her empty car. 'Why don't you give the legendary Richard Malone a call? You could ask him if he's still putting under par, if you like. No, honestly, I don't mind! While you're at it, why don't you ask him why he doesn't give two shits about his daughter anymore? Or ask him how old his new girlfriend is, that's always worth a laugh! Christ, you probably went to school with her. That's right, almost half my age! No, I don't think that's strange. What's that? You could use a bit more gossip for the boys in the parade room tomorrow? Your former supe breaking somebody's face open might not be enough? Well, you just say the word and I'll help out in any way I can! My pleasure!'

She goes on like this, ranting over the steering wheel until the fire burns away, and by the time she pulls up in her own driveway she feels embarrassed and exhausted.

She checks the dashboard clock as she gets out of the car. Alyssa would've been expecting her home hours ago. Linda gave a lot of years to Bedfordshire Police, years she can never get back, and when she finally quit, she swore to spend her nights more wisely. By the time she left, of course, it was too late. Richard was gone, and their only daughter was becoming a young woman. The family chapter of Linda's life was over. She'd missed out. She'd missed everything.

She walks into the house and it's even darker in here than on the roads outside. Like any teenager, Alyssa rarely comes out of her bedroom. Linda tuts, thawing lasagnes tucked under one arm, and begins turning on the lamps, filling the house with artificial life. She dumps the open bottle of wine and the ready meals onto the worktop and gets herself a glass.

'Alyssa! Come down here! You won't believe what just happened!'

No answer. She glances to the empty sink. No dishes whatsoever. This worries her. Alyssa was always a cuddly – OK, sort of chubby – kid, right up until a massive drop in weight around two years ago, and since then, in Linda's motherly opinion, the girl is always just a missed meal or two away from an eating disorder.

'Alyssa? Have you eaten today?'

She turns her ear to the hallway. All she hears is the buzzing of energy-saving lamps warming up around her.

It'll be the headphones.

Linda tells herself that Alyssa will be using her headphones, and why shouldn't she be? There's nothing to suggest otherwise.

And yet there's something about the house. An emptiness. Something almost …

Frightening.

She climbs the stairs, trying not to hurry. Hurry is too close to panic and panic only happens when something is wrong. Dreadfully wrong. Nothing's wrong here.

But the stairs sound too loud. The wood is almost crying.

It's only when Linda reaches the landing that her fright grows into something palpable.

There's no strip of light glowing beneath Alyssa's door.

'Alyssa?' She paces towards her daughter's room and, in her growing worry, she actually prays that she's going to burst in and find Alyssa messing around beneath the covers with a boy. It's bound to happen someday, even to a girl like Alyssa. They don't stay kids forever.

Linda throws open the door, a little harder than she means to, and then she lets the panic consume her.

Alyssa isn't there.

LEVEL TWO

LEVEL TWO

The Game

DEAR PLAYER,
THE PERSON YOU LOVE MOST IS IN DANGER.
TO SAVE THEM, YOU MUST PLAY THE GAME.
THE RULES OF THE GAME ARE AS FOLLOWS:
ALL PLAYERS ENTER ALONE.
DO NOT SHARE THIS MESSAGE. DO NOT SEEK
HELP.
YOUR EVERY MOVE IS BEING MONITORED.
CHEATERS WILL BE DISQUALIFIED.
DISQUALIFICATION IS PERMANENT.
FURTHER INSTRUCTIONS TO FOLLOW.
THERE CAN ONLY BE ONE WINNER.
AND IF YOU LOSE, YOUR LOVED ONE WILL DIE.
WELCOME TO THE GAME.
YOU'VE JUST STARTED PLAYING.

Tap to Download
IMG_1.JPG
1.2MB

The sender is not in your contact list.
Report Junk

11

PLAYER ONE

Maggie Dawson is still in the alleyway behind Nina's coffee shop, shivering against the Minnesota cold.

Her backside is especially freezing after sitting on the ground to pick splinters of broken window from her feet and, while they might eventually feel better for it, she isn't tuned into her physical state enough to notice any immediate relief. Now she's standing in her high-tops again, thumbing her phone so hard she's close to cracking the screen, but her own desperate text messages – more than thirty of them, all frantic pleas and furious anger – go absolutely nowhere:

> WHO THE FUK IS THIS?! WHAT DO U WNT, MONEY?!
>
> Not Delivered

> Pleae don't hurt my boy. Please. Ill do anything jst bring him back to me
>
> Not Delivered

WHERE IS MY SON YOU SICK FUCK!!

Not Delivered

The messages go nowhere because there's no number to respond to. The sender is listed only by those two words: 'The Game'.

She reads it out loud with a mix of disgust and disbelief. For a moment, hysterical laughter almost bubbles up out of her throat. It's like her grandmother's funeral all over again, where she'd giggled all the way through her uncle's touching eulogy; it wasn't because she found it funny, the whole scene was just too much to handle. She needs a smoke. She hasn't carried ordinary cigarettes for a little over a year, but she'd just about kill for one right now. Or a joint. Or a drink. She has the trembling hands of advanced Parkinson's disease, and her legs could go out at any moment.

She takes a long breath and then forces herself to return to the photograph that came through with the text. She stares at it, feeling whatever remains of her heart tearing into much smaller tatters. She tries to convince herself that this could be any little boy. He's mostly hidden in a sleeping bag, curled up on the sort of smooth, nondescript concrete floor you might find in a garage or basement. All Maggie can really see with any true clarity is a tuft of blond hair and a pair of closed eyes. It looks as if he's sleeping. She briefly wonders how the hell he could be sleeping through any of this, and then the horror returns, slamming her in the gut, and she prays to God that he really is just sleeping.

She strokes her thumb against the screen, desperate to feel

his warmth, and feels only hard glass. 'I'm sorry, little man. I'm so sorry. This is all my fault. I'm going to get you out of this. I promise. It's going to be OK …'

She wants to believe that, she really does, but she knows this sobbing damsel routine isn't going to solve anything. She needs to get out of this alleyway. She has to move.

It's surely going to come down to money. The children that truly disappear – those poor kids who take a shortcut home and simply vanish without a trace – are never exchanged for text messages. Their families don't get the luxury of riddles and clues. This dialogue is leading to something and, with every passing moment, Maggie is more and more certain that the solution will come out of an ATM.

Which presents another problem: Maggie is broke. The out-of-court settlement she'd been living off for a long time – garnered from a grossly unpleasant case she'd rather not think about – is long gone, the final paycheque from temping at the bar didn't stretch far through the holidays, and she has only her last surviving credit card to her name. Hell, she doesn't even have anybody she could borrow off, not anymore; her family seldom acknowledge her beyond seasonal obligations, and the only people she can think of who are even *likely* to have any cash just resting in the bank are …

She swallows.

The Taylors, of course. Shaun and Caroline. Jackson's adoptive parents.

It's hard to believe that only twenty minutes have gone by since she first opened the door onto Jackson's cold and empty bedroom, the room which until recently had been nothing more than storage space in her small, cluttered apartment. Twenty dizzying, shattering minutes. How much longer can she put off making a call to the Taylors? The idea makes her shudder with a whole new kind of terror, one that rages between her sense of self-loathing for keeping them in the dark, and her need for self-preservation. The Taylors are his family, and it's only a matter of time before they find out about this. Even if the cops don't reach out to them first, Jackson will surely never keep this a secret, no matter how much Maggie might beg once this is over.

But the Taylors have money – *enough to have bought the boy once already*, she notes with abject disgust – and now that she has stopped to think about it, she feels the slap-shock of a huge puzzle piece go sliding into place. This can't be a coincidence.

Aren't Jackson's wealthy adoptive parents the more likely targets in all of this? Sure they are. The Taylors live in a gated community with alarms and cameras and private security, but their son has recently begun staying over at his birth mother's easily accessible, rented apartment in the neighbouring city. The perfect place for an abduction.

'Son of a bitch!' Maggie unconsciously stamps her heel, fracturing ice underfoot and sending a barb of pain through her sole.

When the next text message comes through with a sudden vibration, she's so startled she almost drops her phone.

Ignoring the flash of sweat across her entire body, she opens it and reads.

YOU LOST THE POLICE. CONGRATULATIONS.
ANOTHER SCREW-UP LIKE THAT = GAME OVER.
THE FOLLOWING MESSAGE WILL CONTAIN A URL.
TO ADVANCE, OPEN THIS URL USING THE TOR
BROWSER ON A PREPAID SMARTPHONE. NOT
THIS DEVICE.
YOUR PREPAID PHONE MUST BE INTERNET AND
APPLICATION READY.
THE URL WILL ASK YOU TO ENTER YOUR NAME.
ONLY YOUR NAME.
YOUR NAME IS: PLAYER 1.
YOU HAVE 30 MINUTES.
SAVE HIS LIFE. PLAY THE GAME.

Once again, Maggie finds herself reading this message from start to finish several times, and it takes the last of her frayed strength to keep from having a total meltdown like before. She has to stay focused.

Player One. Could this be happening to others? No way. Surely, it's some kind of trick ... But then, how could anybody know about her calling, and losing, the police? She glances fretfully to the opening of the narrow alleyway, afraid of what she'll see there, but there's nobody. She starts to imagine microphones in her apartment, hidden cameras broadcasting her most intimate moments to some voyeuristic creep, and perhaps more than anything else, it's this thought of being filmed and watched that most makes her skin crawl.

Her eyes move to the lens of her phone's front-facing camera as it occurs to her that, these days, spies don't need to hide themselves in shadows. She quickly shifts her thumb up to cover the camera, and she's suddenly afraid to make another sound near the microphone.

Before she's had a chance to get her head even a little way around this, the third message comes through. It contains nothing but a shortened URL, which Maggie promptly pastes into Google. When it comes to hitting search, however, she hesitates. She's feeling acutely conscious of her movements on this phone. She closes the search engine.

Right now, she needs another phone. A prepaid phone. A burner. That's what they call them in shows like *The Wire* and *Breaking Bad*, isn't it? Shows she has binged from the safety of her couch. Shows about criminals. Fugitives. Bad guys.

So, what does that make me?

She's pretty sure they still sell burners behind the counters in most gas stations. Probably Best Buy too, but the closest one of those is way out in the suburbs on the north side of the city. There's a gas station about a mile west up Selby. That's, what? At least a half-hour's walk. She's going to have to move quickly, and speed on ice is dangerous.

Her legs have started to seize up in the cold. The skin below her dressing gown is blotchy in all the wrong places, deathly white in the rest. She feels like a zombie; not the shambling, flesh-eating kind, but the old sort, resurrected with voodoo to serve as a mindless puppet. She checks the time. According to the message, she had thirty minutes. She's down to twenty-seven.

'Move,' she tells her legs fiercely. 'Move, damn it. *Move!*'

And, thankfully, her legs are too afraid to defy her.

12

PLAYER TWO

Brett checks his phone twenty or more times between waking up and leaving the house on Monday morning, but it isn't until he's riding the subway west that he has one more compulsive glance and finds the new message alert glowing onscreen. Typical.

He holds his breath. His stomach starts to churn until he realises, with contradictory feelings of both relief and disappointment, that this isn't the long-overdue message from Craig. It's nothing. Just spam.

Brett swallows hard and glances around, wondering if, were this car not so packed, he might begin to weep again. He adjusts his glasses – he rarely bothers with contact lenses in the week – and tells himself that he should be ashamed of his own self-pity, that there are better people in worse situations on this planet, but his grief is real. There's a black hole in his stomach, eating him alive, and its hunger is insatiable. It doesn't help that he's still hungover. That's middle age for you: greying hair and endless hangovers. *Middle age!* Today is Craig's fortieth. Brett has never missed a single one of his friend's birthdays, not even during his years at college, and the torment of this silence stretches out, excruciating. He maximises the volume on his AirPods, letting Prince scream in all the ways he can't.

Martin Luther King Jr Day – or MLK Day – is an American federal holiday observed on this, the third Monday of every January, but you wouldn't guess it was any sort of holiday by the size of the crowd heading from Brooklyn into Manhattan. Brett once read that, on the average weekday, the New York City subway transports almost six million people with up to two hundred squeezed into every carriage. On commutes like this, he'd believe it.

To keep from staring into the faces of those breaching his personal space, he turns his attention back down to his phone. There's no signal below the East River, so he opens the text he must've received moments before coming underground. With his earphones in, he doesn't realise that he reads the message quietly aloud under his breath.

'Dear Player, the person you love most is in danger. To save them, you must play the game. The rules of the game are as follows … Huh …'

There's an image attached, but without signal he's unable to open it.

Never mind. These mobile games typically have cheap, forgettable artwork, and Brett is in a damn good position to judge. That is, after all, his field of expertise.

When he first joined Kickstart Games five years ago, it was still the company best known for its controversial releases from the early 2000s: violent action-adventures like *Hit'n'Run* and *Criminal Frenzy*, as well as a spate of grisly survival horrors. These days, however, Kickstart is revered for its ground-breaking game engine, award-winning storylines, and some of the most cutting-edge graphics the industry has ever seen. As a video editor, it's Brett's job to capture game footage and turn it into trailers for marketing, which means he spends most of his life staring into digital, make-believe worlds.

It therefore occurs to him that this text message might not be random spam after all. It wouldn't be the first time that would-be designers have approached the company using more unique tactics. Brett remembers the pitch for *Cracked*, the heist game that never saw the light of day after its creators sent the plans to Kickstart in an actual cast-iron safe that nobody could open. Then there was *De-fuser*, mailed in a ticking parcel that shut Broadway down for three blocks in all directions. The memory almost makes Brett chuckle. Almost. He hasn't felt much like chuckling since Saturday night.

He takes another closer look at the text message. If this really is somebody's concept, then, even by the standard of cell phone games, it has particularly lousy branding. Without the logo, it doesn't even include a title. Only the sender's tag: The Game.

Brett considers this. Growing up in Brooklyn in the eighties and nineties, a lot of kids were in *the game*. Hustlers, hoppers, wannabe gangsters. *Players* played the game, and plenty of the ones Brett grew up with ended up catching bullets or lengthy prison sentences long before gentrification crossed the river. There were also guys trying to get into the *rap game*, and those who simply *had* game. Brett frowns, thinking of something more specific. The Game. Wasn't that a thing they used to play back in college, gleaned from the internet in its juvenile, dial-up days? He nods to himself. It was. The object of The

Game was to forget The Game existed. A student would burst into class and shout 'I've lost!' and everybody would laugh or groan before declaring the same. Ironic processing, it's called, or the White Bear Principle. Try not to think of a white bear, and the first thing you think of *is* …

He sighs. Just like that, he has unwittingly added another disappointment to this, the start of what is sure to be a thoroughly disappointing week. Until now, he'd been winning The Game for more than two decades and he hadn't even realised.

He locks his phone and slips it back into his pocket.

The train rumbles onwards through the dark under the river, and Brett mouths two words to himself that have never felt more apt in his life.

'I've lost.'

13

PLAYER THREE

Sarah can smell the dog's urine on the grass before she even opens her eyes.

Her entire front is damp from the lawn. In January, rainfall takes days to dry.

This was a bad fall. She's nauseous and trembling. She has no idea how long she's been lying here, facedown in the dirt, but when she rolls over to see the clouds, the overcast sky seems a shade gloomier than it had when she first stepped outside. Back in the house, Archie is bawling.

Sarah sits up slowly, keeping her eyes firmly away from the flowerbed beside her. She knows he's still there, half hidden in weeds, but she can't bring herself to face him again. Not yet. Instead, she blindly reaches out with one hand and buries her fingers into his shaggy fur. What she feels there brings one word to mind: lifeless.

She starts to sob quietly, shaking the dog as if to wake him. 'Duke. No, Duke, no, no, my sweet boy …'

In these seconds, as her heart falls apart at the seams, she tries to work out what the hell has happened. This isn't easy to do without being able to turn towards him to look for clues. All she knows is that, when she first stepped out onto this lawn in her socks, she saw blood. An impossible amount of blood caught on the surrounding greenery like dew. How a German shepherd, enclosed in an overgrown yet toddler-proofed garden surrounded by a seven-foot-high timber fence, could have bled to death is beyond her.

Did he eat something? Something he'd finally dug up from the soil, which has torn his precious insides apart like a knife through so much fabric? The image brings Sarah close to throwing up, and she fumbles in her pocket for her phone.

It is, of course, too late to ring an emergency vet. It'll have to be Neil then, even though the thought of ringing her husband fills her with dread. What a terrible realisation that is, but true; the last thing she needs now is a barrage of blame to add to her anguish and guilt.

Before she can do anything, she finds a text message waiting for her. She sniffs, rubbing tears from her eyes, and tries to make sense of the words onscreen.

Halfway through the text, she shakes her head to expel the grogginess and starts again, but she's still struggling. It's only as she reaches the concluding words – **WELCOME TO THE GAME. YOU'VE JUST STARTED PLAYING** – that her hearing finally locks onto Archie's crying inside the house.

He's really going for it. Loud enough to wake the dead, as Sarah's grandad used to say.

So why hasn't Hannah come looking for her mum yet?

A chill unlike anything Sarah has ever known passes through her entire body. Her hands turn so clammy that the Cinderella plaster slips right off. Her eyes move to the doorway leading back into the house. Somehow, it looks emptier than it ever has before. Except for the floor in the utility area, that is. From this distance, it almost looks like dirt has been trailed inside from the overturned flowerbed, but Sarah scrubbed every inch of those tiles after the episode with Duke last night.

If she didn't know better, she could almost believe that somebody – or something – has entered the building while she's been out here on the lawn. Something quiet and deadly.

'Hannah?' It comes out weak. 'Hannah, don't come out here for a minute, OK darl?'

A good call. The last thing Hannah needs to do right now is walk out here and see her beloved dog dead in the weeds.

So how come Sarah is secretly wishing, more than anything, for her daughter to appear?

Sarah's eyes drag themselves back to the bizarre message on her phone, and she watches, almost powerlessly, as the attached image loads.

What she feels next is akin to one of her blood-phobic blackouts.

It brings the same momentary weightlessness, that surreal disconnection from reality.

It is, quite frankly, absurd.

Here is a photograph of Hannah, wearing the very same outfit that Sarah dressed her in this morning, only she isn't in the living room. She's sitting on grubby blankets in the backseat of an unfamiliar car, which is impossible. She can't be in two places at once. There's a Disney colouring book closed on her lap with a sheath of unopened wax crayons still attached to the front cover, but the girl who looks like Hannah is focused warily on the camera, or whoever is behind it. Without a proper car seat, her belt is wrapped dangerously high around her neck.

Sarah notices that the girl in the photograph isn't wearing any shoes, and she briefly wonders how she made it to the car without getting her white socks ruined in the damp. A strange, pointless consideration.

Then the bliss of shock passes, abandoning her to cruel reality, and Sarah Mulligan begins to scream.

14

PLAYER FOUR

'*Hey! Cinq euros!*'

Noah, who already has one leg out of the taxi, turns back to see the driver glowering and brandishing the fingers of an open hand. Noah is aware he's supposed to do something, but for another second he's too stupefied to remember what.

'*Tu comprends Français?*' the driver barks. 'Five! Five euro!'

'Oh.' Noah takes the phone from his ear and fishes a wad of crumpled papers out of his coat pocket. His hand is shaking so badly that the brightly coloured notes go spilling across the backseat and, among the creased euros, a scattering of small, clear plastic bags containing an off-white powder catch the glow of the car's interior lamplight. Noah flushes, snatching up his carefully portioned bags, and then pleadingly thrusts a ten into the appalled driver's fist.

The tip does nothing to improve the man's mood. As soon as Noah is out of the car, the driver lowers his window and spits in disgust – '*Putain de dealer!*' – before tearing away from the kerb. Across the road, the sign for Harry's New York Bar burns in fierce neon against the night. Fortunately, neither the smokers *huddled outside* nor the doormen hear the driver cursing.

Even now, on a bitter Monday in January, Harry's is filled right up to its famous saloon doors. Sofia loves this place. It's the closest she's likely to get to the Big Apple anytime soon. Maybe ever. Ordinarily, Noah wouldn't come near the building – not because he specifically dislikes tourists, but because he's wary of crowds in general – but tonight is far from ordinary.

Fifteen minutes have passed since he read the text message written in English.

Fifteen minutes that feel more like fifty hours.

As well as the revolver, which is still concealed inside his overcoat, Noah carries two phones while he works.

This is how he was taught, first as a teenager, to sell his boss's wares, and it's a job he has since quit, and found himself pulled back into, more times than he can remember. The last time he left it behind was after Sofia walked into his life and he'd made the decision to go straight. She never knew about the drugs; she simply deserved better than that, he decided. He might have stayed straight this time too – kept on collecting those lapel pins at the Hard Rock Café, and maybe even made shift supervisor in another year or two – if he hadn't just booked the exorbitant wedding of a Hollywood actor, or a rock star, or a drug dealer. Now he carries two phones again, and he hates everything about it.

The first – his iPhone – has been turned off these past few nights, mostly because he's paranoid about GPS tracking while he's out on the streets, but also because the only person who is likely to message him on this is Sofia, and she believes that the phone will be switched off inside a locker in the back of the restaurant until the early hours.

His second phone – the pay-as-you-go burner – takes orders from customers in the area.

Because of this system, Noah didn't see the text message or the photograph on his iPhone until he turned it back on at almost eleven o'clock. Fifteen minutes ago. Somehow, while he'd been roaming the garishly lit streets of Pigalle, the city's red-light district, in search of boisterous stags and drunken backpackers to sell to, his fiancée was taken from him. This is something his mind is having a hard time adjusting to. He has already tried to call her fifty-something times, and the only response he's had has been the heartrending sound of her personalised voicemail:

'*Bonjour, you have reached Sofia's phone! I'm so sorry I can't answer right now, but if you—*'

'*Bonjour, you have reached Sofia's—*'

'*Bonjour, you have r—*'

'*Bonj—*'

He manages to hold himself together well enough to make it past the huge bald men at the door and, after a whirling look between the upstairs patrons, he storms down to the basement level, once more assuring himself that she will be here. Of course she will. She'll be sitting with her agent, Gabriel, and she'll be rosy-cheeked from drink. The way he's feeling right now, Noah would actually be relieved to catch her kissing the slimy bastard. Momentarily relieved, anyway.

He's trying not to think about that photograph, the one that came through with the text message, but the image is seared into the spaces behind his eyes: the tall, graceful figure he knows so well, crumpled in an all too familiar coat, the fur trim now ripped and hanging from her hood; something dark pulled down over her face, a sack or a pillowcase, like that of a convict on the gallows; Sofia on a bare mattress in a dark room. Noah clenches his teeth nearly hard enough to crack them. He is a passenger in a nightmare.

The downstairs bar has an intimate, Prohibition vibe; low ceiling, lower lighting, burgundy plush and a hefty black guy playing the piano over in one corner. The place has always reminded Noah of a set from a David Lynch movie and tonight, with all this quietly discomforting terror, it really could be.

For one mean, fleeting second the world rights itself. Noah sees Gabriel and a young woman sitting together, and relief almost bowls him straight over. Then his eyes adjust to the dimness – he doesn't recognise the curve of her back, and her hair falls over to the wrong side – and his life is mercilessly tossed back into the upside down.

The woman leaning close to Gabriel is not Sofia, but this doesn't stop Noah from charging over and slamming a palm flat onto their table. Glasses jump an inch into the air. Hers topples, spilling the last of some cheap champagne onto the agent's business card still laid out between them, and those at the nearest tables turn to look.

'Where is she?' Noah asks in native French.

Gabriel doesn't flinch. He's white-tanned-orange with fat, sweaty hands. He's in his fifties, going bald. Gabriel has met Noah four times in the past year, but he leaves it a long, blistering moment before he deigns to show any hint of recognition. He takes a black folded napkin from a holder in the centre of the table and drops it onto the spreading champagne.

'Sofia,' he replies, not quite a question.

'Yes, Sofia!'

Gabriel shrugs. 'The last I heard she was on her way here, but that was four, maybe five hours ago.'

'Five. Hours.' Through all his fury, Noah glances down and finds himself automatically moving to mop up the spilled drink with the napkin. A professional habit left over from the day job. He yanks his hand away. 'She never showed up, and you didn't think to worry?'

'I don't have time to chase my clients,' Gabriel says coolly, but his arching brow deceives him, his expression turning curious, concerned. The woman at his table is devouring this strange drama with wide, hungry eyes.

'What was the last thing she said to you?' Noah asks. 'What was it *precisely*, word for word? A text message? A phone call?'

'A phone call. She said she was leaving for the Metro.'

'She said she was leaving, or that she had already left?'

Gabriel swallows. 'I don't know. This was six thirty, maybe.'

'No *maybe*!' Noah hears his own volume rising. He can feel the attention of the room on his back now, the barmen in their white coats and all the cocktail drinkers. His head is pounding. Soon the bouncers will come. The piano plays on, but the tune seems to have slowed. 'Take out your phone and show me! I want to see the call!'

Gabriel only blinks. 'What has happened?'

'What has *happened*?' Noah repeats it feverishly, wishing he was bigger, more confident with confrontation, but his rage sounds too close to begging, his anger too close to tears, and before he can stop it, the yell escapes his mouth: '*Where is Sofia?!*'

The piano player fumbles a note and the instrument goes silent. There's footfall on the staircase.

Gabriel's cheeks redden, his eyes moving around the room in one great, embarrassed sweep, and he lowers his voice. 'You need to calm down, *Noel*. Whatever you thin—'

Noah lunges. It's fast and clumsy, sending the table between them skidding sidewards into the gut of Gabriel's guest, winding her, and he drags the agent up out of his seat by his lapels.

'You ask a client, a twenty-five-year-old girl, to meet you in a bar in the city at night. She doesn't show up for *five hours*, and instead of calling the police, you invite some *whore* to take her place! If something has happened to Sofia, if something really *has* happened to her, then I swear to God, you piece of shit, I will come back for you and I will – I'll—'

He stares into Gabriel's slack, beached-fish expression, his mind on Sofia and the gun, the gun in his pocket.

The hesitation leaves enough of a pause for a man's booming voice to cut in from behind – 'Hey!' – and the next thing Noah knows, he is being dragged easily backwards towards and up the staircase, feeling impotent, a child torn between fury and shame. A few seconds later he is thrown out onto the frosty pavement, dispersing smokers like a leper.

'Fuck you!' he screams back at the bouncers, regaining his balance. There are tears on his cheeks.

Half an hour ago, he was thinking about invitations and stationery while he hunted for customers. He was mulling over which of the dubious characters from his childhood he could have at his own wedding, since most of the invitations would be going to Sofia's guests. Now he is close to a breakdown.

He has to get away from here. Has to reach her somehow.

He takes out his burner phone and uses the speed dial function. The call is answered in an instant.

'Yes?'

'We need to meet,' Noah says.

A cough down the line. More like a snort. The reply is husky, slow and cautious. 'When?'

'Now.' Noah is already moving away from the lights of Harry's Bar, scurrying back into the shadowy, seedy underbelly of the city, a place he has known since childhood, a world he calls his own. 'I'm on my way. I need your help …' He swallows. 'I'm in serious trouble.'

15

PLAYER FIVE

Linda is staring at the text message.

She's studying the words, the language used, checking for anything that might give the writer away. Its composition is simple enough. Vacuous, in a way. All caps, but no exclamation points. Authoritative, not shouting. She brings the bottle to her lips – neat gin from the kitchen cupboard – and hears the neck rattling against her front teeth. She hears it, but she doesn't feel a thing. The bottle has been empty for a while now. She is numb, detached, watching this dreadful scene as if from outside her own body.

She's in Alyssa's room, sitting cross-legged on the bed with her girl's duvet wrapped around her shoulders. It smells of her daughter … vaguely. The smell seems to be fading. Between her legs is one of the only remaining stuffed toys from Alyssa's early childhood, a ragged thing that had been sitting on top of the wardrobe, a knitted dragon named Dragon. For years, this inanimate hunk of wool and stuffing had been Alyssa's best friend in the whole wide world. Now it's dusty, and its black marble eyes are scratched, but it's something to hold onto. Something real. Outside, the winter sun prepares to drag itself up with idle reluctance. It feels like a lifetime has passed since that drama at the Express Food and Wine. Without her daughter, time is a blank dimension, and everything has changed.

Linda knows the proper procedure. What she should be doing. She needs to dial 999 and put a stop to this lunacy before it even starts. If not 999, then one of her former colleagues, that'd be a start. But she can't bring herself to do it. Alyssa is gone. It's too late. The wheel won't be stopped now until, one way or another, this is over.

She glances around the bedroom, which is illuminated only by the soft, white glow from her screen, and among Alyssa's cluttered belongings she sees impossible things in the shadows. Things that make her skin walk over her flesh. Her years on the force are physical monsters, mutated and hideous, and all those faces she'd tried to forget are looking back at her with their own empty, marble eyes.

Amanda Byrne; Laura Collins; Anna Kieszczynska; Kyron Garwood.

Suitcase; riverbed; freezer; furnace.

For each of them, she tastes a tear on her upper lip. How has it come to this? How could it all have gone so horribly, horribly wrong? Absently, she notes the cruel irony of it all. Richard, her husband, her *ex*-husband, said she could never quite separate 'the job' from 'the family'. He accused her of bringing it home to their daughter, that age-old cliché of households behind the thin blue line, and now here she is, alone in the dark, and those opposing worlds have well and truly collided.

Bedfordshire is one of England's smallest counties, yet its

crime stats are comparable to that of most metropolitan cities. For years, drugs, gangs, murder and terrorism were Linda's daily workload. Right now, she is remembering the lost.

Byrne, Collins, Kieszczynska, Garwood.

Four cases – entirely unrelated and separated by years – in which all the officers, volunteers, posters and man-hours she could muster resulted in the same gut-wrenching ending.

Suitcase. Riverbed. Freezer. Furnace.

Dead in four textures, and the law of the land couldn't save them.

So even if she picked up the phone, what could sirens bring to this situation? Nothing good. Forensics turning the house upside down, scouring the homes of every known friend and relative, confiscating phones to sift through private messages and search histories, bagging toothbrushes and underwear for DNA. News vans parked on the front. There'd be alibis questioned, histories scrutinised, paparazzi baying for blood. Nobody wants that. Hers is a cross she should bear alone. She has often wondered how many abductions go unreported every year. There might be hundreds, even thousands, that are solved without any police interference at all. And who could blame them?

Just follow the instructions and make the trade. That's how this needs to be. Clean and simple and over in a matter of hours. Lessons learned and never, ever forgotten. Nobody has to get hurt. She'll do anything for Alyssa, and it all begins with this message.

She trembles and goes back to the words.

There's no way to respond. That was, of course, the first thing she tested.

One-way text messaging. She remembers the training: her squad spread out around desks, eyes front, most of them irritable or yawning because the morning was stifling, and there were no windows or air-con in the room; their guest speaker's sweat patches as he crawled, painstakingly slow, through his PowerPoint presentation.

'One-way messaging,' he'd droned, 'often referred to as bulk SMS messaging, is a system popularly used by businesses in mobile marketing campaigns. I'm sure you've all seen it. Delivery companies use this technology for sending automatic tracking updates, surgeries for appointment reminders, and banks for one-time-authentication codes. If, like me, you enjoy an occasional pizza, then you might have been sent special offers, not from a mobile number as such, but in an SMS sent from a restaurant's name.' Click, and the slide changed. 'There's often no number showing because there really *is* no number. These messages are sent from the internet, and the sender can choose any handle they like. They sometimes come with a virtual mobile number, which is also generated on the net, or a short code to respond to. "Reply 'YES' to reorder prescription", for example, or "Text 'VOTE' to 5404" ... Unfortunately, one-way texting is becoming a powerful asset to cyber criminals who are able to disguise themselves as, among other things, your bank, your dentist, or even your child's school. Now, if you open your designated laptops, I'm going to show you exactly how this works, how these systems are built, and what we can all do to recognise the risks of ...'

Linda rubs her eyes, staring at her screen in the present.

This particular text message has no virtual number to respond to. It isn't going to be that easy. It's a wholly one-sided conversation. The Game is calling the shots.

Linda knows that a whole team could be tracing this already if it had been reported, but where would it lead them in the end? Down into the labyrinth of the dark web? Through fifty thousand portals relayed across China and Russia, and so much impossible international protocol, and all the while sand pours through the hourglass. A door is closing.

Suitcase; riverbed; freezer; furnace.

Gone; lost; dead; forever.

Her stomach is queasy, full of raw gin, what they used to call mother's ruin.

Mother's ruin. That's a laugh. She doesn't smile.

All she has now is this photograph of Alyssa. She goes back to it, to the bound ankles and wrists, and renewed anguish blasts any numbness away. Linda moans loudly. This is her girl! Her beautiful, talented, incredible girl, but the picture captures no humour, no spark, none of the things that make up Alyssa. It is a snapshot of terror caught in wide, startled eyes; panic frozen in her daughter's face like flies inside ice cubes.

Linda pulls the duvet tighter, twisting it around her own neck until she almost chokes, and then buries her face into the old stuffed dragon her girl had loved so much. She has never felt so afraid, so utterly alone, but she knows what she has to do. She is sure that anybody in her situation, anybody facing such total loss, would do the same thing.

There is only one way to end this.

The Game must be played.

The Game must be won.

16

PLAYER ONE

Maggie is heading west along Selby to the gas station that's still at least half a mile away.

She's tramping through gutter slush, spattering herself with grit, because the sidewalks are too slippery for anything more than a cautious shuffle. The streets are getting busier as the city awakens, and her progress is followed by the bewildered stares of passers-by. Her bare legs are pumping machinery, raw, red and near to blistering in the freeze. Where her feet once hurt from splinters of glass, there is now no feeling whatsoever.

She feels like a puppet. Somebody, somewhere, is pulling the strings.

She's searching for a phone, but what she's thinking about is a gun. Not that a weapon could do much to help her right now; she'd just feel better with one in her grasp. There is comfort in iron and firepower. Control, and that's something she is desperately lacking.

She knows that the easiest, and cheapest, way would be to borrow one. This is a hunting state, where more than a third of adults own a firearm. In rural areas, school attendance still drops during deer season, and thousands of Minnesotans shoot trap in high school. Maggie's own team had gone to the State Clay Target League championship, where she hit eighty-six of her hundred targets. She wishes she'd kept it up. She hasn't spoken to anybody from the team in years. Or rather, they haven't spoken to her. Her mind wanders, desperate not to think of things like exhaustion, hangovers, giving up.

For her fourteenth birthday, she chose a gas-operated, semiautomatic Winchester Super X4 Compact with a twenty-six-inch barrel. She sold that gun nine years ago, at the start of what she calls 'the bad times', but she must still be in the system, and she would likely be approved for another shotgun this morning.

Wouldn't she?

There are three things that might affect the instant background check they carry out instore: they'll check for any felony or criminal convictions; they'll look for any reports of domestic violence; and she's pretty sure they'll search for any history of mental health issues too. This last could present a problem. There's also the option of buying illegally, paying cash to have the serial number filed off or something, but she isn't sure if this actually happens in real life.

But then, none of this happens in real life.

Her left foot almost plummets into the mouth of a storm drain hidden beneath snow and she instinctively bucks further out into the road. A car's horn blasts behind her. She glances back, mechanically waving an apologetic hand, and then double-takes.

It's a taxi.

Inside her gut, she feels something alien: for the first time this morning, it is the unlikely touch of serendipity, an infinitesimal flicker of hope.

She slips over to the driver's side, brandishing her phone, and leans down as he stops to open his window. 'You take Apple Pay?' she wheezes. 'Credit card?'

He nods, gaze dropping into the opening of her gown, and she snatches the material shut and, with no other choice, clambers into the backseat.

'The gas station just up—' she starts, then pauses. 'No, wait. Target's open on MLK Day, right?'

The driver shrugs, eyes in his rear-view mirror. 'I guess so.'

'Then Target in Midway,' she says firmly; she nearly tells him to step on it, and this brings another of those dreadful, delirious giggles into her throat.

He drives. She checks her phone. Nothing since the last message. Somehow, seventeen minutes have already passed. What happens in thirteen more? She doesn't want to find out.

Target is a three-minute ride away. It's a monster of a store, a sprawling combination of everything from groceries and furniture to a pharmacy and walk-in clinic. Maggie has been a couple of times since the nearby Sears, Walmart and Kmart all closed down. She knows it has an electronics department. It also sells clothes, which is critical because she has no intention of returning home to get dressed without Jackson. As her driver takes them rolling past the gas station, which was her original destination, she defies every urge to stop. This gamble has to pay off. It has to.

At twenty minutes into her half hour, she uses her phone to pay the driver and then joins the scant smattering of early shoppers wheeling red carts. Her drenched shoes squeak loudly along the aisles, while her expression says there's nothing unusual about her attire. It's a holiday. Give her a fucking break.

As soon as she breaches the border of the electronics department, an attendant clocks her. 'Well, good morning there!' He beams with characteristic Minnesota niceness then he gets a better look at her, and his pockmarked cheeks turn scarlet. 'H-how can I help you today?'

'Prepaid phones,' she says. 'Which ones are they?'

'These here are all prepaid devices. You can choose by either carrier or manufacturer, depending on your needs. Was there something in particular you had in mind?'

Maggie has already stopped listening. She produces her iPhone and pops it out of its protective case, and the credit card hidden in the back falls out into her open palm.

'Oh,' the attendant starts, noticing her phone. 'Is there something wrong with your current device, because we could always look at—'

'This one,' she says brusquely, pocketing her iPhone and snatching a random fifty-dollar handset off its peg. 'This has internet, right?'

'Sure, it's an Android with sixteen gigabytes of data storage and—'

'I'll take it.' She plants her credit card on top of the box and stuffs both into his unprepared hands, and then she leads the way to the check-out at a near jog.

There's a clerk with a nose ring chewing gum there. The boy from the floor steps behind the counter and nudges her. 'Ah, Claire? Could you go ahead and ring this up for this, um, lady?'

The clerk eyes Maggie as she scans the box. 'Would you be interested in extending the warranty on your new handset?'

Maggie shakes her head. *Jackson in a sleeping bag*; she's trying to keep the picture from her mind but it's always there. The colleagues share an awkward glance; for a moment, she's sure one of them is going to ask for identification to go with the credit card, but neither does. The power to embarrass, it seems, is somehow persuasive.

The credit card has barely finished being swiped before Maggie is tearing her way into the box. She finds the battery beneath the instruction manual and slams it into the back of the phone. The screen lights up white, the battery already charged. Thank Christ for small favours. A loading circle spins beneath the Verizon logo. It seems to spin forever. Maggie's palms are slick. She feels another bout of vomit lumbering up her throat. Not now, please God, because if she's going to hurl, she'll do it right here and not waste another minute searching for the restroom. She actually gags. The shop assistants watch closely, engrossed by the spectacle.

Activate your prepaid phone on America's #1 network.

'Money!' Maggie gasps, stomping one sneaker with a squelch, her foot landing as numb and heavy as a brick. 'How do I get money onto this thing?'

The clerk indicates a rack of plastic cards. 'You purchase one of these, dial 611 on your handset, and enter the number from beneath the scratch panel on—'

'All right.' Maggie raps her knuckle onto her credit card and slides it, along with her new phone, back over the counter. 'Load thirty dollars onto it, would you? Quickly.'

The clerk rolls her eyes but does it anyway.

Back on her iPhone, Maggie once again reads her last instructions. 'You ever heard of Tor browser?' she asks. 'Is that something I download?'

'Sure,' the first attendant nods, his interest piqued, and then he lowers his voice. 'I hope I'm not overstepping any lines here, Ma'am, but you haven't by any chance been delving into those conspiracy websites, have ya?'

Maggie blinks. 'What?'

'Well,' he glances pointedly to her gown, and his cheeks fire red again, 'it's just that Tor is generally used by, um ... It protects against tracking, government surveillance, and I just wasn't sure if ... You know what? Never mind.'

Maggie feels yet another swell of hysterics coming on; this kid, who must still be in high school, has mistaken her for some tinfoil-hat-wearing lunatic, the sort you find muttering to themselves under the bridges long after the snow melts every summer. She swallows back the urge to laugh, or scream, and smiles. She wonders how hideous this looks without makeup. She hasn't even brushed her teeth today.

'Could you get the browser onto this for me?'

Maggie sees a warning glance pass from the girl to the boy. The kid hesitates, glancing around. 'Maybe I should get my supervisor, you know, and she can—'

'It's an emergency.' Maggie tries another winning smile, and he awkwardly takes the phone from his colleague and gets to work. His hands seem infuriatingly sluggish.

'Tor bounces its traffic through thousands of relays around the world,' he says, 'which means it can be a little slower than your standard browser, but that's the cost of total anonymity, you know?'

Maggie nods, but she doesn't care. Now that she has come to a standstill, fatigue is catching up with her, clouding her thoughts. She goes back to her iPhone.

Twenty-eight minutes have passed. *Twenty-eight minutes*.

She drums her hands impatiently, leaving sweaty prints on the counter.

Every second tightens her insides further, turning her guts like a ratchet, like some medieval torture device. She watches his fingers, counting the moments in her head, and finally snaps.

'Come on! How frigging long is this going to take?'

The attendant pales. 'Th-there,' he says, handing her the phone. 'All done.'

She snatches it from him like a jealous pitbull. No time to apologise. Onscreen is an application with a vibrant purple home screen. Maggie taps in the shortened URL from the last text on her iPhone. The website it takes her to is almost entirely blank, black, with a single white box for text to be written into. She feels time speeding up, racing to the finish line without her.

For a moment, she flirts with the idea of writing something personal. Something angry and desperate. But instead she writes exactly what she has been permitted to write: her allot-ted name. Then, with only moments left to spare, she hits the return key and drops the phone onto the counter as if it might bite her hand.

It is done.

Nothing happens. Numbness follows. She thinks of her son and takes what seems to be her first full breath in almost thirty minutes.

Glancing up, she sees that both attendants are, naturally, still staring at her. For a second or two, she can hardly remember where she is or how she came to be here. It's a weird feeling on an altogether weird morning.

'Clothes,' she says hoarsely. 'Where can I find them?'

She's pointed in the general direction, and she returns a thumbs-up. Before heading off, however, she leans forward and closes her eyes for a moment. She could faint right here on the counter. It's not a nice feeling.

A brief yet comforting daydream comes to her: a bright orange clay target sailing through a pale autumn sky; the shunt of a gun, a pop muffled by earplugs, and the salty-sweet smell of gunpowder; the shell casing bouncing, smoking on the ground; a distant cheer; a glimpse of a time, and a life, long since lost.

The burner phone beeps harshly, vibrating a little way across the counter, and everybody jumps. Maggie doesn't want to, but she has to look.

There is a simple, rectangular notification onscreen, not much different to that of any regular SMS, WhatsApp or Facebook message, except that the colours are noticeably backwards, white writing on a black background.

It's what Maggie reads between the words that sends a shiver so violent down her back that the store attendants must surely see it.

PLAYER ONE HAS ENTERED THE GAME.

What she reads tells her that this – whatever *this* is – is only just beginning.

17

PLAYER TWO

The US headquarters of Kickstart Games is based in Lower Manhattan, in an unassuming six-storey building on south Broadway. It has no insignia in the windows, and there's a convenience store on the ground floor.

Brett works in post-production in one of the building's many open-plan bullpens, where employees are grouped onto four-person workstations arranged in crosses; this means that if Brett stands up and looks over the rear boundary of his desk, he'll be staring directly into the face of an enormously obese guy called Steve, while Dylan and Amir face one another from his left and right respectively. Brett is a video editor. Steve and Dylan provide various finishing touches to the motion graphics animation, while Amir, a lighting artist, spends his days adding various shines and reflections to digital metalwork and water. Their four interconnected desks are separated up to eyelevel by low, thin walls to provide a sense of personal space without having to return to the infamously drab cubicles of yesteryear. During the dotcom bubble, Brett worked in his own fair share of cube farms.

The actual outer walls of the bullpen boast gigantic murals of concept art from the company's releases: behind the coffee station, two members of the El Loko Gang from *Criminal Frenzy* pose with baseball bats in their hands; over by the restroom there's an Intergalactic Shriek Bomber from cult survival horror, *Empty Space*. There's no uniform required, and every Friday the bosses treat the staff to a takeout lunch; it's that kind of workplace.

For all its cool, hipster vibe, however, a major leak eighteen months ago resulted in Kickstart coming down hard on one thing: personal cell phones.

At first, Brett thought this was a petty, redundant show of force, as every workstation in the building has its own internet access anyway, but then he, and everybody else, began to suffer the seemingly endless ramifications of that breach. Somebody, somewhere, had recorded and shared the final plot twist from the hugely anticipated action-adventure *Endless Fall*; it was a ninety-second clip that delayed the game's release by almost a year and cost untold millions during rewrites.

Now, phones are locked inside small, personal drawers upon entering the building. Because of this, Brett can no longer compulsively check to see if Craig has messaged, and it is driving him crazy. He can, however, see that Craig is listed as *offline* on their workplace communications server. Anybody inside the building should be automatically listed as *online*. So, where is he?

Craig is a junior systems administrator, a position typically held by people half his age. He provides some technical support to employees, but mostly he conducts physical stock checks, moves IT equipment, and carries out the general housekeeping of the storerooms. He wears heavy boots and carries a set of screwdrivers. He isn't into video games. He doesn't come up here often, and he surely wouldn't want to publicly finish whatever they had started on Saturday night, but he has always been impulsive, hot-headed and – let's not beat around the bush here – sort of violent. Perhaps it's a good thing he hasn't showed up today.

Is Brett *frightened* of his best friend? Yes. Craig could put an end to Brett's career, relationship and social standing in one fell swoop, and that's not to mention his physical wellbeing. But Craig isn't here. Yet.

Brett has three flatscreen monitors arranged in a semicircle on his desk. On one, he plays the game, which is currently the beta test of *Endless Fall: Online*. On the second screen, he has a storyboard open. Today, according to the storyboard, he needs a shot of his customisable heroine charging through the sandy, post-apocalyptic wasteland, with the interactive virtual camera swinging out from behind her left shoulder to reveal the cannon in her right hand. These types of shots usually last around two seconds and will take most of a day to perfect, if not much longer. The third screen on his desk captures the game footage; here, Brett can snip and arrange it to create the desired social media trailer. In this respect, he is simultaneously director, cinematographer, lead actor and editor. This morning, the game has been mostly on pause.

Feeling irritable, somehow claustrophobic, Brett checks his personal emails. There's one from Kelly. She sends at least one on any given workday. The subject of the email is a sad face. She says that she hopes his head isn't feeling too bad.

Well, his head isn't feeling as bad as his heart, but he can't really tell her that. His fingers are poised over the keyboard when, from behind his left shoulder, a voice speaks.

'Is that a work message, Brett?'

Brett closes the window with lightning speed and spins his chair around to find Kirk standing over him. 'S-sorry.'

Kirk laughs. 'Hey, I'm only kidding, man! Don't sweat it. Chill.'

Brett scrapes a half-smile out of somewhere and leans back into his chair an inch, trying to look chill, which is the exact opposite of how he's feeling.

Kirk is thirty-one years old and practically runs the entire building, at least on a day-to-day basis. No shit. Perhaps that's why Craig loathes him, though Brett suspects it could be for any number of the following reasons: Kirk dresses well, and he's a trifle camp; he's a gamer, of course, an unapologetic geek; he is woke, he is sober, and, critically, he is almost always pleasant. He is the walking antithesis of Craig Wilson.

'Say, Brett …' Kirk snaps his fingers as if he has just remembered something random upon passing. 'Any chance you could swing by my office for a beat?'

'Yeah, of course.' Brett swallows. 'Is it the trailer, because I wasn't sure about the mutant kangaroo, but I figured—'

'It's not the trailer,' Kirk interrupts him, smiling white teeth. 'The trailer's awesome, dude. The trailer rocks. No, come on, you can message your old lady afterwards, huh?'

Brett often wonders if, in the future, all bosses will speak like this. In New York City, they just might. He stands and follows. His palms are too hot. He feels eyes on his back all the way.

Kirk's office has windows overlooking the mid-morning traffic on Broadway. Instead of another mural, the art in here is neatly framed. There's a bookcase of personal items including awards, photographs and a collection of vinyl figurines spanning precisely the sort of pop culture Kirk likes: Marvel, *Game of Thrones*, *Rick and Morty* … loser shit, Craig would call it, except maybe *Game of Thrones* on account of all the tits.

Kirk invites Brett to have a seat before settling into his own chair. 'How was the game?' he asks.

'*The game?*' Something about these words niggle at Brett, prodding a raw, subconscious nerve, and he feels the strangest tremor. 'What game?'

'The Rangers, man. You were at the Garden on Saturday night, right?'

'Oh!' Of course. Facebook. 'Yeah, the game was …' He hesitates. 'You follow hockey?'

'Only the EA Sports version,' Kirk grins, but the grin promptly vanishes, and he takes on a sorry, puppy dog gaze. 'Look, I've brought you in here as a courtesy, that's all. It's about Wilson.'

'Craig.' Brett's mouth is parched. The ache under his eye, which had been feeling much better today, comes back with a sting. Has Brett been reported for something he can't even remember? He can't be fired, can he? Not in this day and age. *Can he?* 'What about Craig?'

'He hasn't shown up. Again. That's the third time this year, Brett, and it's the third week of January.' Kirk shows his hands like he's a victim in a stickup. 'Now, I like to have a good time as much as the next guy, but if a grown man can't make it into—'

'What did he say?' Brett interrupts uneasily. 'When he called in sick, what reason did he give?'

'Reason?' Kirk shakes his head. 'That's the thing, Brett. He hasn't called in. Not one word.'

'No email? Did you ask HR?'

'Nothing. I'm telling you, the guy's gone ghost.'

'Ghost.' Brett feels a draught from no particular direction.

Kirk pushes into his ergonomic backrest, tipping with the built-in suspension, and knits soft hands at his chest. 'Look, I know how it is, man. You went out of your way to hook a buddy up, and he's let you down, plain and simple. We've all been there. It isn't going to reflect badly on you, if that's what you're worried about. You're one of my guys, you know that. One of my A-team! Hell, if it'll make things easier for you, I can have HR tell this bozo you fought tooth and nail to keep him on the team.'

Brett tries a nod; he's feeling sort of weightless in his seat. 'I should check my cell at least, don't you think?'

Kirk fixes Brett with a level stare; it's this aged, penetrating look that has helped him get to this position in the business. 'This guy is, what?' he asks. 'Thirty-nine, forty years old? He isn't your responsibility. If he really is sick, then it's on him to go through the proper procedure.'

'I know, it's just …' Brett fades into silence because he has nothing more to say, and because he can feel his throat starting to wobble.

Kirk sighs, shifting his chair forward and landing on his feet. 'All right. He's your bud, I get that. Go for it. Check your cell, drop him a call if you like, but I wouldn't tell him about this meeting. Leave that to HR. You're doing good work for us, Brett. You don't need to get involved. You don't need that trouble.'

'No,' Brett agrees. 'No trouble. I like to keep my head down.'

'Correct.' Kirk pauses, eyeing him closely. 'Look, cards on

the table, pal. I know you've got your eyes on the writing and design team, and sooner or later a spot might open up, but the road there is steep with competition. You've worked hard to get here. I know where you started out. We did the background checks after that leak, as you know, and none of that interests me.'

'The background checks,' Brett repeats, adjusting his glasses without purpose. 'Right.'

'Hey, we've all got to start somewhere. What interests me is that you just keep doing *you* now, OK?'

'Sure.' Brett stumbles a little as he gets to his feet. 'Thank you, Kirk, I appreciate the, the feedback, I really do.'

'Don't mention it, kiddo,' the much younger man says.

Brett leaves the room in a calm, collected manner. He closes the door behind him and walks the length of the bullpen as if he's riding the travelator at the airport.

Then he practically sprints through the building without returning to his desk.

His heart, such a tender lump all morning, is now punching, hammering, dangerous.

The security guy retrieves his phone from its allocated drawer in reception.

There's nothing from Craig, as Brett feared.

He reopens the spam message he received this morning and returns to the image he couldn't download on the subway. As he opens the file, he notes the surprising amount of sweat his thumbprint leaves on the screen.

Then the picture loads.

Finally, for the first time since Saturday night, Brett sees his old friend, Craig Wilson.

18

PLAYER THREE

The front door of her house has been opened from inside and left ajar, and Sarah bursts out of it clutching Archie tightly to one shoulder, gasping the same word over and over again as she clears the small front garden in her socks.

'No-no-no-no-no—'

With the hand that isn't supporting her baby, she is trying to get through to Neil on the phone, sequentially hammering the green and red call buttons. He isn't picking up, so she lets it go to voicemail.

'*Neil!* Neil, ring me back, for God's sake! Something has – something has happened! I don't know what to do! Oh God, I don't know what to do! I need you here! Please just, just ring me back!'

She hits the red button in case he might be trying to call her back already – in case she is about to start incoherently bawling – and staggers the length of her road; it's only a short distance, a dead-end of eighteen houses, but Archie is wailing and wriggling against her ribs, and he's too cumbersome to carry at any real pace. If she can only move fast enough, she might still reach her daughter, that's what her body seems to believe. She is moving on adrenaline with complete tunnel vision, the hairs on her neck all screaming electric. She is the frantic, frightened, animal mother.

The cul-de-sac is empty except for a few of the neighbours' cars, vehicles she knows well enough, but the road beyond the junction is long and there's a chance she'll see it there: the car, the licence plate, the *stranger*.

Her head reels with the shrill, crazed chorus of some childish rhyme – *stranger danger, stranger danger, stranger d— –* and it has happened, the dead-of-night dread of every parent since time before mind: her little girl has been SNATCHED.

She reaches the junction, momentarily shunted by grief into denial, half-expecting to see Hannah tottering up the pavement towards her, lost and confused in the way small children so often find themselves. There's no movement in either direction, neither on the paths nor the straight road that stretches both ways into the distance.

Hannah is gone.

Sarah turns desperately on the spot, faced with a fifty-fifty chance, the flip of an invisible coin: left or right?

There's a weight crushing down on her, an impossible mass squeezing the oxygen from her lungs, threatening to steal the light from her eyes. Left or right?

No instinct comes to guide her, no maternal radar, no biological hunch or scent of her child on the air. Left or right? Lost or found? Alive or dead?

She takes neither direction. She goes no further. She falls to her knees in the middle of the road and squeezes her remaining baby almost tight enough to hurt him. She sobs and Archie sobs too, still kicking her left breast, seeming to sense through the simple shapes and colours of his world that something has gone terribly, irrevocably wrong.

Sarah brings her phone to her face. No response from her husband. She dials two nines for the police … and then stops.

For some reason, she can't dial the third number. Her hand has locked up, seized, and it won't allow her to continue. Why?

The text message. She feels her bladder go slack, threatening to give.

Do not share this message. Do not seek help.

An insane idea, since she has never felt so helpless in all her life, not even after those long hours in labour, after the final, agonising push when the baby came out of her body, the baby before Hannah, the girl who never cried, the girl who only hung there from the surgeon's hand like some god-awful—

'Sarah?'

A voice. She turns to it, dazed, with Archie still screaming in one ear and two useless nines waiting on the screen of her phone. The voice is close, but it seems to be travelling very far to reach her.

'It is Sarah, isn't it?'

A little old man is standing in the cul-de-sac. Knitted cardigan, papery skin, bent, arthritic hands. She knows this man. He lives in the house on the corner, his wife used to post Christmas cards to the whole street – the wife died two, maybe three years ago and the cards stopped, and they haven't seen much of the husband since then – but right now, his name is lost to her. That doesn't matter; it doesn't stop her from wanting to fall against him like she once would have done her own grandad, back when a pair of skinned knees were about the worst a day could bring. She nods, answering the question she can't quite remember, and pockets her phone.

The neighbour shuffles closer, slow and rickety, every movement an apparent struggle. His face is all concern. 'What's the matter?'

She shakes her head, unable to say it out loud, unable to make it any more real.

'Come on,' the man says, checking the empty street for traffic, 'let's get you up out of the road, eh?'

He holds out a hand that's twisted like a claw, and she sees him wince with the agony of the gesture, yet she has no choice but to take it. She simply won't make it up alone. If he can offer a hand through his own pain, then she can make it onto her feet. She does, almost dragging him down, hearing his sharp intake of breath, and Archie finally stops screaming to study the new participant in this strange situation.

'What is it?' the man asks. 'What's happened?'

She takes huge, gulping breaths. 'My d—' she stumbles on the word, 'my d—, my d—' and then she stops talking, mouth open. *Do not seek help.* She takes one slow, careful step backwards. 'My ... dog.'

The neighbour – Roger? Robert? – frowns slightly, trying to comprehend. He glances back to her front door standing open at the bottom of the cul-de-sac. 'Your dog? Did it get out? Did it run away?'

She shakes her head ... nods ... shakes it again. Her eyes are darting in all directions. A new sensation thrown onto the pile: suspicion, the feeling of being watched, it brings a new kind of panic.

'All right,' he says slowly, 'we'll go back inside and try ringing—'

'*No!*' It comes out fierce, and she takes another two steps away, circling him now, stepping back into her own road. 'Don't you help me.'

He blinks, showing both hands, and tilts his head. 'It's OK, I'm just trying to—'

'Don't you fucking help me!' This sets Archie off again. 'I haven't asked for your help,' and now, more to their empty surroundings than to him directly, 'I don't want any help! I didn't ask for it! I didn't fucking ask!'

The old man is confused and incredibly hurt, she can see that much, and a dim, more rational part of her knows she'll feel guilty about this later, if there *is* a later, but this is no time for rationality, and all she can think of is the backseat of some stranger's car, and her girl, and that awful, twisted message.

She holds up one hand as if commanding her neighbour to stay, and she walks the entire length of her road like this, backwards, one arm outstretched to stop his advance, the other arm wrestling her baby. The man doesn't move, makes no attempt to follow, and his wounded expression never changes. He's still standing in the very same spot at the end of the street when she kicks her front door closed, blocking him from view.

And as the latch catches, and she turns the key, the next text message, the one telling her to get a burner, arrives.

19

PLAYER FOUR

'You have to help me, Khalid.' Noah clasps his hands together. 'Please. You have to help *her*.'

Noah is back in Pigalle, the red-light district, in a subterranean office without windows. The air in here is sour with body odour, and house music thuds relentlessly through the ceiling from the nightclub upstairs. Khalid owns the nightclub. He owns a moderate portion of the city, but that isn't something he keeps on any books. Paper trails aren't his style.

Khalid is sitting on the opposite side of a vast, ornamental desk. He's massive, weighing close to thirty stone, and beads of unseasonable sweat roll into his beard as he studies both of Noah's phones. For several excruciating minutes, he hasn't said a word.

Noah is seated too, but his black shoes are tapping without rhythm, and he has to push his forearms onto his knees to bolt his restless feet flat to the floor. He can physically feel time wasting, and every second that passes feels like it could be another chance lost. He should be out there searching, but he's down here, in a building he despises, waiting for his oldest acquaintance, his on-off employer, to make up his mind.

As Noah waits, his eyes go from the gigantic, impenetrable safe to the decorative focal point of the room – an AK-47, dull Soviet steel mounted on the rear wall – and Khalid finally glances up. They speak in French.

'It's genuine,' Khalid says. 'The Kalashnikov. Remember how much I wanted one when we were boys?'

'Yes,' Noah replies, remembering without much interest that when they were boys – Khalid a decade older than him but always around, always there – they had wanted a lot of things.

'It was used in the Balkan wars in the nineties,' Khalid goes on. 'The stories it could tell.'

'Yes,' Noah repeats, regarding the weapon with a vague sickness. To him, it brings to mind the terror attacks on Paris and that dreadful night at the Bataclan; his city in mourning and the months of heightened prejudice that followed; the sudden difficulty, for a man of his heritage, in finding work. Hadn't that marked the beginning of yet another stint of hustling? Yes, but it was either move product on the streets or be thrown out to live on them; that's what Noah told himself at the time, and it's what he tells himself now.

Of course, he still remembers the night he was given his own six-shooter from Khalid's extensive collection. A MR73 double-action revolver, the preferred sidearm of GIGN, France's answer to America's well-known SWAT teams. That was three years ago, after Noah had been jumped for his goods at knifepoint, and for a while he had carried that gun as if he was in a Truffaut or Godard movie, swaggering, romantic, untouchable. That thrill, like so many others in his twenties, was short-lived, but he'd held onto the gun. Better to be an armed thug than a dead pacifist, he had decided, though he has never fired at anything other than empty air around a few glass bottles. When Noah quit dealing, Khalid didn't ask for the gun back; it was as if he knew the hiatus would be short, just like the last times, and he was right about that.

The revolver is currently in the custody of the third man in the room, the short, taciturn figure standing behind Khalid's left shoulder. This is Victor. Noah doesn't know him well, because Noah doesn't come down to the club much, but he understands his role. Victor is a veritable caricature of the dour Eastern hardman. The muscle. He has taken the gun – temporarily, he said – until Noah has had a chance to calm down. Noah doesn't see that happening anytime soon, but he is at least consciously aware of his own frantic appearance, and he's doing his best to hold it back. Khalid is a friend, but these sorts of friends are easily spooked.

Khalid sighs through his nostrils, a hurricane sound, and scratches deep inside his beard. 'Before you left tonight, her behaviour didn't seem unusual?'

'She seemed …' Noah swallows. 'Happy. She was herself.'

'And you haven't crossed anybody?'

'I've only been back out there for a few nights. I've kept my head down, like always.'

Khalid nods, watching him closely now. 'And this name, "Player Four", it means nothing to you? You haven't been playing some sort of game on the side, have you Noah? We haven't seen much of you in the last year …'

Noah feels heat in his cheeks. 'No, I swear to God, I don't know what it means. Any of it! Like I told you, she didn't show up at Harry's Bar, so I called you from my work phone; it's new, untraceable, I only bought it last week. I used the same phone to go to this *website*, except it wasn't really much of a website at all. A message told me that "Player Four has entered the game", but that message vanished. I didn't have to delete it; it was as if it had never been there at all. The website must have done something to the phone. Infected it somehow. Bugged it. That was twenty minutes ago. And now—'

'Now *this*,' Khalid finishes, tapping the screen of the burner phone, where the final message is still on the screen.

'Yes.' Noah sighs. 'Now this.'

He can see the screen from here, albeit upside down. It still shows the message, which refuses to disappear even when the screen is locked. In the black box this time, there is an invitation, some kind of code he doesn't recognise made up of letters and numbers. Below that, a digital clock face runs backwards. A timer. The sort you might find on a bomb.

COME AND PLAY.
HD7 6UZ
17:48:59

Victor, who has been eyeing the phones from behind Khalid, speaks. 'What business do you have with the English, Noah?'

'English?' Noah shrugs. 'What English?'

The men on the other side of the desk share a glance, something hard to read. 'This … *invitation*,' Victor says slowly, 'it is to an English postal code, I think. Coordinates.'

Noah feels his stomach plummet. 'No. That can't be right.'

'I think so,' Victor counters. 'I spent two years in England. This is a location.'

'England?' Khalid says with interest. 'Who do we know with ties there? The Corsicans? Definitely not those brats in the nineteenth.'

'No,' Victor says, 'I doubt it. Could be the gypsies, but ...'

Khalid shakes his head. 'It's not their style, this kidnapping, although it wouldn't be the first time they've tried to intimidate us.'

'Gypsies ...' Noah repeats it quietly, clenching his fists. For a while, close to his apartment, half a kilometre of the abandoned Petite Ceinture railway was home to hundreds of travellers squatting in a makeshift shantytown of plywood and tarpaulin. The police eventually destroyed this Romani camp with unorthodox prejudice, its residents were dispersed across central Paris and, in the years since, the Roma have become the bogeymen of criminal activity in the city. Noah's own upbringing in the Maghreb slums had left him feeling largely ambivalent about these people. Ambivalent, that is, until now. Now he is ready to set Paris, and all of the continent, alight if he has to.

'We need to do something!' he says suddenly. 'We need to act now, hit them hard! We have to find them and—'

Khalid raises a hand. 'I understand your frustration, my friend, and I have our people searching, but the last thing we need is to turn this city into a warzone. Not until we're certain.'

Noah mutters something unintelligible, even to himself, while Khalid returns to the photograph of Sofia – Sofia hooded, Sofia taken – on Noah's first phone.

'An Estonian model,' Khalid says. 'She may have been abducted for ...' He looks up at Victor, his stern expression finishing the sentence for him.

'A pretty girl,' Victor replies solemnly. 'It is possible.'

'What's possible?' Noah asks, and then he realises, and he has to force his next words out around a very large stone in his mouth. 'You mean traffickers. You think they are taking her across the Channel?'

'Could be,' Khalid says, 'though that doesn't explain this game, or why they would want you there too.'

'For a cash ransom,' Victor suggests. 'This location may be the drop-off, somewhere they know he will be alone, unprotected. Somewhere we cannot follow.'

'There *is* no cash,' Noah moans. 'I'm working for a wedding. I have nothing.' He twists his hands together. 'If it comes to that, you will help me, won't you? You'll loan me the money?'

There's a fat, dreadful silence.

'Noah …' Khalid appears to be choosing his words very carefully. 'For thirty years, you have been like a brother to me.'

'Yes. So be a brother now.'

Victor raises his eyebrows, clearly unaccustomed to hearing such a tone around their mutual employer. Khalid doesn't bite, he only speaks more slowly. 'If we pay for this girl—'

'My fiancée.'

'Yes. If we pay, then we are only creating an incentive for anybody else who might want to … harm our business in the future. You understand that, don't you?'

Noah understands that right now he doesn't give two shits about Khalid's business.

'So we play,' Noah says, 'but we play this my way. We find them first. They say they're monitoring me. Is there a way to reverse that? If they can see me, then how do I see them?'

'I don't know,' Khalid admits, shifting backwards in his seat, moving his face away from the two phones. 'If either phone is bugged, then do they hear us right now? Can they see us, Victor?'

Victor leans over his shoulder, staring down into the lenses of the front-facing cameras as if to find somebody staring back at him. 'I don't think so. There's no service down here for them to connect to, even if they are trying. So long as we remain underground, I imagine we are safe.'

'Good,' Khalid says. 'For now, Noah, you must let us do our thing. Once we have some answers, we can re-evaluate the situation and—'

'No. If they are taking Sofia to England, then I am going to England. With or without money, I am going tonight. I'll be there when the timer reaches zero. Only, I don't have a passport …'

'Noah—'

'You can get me there, can't you? To England at least. You can get me across the water?'

Khalid hesitates, pinching his eyes shut. 'It is a bad idea; I promise you that. No good will come out of doing their dance or playing this game.'

'I agree,' Victor adds. 'You are much safer in Paris.'

'And Sofia?' Noah can feel his voice breaking. 'Is *she* safer if I stay in Paris? Khalid, please. All my life, I've never asked you for a thing. Sofia means everything to me. She's my family. My world. *Please.*'

More silence between them. Just the pounding of the bass upstairs while, on the screen of Noah's burner, the clock counts down, down, down without pausing.

Finally, Khalid sighs. 'It will not be pleasant,' he says, 'but for you, I can make it happen. If this is what you want.'

'It is. If it means having her back, then I'll go anywhere. I'll do anything.'

'Yes,' Khalid agrees. 'I think they know this, and that's what I'm afraid of. You will need to leave this one,' he gestures to the iPhone, 'behind. It can be traced, and I can't allow that, considering the journey you're about to take. I'll keep it here. Leave the product too. They'll have dogs at customs.'

Noah reaches out and touches the photograph of Sofia on the screen of his own phone one last time, and then he leaves it on the desk and instead pockets the burner.

'There's one more thing I need,' he says, getting to his feet.

Khalid looks at him both warily and wearily. 'What else?'

'If I'm doing this,' Noah turns to Victor, 'then I'm going to need my gun back.'

20

PLAYER FIVE

Linda opens her eyes, woken by her bladder, and with instant, lurching sickness she can tell from the light around the closed curtains that it's almost the middle of the day. Tuesday.

She sits upright, tossing Alyssa's duvet aside, and looks at the digital clock on the bedside table. Sure enough, it's coming up to afternoon. Impossible. She grabs one of the bed's pillows, slams it over her face and shrieks into it.

How could she have slept? She smacks herself through the pillow, rousing her senses with a blunt ringing across her jaw, and kicks her feet as if she's more than fifty years younger and in the throes of a tantrum. How did she allow this to happen? She thinks back, recalling her final moments of consciousness.

There'd been some back and forth on her phone.

Player Five. She is now Player Five and, like any game, she'd been forced to wait her turn. And so, she had waited. The phone remained silent. There was nothing more she could do. Dawn had come, the temperature in the room dropping until she could see her own breath around her, and that's about the time her adrenaline must have given up the ghost. The gin had dragged her off to some deep, dark place, and she'd sat here, wrapped in her daughter's quilt, and done what? Cried herself to sleep holding her daughter's stuffed animal? Faded out like a dying battery?

A brief slip of the eyelids, that was all, and hours have been lost. Crucial hours. So much training, so many years on the force, and now that she's playing for her daughter, playing for keeps, she *falls asleep*. She clenches her fist, frustrated enough to smack herself again, but refrains. Instead, her hands rummage through the tangled bedding for her phone.

She finds it and sees, with horrible relief, that the next instructions have been sent while she slept. Fortunately, this message requires no immediate response; if it had, then this whole thing might have fallen apart already.

It's the invitation. She stares at the postcode, the timer, absently rubbing her lower lip. This is 'the meet'. The postcode starts with HD, which is Huddersfield, West Yorkshire. There's a little over five hours left on the clock, and the numbers are falling by the second. The timer will end at five o'clock today. One way or another, this could all be over by late afternoon.

No. Not one way or another. Just one way. Her way. She has to move; she has wasted so much time. If she can get there early, she can survey the location. She should be there already, waiting, watching.

Watching for what? For whom?

Another sharp twinge in her abdomen, calling her to the bathroom. She moves, swinging her feet onto the floor, and hears a voice as clear as day.

'*Can't you play it with me, Mum? Just one game!*'

For a heartrending moment she imagines it's real, that her daughter is here in the room with her, and she spins around so fast she almost empties her bladder on the spot. But the room is otherwise empty, the voice incredibly young. It's nothing more than a remnant of a dream she'd been having, torturous in its authenticity. A memory, she thinks, but a memory of what? Something random, something bad. Linda allows herself a painful glimpse back through time.

Alyssa on her birthday – sixth? Seventh? Too many years ago now – holding a white box, surrounded by scraps of pink wrapping paper. That bloody Nintendo, the one that had sold out across the country, which Linda and Richard had had to drive into London to find. Alyssa's face, so pretty even then, at first ecstatic and then fading, frowning, because she'd barely finished opening her presents and her mum was already putting on shoes and eyeing the exit.

Linda in uniform, moving in for a kiss: 'You'll have to get your dad to set it up for you, I've got to get to the station.'

'But we can all play it together! We can do bowling and it'll be like a real tournament, and you can make yourself on the game, you choose faces and clothes, and you move your arms around with the controller like it's a real—'

'Later, Alyssa.' Getting short now, snappy, exhausted. 'Just entertain yourself for a while, all right? Ring Georgia and see if she wants to come over and play it with you.'

Alyssa's face darkening, turning away.

Richard by the front door, crossing his arms: 'She hasn't spoken to Georgia for almost a week. She says she stole her gel pens, the smelly ones. I told you this.'

'Gel pens, right, of course. The smelly ones. What do you

want me to do, Richard, file a report? They're kids, they'll be fine in another day or two, you know what they're like.'

Richard's expression, that look she hated, the one that would finally end them. 'It's Saturday, Lin. Her birthday. You said you'd get it off. You *always* say you'll—'

Linda opens her eyes and shakes her head, chucking the memory away because the memory only hurts. It has nothing to do with now. It starts to fade, but the echo remains.

We can all play it together! We can—

Linda halts, pressing her hand against the aching side of her head, considering the dream-memory, the message from her own subconscious.

Player Five. She is Player Five, standing by her daughter's bed in Luton, England, at almost twelve o'clock on Tuesday. She is Player Five.

So where are Players One, Two, Three and Four?

She balances her laptop on the bathroom sink and powers it up while she empties her bladder, then she carries the computer into the living room and opens her browser. She only has to type the first two letters before the predictive address bar takes her where she wants to go; it's a place she visits more and more often.

The website has a start-up page with a graphic of a seven-pointed star above two truncheons crossed over in an X. The colour scheme is, naturally, blue.

The Billy Club
An informal global community for serving and veteran police officers

She clicks on the button marked ENTER, dismissing the pop-up and its conditions with which she is now well familiar:

> *The BC is independent of any police service. It is a place for officers from across the world to share their personal ideas and views in absolute, encrypted anonymity. It is not recommended that any investigations, ongoing or historic, are discussed in any detail. The BC takes no responsibility for the content within. We are a self-sustaining community started by veteran officers, for veteran officers.*
>
> *By entering this site, you agree to appropriate behaviour, as detailed in our <u>terms and conditions</u>. The Internet has a million homes for pornography – this isn't one of them.*
>
> *For legitimate support, we provide a list of worldwide charities <u>here</u>.*
>
> *Thank you for reading and thank you for your service. THE BILLY CLUB, est. 2001*

Inside, the website is organised like so many online forums, with categories upon categories upon categories: POLICING NEWS with a dropdown list of countries, mostly from the Western world; GENERAL POLICING DISCUSSIONS AND SPECIFIC INTERESTS (FIREARMS, ROAD POLICING, RETIREMENT AND RESETTLEMENT); BODYCAM CLIPS AND KIT TALK.

When Linda first discovered this website – and she can no longer remember exactly how or when that was – she had cringed. The name was stupid, the grown men and women spilling their guts inside even worse. Thousands of cops from across the world reminiscing on the good old days, or else lamenting them. Mostly the latter. There were private dicks looking for tips. Silly old sods trying to rouse vigilantes. Losers looking for love.

Now she's on here a lot, talking to the friends she has made, chatting with people who simply *get her* in the way her own family never have. Once upon a time, she'd scoffed at the idea of dating services for uniforms too, but now she understands; it really does take one to know one.

She opens a category with the clumsy comic title of INTEL, DIRT AND RUMOUR. Some of the most popular recent posts here include: *Vehicle Theft, East London Action Team*; *Meth Dealers of Chicago, Named and Shamed*; *Gangs in Paris, Who's to Blame?*

She hesitates, cursor hovering over the search button, and then clicks and types. Despite the website's initial warning, ongoing cases – particularly the strangest of those – are often discussed here, chain of evidence be damned. This, though, is surely a needle in a haystack. Even if Players One, Two, Three or Four *have* somehow made it onto the radar of God only knows which police forces, the chances of it ending up in the public domain are infinitesimal.

And, of course, she is correct.

She finds nothing immediately relevant in ABDUCTIONS, and when she types in 'The Game', it returns ongoing debates regarding policing fitness standards, along with light-hearted banter surrounding a continuing football rivalry between the police and fire brigades of Kent. Nothing new.

She gives up after nine minutes, conscious of the clock, and closes the laptop.

Time to move.

If she had scrolled down to the very bottom of the results page, then she might have seen an old, all but forgotten post, and an adjoining article regarding a crime of crucial importance.

Not that anybody would be likely to see the connection on first glance.

That game, after all, was played a year and a half ago, and it happened in another part of the world entirely.

21

PREGAME

EasyJet's flight 2125 touched down fifteen minutes early, and the passengers – mostly Britons dressed in shorts, ready for August proper – filed off the plane from the frontmost exit and made their way through customs. Of these two hundred or so travellers, only the young woman with the fierce cobalt pigtails paused to take a selfie in front of the bilingual sign in Arrivals.

Bienvenue à l'aéroport Nice Côte d'Azur Terminal 2
Welcome to Nice Côte d'Azur Airport Terminal 2

Dodging the moving herd, she stuck out her tongue and threw two fingers up in a gesture of peace. She purposely angled the shot to include her chest, T-shirt a little too tight over braless breasts, nipple piercings pressing against the thin white cotton and the bright purple letters printed there; the letters, in a pixelated font, spelled PWN ME.

Happy with the photograph by the third take, she then took several more in front of the sign, these versions all *sans nips*.

The first image she would upload to her Premium Snapchat, while the latter would go to her regular accounts on Instagram, Twitter *et al*. She wheeled her carry-on case along blindly, eyes on her phone, mechanically consenting to the terms of the airport's Wi-Fi. She added soft filters before uploading the pictures to the relevant accounts, where she went by the name that she used for all her social media, the improbable name that would never appear on any nation's passport: Glitch Valentine.

Across, below or above the pictures, she posed the same simple question in text.

Who's ready to play?

Immediately, the Likes began to amass.

She smiled, feeling an immense sense of relief. The flight was over. The weeks of secrecy and deceit since she had first received the invite were now behind her. She'd made it, and she'd done it alone.

Come and play, the invitation had said, and here she was.

'OK, Glitch,' she said to herself, surveying the terminal. 'Now what?'

A good question.

The terminal was busy, feverish with summer heat, and the pulse of the entire airport seemed to be at its most hectic. Families stood together in loose clusters waiting for loved ones to emerge from the baggage carousels. Older children squabbled while younger ones simply screamed. A voice from the overhead speakers warned against unguarded luggage in French, English and French again, and the squeak of shoes and suitcase wheels was constant.

This was her first time alone in any airport, and it would be all too easy to let herself get dizzy and become overwhelmed. She couldn't allow that. Not here. Not now. This was a new beginning. For too long she'd been controlled by her own anxieties, but that girl was somewhere far behind. Away from home, she could be anything she wanted.

Out here, she was Glitch Valentine.

She spotted a line of chauffeurs standing by the exit, all fully suited and making the most of the indoor air-con. Each was holding a sign with a handwritten name upon it. She approached at a brisk walk, excited, but quickly realised that none was waiting for her. A shame, because she'd always wanted to ride in her own limousine, but there'd be time for that yet. If she won this thing – a big *if*, she reminded herself – then she'd probably treat herself to first-class luxury all the way back to England. And why not? In terms of sheer Instagrammability – a word she loathed and now found herself using as a blanket term for all social media – a few uploads from the first-class cabin might pay for themselves in new followers. Well, not literally, not penny for penny, but the rule of thumb was simple enough: in this game, you faked it until you made it.

Followers led to paid subscriptions. Subs attracted sponsors. Sponsorships attracted exclusivity deals, and they brought the *serious* money.

She had decided to get out of the heaviest footfall – to claim a quiet spot on the outskirts of the terminal where she could read the invitation for the hundredth time – when somebody caught her eye. An Asian American of six-three with tattoos up her neck and a harsh punk undercut through bright pink hair, the woman would've been difficult to miss.

'You're joking,' Glitch whispered to herself, and then she was moving for the exit again, following at a jog before the new arrival was swallowed in the hurrying crowds. Outside, the heat smacked her like a fist, but she didn't slow down until the woman ahead had stopped to vape in the smoking area.

'Hey!' Glitch said, leaning on her case's handle to catch her breath in the baking Riviera heat. 'Sorry, pardon me. You're *Infinitear*!'

It wasn't a question. She knew well enough; she'd been following her for years.

The woman looked her up and down, exhaling a monumental cloud of whitish vapour, and smiled. 'Right,' she said, 'but when I'm not creating, I just go by Amy.' She offered her hand, which was pumped enthusiastically, and nodded to the carry-on luggage. 'Digging the Pokémon case.'

Glitch beamed. 'It's limited edition from the nineties. Gen One, obviously. I got it shipped over from Kyoto, which was a nightmare because it got stuck at customs and I thought it was lost for good, then it went to the wrong post office and …' She cringed. 'Sorry, I'm rambling, I'm just so psyched that you're here. I saw your post saying you had something exciting happening this weekend and I knew, I just *knew* it had to be this!' She paused, glancing around at the smokers and the families sweating in lines for taxis, and dropped her voice. 'You *are* here to play, aren't you?'

Amy winked, speaking between puffs on her enormous e-cigarette, which looked like a psychedelic cyborg-phallus. 'Be some coincidence if I wasn't, don't you think?'

Glitch laughed a little too hard and blushed. 'Well, I have to say, you look *amazing*.'

'Ah, please!' Amy waved a hand, feigning bashfulness, and put on a pair of perfectly round shades from her pocket. 'Sugar, I look like shit, OK? Flew outta Austin yesterday morning, had a three-hour stopover at London Heathrow, now I don't know what day it is or what time zone I'm in. Let's just hope they got showers at this place, wherever it is, because I got my monthly last night and it's like *Shark Week* in these goddamn cactuses they call leggings.'

Glitch felt momentarily light-headed, hypnotised by the Texan drawl that seemed thicker, almost syrupy, in real life, even after listening to it for hundreds, literally *hundreds*, of hours in the past. Amy Choe – Infinitear to her legions of fans – was only twenty-five years old, as Glitch recalled, but those few years' difference had always made her seem to Glitch – online, at least – to be so much more of an adult, a professional, a real person. Now she was here, in the French sunshine, talking about her period.

'What's your name, anyway?'

'Oh.' A clear of the throat. 'It's Glitch Valentine.'

'*Glitch Valentine*.' Amy considered it for a moment. 'I like it. Makes me think of *Resident Evil* gone wrong. How old are you?'

'Eighteen,' she says a little too quickly. 'People say I look young for my age.'

'You look just fine to me. You're doing good, right? Think I've seen you around.'

'Ah, I don't know,' Glitch shrugged, her turn to play coy, 'nothing like you. What do you have now? Over a million followers?'

'One point two on TikTok. One point nine on Twitch.'

'One point nine!'

Another thick, vaporous exhale. 'You seen anyone else around?'

'No. I just landed.'

'Same. I'm all for suspense, don't get me wrong, but talk about a vague invitation. Seriously, I half-expected it to be BS ... until they paid for everything.' She pocketed her vape and stretched, yawning. 'I guess we ought to stick together. I still got to post though. You want to get in it for a mention?'

'Seriously? Yes, that'd be amazing!'

'All right, Valentine, let's do it.'

They followed signs for the shuttle buses, Amy holding her phone on a selfie stick and talking as they went.

'What's up, everybody? Infinitear here, sending a big, fat, Texas *howdy* from the glorious French Riviera! Excuse the shades, guys, I've been travelling for two days and I look like *hell*. I do, however, have to give a special shoutout to Alt Threads dotcom for their latest haul. Their Lazy Leggings kept me cosy and sane all the way over the Atlantic. Seriously, you got a long journey coming up, here's my advice: take sixty bucks and get yourself a pair, they're unisex and you won't regret it. I'm not joking. Do it and thank me later.

'As y'all know, there's going to be some disruption to my usual streaming schedule this weekend, but I promise it'll be worth it. Hang tight, and all will be revealed in the next few hours. Oh, and if for some strange reason you *don't* know this smoking hot stuff walking alongside me, this is Glitch Valentine! Blow them a kiss, girl!'

She did, feeling a little dizzy. 'Hello, guys!'

'I know, I know, she's a British babe, right? Check her

out in all the usual places, we'll try to get some links put into the description after this goes up, as well as the link for those *amazing* leggings I mentioned, and links to all my other platforms too, including my eighteen-plus communities where I'll be doing stuff I can't do on YouTube or Twitch. So, yeah, subscribe, hit that Like button, turn notifications on, and all will be exposed very, very soon. It's going to be wild, I guarantee it. Mwah!'

She signed off by blowing a fat kiss of her own, and then silently busied herself on the phone.

'Wow,' Glitch said, 'you're so *natural*.'

'Practice, that's all. You stream more than eighty per cent of your life, waking *and* sleeping, and you get used to it.' She glanced up from her phone as they turned the corner. 'You think this is us?' The question was rhetorical.

Glitch caught her breath. There were more than a dozen people, most of whom she recognised despite never having met them in real life, crowded around a white, titanic, stretch Hummer. Some were talking excitedly in groups, but most were performing into their own cameras with the vehicle in shot behind them. The limousine had a printed sign in the front window.

PRIVATE: HAVE INVITATIONS READY.

'Nice ride,' Amy said.

'That's *Fyrestarter*,' Glitch replied in a hushed voice, 'Streamer of the Year at the last Shortys, and there's Stacey Sargent, and *LOL-eater* …' Intimidated, she took an involuntary step backwards. 'Is this an all-girl tournament? I didn't realise …'

'Fucking sweet if it is. These things are usually *crawling* with creeps, you wouldn't believe.'

Glitch nodded, but she didn't move.

'You OK, Valentine?'

Valentine. You are Glitch Valentine and you can do anything. You have a right to be here. You deserve to be here as much as anybody else.

She exhaled, regaining her composure, and allowed excitement to suffocate her nerves.

'I'm OK. Just play the game, right?'

'That's what they say,' Amy said. 'Play the game, and may the best woman win.'

22

PLAYER ONE

The studded tyres of her present taxi come to an easy enough halt in the snow, and Maggie asks the driver to wait here at the roadside.

He taps the meter. 'I'll have to keep her running.'

'Fine,' she says, 'this shouldn't take long. A few minutes. I'll leave my bag here, OK?'

The driver eyes her for a moment and, apparently deciding that this dishevelled yet cleanly dressed young woman isn't going to run out on her dozen-mile journey without paying, he nods, reaches into the map pocket of his door and takes out a rolled newspaper.

Leaving the car, Maggie notices one last Target clearance label hanging from her new hooded sweatshirt and yanks it away with a snap, absently dropping the litter into the gutter. She closes the taxi's door behind her, leaving a shopping bag with her dressing gown on the backseat, and takes several paces away from the car before checking the phone.

Twenty-five minutes ago, a ticking clock appeared on the screen of the burner. With it, an invitation, and something as insane as anything else this morning: a postal code, according to her quick, couldn't-be-helped search on Google. A *British* postcode. Somehow, Maggie has a little less than twenty-five hours to reach her next destination.

Her next destination is four thousand miles away.

Four thousand miles in the wrong direction, if finding Jackson is the goal here.

Has she been given a voice to argue the point, or time to consider the demand? No. Just these numbers that run down relentlessly, draining her fight – and, it seems, the beginnings of her sanity – as they go.

She has no business in England. She has never left the United States. In her experience, Minnesotans don't do much overseas travelling; why leave the greatest country in the world, when this country has almost any climate you could find elsewhere on the planet?

The idea of willingly fleeing the country now, of abandoning Jackson, goes against every instinct she has.

The fear of disobeying The Game, however, is somehow worse. She doesn't know what will happen if she leaves, but she has a damn good idea of what could happen if she stays.

Remember the plane guy, she keeps reminding herself, unable to recall his name but remembering the story well enough from high school. The *plane guy* – not Hughes, who was played by DiCaprio in that long, long movie, but the other – was told not to involve the police when his kid was taken for ransom in the night. He called them almost immediately, and the cops led to the military, and the military led to international press, and that brought mobsters, vigilantes and the president along for the circus.

And the kid?

OK, so maybe it's not the best thing to be thinking about right now, but it's serving well as a lesson in obedience. Follow the demands and get Jackson back unhurt. Follow the rules.

She enters another alleyway, her second of the day, and aims for the neighbouring street. She couldn't leave the taxi running directly outside her actual destination, so she has to approach the house from behind. She's in Minneapolis now, the sibling to her own Saint Paul in the great Minnesotan Twin Cities, and that's fitting because the yard she's now vaulting into belongs to her own big sister.

Maggie has no passport, but she knows that Karen does. Karen spent Christmas in Paris. Maggie's mother posted, and boasted, about it at length on Facebook. The sisters share a remarkable resemblance, despite the five years between them. Or, at least, they used to. Once upon a time, they might have been twins.

Over the low point in the hedgerow, shaking a dusting of snow to the ground, she lands on a narrow, salted walk that runs from the rear gate, up through the immaculate garden to the back door. She freezes here, watching the windows for any sign of movement. She doesn't have to wait long to know the house is empty. Karen hasn't spoken to Maggie in years, and might never speak to her again, but she's always been a traditionalist. As it famously boasts on its licence plates, Minnesota is the land of ten thousand lakes, and on any three-day weekend such as this, Karen, her husband and the kids will be up at Bobcat Pines, the family's lake house, with Maggie's parents. You could bet your bottom dollar on that.

Even today this stings a little, and jealousy rises like bile.

If Maggie had been invited, if Jackson had spent the weekend with his biological cousins, then none of this would be happening.

Her mind goes out to the lake, a place she'd once believed to be bottomless, its faintly fishy, mineral smell now undoubtedly trapped beneath a surface as smooth and solid as polished diamond. Kayaking, fishing and sailing in the summer, skating in the winter, hot cider and toasted s'mores. She imagines her three nephews playing hockey on the ice, each boy with as much Dawson blood in his veins as her own child, each boy accepted into the family in a way Jackson never will be. Maggie has never met her nephews, but she's seen photographs, and her mother still discusses Karen as a sort of commonality whenever they speak, as if the sisters are still friendly, as if nothing ever happened.

Nine years, more or less. Has it really been so long?

Approaching the house now, all the old guilt tries to force itself upon her, and she pushes it back to where it belongs: in the past. She can't dwell on that today. She's already maxed out on guilty feels.

But aren't the similarities sort of ... uncanny?

They are, and the realisation makes her shiver.

Nine years ago, Maggie borrowed her older sister's ID for one night. She took it without permission, a spur-of-the-moment decision, and everything changed.

Karen was a senior in college at the time. She'd come home one weekend thanks to the worst menstrual cramps of her life, and though that reason had no specific bearing on things to come, Maggie always remembers that part. While Karen was curled up around a hot water bottle, being doted on by their mother, Maggie, a sophomore at high school then, had slipped the driver's licence from her sister's purse with the deft ability of any teenage shoplifter.

With tailored makeup and the tallest heels she owned, Maggie could add years to her image, a trick adolescent girls pull off so much better than their pimpled, fluffy-cheeked male classmates. In fact, despite her sister later referring to the look as 'the Halloween-slut version of herself', it would've been good enough to fool anybody other than close friends and family from a distance.

That was precisely the problem. That's how everything went so wrong.

Now history is repeating itself. Or rather, history is being *forced* to repeat itself.

Coincidence? She tells herself that it has to be. Surely, it has to.

The back door is locked, of course, but Maggie quickly spots what she's looking for attached to the external wall of the house. It's a family habit, something the sisters had instilled into their own childhoods because their parents were usually at work when the school bus dropped them off at home, and because both sisters were clumsy enough to have lost their own set on more than one occasion. What she finds is a small, steel key safe. Biting her lower lip, Maggie spins the stiff dials. For a second, she thinks it hasn't worked, that old habits actually *haven't* lasted, but then the cold mechanism shunts, the face of the box drops open, and the key falls into her open hand. The code is their mother's birth date, same as it ever was.

She sighs, half relieved, half rueful. 'Predictable, Sis.' Then she holds her breath as she unlocks and opens the door.

No sound inside. No alarm. Linden Hills is a good neighbourhood. There's always the chance of surveillance, a hidden camera or two, but she's in too deep to worry about that now. Better to get this over with. The taxi is waiting, and the clock is, quite literally, ticking.

She looks around. Nice place. A palace compared to her apartment, though that's not a very high bar. This is the first time Maggie has actually been inside. On several occasions, after their excruciating mother–daughter trips into Minneapolis or down to the Mall of America, she has waited in the car while her mom has dropped something off for Karen or the kids. Maggie has never even seen their faces at the windows.

It's all very clean. Very Karen. Apart from a few drawings on the fridge, and the framed photographs, you'd be hard pressed to believe that three boys actually live here. Cute kids though, she has to admit it. They look a lot like their dad.

Don't all boys?

Maggie's stomach turns violently at the passing thought of Jackson's father and she presses on, rapidly opening and closing each of the kitchen drawers in turn. No luck. It's a big house, and it takes her a couple of minutes to find the study upstairs. Wood-panelled. Fancy, but a little ugly too. Sort of dated. She starts with the desk, rifling through paperwork in the top drawer, praying they don't use a safe for their more valuable documents.

Could you blame her if she did, she asks herself, *after what happened?*

Fortunately, safecracking is something she never has to consider. The passports are there, all of them, held together in a plastic wallet. One happy family.

She takes Karen's, pausing for a moment to look into her sister's blank, formal stare. She plants a soft, sad kiss onto the laminated page.

'Forgive me,' she whispers, knowing she never would and never will, and then she slips it into the pocket of her new jeans with a revolting sense of déjà vu, before carefully returning the wallet and closing the drawer.

The whole way down to the back door she expects to hear the family car pulling onto the driveway, or the key turning in the lock at the front of the house. Neither happens.

She almost wishes it would, so that somebody might put a stop to this, but she leaves without incident, locking the door and returning the key to its safe, already quite certain that she will never see her sister again.

23

PLAYER TWO

'Come on, Craig, quit jerking me around.' Brett knocks again, harder now, another step towards pounding. 'I'm not playing. I refuse to, so just open the goddamn door!'

He waits. Nothing happens. A tiny part of him, a part where his deepest cowardice lurks, is relieved. This needs to be handled delicately, and delicacy has never been Craig's strong point.

From his place in the narrow, gloomy corridor, Brett listens. He hears the low, indistinct chatter of TVs from the surrounding apartments. A jackhammer outside. An infant crying and Latino music thudding somewhere overhead. Nearer still, one of the immediate neighbours coughing in huge, ripping hacks. They say asthma rates are higher in Mott Haven, this southwestern section of the Bronx, thanks in part to the waste yards on the riverbank and the elevated roads by Willis Avenue Bridge. This is a neighbourhood built around meat markets and metal workers. The sort of place you'd expect Craig to have found work without issue, but jobs are hard fought for in any corner of the Apple and, for all his bravado, Craig often needs a hand as much as anybody else.

Brett hears all these sounds, the rich tapestry of the Bronx, but he doesn't hear Craig.

He presses his forehead against the door, cool cracked paint on his flushed skin, and talks.

'All right man, you got me. I don't know what happened after the hockey, I was so damn wasted, but I must've screwed up big time. I accept that. I was obviously trying to push your buttons, and I guess I took it too far. I was goofing on you, plain and simple, and now you're doing the same to me, right? ... Right?'

Wrong. This thought is so clear in Brett's mind that, for a split-second, he believes he really hears it through the door.

Wrong, because this isn't a prank and you know it. You know Craig. You've known him almost all your life.

That's true, and in all that time Craig has never shied away from confrontation. Craig has never schemed. On the contrary, he charges at his problems without the luxury of rational thought, hands balled into fists.

Can Brett honestly picture Craig faking a head wound with a bottle of market-brand ketchup, sticking a strip of tape over his own mouth and tying himself to an old chair in front of a camera set on a timer?

No, Brett can't see him doing that. The notion is almost laughable, but so is the idea that his friend really is shackled to some chair like that doomed cop in *Reservoir Dogs*, dressed only in his Rangers jersey and underwear.

There *is* a photograph, it's right there on Brett's phone, but that doesn't mean much. Not in the age of Photoshop. There's also the text message to consider. *The person you love most is in danger.* If that was the case, then – God forbid – it would be *Kelly* in that picture.

It would be Kelly.

Wouldn't it?

A narrative is still forming in Brett's mind, the same ugly story that has, in some shape or another, haunted him for two days now, his own imagination filling the empty, drunken void. Saturday night at Madison Square Garden, the two of them up in their high seats, or at a neighbouring bar after the final buzzer. Maybe they were just outside, pissing in the frosty street. It doesn't matter. What matters is the talking started, and the talk got deep. Brett would've been sloppy, getting weird and needy, and Craig ended up putting him on his ass. It's happened before. OK, so they were teenagers the last time, boys who had tried to drink the whole world, and Craig had always pulled his punches back then, but it could've happened again. Tequila brings out the worst in everyone.

Brett remembers something then, words coming from that black hole in his memory, words spat with such disgust that the voice of his friend is nearly unrecognisable to him.

'*You snake! You filthy fucking snake! You dirty, lying, deceitful little—*'

'Enough!' In the hallway, Brett is clenching all over, clasped by the rigor mortis of shame. The memory ends there – if it *is* a genuine memory – and it's enough to confirm his worst dread. Craig wouldn't want to see him after such a betrayal, wouldn't want to step foot in the same building on Monday, which would leave him out of a job.

This, then, is Brett's punishment. Extortion, plain and simple.

'Don't do this,' Brett pleads to the door in his face. 'It doesn't have to be like this. It was a dumb joke, that's all. I was pulling your leg. Playing a stupid—'

Game. It's one sentence he can't bring himself to finish. He takes out his phone and looks, once again, at the latest message. He has been told to buy a disposable phone. A burner. Something to do with a website. In three minutes, the half-hour he has been granted to do this will be up.

'And what happens then?' he asks the door, pocketing the phone. 'How far are you willing to go? You going to start posting me your own severed toes? Answer me!'

He does something instinctive, something so ludicrously simple that it hasn't occurred to him to even try it until this very moment; for the first time since the old geezer downstairs let him into the apartment building, Brett tries the handle on Craig's front door, and the front door opens easily.

He watches it swing inwards. It moves with an eerie, silent grace as if the hinges are broken, and a childhood memory comes back to Brett, of the haunted house at the fair.

'Craig?' he calls because it's what you do when you let yourself in, not because he expects a reply. He isn't expecting a reply because now he can see the damage to the doorframe. The steel strike plate is bent out of shape, hanging on by one twisted screw. The wood behind it, the part of the frame that holds the latches in place, is cracked and splintered. Something heavy hit this door, shunting the deadbolt straight through. He couldn't see it in the gloomy corridor, but now that the door has swung inwards – and all the lights inside are turned on, despite the hour – Brett can see a solitary boot print on the wood.

For a moment he almost runs, but his nerve holds. He steps forwards into the apartment, into a growing sense of cold abandon. He doesn't close the door behind him, doesn't want to trap himself inside, which is plainly ridiculous because he doesn't believe this at all … Does he?

This is Craig's apartment as he knows it. Not a total dive, but a bachelor's place all the same. It smells how he imagines a cave might smell with a dash of Brut spilled inside. This is the habitat of a grown man with adolescent values, the sort that are usually stripped away early by any long-term relationship, and there's a general mess here that Brett could never get away with at home. An open pizza box full of crusts, empty containers from Dunkin' Donuts. No framed photographs on the walls, no trinkets, no memories. Just beer cans on the coffee table, alongside – no kidding – a bottle of lotion, a clutch of unused kitchen towel and a couple of stroke books.

The sight makes Brett feel very uncomfortable and his cheeks begin to burn. Do people still go out and buy porno magazines? He glances at the cover of the nearest issue, the one that isn't spread fully open. *The Girls of Penthouse, September/October 1999*. An old favourite then.

Is this what Craig would have Brett believe he was doing when the door burst open? Sitting here with his pants around his ankles, jerking it to a magazine he's held onto for twenty years, something he picked up while Brett was off at college? Brett's initial embarrassment transmutes into pity, but he still finds himself unable to buy into this. It's all too … perfectly wrong, somehow. It's like set dressing. And is that blood on the back of the couch? Sure it is, around a dozen flawless, penny-sized drops. He shakes his head. No way. Not biting.

A vibration in the pocket of his overcoat startles him. Another text message, this one short.

TIME'S UP.
CONTINUE?

He shakes his head, pocketing the phone.

Objectively, he understands the concept of denial. He is even aware, on some base level, that he might be experiencing it right now. Probably is, in fact. He's looking at the situation clinically, but that's surely better than hysterics. It's safer to be sceptical than gullible. That was something he learned as a kid.

So, what *did* happen here? Catching a man with his pants down would give any intruder the upper hand, but then what? Is Brett supposed to believe that they – whoever *they* are – pistol-whipped Craig across the back of the head like they do in the movies and then carted over two hundred pounds of unconscious bulk into the trunk of some waiting car, via the elevator? Or did they march Craig out of the building on the muzzle end of a handgun or the old banana in the coat pocket? This may be the Bronx, but that feat seems especially doubtful considering what faces this building …

Brett sidesteps the couch, ignoring the ketchup – *blood, it's blood, when are you going to wake up and get that into your thick head* – and looks out of the fourth-storey window. Directly across Alexander Avenue, right there on the opposite corner, is the NYPD's 40th Precinct. He can see blue uniforms gathered on the steps there now. Day and night, police vehicles fill reserved spaces on both sides of the road, including the area directly outside the entrance to these apartments.

'I wasn't born yesterday,' Brett says to the room. 'You think you can blackmail me, Craig? Think again.' He unlatches and opens the window. Cold air rushes in, blasting away the lingering cologne and the faint-popcorn smell of old, unwashed fabrics, and the apartment is filled with the noise of traffic and the ceaseless din of a nearby jackhammer.

Brett leans out of the window, his usual shyness overruled by something close to delirium, and cups his hands into an improvised bullhorn. '*Hey! Hey, Officers! Up here!*'

There are three cops on the steps down there. They're lost in some anecdote, laughing among themselves, and they don't hear him; the sound of the hammer swallows his voice without effort. Brett frowns, looking up the road in both directions, but he can't see where the racket is coming from. A private company, he guesses, because he's sure the Department of Transport doesn't work federal holidays. Only one person seems to have heard him: a tattoo-faced meth head with peroxide, Slim Shady hair on the nearside pavement has stopped, mid-phone conversation, to stare up at the man leaning from the window. Irritated, Brett tries again.

'*Officers, hey! We have a problem here! Do you hear me?*'

They don't. He yells a couple more times, and then grits his teeth and slams the window shut.

'No worries,' he says to the apartment, 'I'll just go down and get them. This is your last chance to put a stop to this! What's it going to be?'

He waits a whole minute or two, as if Craig might appear with a grin and his hands in the air – *OK Brett, you got me! I was in the closet all along. Get it? Joke's on you, ha-ha-ha!* – then he storms out.

Inside the elevator, his pocket starts to vibrate, but it's almost immediately cut off when the sliding doors close and the signal is lost. He takes out his phone. It was an incoming video call, ID withheld.

Craig then, now that his bluff has been called. Brett was right all along. He'd like to be smug, but all he feels is utter relief.

What a stupid game. Somebody could've been hurt.

As soon as he steps out onto the ground floor, his phone begins to vibrate again in his hand. Another video call. This time he answers, though he presses his thumb tight over the front-facing camera so that it only shows darkness on his end; he hates the unflattering angle on these things, and he isn't in the mood to be seen right now. He doesn't want Craig to know how badly he had scared him.

The call takes a moment longer to connect, and then the livestream begins.

All at once the empty entrance lobby around Brett, the rest of the apartment building above him and the whole of New York City seem to slide into mute. The jackhammer outside finally falls silent.

It's Craig onscreen – he was correct about that much – but Craig remains zip-tied to the chair, as previously modelled in still life, dressed in the same hockey jersey, underwear and silver duct tape combo. The blood on his face is darker now. His eyes are open, dog-tired but glaring. There's no sound from the other end, only visuals, and there's something doubly unsettling about that.

The phone doing the filming is moving around with its flashlight on full, picking out the wet patch on Craig's boxers and the doubled-up zip ties holding his wrists to each of the chair's arms. The signal must be slight because the picture keeps stalling as if it's going to cut out at any second.

Brett hadn't paid the chair much mind in the photograph, but now that the camera is moving around, he can see it is dark, tattered leather with a mechanical footrest, which is where Craig's ankles are also zip-tied. An old-fashioned dentist's chair maybe, or the sort you'd find in a vintage barbershop, one so heavy it might as well be secured to the ground. The light momentarily catches a web of green copper pipes on the rear wall, like those in a basement or boiler room; very *Nightmare on Elm Street*.

'*Craig?*' Brett cries this out thinking that he won't be able to hear him, but Craig's eyes bulge in response and his mouth starts to work frantically against the tape. The sight is horrifying. The filmmaker takes a step back so that Brett can see the whole picture at once.

In the darkness behind Craig, something moves.

Its head rises above the back of the chair, looming over the oblivious captive, and there's something terribly wrong with its face; it's all black stitching and twisted metal, the face of Frankenstein's monster, and Brett bites back a scream.

But it isn't a face. Not really. It's a mask made up of padded leather straps that wrap around the skull, chin and forehead, all held together with thick surgical stitching. Across the face is a wire cage, like some medieval horror. It's almost impossible to see the face within the cage. Only the whites of the eyes catch the flashlight at first. Then the teeth, which come out in a gap-filled grin.

It's a catcher's mask, Brett realises, the sort they wore fifty or sixty years ago. A common sight in baseball. A regular part of the – *game* – sport.

'Craig!' Brett is yelling now, oblivious to the apartments above him. 'Craig, behind you!'

Useless, of course. Craig can't do a damn thing about it.

The newcomer's arms come into view, and gloved hands place something onto Craig's torso. It's a single sheet of nondescript printer paper. The words are handwritten, badly, in black marker pen:

NO COPS
NO CHEETING
PLAY THE GAME

Distantly, Brett feels his bowels turn loose. His first instinct is to run for the police outside anyway. They're twenty paces away. He could make it. His own camera is still covered; the cops could be watching this, taking notes, getting moving.

Then the enormous bat comes out from behind the chair and Brett doesn't move a single inch.

It's a Louisville Slugger. Ash or maple, the sledgehammer of the batter's arsenal. The guy in the catcher's mask – stupidly, savagely grinning – pulls it over one shoulder, ready for the first swing.

Craig is still staring into the camera, all eyes in the white light.

He looks like roadkill.

He never sees it coming.

24

PLAYER THREE

Sarah has the postcode, and less than three hours left on her timer to reach it.

By five o'clock this afternoon, she must be in a location about an hour outside of Salford. It is a place she dreads, a dreamscape from her worst nightmares, a setting that taps into the fundamental terrors of every parent alive, particularly those in the northwest of England.

The moors.

More precisely, the outskirts of Saddleworth Moor, that vast, ghostly panorama of blanket bog, wild heather and lost, murdered children. By choosing this site for whatever handover is coming, the abductor's message is clear, his warning obvious, and Sarah doesn't want Archie anywhere near it.

That's why she is currently hurtling her very-used Nissan Qashqai through suburban roads, driving like Cruella, mounting kerbs on every tight corner; a few moments ago, she scraped along the entire length of a parked van, snapping her wing mirror back and causing Archie to scream in his booster seat, and she never paused to check the damage. She is on her way to the only place to go in times of such confusion and anguish. She is driving to her mum's.

Standing upright in the nearest sticky cupholder is an old pay-as-you-go that she found in a shoebox full of obsolete phones she's been meaning to sell for a decade, all of which are now worthless. The timer is onscreen, white digits in a black box that occasionally flickers. Something must've downloaded itself – malware, she's heard it called – and it looks buggy.

Neil hasn't returned her calls, which she finds simultaneously worrying, infuriating and utterly insane. Isn't this precisely the sort of emergency that phones are carried for? Paradoxically, however, she's also relieved. Or, as close to relieved as she can be under these circumstances. When he finds out, Neil will fly off the handle. His grief will be ballistic. There'll be no conversation, no chance of getting him to follow the rules, and that could provoke an outcome that was never a part of the kidnapper's plan.

And what *is* the plan, anyway? Why is this happening?

Sarah has come to believe, or simply hope, that this must be about her winnings. Somehow, somebody knows about the money. An employee at the bingo company who has snooped through customer files, maybe, or one of her online friends. She has, after all, never *seen* Jill, Mandy, Sue, Mo or Jen. She's never told them about her winnings – nothing beyond an occasional boast – but who's to say that Mandy from Barnsley isn't actually some twenty-year-old scammer playing the long con? Or Sue really might be a sixty-year-old woman from Wolverhampton, who also happens to extort families for a living. A four-figure sum may not be enough to turn ordinary people to abduction, but to a career fraudster it might seem like fair pay for a single afternoon's work. The important things here are maintaining a dialogue and following the rules. Hannah isn't hurt – she didn't look it in the photograph, at least – and there's no reason that she has to be.

Duke is dead.

A sad, mournful wail in the back of Sarah's mind keeps reminding her of this because, in the uproar of losing her daughter, she has been given no time to grieve her gentle, loving dog. The puppy that was her baby when she thought she could never have children of her own. He was a member of her family, and somebody butchered him for nine measly grand. They should've just knocked on the front door and asked; Sarah would've gladly paid it all to spare his life, and to stop this from ever happening.

There is a chance that Neil, frightened by the missed calls, is already speeding the company van towards an empty house and a murdered dog. What then?

Sarah doesn't know. She is taking this one step at a time, and that begins with dropping Archie off at his grandmother's.

Her regular phone is connected to the car's hands-free system. When Sarah has her breathing under control, and she is fairly sure she'll be able to keep her shit together long enough to form a complete sentence or two, she calls her mother to tell her the terrible half-truth that she has decided upon.

25

PLAYER FOUR

Noah is somewhere on the outskirts of Paris. That's all he knows for sure.

Victor, his boss's hard-faced assistant, has come this far with him, though they haven't spoken since leaving Khalid's nightclub.

'Once we get back to ground level,' Victor had said as they left the basement, 'we don't speak. Not in my car, not afterwards, not unless I think it's safe and I speak to you first. Assuming your phone is compromised, they'll be listening from the moment it returns to full service. They probably have access to its cameras. Keep it in your pocket with your hand over the microphone whenever possible, OK?'

Better than OK. The silence is fine by Noah. His mind is fully occupied, his stomach too unsettled for him to hold any real conversation.

They are walking through the maze-like back quarters of an industrial building Noah doesn't recognise. Victor is leading the way down corridors, past empty offices, through dim, cluttered storerooms filled with pallets of nondescript cardboard boxes.

The last storeroom is crowded with people. They're huddled on the floor, dozens of them, watching Noah with wide, frightened eyes from inside big coats and sleeping bags. He sees Asians, Africans, Europeans; there are children sleeping among them. He does his best to keep his eyes pointed forwards, following Victor, thinking of Sofia.

The tour ends in an enormous warehouse. The rolling doors are all closed but it's incredibly cold in here, and there's an articulated lorry, at least fifty feet long, parked in the centre of the loading bay. Several sodium floodlights have been arranged around the lorry, and their harsh yellow beams pour onto another twenty or more of the bewildered storeroom people waiting in a line. Two men in hi-vis jackets are herding the queue into the back of the lorry, and they're not doing it with much grace.

'Hey!' Victor whistles through his teeth and raises a hand.

One of the hi-vis foremen – that's how Noah thinks of them, as if this is any ordinary warehouse job – turns around. He nods, spits on the floor, and beckons them closer. Noah hesitates, and Victor leans in to whisper in his ear.

'When you need us, you use a payphone from the other side.' He hesitates. 'If you make it. I'll try to have a ride waiting for you there.'

He claps Noah on the shoulder, sombrely, and gestures for him to go to the waiting truck. This is the first time that Noah registers a major shift in his nerves; now they are not just focusing on Sofia's safety, but also his own. He approaches the lorry with heavy, reluctant footsteps. At the same time, the nearest foreman is marching to the back of the dwindling line waiting to enter the lorry. The final passengers are a trio.

A family: father, daughter of about eight or nine, and mother bringing up the rear.

The father is dressed in an incongruous Disneyland sweater, Mickey Mouse in bright, nineties colours, though he doesn't look like he's ever seen a theme park. The jumper is threadbare at the cuffs. These souvenirs often wind up in charity parcels around Paris. Some injury has left his face badly scarred. The foreman sidesteps between the little girl and her mother, who is the last in the queue, separating them.

'No,' the foreman says to the mother with a tone more often saved for dogs. 'You have to go back and wait. This is full.'

Her husband, in the Disney sweater, tries to reach for his wife. 'We already pay!' he cries in stumbling, broken French. 'Three nights we wait here! Three nights!'

The foreman is big, and it takes little effort for him to shove the couple several feet apart. He holds up two fingers and shouts in their faces. 'Two go! One wait!'

Noah watches the ensuing struggle from a short distance away; his sense of shame is nearly unbearable. He isn't sure how long it goes on for. First the anger, then the begging, and they aren't begging the foreman now, they are begging *him*. The father, struggling to find the proper language, uses his hands to show Noah his family, his wife, his little girl, all he has in this whole world. He clasps his palms together in a sickening imitation of prayer. The mother actually drops to her knees. The child sobs, bewildered and afraid. It seems to go on forever, and it is truly hell.

Noah glances back to Victor, who is watching impassively. Stay or go?

What would Sofia think of him now, in this very moment? What would she say?

She won't be saying anything at all, if she ends up dead.

'I'm sorry,' Noah mutters. 'I really am.'

He doesn't wait to see who stays behind in his place. He doesn't want to know whose ticket he has stolen.

The second man in hi-vis, the one now inside the lorry, calls him forwards and he goes, turning his back on the family. The father starts yelling, cursing in a language Noah doesn't speak but understands perfectly well. He yells until there is a loud smacking sound, a thump on the ground, and then there is only wailing.

Noah looks across to Victor one last time. The man nods his farewell. Noah climbs up into the rear of the truck.

Inside, a magic trick has occurred. The twenty or so people he watched enter have somehow vanished among the stacks of boxes. It's like those clown cars from the circus, although there's nothing amusing here. Noah is beckoned through a narrow gap between the merchandise. Up at the front, the cab end of the trailer, a portion of the steel floor has been lifted. It's about the size of a coffin. Looking down into that tiny space, he feels his stomach tighten. The man in here, the second hi-vis, speaks to him; his voice is very dense in their tightly packed surroundings, and his breath smells like shit.

'French?' the man asks.

'Yes.'

'OK.' The man looks noticeably relieved to be speaking his native language. 'You go in on your stomach, head this side,' he points, 'and shuffle right until your shoulder touches the next person. If anything happens, if anything goes wrong, you never saw me. You were never here. You're on your own. I don't need to tell you what would happen if you talked. You understand. You're in the game.'

'What?' Noah tries to take an instinctive step backwards and comes up against the boxes stacked there. 'What did you say?'

The man frowns. 'You work for our mutual friend, don't you? You're no immigrant, you're in the game.'

'Oh.' Noah nods and takes a deep breath, looking into the hole. 'How long will I be down there?'

The man shrugs. 'Four hours to Calais. Two more to cross. That's without traffic, queues, customs.'

'So, all night,' Noah says grimly.

'You want comfort, get a passport.'

'Never needed one,' Noah says. 'Now I don't have time.'

From the rear of the trailer, beyond the boxes, the first foreman yells. 'Get a move on, huh? We've got two more out here!'

Noah has a moment to wonder if he's doing the right thing after all. Once he's inside this hole, there's no helping Sofia. No checking his phone. It's a gamble, and it could mean life or death.

'Hey,' the man says, snapping his fingers in front of Noah's face. 'It's time.'

Numbly, Noah crawls down, squeezing into the dark, rank bowels of the lorry bound for England.

26

PLAYER FIVE

Linda is standing in front of her full-length mirror, side-on, studying her own outline in the reflection.

She's dressed in dark clothing, boots and gloves with a long black parka zipped up to her neck. Fastened like this, the coat just about belies the shape of the stab vest underneath, as well as the old kit belt wrapped around her hips. She runs a hand over the belt, knowing by haptic memory the positions of her Maglite torch, the pouch for disposable latex gloves, the cuffs with their keys clipped onto swivels; it's better to be overprepared.

'You can do this,' the greying lady in the mirror tells her. 'You can, but you have to go now.'

She almost resists the urge to have one final look around Alyssa's room – she can't afford to spend any more time pining over the inanimate and the sentimental – but halfway down the staircase she doubles back. Her daughter's tattered wool dragon is lying facedown on the bed where Linda left it.

'You can keep me company,' she says, and she picks it up and takes it with her.

It's cold outside. Not such an inconvenience, considering Linda's extra layers, but the temperature brings a spontaneous sort of word or image association to her mind – *cold; freezer; morgue* – and she doesn't like it one bit. She unlocks her car, goes to open the door and pauses. She has only just looked down her driveway.

'No. Please. Not today.'

In Linda's neighbourhood, there is an ongoing dispute with the council over public parking. Each week, rather than paying the extortionate airport fees, hundreds of passengers simply dump their vehicles in these residential areas and either walk or taxi the rest of the way to the airport, leaving their cars kerbside for ten days, two weeks, sometimes longer. The council refuses to introduce permits because the local residents all have private driveways, but the fight for space has a knock-on effect on legitimate guests, delivery drivers and local workmen.

Today, not for the first time, there is a nondescript white van parked with its rear end sticking over the opening of Linda's driveway, blocking her in. There's a scribbled note in the window: BACK IN 20!

She could honestly scream. She looks desperately in all directions.

'Why wouldn't you leave a phone number?' she asks the empty road. 'What's *wrong* with you!'

With her hand that isn't, quite ludicrously, still holding the stuffed dragon by its paw she checks the timer on her phone: four hours and change remaining.

If the van has been here for eighteen minutes already, then she *might* be able to wait.

If, on the other hand, it has only been here for two minutes …

She pockets her phone, muscles tightening, and looks at the front of the van. There is, infuriatingly, about a foot of space between its bumper and the next car along; if the driver had only filled that gap then she could probably squeeze her BMW out.

After waiting for as long as she can bear to – about twelve seconds – she reaches beneath her coat and, automatically finding the correct slot on her kit belt, takes out her retractable baton. Still holding the dragon in one hand, she whips the weapon out to its full length and quite easily crunches it through the safety glass of the driver's side window. The alarm blares out, but she doesn't bother looking around to see if anybody is watching. Instead, she calmly pops the lock, opens the door, leans inside and releases the handbrake. Her road runs on a slight decline, enough for gravity to finish the job, and the van rolls into the next car in line.

In her own car, she starts the engine. The stuffed toy – once her daughter's favourite – is on the passenger seat. Linda glances at it as she puts the car into reverse. 'You know what we're going to do, don't you?'

She replies to herself in the high-pitched, croaky voice that she hasn't used in years; the voice that had made Alyssa giggle every time; Dragon's voice.

'We'll breathe fire on them,' Dragon says cutely, and a tear rolls down Linda's cheek. 'We're going to find whoever's responsible, and we'll burn them all.'

'That's right,' Linda replies. She licks the tear from her upper lip as she squeezes her car through the gap at the end of the driveway. 'Burn them all.'

The alarm is still ringing, and an outraged workman in a hard hat is running down the pavement towards his van, waving his arms and yelling for her to stop, but she never gives him so much as a single glance.

27

PLAYER ONE

MSP International is full of clocks, and they all seem to be going too slowly.

Maggie finishes her beer and orders another with a gesture of her hand. The beer went down surprisingly easy. The burger's going nowhere. She picks it up and tries another bite. It's lukewarm now, about as flavoursome and appealing as ash in her mouth, but her body needs *something*. She feels weak and the single beer, the only thing she's had since waking up mildly hungover this morning, is already making her head swim. She feels all mixed up inside.

She's sitting in a bar that's supposed to resemble an outdoor patio area within the airport. There's a parasol over her table, blocking nothing more natural than the rays of the overhead lamps. Both phones are on the tabletop. From here she has a pretty good view of the terminal. Unfortunately, that view goes both ways, and the place is packed full of men and women in blue uniforms; she keeps fooling herself into thinking that they're looking right at her, ready to charge. TSA officers don't carry guns. The cops, and the undercover Federal Air Marshals who could be everywhere, do. This is a fact she can't seem to shake from her mind.

She used her phone to book the flights, despite being seated on a bench outside the airport doors at the time. She could've bought them in person at the Delta gate, but she didn't dare walk up to the counter with a passport in one name and a credit card in the other. She sweated nonstop as she passed through the security checkpoint with her single item of luggage, the Target shopping bag with her scruffy dressing gown inside. It was only once she was through security, properly inside the terminal, that she realised she was still carrying the bag at all and dumped it into the trash.

The tickets cost a thousand dollars. One thousand dollars. Her card is almost maxed out.

To travel to the UK without a visa, North Americans have to book a return flight within six months. Since Maggie is supposed to be in England late tomorrow afternoon – Tuesday, GMT – the earliest return flight she could buy a ticket for doesn't depart from Manchester until midday on Wednesday. Two days. Somebody will have Jackson from Sunday night until at least Wednesday evening, and Maggie will be a world away. She has considered the idea that Jackson is also on his way to the same destination in England, but this seems unlikely without his passport and under duress. During the outgoing flights alone, Maggie will be without phone service and off the grid for more than eight hours. Anything could happen in that time.

Are they feeding him? Is he alone? Are they hurting him? There's no way to know the answers to these questions. There's nothing to do but follow the rules.

She sits, waiting for her flight to begin boarding; for her sister to call the cops; for a new message to come through demanding she strip naked in the middle of the airport, or scream that she has a bomb, or steal the sidearm from a passing cop's holster and wave it in the air until she's shot dead. Why not? It's just a game, after all.

The next beer is placed onto her table and she jumps.

'Gee, sorry,' the waiter says. 'I didn't mean to startle you.'

'Forget it.'

He's about her age, this waiter, maybe a couple of years older, chubby with a ponytail. His gaze bounces back and forth between her face and her mostly untouched meal. 'Something wrong with the burger?'

'No. No, it's fine.'

He nods. 'Nervous about flying?'

'You got it.'

He smiles, his eyes on her like a magpie on a coin. 'Nothing to worry about. A couple more drinks and you'll be fine.'

'I'm sure you're right.' She considers her own smile in return. It feels ugly before it's even out of the gate, so she doesn't bother. Instead, she sips the beer.

The waiter falters. He's hovering by the table, looking at her closely. 'Hey, I don't mean to be rude, but … Do we know each other? You seem really familiar to me.'

'No.' It comes out like a bullet, a jab, an answer she's been giving for years. 'No, I don't think so.'

'Really?' He stays put, holding his empty tray. 'You've never been on TV? You look so darn *familiar* to me.'

'Just one of those faces, I guess.' She catches herself tugging at the loose strands of her hair, an old painful habit, and forces herself to stop. She's just about to tell him to take a hike when her phone – her own iPhone – vibrates across the tabletop. She's actually grateful for the interruption. 'Sorry, I need to read this. Do you mind?'

'Not at all. Just give me a shout if you need anything else, OK?'

'Sure,' she says, already knowing that her next steps will be to finish this drink as fast as possible, pay up – sans tip – and get the hell away from here. She waits for him to go before she reads the message.

It's from Caroline. This is, of course, an inevitability, something Maggie had to face up to sooner or later, but that doesn't make her feel any better prepared, or any less guilty, for it.

Hi Mags, all good? We should be there in 30 mins ok?

Maggie responds with fumbling hands: **All gd. Spk soon.** Except, all they'll find in thirty minutes is an empty apartment, and quite possibly a police presence. They're going to go out of their minds.

Maggie's thoughts go back to the first time she met Caroline Taylor.

Maggie was sixteen years old. Caroline and Shaun were both thirty-one. They were beautiful, and they lived in the biggest house Maggie had ever visited.

She remembers sitting on the back porch, gazing across a manicured garden towards a private tennis court. The lingering heat of summer was stubborn, refusing to let the coloured leaves claim the season. Shaun and Caroline, two young orthodontists, sat on one side of a table in the shade. Alongside Maggie was her facilitator, Diane, a woman of around sixty who worked at the agency.

At first, Diane did most of the speaking.

'As you know, law dictates that the mother has thirty days after birth to make up her mind. Nothing's final before that point, although Maggie can release the baby to you guys straight away, should she choose to. You've had time to study Maggie's personal adoption plan, so you've seen she's opted for a semi-open adoption. This means she can have access to letters, pictures and contact if she so desires. There are post-adoption contact agreements we can draw up in the presence of an attorney, though I have to tell you now that, in all honesty, these are only occasionally enforceable in the state of Minnesota. From what I understand, both parties seem to be on the same page regarding correspondence?'

'Absolutely,' Shaun replied. 'We'd want this to be as transparent as possible for the child. I was adopted, and my parents went to huge efforts to keep that from me. I didn't find out until my early twenties. Since the moment we decided to do this, we've said that the birth mother should be involved from day one.'

'If you wanted to be,' Caroline quickly added.

'Right,' Shaun said, 'of course. However much you wanted to be included would be up to you.'

Maggie glanced down at her own swelling body. 'I *guess* that would be cool …'

The Taylors were gazing there too, their eyes desperate, longing, almost starving, and Maggie would've closed her overshirt then if the buttons still met in the middle. She was only a couple of months into this, but already she felt as if she was getting bigger every day. She'd assumed she would have until her final trimester before she needed to think about buying new clothes. She'd been wrong.

Caroline must've intuited her discomfort, because she snapped her eyes away from the belly and gave a soft, awkward laugh. 'This all feels a little formal, doesn't it? Is there any chance of Maggie and me having a minute alone together? Sort of, *mom-to-mother*. Would that be all right?'

'Well,' Diane said, 'I'm not actually obliged to be present, but it does usually help for me to be here to answer any questions either side may have. Maggie, what do you think?'

'It's cool,' Maggie said. 'I think I'd like that.'

Caroline smiled gratefully, while Shaun nodded and got to his feet. 'You're in luck, Diane,' he said. 'You now get to witness the Minnesotan mocktail master at work!'

'How could I refuse an offer like that?' Diane laughed, following, and then they were alone: just Caroline, Maggie, and the fifty-thousand-dollar child growing in Maggie's womb.

For a moment, they said nothing. The Taylors had set up an electric tower fan beside the pregnant girl, and it hummed gently as it pivoted and blew.

'Are you anxious?' Caroline asked.

Maggie considered this. 'No. I don't think so. Are you?'

'Honestly? Extremely.'

'Diane told me this isn't your first go at adopting?'

'She told you that?' Caroline crossed her forearms, cupping her own elbows in each hand as if she was momentarily cold, a doe suddenly vulnerable, and sighed. 'Yes, I suppose they tell you everything. We had another mother lined up last year. It … didn't work out. She let us down.'

'How far through?'

Caroline looked at her carefully, hesitantly, before replying.

'Forty weeks. Birth. We had the nursery ready. Bottles sterilised and our bags all packed. We were waiting for the call to meet her at the hospital and the call just … never came. By the time we got through to her, it was all over. She'd taken the money, and she'd taken the baby. Her baby. I hope she's happy, I really do.'

Maggie felt an urge to reach out and touch her, this poor stranger, but she never did; Caroline looked so perfectly cool in her designer sundress, so silken and toned, and Maggie's hands were swollen and clammy. Instead she simply said, 'You can trust me. I won't let you down.'

'Oh honey, you don't know *what* you'll do when the time comes. You don't know how you'll feel.'

'I know. I don't want this child.' There it was, a statement so obvious – she was here to discuss adoption, after all – and so grotesque that she startled herself and felt the tops of her ears begin to burn with shame. 'I mean,' she quickly backtracked, 'look at this place. I can't provide anything like this. I should be in high school.'

'What about the father? What does he think about it?'

Maggie clenched all over. 'There is no father. This should never have happened. At least now, something good can come out of this mess. I can make a difference.'

'Yes,' Caroline said. 'You really can. I just want to be a mom, Maggie, that's all. A good mom.'

'You will be. You have any idea what you might name him?'

'Him?' Caroline caught her breath. 'What makes you think it's a boy?'

Maggie shrugged. 'Not sure. Just a feeling, I guess. What would you call it if it was?'

'Jackson,' Caroline said without hesitation, her eyes shining desperately. 'We'd call him Jackson.'

'Jackson?' Maggie looked down at her belly, head cocked, and rubbed herself there where the flesh was tough and warm. 'Jackson Taylor.' For the first time in weeks, she really smiled, inside and out. 'I love it.'

*

In the airport, years later, there is one part of this conversation that now ricochets around Maggie's head; it's her own voice saying *I don't want this child, I don't want this child, I don't want this child* …

About two minutes after she has replied to Caroline's text, while Maggie is hurriedly chugging the last of her beer, the burner phone vibrates on the tabletop, and she coughs suds. Blind to the surprised gazes of the surrounding passengers, she wipes her teary, choked eyes with a napkin and reads.

THIS PART OF THE GAME IS CALLED
HIDE AND SEEK.
YOUR SUCCESS GOING FORWARD
WILL DEPEND ON YOUR ABILITY TO
DISAPPEAR COMPLETELY.
HINT: CREDIT CARD PAYMENTS ARE EASILY
TRACKED.
SO IS YOUR PERSONAL PHONE.
DESTROY IT BEFORE REACHING YOUR
DESTINATION,

Finally, after fighting it throughout the whole of this long day, she laughs out loud. Really laughs. That punchline is a real zinger. Somebody, it seems, has a sense of humour. Good for them. Unable to respond, she looks directly into the front-facing camera and raises her middle finger.

'How's this for a safe journey, you sick cunt?'

She slams the burner down and turns her attention back to her *actual* phone, the one she has just been ordered to destroy. It contains her whole life. Thirty thousand photographs chronicle the end of her teens into adulthood, and she doesn't remember the last time she backed them up.

She knows none of its saved contacts by heart – because who needs to anymore? – and there's also the evidence to think about. The Game is doing a brilliant job of forcing Maggie to write her own criminal narrative here, and it doesn't even need to try very hard. Since she woke up this morning, somebody has been saying jump, and she just goes on asking how high. *Thank you, sir, may I have another?* Well it isn't happening. Out of sheer principle, she won't destroy another piece of evidence.

But will they know? She isn't sure. Can a turned-off phone still be traced?

She's wondering this when the phone in question starts to ring.

It's not The Game, but it's not much better. Maggie holds her breath, as if a strong exhale might trigger Accept, until it stops ringing.

She finally releases her breath, and the phone immediately starts ringing again.

'Fuck! Fuck, fuck, fuck!'

She has delayed it for as long as possible, and it is finally about to catch up with her. Answering the phone will be like putting a loaded gun to her ear in Russian roulette; there's no way to know, until she answers, what the Taylors have or haven't realised, and if she *doesn't* answer, and they get no response when they buzz her apartment, then they will probably call the police anyway.

Would that be such a bad thing? To have the cops searching while she's off in England, obeying the rules? Maybe not, although the cops would be hunting *her*, and she might just end up stepping off the plane into a pair of British handcuffs, which brings her full circle, because if she can't complete the game, and if she can't make it to the location on time, then Jackson will suffer the consequences.

Her head feels like it's about to explode, and before she knows what she's doing, she is paying the bill in a daze and rushing for the nearest bathroom with both phones in her hands.

The restrooms at MSP have classical music being pumped into the stalls. It's not ideal, but it's better than the public address system calling flight numbers in the background.

Maggie shuts herself into an empty stall and, when she finally thinks she isn't going to just throw up into the bowl, she answers Caroline's fifth consecutive attempt at getting through.

28

PLAYER TWO

'Alexa, pause.' Kelly's voice, cautious, coming down the hall from the kitchen. The *Hamilton* soundtrack, which had been playing when he opened the front door, stops. 'Brett, is that you?'

'Yeah, babe. Only me.'

The house smells rich with paprika and chorizo, Kelly's 'famous jambalaya', but Brett makes no detour for the kitchen on his way to their bedroom. He hears pots and pans being shifted around, but the music doesn't restart.

'You're home early.' Kelly is somewhere down the hallway now, coming closer. 'They let you off because it's MLK Day?'

'Sort of,' he calls back. Then, 'Actually, there's this meeting we've got to go to, it's affected our shifts, real last-minute stuff. Honestly, it's kind of chaos.'

He's in the bedroom for a couple of minutes, bouncing around like a bird trapped indoors, before she appears in the doorway. Her wide eyes move from the small suitcase, thrown open on the bedcovers, to the brand-new phone beside it. The phone is a burner, the kind preferred by drug dealers and partners with double lives; it's this phone, more than anything else, which makes her feel uneasy.

'What's going on?' she asks warily.

'Work, like I said.' He doesn't meet her gaze, only tosses a change of underwear into the case, considers the single pair for a second, and then adds another. 'There's a problem with the beta test, something serious. It's a mess, a total screw-up. We're being flown out to London for an emergency conference.'

'London! When are you supposed to be going?'

'Tonight.'

'*Tonight?*' She laughs, but it isn't like her usual laugh at all. Far from it. 'They expect you to drop everything and get on a plane to England this evening?'

'You know how they are since the big leak. Paranoid, Kelly. Out of their minds. It's all a mess, honestly, a total screw-up.' He's repeating himself; he'd only managed to plan a rough outline for this conversation, and the wheels are coming off. 'They gave us these phones – you know how they are about personal phones – so I'll be sort of *off the grid* for tomorrow, but it's not the end of the world. Give you some peace, right? Where are the passports?'

'You put them in the safe.'

'Right, the safe, sure.'

The safe is in the bottom of the closet; it's a Yale fingerprint model hidden beneath the tails of clothes hanging from the rack. He parts the fabrics roughly, yanking them aside like curtains, and one of the plastic hangers breaks with a loud, startling snap. It sounds like bone and he recoils in horror.

His leg! his mind shrieks. *They broke his fucking leg, snapped it like a goddamn wishbone, made him pass out with the agony, put the bone right through the fucking skin—*

He clenches his fists until the fingernails dig into his palms and hot tears flood his eyes.

Kelly moves as if she's going to step into the room, as if she might be coming to comfort him, but she hesitates. It's an awkward, obvious move. He glances at her and, for just a moment, she actually looks fearful of him. She's tugging at the cuffs of her sweatshirt.

'Brett,' she says quietly. 'What's happened?'

He shakes his head and kneels down to the safe, pretending to adjust his glasses but drying his eyes with a pinch of the fingers. He pockets his own passport and closes the door, which locks again with a beep. This is in accordance with the demands of The Game, the latest in a series of instructions that have come through in the hour since he bought the burner in the Bronx.

First, he received the invitation. Then, after he'd booked his plane ticket in the taxi back to Brooklyn, he was told to destroy his phone and to stop using credit cards. He got the taxi to pull over while he withdrew cash, and then he smashed his own phone up and dropped it into a trashcan. Now Brett Palmer is up to speed. It's Monday afternoon in New York City. At five o'clock on Tuesday evening, local time, he is expected to be in a part of England he has barely heard of, and he has no idea why.

Craig's right ankle is shattered. They did it with a baseball bat – a *baseball bat* – as if this was all some scene out of *Criminal Frenzy*, the gangland video game produced at Brett's place of work. The bat had swung too fast for the stream's framerate to follow, but it had landed again and again, and Brett could see blood, and the white bone protruding through flesh, and—

'Is—' Kelly takes a deep breath; her voice is shaking now, turning something ordinarily so joyous, so confident, into the wounded squeak of a child. 'Is this it, Brett? Are you leaving me?'

He halts, halfway through zipping the case shut, and turns his face fully towards her for the first time this afternoon. Looking at her like this is like seeing Craig with the tape over his mouth; it's seeing a person he loves so sincerely being deeply, truly hurt.

'What? No! Kelly, it's work, that's all. I swear to—'

'You're lying to me.' It's the flatness, the absolute fact of the matter, in her voice that scares him the most. The surety. 'Something happened on Saturday night.' She's crying freely, though the tears are silent now, but her eyes are strangely sympathetic. Understanding, almost. 'Did you meet somebody?'

He turns back to the zip on the case, finishing the job. 'This is stupid. It's a meeting in London, I'll be gone for a day or two and you're here trying to guilt-trip me about—'

'It's OK, Brett.' Close to sobbing now, still silently though, as if she is herself talking through some distant video call. 'I … know. I'm not stupid. I know.'

Once again, everything seems to stop. Even on a day of incredible moments, when he is sure his guts have taken all the pounding they can get, this one hits the stomach hard. It's in her face, and in the words she doesn't say. Brett's mouth is too dry to speak, and even if it wasn't, he doesn't know what would come out of it.

'I know you love me,' she continues, sniffing now, wiping her nose on her cuffs. 'I'm sure you do, and I love you so much. You're my best friend. You know that, don't you? You could tell me anything.'

'I don't know what you're talking about. I don't know where this is coming from, but I don't need it right now. I've got so much stress you wouldn't believe.' He has to get out of here. It suddenly feels as if the building, their home, is collapsing in on him and he can hardly breathe. He pockets the burner and picks up the case. 'A – a couple of days,' he manages drily, and he even forces half a smile. 'You're making a big deal out of nothing, I promise. It's stress, that's all. I've never been so goddamn stressed in my life, and I just need a little support, OK?'

She opens her mouth to answer and he cuts right over her.

'Don't answer. I have to go. I'll be back and we can talk about whatever you want … but don't worry about me. Please. I'm not leaving you, and I love you. Know that, Kelly. I love you.'

And just like that, the encounter – which has lasted two minutes – is over.

He stops on his way out of the room, on his way out of the house, and kisses her, his partner of almost a decade, for the last ever time.

29

PLAYER THREE

'Is there something wrong?'

Sam had asked it, speaking the exact words that were stuck in Sarah's throat. He was still smiling, kind of, but the beam – the one that had seemed to illuminate the entire darkened room only moments ago – was shrinking.

Their baby was still onscreen – the miracle of the head, body, arms and legs they had created – but the sonographer had gone very quiet. She was pressing the transducer into Sarah's abdomen with increasing force. Sarah was on her back, Sam sitting beside her, holding her hand. One of their palms had suddenly turned very cold and incredibly damp; it was hard to tell whose.

They'd been so excited. So expectant. So damned naïve. They'd already begun to paint the nursery in neutral emulsions, taking it for granted that intercourse equals pregnancy equals child, the proof is in the billions. They were in their twenties and, all around them, their friends were having kids, seemingly without much effort. It was a good time to start a family. Sarah had been with Sam for six years and they were engaged to be married; they were yet to set the date, but they were in no rush. The decision to stop using contraceptives had been a mutual, exhilarating one. They were happy together, and they were ready to share that happiness with a child.

And Sam was such a sweetheart. Sarah knows that now. He was kind, considerate, generous in the bedroom. Chubby and a little insecure, never quite realising how good looking he actually was. A lot of girls thought he was soft. His exes certainly must have, because they had all ended up cheating on him. For years, Sarah hated them for that, these strangers who had chipped away at her fiancé's self-esteem with acts of thoughtless lust and pointless cruelty.

In the end, of course, Sarah had done the same, but that all happened later.

This was the twelve-week scan. They'd come to the hospital with more grins than nerves between them, expecting to leave with the estimated delivery date. It was just another happiest day of their lives.

Then Sam had asked that dreaded question: is there something wrong?

The sonographer's answer, so simple and so final, would go on to haunt Sarah's dreams for years.

'I'm … I'm struggling to find a heartbeat.'

And she never did.

*

Something from that day plays over and over again in Sarah's mind as she drives the ten minutes to her mother's house on Tuesday afternoon.

Everything after the ultrasound had happened in a peculiar daze, not so dissimilar to the one she's experiencing now. Their child, they were told, had been dead within her for about a week. For seven nights, while she'd been imagining movement, convinced of life – every time Sam had pressed his head against her tummy and talked softly, kissing the skin – there had been only death inside. She'd called her mother from outside the hospital. She told her they'd lost the baby. Her mother burst into tears, and what she said then, the words that spilled out of her mouth upon hearing the terrible news, comes back to Sarah now.

'I've already told so many people. What are they going to say?'

Sarah had hung up the phone. Later, her mother put it down to shock, a reaction wrenched from her own winded gut, and that was probably the truth.

Still, years on, here it is in Sarah's mind. *What are they going to say?*

She's careful not to actually drive past the bungalow, since her mother is likely to be looking out of the window by now, and she kerbs the car a couple of houses down despite there being ample space directly outside the front gate. She moves quickly, racing to unbuckle Archie before his grandma has a chance to come out and greet them, which she usually does. She will expect to see Hannah, even if it's just for a minute or two, but all she'll see if she gets too close is her granddaughter's empty booster seat.

Sarah at least makes it through the gate, carrying Archie and his Peter Rabbit changing bag, before the front door opens.

'Oh, Sarah!' Her mum comes shuffling out, clutching her

cardigan tightly against the afternoon air. It must be cold. Sarah had hardly noticed. Sarah's first, most basic impulse is to run for her mother; she wants to be held, and she needs to be loved, but she manages to grip onto her strangely detached composure.

Ann takes the baby from her daughter, only after checking the street with a cursory, almost imperceptible glance. Ann is fifty-eight, but she's been out of work and claiming disability for most of her life. It used to be for her back. Now it's for another long-term condition called fibromyalgia syndrome. Despite the affliction, she manages both baby and bag without much struggle, though she's frequently paranoid about being seen.

'How on earth did it happen?' she asks. 'You said he was in the back garden?'

'What?' Once again, Sarah had momentarily forgotten about her own beloved, murdered dog. 'Oh, Duke, the garden. I'm not sure. I mean, I don't know how. Sorry, my head is just pounding.'

'You do look awful.' Her mother hikes the baby a little higher. 'Poor thing, he was such a sweet dog. You ought to report the bloke you got him from, you never know what condition they're being bred in. You might even be able to get some compensation. They were showing these puppy farms on ITV last week and I swear to God, Sarah, some of the states of these—'

Sarah is already backing towards the gate when she interrupts. 'I've got to get going.' She half-heartedly gestures to the car. 'Hannah, you know, I'm going to take her for a Happy Meal. She's so upset.'

'I bet she is.' Ann cranes her neck, trying to peer through the rear window of the car parked almost a dozen yards away, and starts to follow. 'She doesn't want to give her nana a big fat cuddle?'

'No.' Sarah quickly closes the gate on her mother. 'Sorry, maybe later, she's sleeping at the minute. I think it's all just too much for her to understand. I'm going to take her out, like I said. Try to explain.'

'Oh.' Ann's face, as so often, is difficult to read. Understanding? Offended? Suspicious? Sarah can't be sure, and she doesn't have time to stand here deciphering the creases and the lines. 'Tell you what,' Ann says, turning on the spot. 'Let me give you some pennies to give to her ...'

'Mum, honestly, I really need to be—'

'I won't be one minute, Sarah. Am I not allowed to give my own granddaughter a little bit of pocket money on a day like this ...?'

Sarah watches, feeling close to another meltdown, half-tempted to run, as her mum shuffles into her bungalow's hallway, puts down the changing bag, and rummages through her own handbag with Archie still wrapped around her.

She returns and places a handful of shrapnel in her daughter's hand, which Sarah dumps into her coat pocket.

'I need you to do me one more favour. I ...' Sarah hesitates, reluctant to do this, knowing she has to. 'I need you to get hold of Neil for me. You'll have to tell him what's happened.'

'Christ, Sarah, you haven't told him yet?'

'I haven't had a chance! He's a nightmare to get hold of when he's working, and now my phone is dead. Well, not dead, it's broken.' Stumbling on excuses now, tripping on lies in the minefield of her own throbbing head. She takes a deep breath. 'Look, I just need you to explain the situation to him. Duke is in the garden, and I can't deal with what needs to be done. I'll be out until it's sorted, and I don't have my phone.'

Her mother rolls her eyes to show how put out she is by all this, but they both know it's precisely the sort of drama she loves to be involved in. Besides, she has a lot of time for Neil. He is, in her own words, a 'proper bloke', and she respects that. 'Not like the last one,' she usually adds. Ann didn't like Sam. She never said so during the course of Sarah's relationship, not explicitly, but it was obvious enough. Sam was a bit of a geek. Sam was weak. Sam was almost certainly the reason they couldn't produce a grandchild, and never mind what the doctors had to say about it.

Of course, Ann doesn't know everything about Neil. She doesn't know about the four grand he lost in bad stocks – a market he knows nothing about – when Hannah was a baby; nor is Ann aware – thank God – that the married couple haven't had sex in months, probably because Neil would rather get his rocks off to the videos Sarah once found on his laptop, the websites where he goes by the charming handle of NEIL_B4_ME, his own secret online world; if those are the things that constitute a *proper bloke* …

Sarah nearly has her hand on the driver's door handle when she turns and hurries back to her mother, who is standing at the edge of the garden, watching closely.

Sarah leans over the gate and presses her face against Archie, kissing him on the head, smelling the powders that make her heart ache with longing. Her eyes are closed, fighting back tears, and she whispers, 'You do keep your doors locked, don't you, Mam?'

'Usually. Why? What's wrong?'

'Bad day, that's all. Just … lock them, yeah? Lock them all.'

She doesn't wait for a response.

She checks the street in both directions before getting into her car, and then she starts the engine, takes one more look at her youngest through the rear-view mirror, and sets off on the drive to get her daughter back.

30

PLAYER FOUR

Darkness. Absolute black.

Noah is lying prostrate on cold steel. He has managed to wriggle his arms up, with his elbows now bent above his head, to form a sort of pillow on crossed forearms. This, at least, stops his face from smashing into metal each time the lorry hits a bump in the road, though it raises his head far enough so that the back of his skull collides with steel above instead.

The tyres are cacophonous. For a while, once they had begun moving, Noah thought the sheer volume might drive him mad. Then, whenever the lorry came to a brief standstill at junctions, he began to hear weeping in the dark. Now he's thankful for the sound of the wheels.

The passengers must be arranged top to tail; more than once he has felt shoes bump into the upper half of his body. Whoever entered the vehicle before him is lying on his right side, their shoes no more than a couple of inches away from Noah's raised elbows. The feet of the person on his left, the one who came after him, only just reach his hips, which suggests that it's probably the child he saw outside. Noah is in the place where this little girl's father should be. He wishes he could change things, but he can't.

The air seems thin, as if it's being used up faster than it can enter whatever holes have been drilled into the undercarriage, and the fumes of diesel are nauseating. The world shudders and rattles constantly, even when the truck is stationary. Quite recently – time is impossible to measure – somebody vomited. Not a great deal, perhaps, but the stench is inescapable. Noah wonders if the culprit had turned to the side, showering their neighbour's shoes, or simply made a puddle around their own face. Some choice. Noah himself could use a bathroom. Now that he's been forced to a halt, the stress is tearing his bowels apart. A best-case scenario, as he currently sees it, will probably involve him having to urinate into his own trousers before the journey is through. If that doesn't relieve some of the pressure, he may end up defecating.

Has it been one hour? Two? How long is a night without moonlight or air? How does time pass in a coffin?

Often, he doesn't know whether he's awake or sleeping; nightmares come regardless. Grotesque men take turns on his fiancée. Every vile act his mind can summon is inflicted upon her. In most of these repulsive visions, she screams in horror. In a few, and somehow the worst, she screams with pleasure. More than once, Noah is overcome by the idea that he has made a rash, potentially lethal decision. Sofia is in Paris, and he is moving further and further away from her. The thought makes him want to scream to be let out, released before it is too late, as if the driver sitting in the heated cab would even hear him. This journey, already the worst experience of his life, could also prove to be his greatest mistake.

He asks himself a question: *How did I get here?*

And, since there is nothing else to see, the dark actually answers.

*

Noah was the odd one out in a building full of world-class beauty; long bare legs of every shade, vibrant fabrics and fierce makeup, the flash of cameras and the sparkle of diamonds.

He was walking through the crowds with his face lowered, feeling – compared to the ladies around him – like anything else that preys in shadow: cockroach, rat, bloodsucker, parasite. He didn't know what the event was for, but that wasn't unusual. Modelling conventions, fashion shows, charity fundraisers and galas; these sorts of parties were a good source of income, as long as his connections could get him through the doors, and they usually could because Khalid ran one of the biggest security outfits in the city.

The women were the main attraction, but it was the men who spent the big euros. Agents, directors, producers, designers; they were all on blow, and they loved to make it snow for their girls. It wasn't unheard of for Noah to finish a night's work with a five-figure sum in his coat pocket.

Looking back now – and this is something he has planned to include in his wedding speech – it seems implausible that, in a room filled with the most beautiful models and influencers in the world, there was only one girl that stole Noah's eye. Yet that's precisely what happened. More implausible still is the fact that this young woman, this otherworldly deity surrounded by male models and millionaires, returned the pauper's gaze.

Noah – who, in spite of dealing, or perhaps because of it, had never had much interest in taking drugs – had floated across the room towards her like a man dazed by some hallucinogenic of—

A sound breaks through the darkness now, cutting even through the rumble of the lorry's wheels and the rattling chassis, and it yanks Noah from his own memory like a fall in a nightmare. He doesn't exactly *hear* the stiffening of the bodies around him, and he isn't actually touching anybody, but he somehow feels it in the thin air.

The sound is a siren, racing up to the lorry from behind. Noah squeezes his eyes shut, for all the good it does, and he begins to pray.

The lorry sounds as if it drops a gear, slowing down. Noah gets the feeling that, all around him, people are reaching out to their own Gods.

The siren maintains its approach, and then it overtakes and screams off into the distance.

False alarm. Noah allows himself to relax, but not too much; his bladder and bowels are still too uncomfortable for that.

He closes his eyes, searching for the memory, looking for Sofia …

But he doesn't find his way back to her tonight.

31

PLAYER FIVE

Her urge to speed rises and rises, yet Linda just about manages to restrain herself for the time it takes to crawl up the length of the M1. These are three desperately lonely hours.

Putting her foot down might gain her a few minutes, but what happens if she's snared in a speed trap or wiped out in a head-on collision? She'd become another footnote in Radio 2's traffic updates, that's all, and it would be days before an investigator starts to put all the strange pieces of the puzzle together. She'd be left in a coma, or scraped into a body bag, and Alyssa would be forgotten.

So Linda sticks to the limit, and after almost two hundred miles on the same stretch of road with only her own frightening thoughts for company, the GPS finally guides her onto more scenic secondary roads. This is rural Yorkshire, all farms between patchwork fields, and then the land becomes sparser as she moves west towards the moors. It isn't even four o'clock in the afternoon, but the day is beginning to fade. Night is coming early. The end, she feels, is getting nearer.

The GPS brings her to an A-road several miles north of

Saddleworth Moor; it's little more than a track wide enough for a tractor to pass through, and there's nothing much to see when the satnav plays its short, triumphant jingle: 'You have arrived at your destination.'

She peers through the windscreen at bare trees, tangled winter hedgerows and small walls of stone. 'You sure about that?' she asks, letting the car roll slowly forwards. She has never been here, but she studied the place on Maps before coming, of course, and there's only one building listed at this postcode. After another twist in the road, still rolling with the weight of the car, she sees a sign pointing up an even narrower gravel track.

THE GAMEKEEPER'S INN.

'What do you think?' she asks the stuffed dragon on the seat beside her. 'Too on the nose?'

Dragon remains noncommittal.

Linda briefly considers leaving her vehicle further away, avoiding the car park and completing her approach on foot, but decides there's not much point. The element of surprise seems worthless. Later, once this is over, however this all ends, she won't be difficult to follow so far. ANPR cameras will have marked her progress right up the country and stashing her car around one more corner is hardly going to make a difference. She turns, drives slowly up the gravel and pulls into the cracked painted lines of a parking space, facing the inn.

She keeps the car running and studies the building. It's quaint. Exactly how you'd expect an old Yorkshire pub to look. A thin stream of smoke rises from the chimney above three floors, and a sign at the entrance advertises rooms within. Two cars are parked in the area marked for staff; both have remained still long enough to glisten white with frost.

Linda waits for a while. Nothing happens. Nobody comes. At five past four she turns off the engine and finds herself unable to move.

'Get out of the car,' she says to herself. 'You've come this far. You're almost there. Get out of the car. Just do it.'

She does, but not before kissing Alyssa's old stuffed toy and leaving it sitting upright on the passenger seat.

As she locks the door and starts across the car park, she feels like an animal being watched. She feels like prey. She wonders if this is how the others have been feeling, wherever they are. It's zero degrees now, and the ground is literally freezing. Puddles in the myriad potholes crack beneath her stride. She takes one last look around the deserted area and steps inside the building.

There's a short entrance corridor with hooks for coats, all empty, and a staircase ahead going up to the guest rooms. Her movements seem very loud. A left turn before the stairs brings her into the reception area, which is warm and inviting but vacant; it smells of filter coffee and the dusty-metal odour of coal burning in a nearby fireplace. The décor is traditional British hunter: dark panelling on the walls and a solid wooden counter, its surface oiled and splitting with age; above the panelling, mounted on a picture rail, looms a vast collection of taxidermy; grouses, pheasants, rabbits and a small fox watch Linda cross the room with blank glass eyes.

There's a door behind the empty counter, pulled to, and Linda can hear a television beyond it. An audience cheers on one of those afternoon gameshows. With her palm she rings the bell, striking it harder than intended, and the door opens halfway.

A woman leans into view, tipping back her chair to peer

through the doorframe. 'Oh!' She's a big lady with tight curly hair, aged anywhere between forty-five and sixty, Linda guesses. She's eating something flaky, a sausage roll, and she hastily brushes crumbs from her jumper as she switches the unseen television either off or to mute. With a kicking, paddling motion she scoots her office chair through the doorway and up to the rear of the desk.

'Sorry, love, I was in a world of my own.'

'That's all right,' Linda replies mechanically, watching the woman closely.

'It's bitter out there, isn't it?'

'Very,' Linda says.

A moment of silence. The woman smiles expectantly, natural and relaxed; it's a smile that says she is not only down to earth, but the salt of it too. A real Yorkshire lass. Linda's eyes trail to a plaque standing on the countertop; where there might ordinarily be a title, there are three words engraved in the brass there: BEWARE THE MOON.

The proprietor notices and rolls her eyes. 'You know that film? The werewolf? The boss's idea of a joke, I'm afraid.'

'The boss?'

'My husband.'

'You own the place?'

'Fifteen years now. I'm Pat.'

Linda doesn't offer her own name in return. Instead, she turns her ear to the corridor behind her. For a brief moment, she's sure she hears a rushing draught as if the front door has been opened, but there's nothing more.

'Your husband,' Linda says slowly, 'is he the taxidermist?' With a tip of her head she gestures to the carcasses above.

'Derrick?' Pat laughs once, a funny sort of *whoop* sound. 'No, the grounds belonged to a manor that burned down in the twenties. This would've been where the gamekeeper lived, and when they renovated it into a hotel in the seventies, they kept the animals. When we got the keys, we did the same. They gave me the willies at first, but now I can't picture the place without them. Funny how that happens. We still get the shooting clubs up here and they like them well enough …' She pauses. 'I'm sorry, was it a room you were after?'

'I'm not sure. I was told to be here at five o'clock.'

'Oh, you're with this game, are you?'

Linda nods stiffly. 'I am.'

Pat lifts a laptop out from behind the desk. 'World of my bleeding own,' she repeats, putting on thick glasses. 'Let me just find your *email* …' She squints as she scrolls, clicking at times, and then nods. 'Right, we've got the old parlour set up for you, as requested, and I'll have a lass on the bar from five. You're booked in for a couple of hours but, as you can probably tell, we're not expecting a busy one. If you end up wanting to stay the night, I can offer you an excellent rate on board and breakfast. Roads get treacherous out here. I have it down that there'll be five of you. What is it, some sort of murder mystery? We get them from time to time.'

'I hope not,' Linda says. 'This was an anonymous email, was it?'

Pat leans closer to the screen. 'Just "*The Game*". To be honest, we weren't sure you were actually coming. Derrick swore it was a wind-up, but it doesn't cost to hold the room, not when it's quiet like this, so I got it laid out for you.'

'Is it just you here at the moment? I noticed *two* cars outside …'

'Just me and Mike, our cook.' Pat blinks over the top of her spectacles, looking at Linda closely. 'Is everything all right, duck?'

'Yes. Sorry.' Linda forces a smile and, concealed by the edge of the counter, she runs her hand along the belt beneath her coat and produces her long-expired warrant card, which she flashes briefly. 'Old habits, that's all. Thirty years with the police will do that to you.'

She isn't sure why she does this, except that it has always given her some sense of control in the past, and it works well enough now because Pat looks significantly relieved.

'My nephew's a copper. Hard work.' She checks the time, returns her laptop to its hiding place and heaves herself up out of the chair with a sigh. 'Can I get you a cuppa while you wait for the others?'

'That would be nice,' Linda says, meaning it. 'Black coffee. No sugar.'

'My pleasure. Feel free to make your way to the parlour, it's through that door and down past the bar. I'll bring the drink through to you there.'

'Thanks.' Linda waits for her to leave for the kitchen.

'You know something,' Pat pauses in the doorway, 'you ought to let whoever's in charge know it isn't wise to go calling yourselves "the game", not on the moors.' She chuckles and points up to the taxidermy. 'Around here, *that's* what happens to the game!'

Then she exits the room, still chuckling to herself, leaving Linda feeling very cold despite the warmth of the reception.

Once alone, Linda backtracks the way she came through the short corridor with the empty coat hooks to the main entrance. She presses her face against the glass in the door; it's dark outside now, and lights have come on over the car park. There are no new vehicles out there.

She still has her nose pressed to the glass, watching her breath leave foggy impressions on the pane, when somebody speaks from behind her.

'I heard you.'

Linda turns, startled, and sees a woman lurking on the staircase at the rear of the corridor.

Linda doesn't know this woman, doesn't recognise her at all; she's either close to her own age or considerably younger – thirties, maybe – only aged by some helpless trauma; she has faded golden hair that might once have been red, and she is clenching and unclenching her fists in slow, shaky rhythm; her eyes are those of a woman enduring the worst day of her life.

'Sorry?' Linda replies.

The stranger breathes two words: 'The Game.'

Linda's gut goes into freefall and it must show on her face because the woman on the stairs begins rushing towards her.

'Wait!' Linda brandishes one authoritative palm, a cop's gesture. 'Wait a minute! Who are you?'

But the woman doesn't slow. 'Where is she? *Where's Hannah?*'

And before Linda's brain has any hope of catching up, the woman is upon her, hands reaching for her throat.

32

PLAYER ONE

Where are you, Jackson?
  Are you down there?
  Are you afraid?
  Where are you?

Maggie's face is pressed against the acrylic porthole window, and she's looking down over the lights of the Twin Cities and the vast, empty whiteness of surrounding Minnesota. The plane banks as it goes upwards, and then the city lights are swallowed by clouds and the land is simply gone. It's around eight o'clock, Central Time, on Monday evening. By the time she reaches full altitude, Maggie will be travelling at about five hundred miles per hour. She has never been overseas, but she made a few domestic flights when she was a kid and that figure has always stuck in her memory. Five hundred miles per hour; that's approximately eight miles further away from her son with every passing minute until she changes flights at Kennedy International.

She pulls down the shade and closes her eyes, and the phone conversation with Caroline plays over and over like a bad song caught in her head. That was hours ago. The Taylors must be going out of their minds, and Maggie can empathise. Seriously, she gets it.

She'd been on her knees in the stall when she'd spoken to Caroline, doubled up on the polished off-white terrazzo in case of vomit. Not so long ago, the restrooms at MSP were big news. They were the focus of a hundred-million-dollar revamp, and their gigantic cubicles, clerestory windows and mosaicked walls had won them the title of the best airport johns in America, or something like that. Maggie had been thinking of that when she answered the phone and spoke over the sound of classical music being pumped into the stall.

'Caroline! Hi!'

'Maggie? Jeez, I was starting to worry.'

'Sorry, the service out here is garbage, you know.'

'Out here?' The first sign of unease in Caroline's voice. 'Where are you?'

'Where?' A toilet in a neighbouring stall flushed, and Maggie scrunched her eyes tight. 'A restroom. I'm in a restroom. Jackson is outside.'

'A restroom? A restroom *where*? We're only twenty minutes away from your apartment.'

'OK, great, it's just …' Deep breath. 'Look, I have something to ask you. It's a little, um … Well, no, it's not little, it's a huge favour actually. My parents, you know, they want to meet Jackson, so they've invited us up to their cabin and I was sort of thinking, well …'

'Jackson has school tomorrow.'

'I know he does. I get that but, you know, this is really important to me. It'd only be a day, two at the most, and—'

'Absolutely not. There's no way we're pulling Jackson out of school. I'm sorry, Maggie, but it's out of the question. When we agreed to this, the deal was—'

'I know.' A twinge in her gut; even through the lies, and the horror, was it a twitch of jealousy, of anger? Was she really ready to argue over a fantasy she was creating? Yes. 'They're his family too, Caroline. They've waited years to meet him, and it'll only be a couple of—'

'No.' Caroline's voice, colder now than Maggie had ever heard it. 'We're patient people, and we've been more than accommodating throughout all of this, but when it comes to Jackson's education you can't expect us to—'

Maggie had tuned out then, swallowing hard. Words were like bugs clawing up her throat, and any moment now she would say it, say it all, and they could have the damn Game, Shaun and Caroline could play it together, they could take her flight to England and prove how much they really wanted Jackson.

'Look,' Maggie heard herself say, 'you're cutting out. I'm sorry, but I'll have to call you back.'

She hung up, hands shaking, and the phone began to ring again. She switched it off.

Now the thought of destroying it, as instructed in her last message, didn't seem so bad. In fact, she began to worry that she had already held onto it too long. She lifted it over the bowl, wondering if it would flush, knowing it probably wouldn't. She thought about smashing it, hiding the pieces somewhere, but she couldn't leave it for *anybody* to find. Airports are more than a little cautious about security, and if the phone ended up in the hands of a police officer …

She'd closed her eyes, clutching the phone, thinking hard. *Where do you lose something inside an airport?*

The thought gave her an idea, a way she could leave the phone behind and then collect it again once this was over, and she left the restroom and made her way to the nearest helpdesk.

'Excuse me,' she said to the man there, 'you have Lost and Found, right?'

'Yah sure,' he said, 'our Lost and Found office is down on the valet level of the terminal. We don't have one this side of the TSA checkpoint, I'm afraid. You can't collect lost property *after* having your luggage checked, you know.'

'Of course,' Maggie said weakly. 'I just found this phone in the restroom ...'

She handed it in, and the last strand of communication connecting her to the Taylors was severed.

The plane now rights itself, the seatbelt light goes off, and the terrible phone conversation chases Maggie down into an exhausted, semiconscious memory-dream.

Maggie was only sixteen years old when she went into labour, but her parents weren't allowed to be with her in the theatre. Shaun and Caroline, on the other hand, were. At one point during the delivery, the Taylors actually held one of Maggie's hands each, framing her like solemn, anxious pillars on either side. Sometimes Caroline cried and Shaun soothed her, telling her that she, *Caroline*, would get through this, that it was all going to be OK, that she just had to breathe, breathe, breathe. The entire ordeal was fucking ludicrous.

For Maggie, that night truly redefined the word *labour*; it really was laborious. The Taylors had paid almost fifty thousand dollars – after medical, legal and agency fees, as well as living costs now that she had been thrown out of her family home, Maggie would get about ten thousand dollars – and that evening she would've said they got their money's worth, every single cent. Her entire lower half felt like it was being yanked, pulled, clenched, stabbed; her spine was being twisted and her hips drawn apart; at one point it felt like the worst menstrual cramps of her life and she actually laughed out loud, thinking of her sister coming home from college with period pains on that weekend – forty weeks prior – that Maggie had taken her ID.

In the end, for all the supposed beauty of childbirth, it had felt like she needed to take the world's biggest shit in a room full of strangers. Unable to deliver on her back, she'd finished the job on her knees, thinking deliriously of how funny life sometimes is, how things so often come around full circle; this had all begun with her on her knees, and it ended the same way.

Jackson was born at 10:14 after a gruelling eighteen hours. By law Maggie could've kept him, even then, and the Taylors would've lost everything. She held him for maybe five minutes before handing him over to Caroline. It was the right thing to do. The only good to come out of that abysmal ordeal.

Maybe one day, she'd thought, she might be grown up enough to be a part of his life.

One day when all the crazy shit was over.

But for some people the crazy shit is never really over.

33

JACKSON

'You don't have to go if you don't want to, son. You know that, don't you? You shouldn't feel obligated.'

His dad had said this just as Jackson was coming down the stairs with his backpack, ready to leave, and it had caught him by surprise.

'What's *obligated*?' Jackson asked warily.

'Well, it's when you feel you ought to do something, even though you don't really want to, just because you're scared of hurting somebody else's feelings.'

'Shaun …' That was Mom. 'We can't let her down now.'

'I'm just saying, he shouldn't be made to feel guilty if he's not as, uh, *enthused* about going as he used to be. Besides, what if he, you know …'

'I want to go,' Jackson said quickly, doing his best to sound as *infused* as he could. 'I do, honest I do.'

That wasn't strictly true, and his parents had obviously guessed as much, but his father didn't press the topic. He agreed to 'put a pin in it', which meant that it was done for today, but it would come back around soon enough. Shaun Taylor is always putting pins in things.

Jackson has thought about this conversation a lot. In this strange room, in this unfamiliar building, there's not much else to do but think about the moments that have brought him here.

It had only been a white lie anyway, the nice kind, because Jackson knows how much Maggie enjoys his company, and he likes to make her happy. She lives in an apartment, which is surrounded by people in noisy, neighbouring apartments, but he still worries about her being lonely. She often seems a little sad, and sometimes, when he's in his own big home, he dreams about her, all alone in her tiny apartment, and he wakes up feeling bad.

At first it had been cool, the thought of having two moms; two birthdays each year, two Thanksgivings, two Christmases. His parents never lied about his adoption, so he'd always known she was out there, somewhere in the Twin Cities.

He first met her on a Saturday afternoon at the mall. Maggie cried when she saw him, and he cried, and his mom cried too.

Somehow, Jackson had known right away that he loved her, this stranger, his mother.

He loves her still, so darn much … Just not like he loves his mom and dad.

She'd been *drinking* on Sunday evening. He'd never tell his parents that, because he knows it's a bad thing, but he isn't stupid. He'd seen her pouring *the drink* into her Sprite, and she'd been getting sillier, funnier, cuddlier by the time *The Iron Giant* had finished; it's an old cartoon, and he's seen it too many times to count, but he didn't want to hurt her feelings by telling her that; Maggie doesn't own many movies. Not long after he had gone to bed, just before falling asleep, Jackson had smelled the thick, fruity cigarette smoke coming in through the gap under the bedroom door, and once again he'd found himself feeling sort of bad for her and he wasn't even sure why.

It was very late when he was taken.

He'd woken up cold, and for a moment he thought he was in his own bed. Then he recognised his surroundings, the sparsely furnished bedroom at Maggie's, and panic and shame engulfed him. His pyjama bottoms were soaking wet, his groin sticky and itchy. He scrambled onto his feet and snatched up his Spider-Man blanket, which had fortunately absorbed most of the pee, and – like a stupid baby – he began to cry. He was alone in the room, but his face was burning hot. This unwelcome night-time habit had started happening a few weeks ago, and now he desperately wished he'd stayed at home, where he could knock quietly on his parents' door and Dad would help him shower and fix him clean bedding without judgement.

Had his parents warned Maggie that this might happen? Perhaps. Even so, that didn't mean he wanted to wake her up now and show her what he'd done. He didn't want her to *feel obligated*.

He was still clutching the blanket and thinking about how he was going to get himself out of this situation when he heard the noise at the window and, like a dream suddenly remembered, he realised that it wasn't the wetness that had actually woken him up; it was that *sound*.

He froze, and the heat of humiliation that had filled his cheeks abandoned him in an instant.

There was a scraping, squeaking, wriggling sound coming

from behind the roller shade. It made Jackson think of old branches in the wind, or how rats might sound if they were trapped alive inside a wooden barrel, waiting to die. He shuddered. There were no trees outside the window, no overhanging boughs to creak and moan, but there *was* an old metal fire escape. Could that be moving in the wind?

What wind?

The hairs stiffened on the back of his neck.

The night was still, dense with the thick silence of snowfall, and yet the sound came again, wriggling and sly.

Heating pipes? Not inside the window.

He was starting to get scared now, frightened like a dumb baby with a piss-soaked blanket, and without allowing himself to think about it anymore he reached for the cord by the window, reached out to show himself that he was no baby.

He raised the blind quickly, with one sharp tug, and then he knew, for the first time in his life, what it was to be petrified.

There were eyes staring in at him through the glass. Wide, white eyes, and in that moment Jackson forgot all about the fire escape, the steel platform, and he saw only a spectre floating five storeys up, a vampire clawing to get in. He thought he was screaming for help, but he wasn't. He never made a sound.

*

He sits up now, woken by the nightmare of reliving that terrible moment, and once again his groin is wet, the skin on his thighs irritated and sore.

It is Tuesday morning, and he is locked inside a basement.

'No,' he moans, peering down into the sleeping bag on the smelly folding mattress. 'No, please ...' He starts to cry.

'It's OK, kid.'

Jackson spins around so fast he actually hurts his neck. *He* is in here. The man. The one who took him. He must've come down the stairs while Jackson was thrashing through his own nightmare, moving like a whisper despite his size.

He is still wearing the mask, of course. He'd been wearing it when Jackson had first seen him through the window, and for all Jackson knows he has been wearing it ever since. Probably not though. That wouldn't be very practical. It's a simple ski mask, not an entirely foreign sight in Minnesota where the winter air can blister bare skin in minutes. When Jackson had first seen him, he had been levering at the bottom of Maggie's window frame with some sort of steel bar; on seeing Jackson, he repositioned the tool and simply punched it through the glass.

Now he is holding a bundle of various fabrics that are hard to distinguish in the gloom; the only natural light comes in through gaps around the wooden boards that have been screwed over the small, high-up windows at street level. Jackson never hears any traffic up there. The house has an abandoned feel, an empty smell.

The man's voice is overly gruff, like a bad imitation of Batman, and Jackson is sure he's making it up.

'I knew that smell yesterday,' the man says. 'Should've done something about it then, but ...' He sniffs. 'Shit was crazy, wasn't it?'

Jackson doesn't say a word.

'I wet the bed until I was fourteen years old. You ain't got nothing to be ashamed of. Got you some fresh blankets here. Clean sweater. Some of them moist towelettes. You can go ahead and leave your clothes out. We'll get 'em washed up.'

'I want to go home,' Jackson whispers, not for the first time. 'When can I go home?'

'Not long now,' the man says. 'Be over soon enough. One more night, I think.'

'Another night?'

'Sorry, kid. Like I told you yesterday, this ain't personal.' He places the bundle on the concrete floor and moves quietly, ghostlike up the staircase. 'It's just work. Be over soon enough. One way or the other.'

He leaves the cellar, closes the door and slides the locks back into place.

All of the locks.

34

PLAYER TWO

'There's nothing you can do this evening?' Brett asks. 'What about cancellations? Wouldn't it be worth hanging around for a seat on a direct flight?'

He's already tried this with British Airways, KLM and Virgin Atlantic, and now the man at the Delta counter gives him more or less the same answer: no, Brett isn't going to be flying directly to England tonight.

'I'm sorry, but right now the best we can offer is the 23:50 to Paris Charles de Gaulle, which would land at one p.m. tomorrow. From there you can fly with Air France. That departs at 14:50 and lands in Manchester at 15:20, local time.'

'15:20?' Brett closes his eyes, doing the quick maths. Will that be too late? Suppose he can't get a ride from the airport on the other side! He wants to shake this man, make him understand that this could be life or death, but of course he doesn't. The man at the counter says he's sorry, again, and Brett books the flights along with a return on Wednesday morning.

'Any suggestions on what I'm supposed to do for the next

seven hours?' Brett asks, pocketing his wallet with the receipt inside.

'We generally advise arriving at security three hours before any international flight. If it were *me*, I'd consider a four-hour Daytripper stay at TWA, our on-airport hotel.'

'TWA, huh?' Brett extends the telescopic handle on his overnight case and pats the edge of the counter with one hand as he turns away. 'Thanks.'

If he leaves now, he could be home in sixty minutes. He could heat up some of Kelly's famous jambalaya and stretch out in his own gorgeous bed; it's only five o'clock, but God knows he feels tired enough to do it. He could try to smooth over his abrupt departure from work.

He'd have to look Kelly in the face though. He'd have to subject himself to her probing questions, offer up his secrets to her prying fingers, and in his current emotional state that seems like far too much to handle.

He's thinking about the things she said, and mostly the things she didn't, as he starts in the direction of the TWA.

*

He sleeps – he's sure he does – but his rest is paradoxically frenzied. It reminds him of the time he had a bad reaction to penicillin. Feverish images scream in the dark, and he dreams of video calls in which he's forced to watch as Craig's throat is sliced as cleanly as sashimi, and his eyeballs are plucked from his head.

That broken ankle is with Brett always. It's there when the alarm on the burner goes off at eight o'clock that evening, and it's with him in the hotel shower. It's the cracked ice floating in the Old Fashioned he forces down in the terminal, and it's the closing snap of the overhead luggage compartments in the cabin.

How long can a person remain strapped to a chair?

How long before the ruptured flesh swells, strangling veins and killing the leg, if not the heart?

How much pain can a man really take?

The plane starts down the runway of JFK and Brett closes his eyes.

Among all the things he can't connect, and all the questions he cannot answer, there is the mystery of England. As far as he knows, Craig has never been. Wouldn't go, in fact. Craig refers to the English as tea-sipping faggots, or buck-toothed limey bastards, or some creative variation on the theme.

Brett has been to London twice, both times with Kelly. On the first trip they did the tourist circuit: rode a red bus and the London Eye, took selfies outside the palace and Big Ben. The last time they went, for her birthday four years ago, he'd taken her to that *Harry Potter* play in the West End. It was showing on Broadway, of course, but he wanted to make a long weekend of it, and – as he said to Kelly once she'd opened the envelope and screamed with delight – if you're going to do Potter, you should really do it in Britain. They were good times, those trips. They really were.

Now, somehow, he is flying to England again. It's surreal. He's travelling the breadth of the world to do something an online bank could do in a nanosecond. That's the conclusion he has come to. Online banking leaves digital fingerprints, and he is being forced to go back to analogue. Some international organised crime outfit must be working in a pincer movement; on one side of the world, they kidnap the target, and on the other they take the money. The action is on burner phones, the evidence disposable, and the victim does all the hard work himself.

So, he wonders, *what are the demands? Where's the ransom note? What's this going to cost?*

He needs to know, and the sooner the better, but he still doesn't want to. It may be a price he can't afford. He's a video editor making trailers for a games company, for Christ's sake. He lives in a beautiful duplex, yes, worth almost one million on paper, but that's just New York value. That doesn't make him *rich*. Besides, it was Kelly's inheritance that secured the damn place, and it was nothing more than a rotting shell when they first got the keys. What's he supposed to do? Hand his house key over to some cockney geezer in a brown envelope and say good luck with the neighbours?

The *Game*, The *Game*, The *goddamn Game*. Why do they call it The Game?

Because maybe this isn't about money at all.

The last leak at Kickstart Games cost the company millions, but what if the 'leaker' didn't do it for personal gain? What if he or she was *forced*, and Brett is about to suffer the same fate?

Somewhere over the Atlantic, despite his mind still whirling with these thoughts, Brett manages to drink himself back to sleep. It doesn't take much, just a couple more glasses and a blanket on his solitary three-seat island; the crowded direct flight would've been better for timing, but it would've stolen the last of his sanity. He doesn't wake up until they're passing over England, frustratingly near to his final destination, and he finds himself lost in the peculiar time warp that is simultaneously dawn in New York City and lunchtime in Paris. He picks at his complimentary breakfast baguette for nothing more than essential sustenance, and soon the plane begins its descent.

He has an hour and a half wait before they'll even begin boarding at Charles de Gaulle. There are a little over four hours left on the timer on his phone. It's going to be close. His stomach hurts, forcing him to the restroom. He goes seven times in a single hour, doubled over, passing little more than foul water. It's stress. Painful and gross, but he's relieved it is happening now, *after* the seven hours in the air and before whatever's coming next. Once his guts have given all they can, he sits at the gate feeling shaky and exhausted all over again.

It's early afternoon on Tuesday. The plane to Manchester looks set to be only a quarter full. His eyes move over a large family of Muslims draped in cottons and a few men in suits, working on laptops. There's a young blonde pacing back and forth so hectically she makes him dizzy; she doesn't have any luggage whatsoever, and she looks almost as dishevelled as he feels. Wasn't she on the flight from JFK? He thinks she was.

His gaze eventually comes to rest on a couple of young men, intertwined on their plastic seats. Late teens or early twenties, both dressed in Disneyland merchandise. They're cuddled up around a Nintendo Switch, occasionally exchanging soft kisses on hands or foreheads. Brett watches them with a strange combination of fascination and sadness.

The plane seems to spend an exasperating amount of time screwing around on the runway, and Brett feels like tearing out his own fingernails with his teeth. It boards, flies over the Channel, and lands in Manchester, England.

Once his feet are on the ground, Brett puts them to good use by storming through the shuffling customs crowd at a near jog. Somehow, despite his best efforts, he still arrives at the helpdesk *behind* the young blonde from his flight.

He shakes his head in disbelief: *Christ, what did she do, sprint here?*

There's nothing he can do but wait a little longer.

The blonde is leaning right over the counter, showing the clerk something on her phone. Brett tells himself that she has an incredible ass, but his heart isn't in it anymore. Her passport is sticking out of the back pocket of her jeans, and Brett briefly thinks, not for the first time, how strange it is to see somebody travelling with not even a handbag or purse.

He checks his own phone, watching the timer as it falls into its final hour, and when he looks back up the desk is empty and the employee there is looking at him expectantly.

'Welcome to Manchester,' she says, 'what can I do for you?'

'I have this, um, *zip code* I'm trying to get to …' He considers showing her the postcode and timer onscreen but then asks for a pen and paper instead. He jots the code down and slides it over the desk to her.

She looks at the jumble of numbers and letters for only a moment and smiles, apparently bemused. 'The TransPennine Express train would get you to Marsden or Slaithwaite, those are the closest stations, but you'd still have to get a taxi the rest of the way.'

'What about hiring a car?' he asks.

'Absolutely, we have eight providers in our Rental Village including Avis, Hertz and Enterprise. There's a free bus transfer departing from the terminal every ten minutes.'

'Great,' he says, reaching for the paper, and then pauses. He looks down at the scrawl, which she has slid back to him. 'You know where this is, just by the code? You didn't need to put it into your computer or anything?'

She laughs. 'No, I'm not that good. It must be a popular place.'

Brett blinks, bemused. 'Why's that?'

'That young woman before you; she just showed me the exact same postcode.'

This is when Brett begins to run.

35

PLAYER THREE

Sarah has been on the staircase inside the Gamekeeper's Inn for several moments, eavesdropping on their conversation:

'*Your husband, is he the taxidermist?*'

'*Derrick? No, the grounds belonged to a manor that burned down in the twenties ...*'

Neither of the women in the reception area saw her enter the building.

Sarah had first driven around the car park, glancing over the two vehicles in the staff area, before deciding she didn't want to park here. The place gave her the creeps. Instead, she left her car five minutes away, concealed behind a grass verge in a rural turning circle, and traipsed back to the inn through the surrounding fields. The wet ground was turning to ice, and her shoes crunched over whitening grass.

She was on the other side of a treeline, parallel to the gravel track leading to the building, when she heard the approaching car rolling along. She froze, pressing herself against an oak, and listened. The car waited a while, then turned onto the crunching stone.

Sarah had peered out from her gloomy hiding place, heart pounding, and seen the black BMW rolling into the car park. It stopped, facing the building, and just sat there with its engine idling.

Was Hannah in the backseat? She couldn't tell. She was looking at the car side-on from twenty yards, and the most she could see was the basic shape of the driver. It looked like a woman, and she wondered once again if it was one of her bingo buddies turned extortionist.

Minutes passed, and Sarah remained perfectly still, her breath pluming up in rapid, stuttering clouds. She told herself that all she had to do now was run up to the car and tear open the door, but she was too afraid of what she might find, and what sort of person she might face. She was clutching the pay-as-you-go phone tightly, waiting for instructions, but nothing came through. She was early, and the timer was still counting down.

The engine was eventually turned off, the headlights went dark, and the driver sat there for a moment longer. It almost looked as if she – and by then, Sarah was sure it *was* a *she* – was talking to somebody in the car. Someone too small to be visible through the side windows. The driver got out, but not before leaning over to *kiss somebody* in the front seat. Sarah grabbed onto the surrounding foliage, tethering herself in place. The driver locked the car and walked into the building, her stride confident, self-assured.

The moment she was out of sight, Sarah made her desperate break for the BMW.

She threw herself against the passenger window, ready to claw her way through the glass if she had to … but there was no child. There was only a tattered teddy of some breed, an infant's plaything, sitting creepily on the seat. Had this been used to pacify a stolen child? She couldn't be sure, but she didn't think so. She looked into the backseat. It was free of blankets and more modern than the car her daughter had been photographed in. Sarah moaned, knowing that she would have to enter the building.

At least, she told herself, it was a public place.

It didn't *feel* very public.

She held her breath and let herself in through the entrance as quietly as she could. From along the short corridor, coming through the opening on her left, she first heard their voices. As she crept along the hallway, she chanced a peek into the reception. The woman who had been driving was facing the other way, blocking the sightline of the employee at the desk, and Sarah took this opportunity to slip past and reach her spot on the staircase.

This is where she is standing when the conversation turns.

'*I was told to be here at five o'clock.*'

'*Oh, you're with this game, are you?*'

Sarah's legs unhinge and she has to catch the handrail to stop herself from rolling down the bottom three steps.

'*I am,*' the woman says, and Sarah strains to hear the rest through the deafening rush of blood in her own ears. They're not making much sense, these two women, and neither seems to know exactly what's going on. The woman from the BMW says that she's with the police, and Sarah doesn't know whether she should run *to* her or, in accordance with *the rules*, run away from her. Is this some kind of *sting operation*, if such a thing exists, either on behalf of the police or set up by The Game itself? Some kind of trap? The woman could, of course, be lying.

Before Sarah has decided upon her next move the conversation is over and the woman from the BMW is here, right *here* at the bottom of the stairs with her back turned. She peers out through the glass at the entrance, and Sarah hears three words coming out of her own mouth.

'I heard you.'

Startled, the woman turns towards her. She has a hard face, not unattractive though, and she must be almost the same age as Sarah's mum, but that might just be the grey.

'Sorry?'

'The Game,' Sarah says, and the woman's face drops because she knows, she knows *something*, and before she can stop herself, Sarah is off the staircase.

'Wait!' the woman says. 'Wait a minute! Who are you?'

'Where is she?' Sarah shrieks. '*Where's Hannah?*'

She reaches for the older woman's throat, spurred by a fury she's never felt in her whole life, but the woman bats her away with practised ease, despite her age.

The next thing Sarah knows she is pinned against the wall with a hand over her mouth.

'What number?' the woman hisses into her ear. 'I'm *Five*, OK? *Player Five*. They have my daughter too. You got the messages? What number are you?'

Sarah struggles until she can't struggle anymore, and when she presses her forehead against the wall by the empty coat hooks, subdued, the hand is finally removed from her mouth.

'Three,' she says miserably. 'I'm Player Three. Somebody took my girl. Somebody took my baby girl.'

The woman behind her says, 'Oh Jesus Christ,' and gently lets her go.

*

They're sitting in the parlour by half past four, only minutes after meeting, and Sarah is clutching a cup of tea with both hands. The chairs are comfortable, real leather, and somebody has laid a fire before they arrived. It could be soporific if it wasn't so disturbing. The chairs are arranged around a round table of dark wood in the middle of the room.

Sarah looks down into her milky drink, which the proprietor poured after showing the shellshocked women in. The proprietor is gone now. The door is closed. Sarah is desperately thirsty, but something is telling her not to take a sip. She looks at the other mother, who is closest to – and facing – the fireplace. Player Five's face is an absolute blank.

'What is this place?' Sarah asks hoarsely. 'Do you think the owners have something to do with this? What does it mean?'

'I don't think it means anything,' the woman replies in a hushed tone. 'I think it was probably chosen for its name and nothing more complicated. Probably picked from a list of places online. Maybe it was somebody's idea of a joke. They wanted us to find this place, that's the important thing. They wanted us to know it when we saw it. They *want* us to meet.'

'What for?' Sarah continues whispering. 'Money? One big pay out?'

'I don't think so. I'm not sure that this has anything to do with money, and that's the most frightening thing about it. I think this is only the start.'

Player Five sips her coffee, and Sarah follows suit with a cautious mouthful of tea. If it's been spiked then the drugs aren't immediately obvious.

'Your daughter,' Sarah says. 'How old?'

The woman is quiet for a moment. 'Seventeen. Alyssa's seventeen. What about …?'

'Hannah. Two.'

The woman glances over, directly at Sarah, and her tired eyes are full of sorrow. 'I'm so sorry.'

Sarah turns her face to the fire. A log pops inside, shooting sparks up into the chimney. 'What's your name?'

'I'm not sure if we should share our real names.'

'I'm Sarah.'

The woman sighs. 'Linda.'

'Linda.' It feels better to have a name for the face; Sarah can't stand the inhumanity of the numbering, and she supposes that is the point of it. 'I heard you say you were police. Is that true?'

'I was. Thirty years.'

'Does that mean I'm breaking the rules by talking to you?'

Linda considers this. 'I don't think so.'

'Good, because I'm glad you're here.' She winces, feeling foolish. 'I'm sorry, I don't mean that, I wouldn't wish this on anybody. It's just that I've been on my own all day and … I've been going out of my mind.'

'It's OK. I know what you mean.'

Sarah presses her head back against the leather and sips her tea, which has no taste at all. She feels utterly drained. This is how she felt after the miscarriages, more of a husk than a real person. Useless. Helpless. All round *less*. If Neil has, for some reason, *still* failed to see her messages, and if he hasn't already gone home early, then he will be finishing work in the next hour. Sarah's phone is switched off inside her car with its SIM removed, which was as close to destroying it as she managed to get. It won't take Neil long to realise that something is very, very wrong.

'She can't be out there all night,' Sarah says. 'Not my Hannah. She's just a little girl. She needs her own bed, her *stuff*, and …' She can feel herself going again, slipping into the dark, teetering on the edge.

'Sarah.' Linda speaks softly but firmly, catching her before she falls. 'She'll get through this and so will you. We've just got to keep on doing as we're told, and there'll be no reason for anybody to get hurt. That's one thing I *am* sure of. If these people, whoever they are, wanted to hurt our girls then they would've done it already. They wouldn't be stringing us along.'

Sarah desperately wants to believe that, but she can't. Not until Hannah is safe in her arms. 'Do you think they're both together? Our girls?'

Linda's eyes fill up, reflecting flames, and she quickly swipes at her cheek. 'If they are, then my daughter will do everything she can to look after Hannah. Alyssa is the—' her throat catches, just briefly, and she swallows hard. 'She's the smartest, bravest girl. She really is. She wouldn't let anything happen to your child. I know that for a fact.' A pale smile passes across her lips and she wipes at her cheek once more. 'She's so good with kids, better than I've ever been.'

'Can I see her? Have you got a picture?'

Linda raises her eyebrows, a cloud of suspicion passing over her features, and then she rummages through the pocket of her coat.

'Aren't you hot in that?' Sarah asks, only just noticing how high the woman's coat is fastened. Sarah is wearing a coat too, but it's unfastened, and she still feels hot and uncomfortable. 'You're sitting right next to the fire.'

'Been feeling cold all day,' Linda replies distractedly, and she takes a photograph from her purse and holds it up to Sarah without handing it over.

In the picture, the girl is a few years younger than seventeen; she still has the chubbiness of prepubescence, the puppy fat around her face, but she's quite gorgeous, and Sarah thinks that she just might grow into a truly beautiful woman. Assuming she gets the chance.

'It's a few years old,' Linda says ruefully, taking one final, yearning look herself before slipping the photo back into her purse. 'All my recent pictures are digital and …'

'I know,' Sarah says. 'I was told to leave my phone behind too. It's got everything on it. When this is over though, I'll be getting hard copies of every photo I've ever taken, every single—'

The door to the room opens without warning, cutting her off mid-sentence, and she automatically shrinks in her seat. This time there's no fight or flight reaction. She's too surprised, too slow, and all over her skin she feels her hairs turn into needles.

Even from a distance, she actually feels Linda's body mirror her own tension as she turns from the fireplace, but Linda doesn't get to her feet so neither does Sarah.

Two people enter the room.

The first is a young blonde, little more than a girl herself, dressed in a hooded sweatshirt and red high-top Converse. Her face is drawn, shattered, afraid.

From behind her, a more smartly dressed man in a scarf and overcoat ducks inside. The first thing Sarah's eyes go to is the thing at his side, the thing he is wheeling, and all she can seem to think is that the suitcase is very full, the suitcase is perfectly Hannah-sized, and all of her worst fears are about to become reality; the case is going to be unzipped and her mind will follow when she sees what's inside, her brain simply tearing like crepe paper, and there'll be no going back, no more sanity, no escape.

The man, however, does not open his case and, as her initial scare passes, Sarah sees that his expression is also one of confusion and dismay. He looks sick and dehydrated, as gaunt as a person with food poisoning, sort of weedy for his age. There's stubble on his wooden face, and his eyes move from Sarah to Linda and back again.

'What the hell is this?' he asks, his accent American. 'Who are you people?'

'You first,' Linda says. Her face is cool, but her body seems somehow tight and her eyes are close to crazy. 'You can open that suitcase too, while you're at it. Let us all have a good look inside before we go any further.'

He shakes his head, large glasses reflecting firelight. 'I've travelled four thousand miles to get some answers. I'll ask the damn questions here.'

'It's not going to work like that,' Linda replies flatly, staring him down. 'If you wanted to call the shots then you should have got here first.'

Sarah isn't exactly sure that that's how this works, but either way it's the youngest woman in the room, the one beside the man, who tentatively asks the next question. 'They gave you a number, right? What numbers are you? Which … *player*?' She says this last word with obvious distaste, forming it in her mouth like a curse word, a taboo.

Sarah swallows, and then points to herself and Linda in turn. 'Three. Five.'

The new girl nods, reflecting the gesture for herself and the man beside her. 'One. Two.'

'OK,' Linda says. 'Fantastic. We're all introduced.'

'Almost,' Sarah says quietly, checking her burner. 'There are twelve minutes left on my timer.'

The man shrugs. 'We're here, aren't we? This is as far as we've been told to come. We made it.'

'Maybe,' Sarah says, 'but where's Player Four, and what happens to us if they don't get here in time?'

36

PLAYER FOUR

Noah is woken for the last time in the blackness by the sound of the trailer's enormous rear door rattling open in the world above him.

The lorry has stopped completely, and this time it doesn't seem to be on a ferry or an underwater train. Noah has no idea which course the trailer took across the Channel, but for several hours in the night the engine had stopped, and Noah had been forced to try to sleep through first the excruciating cramps and then the sickening numbness as the lorry rocked queasily from side to side.

This time, even the sensation of some greater movement has altogether ceased. The journey is over. Boxes are being shifted now, and voices are rumbling. Men's voices. In the pitch-dark bowels of the trailer, nobody breathes. When the hatch eventually opens, it doesn't sound like any border officer calling down from the topside.

'Wakey-wakey, you dirty sods! Out you come!'

There's laughter up there, deep guffawing, and Noah has no choice but to join the wriggling procession of assorted migrants leftward, towards the exit. As soon as he reaches the opening, strong hands seize him by the back of the coat and haul him up through the hole. His legs are dead, and he slumps against the inner wall of the trailer as blood returns to his feet and his eyes adjust to the light.

'Chop-chop!' the man says, shoving Noah away from the hatch so that he can reach inside for the next in line.

'OK!' Noah says irritably, catching his balance before falling. The man looks like a border cop about as much as he sounds like one; he has a silver tooth and faded tattoos on his face. The boxes Noah had previously navigated between have all been tossed unceremoniously onto dewy grass outside, and the sight of them thrown out of the door like that makes him feel acutely nervous as he eases himself down onto an unkempt verge.

It must be mid-morning. Overcast and chilly. Noah's eyes sting in the daylight, but his lungs welcome the fresh air. Stretching his limbs, he sees empty greenery in all directions. Winter greenery muted to greys. A handful of sheep graze in a distant field. The lorry is parked haphazardly beside a rural road, and around the lorry there are three stationary vehicles: a silver Mercedes saloon and two unmarked white box vans. One of these vans is parked across both lanes ahead; it's a road-block but there are no flashing police lights.

Noah counts six men: two in the trailer still hauling out passengers, one standing over a subdued man – Noah's former driver, he assumes, though he hasn't seen him until now – sitting on the verge, and three more keeping eyes on the road in both directions. Victor said there'd be a driver waiting for Noah; the Mercedes, he decides, is probably here for him, while the vans are for the other passengers. The border-hopping mother and daughter from last night are already on the grass among the tossed boxes, and more people are being shoved out behind him. Noah can't stand to be over here with them, so he delves through his pocket and rolls a cigarette. Lighting it, he begins to walk towards the nearest bare hedgerow.

One of the Englishmen on the ground, a bearded one wearing a knitted flat cap, spots Noah moving. 'Where do you think you're going?'

'*Je dois aller pisser*,' Noah says, cupping his genitals with one hand for illustration. 'I need to take a piss, man.'

'Fucking animals, the lot of you,' the man grumbles, turning to one of his partners. 'Keep an eye on him, Ricky. Don't let him wander too far.'

'All right.' Ricky is obese in a huge waxed jacket with tattoos up his neck. He follows Noah closely, heavy boots churning the ground.

Noah reaches a semi-sheltered spot, starts to undo his zipper and glances back over one shoulder. 'Privacy?'

'Get on with it, Frenchie.'

Noah shakes his head. He empties his bladder, sighing around his cigarette and shuddering with blessed relief, then fixes his work trousers and flicks the remains of his smoke off into the bushes. He's trudging back towards the bewildered crowd now gathered behind the lorry when he takes out his phone to check for updates. Nothing new. It's 11:42 on Tuesday morning, local time; it's later than he thought, and the timer is still counting down relentlessly. This brings back the nerves. This makes him want to—

'Uh-uh!' Out of nowhere, the man called Ricky easily plucks the phone from Noah's hand.

The terror is surprising, instant, as if he has just been stripped naked where he stands. 'What are you doing?'

'You won't be needing this, mate.'

Noah reaches for the phone – his only connection to The Game, his last link to Sofia – and the man shoves him in the chest, hard, sending him stumbling backwards.

'You're making a mistake,' Noah says through gritted teeth. 'I'm the one you're picking up, idiot! I'm not like the rest of these people, I'm here for business! Khalid sent me!'

Still holding the phone, Ricky turns to his partner who is standing by the lorry a dozen yards away. 'Hey, Johnno! He says he's here on business. Says *Khalid* sent him!'

'Oh, Khalid?' Johnno replies.

'Yes!' Noah says, relieved.

Johnno in the flat cap regards him for a moment, and then does a fake, pantomime tremble. 'The only business you'll be doing is picking fruit for the next year like the rest of your mates.'

'What?' Noah looks once more at the vans blocking the road – at the fearful travellers huddled together, and the lorry's driver sitting further along the grass verge – and cold realisation slips over him like a flash flood.

This isn't their destination. This is a shakedown. These men are pirates, and the passengers ... they're the loot.

'What is this?' Noah asks, panic rising. 'Is this part of The Game?'

Ricky laughs in his face. '"*Is zis part of zee game?*" Jesus, lad, get back with the others if you know what's good for you.'

Noah stays still, holding out his hand. 'I need that phone. Give it to me.'

'Oi, Ricky!' Johnno again, from far away. 'We've got to get off this road sharpish. Introduce that dickhead to Blighty, why don't you?'

Ricky grins, and the next thing Noah sees is a flash of fat fist, and then he's lying on his back staring up at a grey sky full of spinning white dots with the left side of his jaw ringing.

He tries to roll over onto his front, to get some purchase on the wet grass, and a filthy boot connects with his forehead, detonating his world in blinding white light. Heat pours over his face, drowning his right eye; it's his own blood.

Through the red film he sees Sofia, laughing in the bathroom only last night; he sees her smiling on the terrace of the Shangri-La hotel; he sees her with the hood over her face. He isn't going to make it. There's still an entire country left to cross, and the clock is ticking. He isn't going to get there in time.

He manages to get onto his knees and, with one sleeve, frantically wipes his stinging eye free of blood. He looks up, dazed. The man called Ricky is still grinning when he drops the phone onto the ground; he's still grinning when he lifts his boot over it, ready to stomp it into pieces; and he's still grinning when he sees the revolver in Noah's hand, though the grin is more puzzled than amused.

Ricky has time to blink, one leg still raised, before Noah pulls the trigger.

It's not like in the action films Noah loved so much as a kid, those stolen videotapes they'd watched together on the only television in the slum. The gunshot is more of a pop than a deafening bang, and the man doesn't fly several feet through the air; at first, he doesn't even fall. He just lowers his foot slowly, missing the phone on the ground, and then stands there looking perplexed. The bullet has grazed the left side of his head, erasing a moderate chunk of his ear, and blood cascades over one shoulder of his waxed jacket. A fraction of a second later, his body seems to realise what has happened and he hits the floor like a sandbag.

Voices bellow, and the lorry's passengers begin to flee in all directions. Noah turns his aim on the advancing men.

'Stay there or I shoot!' he cries, voice cracking.

They stop, reluctantly, some of them now wielding sizeable blades, and watch as Noah picks up his phone – briefly checking the timer on the miraculously undamaged glass screen – and pockets it.

The man in the flat cap says, 'You've just fucked up big time, son. You're in for a world of—'

Noah fires another shot off, making everybody crouch with their hands raised, as he walks backwards into the road, swinging the trembling muzzle from one Englishman to another. Sweat and blood are now pouring into both eyes, nearly blinding him, but when he reaches the Mercedes and chances a glance inside, he sees that the keys are in the ignition. He opens the door behind his back, blurry eyes on the traffickers.

'Anybody moves, I'll kill you all!'

They glare, shake their heads and threaten, but nobody moves until Noah has fallen into the supple leather driving seat and slammed the door shut. By the time he sees them sprinting up from behind, growing in the mirrors, he is already bouncing the car over the grass verge to bypass the van blocking the lanes ahead. When he rockets past the last refugee on the road, Noah is driving at ninety and the adrenaline explodes out of his mouth in a scream of triumph.

He drives without direction for a while, half-blind, on the wrong side of the road and interested only in putting some distance between the scene of the shooting and this stolen vehicle, and then he stops by a ditch to mop his beaten face with a rag from the glovebox and enter the postcode into the car's built-in satellite navigation system. He doesn't stop for long.

Once he is moving again, he tries to call Khalid, but Khalid never answers. Noah has the feeling that this is no accident. Khalid has no intention of putting his hand in his pocket. Noah is on his own.

He glances at the screen in the dashboard. There are over two hundred and seventy miles left to go, and the satnav says he can drive that in just over five hours without stopping. It's already a little past noon.

On the timer, the numbers fall.

04:52:01

With just a country left to go, Noah presses his foot down harder.

37

PLAYER FIVE

They are sitting around the table in the parlour, divided into two factions of two: Linda and Sarah on the fireplace side, the Americans on the other. There is one more chair in the room; it sits nearest to the closed door, separating the two pairs, and it remains empty.

Linda has one eye on the clock. Eight minutes to five. Time is almost up.

The American man says, 'Satisfied?'

Spread on the table before him, opened out like a pair of autopsied lungs, is a suitcase full of suitcase things: underwear, toiletries, nothing out of the ordinary.

Beside Linda, Sarah nods and he zips his case closed and shoves it under the table.

'Did you really travel four thousand miles to get here?' Sarah asks, sounding hopeless.

'Yep. Amazing what you can force somebody to do with just a message and a timer.'

'And a kidnapping,' the girl beside him adds timidly. 'Don't forget that part.'

'Strangers from two different states,' Linda says, eyeing them both, 'and we're supposed to believe that you just happened to bump into one another on the flight over here, is that right?'

'The cab, actually,' the man says, 'but yeah, I guess we shared the flights too.'

'I get how that must look,' the girl says, 'but the two of us are in the same position over on this side of the table. We have no choice but to believe that the two of you don't already know each other, you know. All we can do is trust that we're in this together. For now, at least.'

The words have barely finished coming out of her mouth when the noise begins.

At first, it's an engine, something loud that penetrates the walls of the inn. The sound of the engine is followed by the screech of brakes, and then there are a few seconds of quiet. The yelling begins a moment later, echoing through the building, and together the players shrink like war-weary citizens beneath a passing jet, waiting for an airstrike. Linda feels the spark of old electricity in her belly, the nerves and excitement and fear. From around the parlour their eyes meet in fretful glances, their bodies frozen. Combined with the senseless shouting, adding to the distant cacophony, there is the ceaseless hammering of the bell in reception.

ding-ding-ding-ding-ding-ding-ding—

Linda can't make out the words, but she's the first to move, her feet dragging her out of the parlour, bouncing on soft patterned carpets past the bar and dining room at a jog. Halfway along the corridor a swing door opens and Pat, the building's owner, comes out of an empty kitchen looking perplexed.

'It's OK!' Linda says, brandishing that familiar *stay back* palm. 'It's for us.'

She isn't exactly sure why she says this, it just falls out of her mouth, and yet she knows it's the truth and Pat turns back into the kitchen. Whatever awaits Linda and the other players around the next corner, it is strictly a burden for the four of them.

The man in the reception area looks younger than she'd been expecting. She finds him twirling beneath the taxidermy like a punch-drunk boxer ready to be rushed from all sides. He's bug-eyed, there are traces of dried blood on his face from a coagulated wound on his brow, and when he yells up at the dead animals, he does so in two languages.

'*Je suis là! Où es-tu? Je suis là!* Come on, I am here! You want to play? Let's play! Where is she? Where i—'

His dark gaze falls on Linda standing in the doorway, and she feels every muscle tighten. It's not that she's afraid of him, at least not in a way she'd ever like to admit to herself, but she is somewhat relieved when the other three players appear tentatively at her sides.

The Frenchman is holding a phone tightly in one fist. His empty hand twitches towards his coat pocket, and for a moment Linda almost fools herself into believing that he's reaching for a weapon. She goes to reach for her own kit belt in turn, ready for some kind of Clint Eastwood quickdraw, but his hand stops short and so does her own. It's obvious from his heavy, puzzled silence that these aren't the faces he was expecting to confront here: a very pretty blonde who looks almost like a teenager, a chubby suburban housewife, a well-groomed man in thick designer spectacles and herself, Linda, who is fast becoming an old British lady.

They stand like this, facing off, for what seems like a very long time until the American girl eventually breaks the silence.

'Well,' she says, 'I guess *this* is Player Four.'

*

They manage to coax him back to the parlour. He comes hesitantly, maintaining a wary distance, and then the five of them are finally together.

Linda returns to her seat nearest the fireplace in as collected a manner as she can. Beneath the surface, however, her nerves are shot. She can feel a sort of helpless violence inside her, a sheer desperation that wants to break these strangers apart in search of those answers they claim not to have.

Why isn't Alyssa at home, safe, where she belongs?

Why is this happening?

What have they each done to deserve this?

There's blame in this room, she's sure of that much, but she has to keep control. She's in a powder keg, a pitch-black mineshaft choked with gas, and an explosion of personalities now could quickly bring this day to an ugly, unthinkable end.

Follow the rules, she reminds herself. *Play the game. Get through this.*

She watches the newcomer as he shuts the door, always keeping his back turned against it. She feels no real sympathy for him. Not like she had for Sarah. She'd never given much credit to anything so fey as some unspoken maternal bond, but now she wonders if maybe there is such a thing after all. Indeed, it's the mothers of the room she feels sorry for.

This latest arrival, on the other hand, looks insolent and

shady, his face so much like those of the drug dealers they used to pin up on boards at the station, the corner boys who were too idiotic to know they were nothing more than dogs to their wealthier bosses. In fact, that's sort of what he reminds her of: those dogs on the charity adverts, the ones with bald patches and too many ribs on show, the kind that bare their teeth out of fear, confusion, stupidity. She can smell him too; there's a fusty, sweaty stink about him as if he spent last night somewhere cramped, diseased and foul. He smells like a fox ought to smell.

She once more finds herself bracing as he rummages through his coat pockets, but all he pulls out is a crumpled packet of tobacco with which he efficiently rolls a thin cigarette. He perches it between his lips and fumbles for a light. His hands, she notices, are shaking.

'You can't smoke that in here,' she tells him.

He eyes her for a moment – insolent, as she'd expected – then pockets the roll.

Sarah is standing to Linda's right, where she'd previously been sitting, her hands now gripping the back of her former chair. The Americans are both back on their side of the large table, a unit of their own, standing close – but not *too* closely – together behind their own seats.

'Who are you?' the American man asks. 'What's your name?'

'Fuck you,' Mr French replies, 'that's my name.'

'Hey, asshole,' the American girl bites. 'We're all in the same boat here, you know. We were all told to come here. We've all lost—' She stumbles, hesitates, losing stride. 'We've all had somebody taken from us.'

The Frenchman eyes them suspiciously, one by one. 'I don't

know you. I am told to come here, and here you all are, waiting together. Maybe you did this. Maybe you have her.'

A strangled noise escapes Sarah's throat, capturing his attention. She speaks quietly, unsteadily, punctuating her words with short hitches of breath. 'My daughter is – gone. Somebody – somebody *butchered* my dog. My sweet, harmless dog. They came into my home today – where my children were sleeping – and they stole my little girl. My husband doesn't even know! And now you turn up here – looking like *this* – barely able to speak English – and you have the nerve to stand here and accuse *us*?'

He doesn't respond, but Linda sees his eyes flicker away, momentarily shamed.

'She has a point,' the American girl says. 'I mean, look at this guy. You ever see *Taken*? These French Arabs, you know, that's all real. It's what they do.'

'Hold up,' her male counterpart says, 'we can't be sure. There's no way to prove anything.' He flashes a guilty look towards Sarah. 'And I'm sorry, but that goes for you too.'

Her eyes widen. 'Why would I make this up?'

'I'm not saying you are,' he quickly shows his empty, disarming palms. 'Maybe this guy has lost someone, and maybe not, but we can't go making racist assumptions based on some Liam fucking Neeson movie. If we're going to move forward, we need to show a little trust and work out how we got here.'

Sarah shakes her head. 'I can't trust him. I can't trust you either. A man did this. It's *always* a man, and I won't trust *any* of you until my girl is …' She doesn't finish. She looks as if she's going to weep again, only her sore, bloodshot eyes can't quite manage to form the tears.

'Again,' the American girl says slowly, and she points a thumb to the man beside her, 'I can't vouch for anyone, but if your girl was taken today, then it couldn't have been him. Like we already told you, we were on the same plane from New York. I know that much at least. I saw him board on the other side.'

'Thank you,' the man says.

'Do I really need to point out the obvious?' Linda interjects. 'We're talking about five abductions across the breadth of the globe. Whether you saw him in New York or not, this wasn't the work of one man. This was something organised. This is something bigger.'

The gravity of this – such an obvious statement – hits hard and the palpable tension in the room morphs back into subdued, bewildered fear.

The American man takes his seat, and he glances between the others. 'Sit down, why don't you? Y'all are making me nervous.'

'I don't feel like sitting,' Sarah mumbles, but once everybody else is seated she does it in automatic acquiescence. Even the French one takes a chair, which is probably a good idea because he looks pale and increasingly weak.

To Linda, the five of them, all gathered around the table in this cosy room, now look like so many exhausted witnesses; she wonders what stories they will tell.

'All right, look,' the American says, 'I'm going to start things off here. My name is Brett P—'

'Wait,' the girl beside him interrupts. 'Do you think it's a good idea, sharing our names?'

'Why not? I've already told it to you, and I know these

people just as well as I know you, don't I? Besides, whoever is doing this must know a lot more about me than just my name. I've got nothing to hide.' He takes off his glasses and slowly, methodically cleans the lenses with his coat sleeve. 'My name's Brett Palmer. I'm thirty-nine years old, born and raised in New York City. You can check me up on Facebook if you don't believe that, but there's not a lot to see. I'm just an ordinary dude. I'm not famous. I certainly ain't rich. I don't piss people off more than anybody else, so far as I know, and I've never had an affair or broken the law. I wouldn't go out of my way to intentionally hurt anybody. I guess what I'm trying to say is that …'

'You're innocent?' Linda suggests.

'No. No, maybe not that.' He replaces his glasses. 'All I'm saying is that there's nothing *exceptional* about me. I look around this room and I recognise nobody. I don't know this building. I've no connection to this *country*. In other words, there's no parallel I can draw out of this. And I'm guessing by the look on everybody's face that I'm not the only one. As far as first impressions go, it seems to me like the one thing we have in common is having nothing in common whatsoever. Of course, if I'm wrong about that then say so, please, because I've just flown across the world to get some answers, and right now I don't feel any closer to seeing the whole picture.'

Somewhat to Linda's surprise, Sarah is the next to speak. 'I'm Sarah, and nothing about this makes any sense to me. I don't recognise you people. I don't know why this is happening, but I don't deserve this. Nobody deserves this. It's twisted. It's evil.'

Around the room, silent agreement. The fire is shrinking

into glowing embers. Without pausing to consider whether or not they are strictly decorative, Linda reaches out and adds another couple of logs from the nearby stack. They smoulder for a moment.

'Linda,' she says, and that's all. The wood reaches temperature and bursts into orange flame.

'I'm Maggie. My son was taken almost two days ago. I haven't spoken to him since. I don't even know if he's still …' She takes a deep breath and wafts at her eyes with one hand as if she is wearing mascara; she isn't. 'He's eight years old, and he's half the world away right now, Jesus knows where, back in Minnesota. All I've had is one photograph, and then nothing but these stupid fucking messages.'

'Two days,' Sarah whispers, burying her face in her hands. 'Oh God.'

'Has *anybody* been able to respond?' Maggie asks. 'Has anybody had, I don't know, a *dialogue* with these people?'

Shaking heads.

'Just the messages,' Linda says. 'One-sided instructions. No demands for any sort of ransom.'

'But it has to be for money,' Sarah says. 'Why else would anybody do this?'

Maggie sighs. 'I don't think it's about money. I did at first, but … It can't be. The plane over here cost me almost a thousand dollars. They – whoever *they* are – could've had that money. They could've had a thousand dollars for a single night's work, and my son would be home by now. Instead, it's like they actually *wanted* me to waste the money on that flight. They wanted me here, in this building, with the rest of you people. Why *here*? Anybody figured that out? Who even owns this place?'

'The woman out front,' Linda says, 'she's the owner, but I don't think she has anything to do with this. She told me they'd received an anonymous reservation for this meeting, and I believe her. Honestly, I think the building was chosen for its name and nothing more. Something obvious for us all to find. A hidden place to meet.'

'Oh yeah,' Maggie says, 'the Gamekeeper's Inn. Because this is all just a game, isn't it? Some good old-fashioned fun. Am I the only one missing something here? Is this all some kind of joke?'

'You don't ...' Brett starts, stops to clear his throat, then starts again. 'Do games have any relevance to anybody? I mean, y'all don't play games, or, you know, *work* with games or anything like that?'

'Do I look like the gaming type?' Linda asks.

'No. No, I guess you don't.'

'I play a little online bingo,' Sarah says, the first bit of colour Linda has seen there mounting in her cheeks. 'Nothing serious, a few games here and there. One of the first things I thought when ... when this happened, was that my phone had been hacked through the website. That maybe I was being blackmailed for my winnings. Do any of you do any sort of online betting?'

More shaking of heads.

'*Gamekeeper's Inn,*' the Frenchman says, joining the conversation from the sidelines. 'This cannot be, uh, coincidence.' He looks at Linda. 'You say you believe her, this owner. Why should we believe *you*? I think we bring her in here.'

'And do what?' Brett asks. 'Put the screws on her? Pull some fingernails? OK, and after that we'll get some jump leads and a car battery, start torturing the truth out of each other too. That ought to solve this.'

'Sounds fair,' Maggie adds, glaring at the Frenchman, 'and I think we all know who we should start with, don't we? That cut on your head looks nasty. Some kind of struggle?'

The young man only scowls back, hands in his pockets beneath his side of the table.

'This,' Sarah says, 'is why we have only one option here. There's only one way to prove who we are. We go to the police. Together. If *none* of us are playing by the rules, then surely they can't—'

'No police,' the Frenchman says abruptly.

'Why not?' Sarah rounds on him. 'What do you have to hide?'

He doesn't answer, but Brett does. 'I … I don't know if you'll want to hear this, but …' All faces turn to him at once; with the sleeve he'd used to clean his lenses, he dabs at a line of new, visible sweat on his forehead. 'At first, I thought it was a hoax,' he says. 'Blackmail or something. Y'all probably thought the same thing. So I tried to call their bluff, you know? I tried going to the cops.'

Stony faces wait for him to continue. Linda feels her stomach clench; she doesn't want to hear this next part out loud.

'And?' Sarah whispers.

'They were watching me, I guess. Somehow, *somebody* was watching me. Or maybe it was because I ran out of time. I don't know, but before I got to the station, a call came through. A video call. They … They made me watch while they …' He scrunches his eyes tightly, wincing, and when he opens them again, they're full and wet. 'Ah *shit*. They broke his fucking leg. They smashed it with a bat, man.'

The only sound is a log crackling in the fire.

'Oh Jesus,' Maggie says, hands clasped over her mouth. 'Oh no.'

Sarah is already up out of her seat, pacing on wobbly legs, breathing hard.

'He had tape over his mouth,' Brett goes on, 'but he was screaming. I could see that. He was … screaming.'

'I can't,' Sarah says. 'I can't.'

'You saw them?' the Frenchman asks. 'They were in this video?'

'I saw somebody. There were two, one doing the filming and the other doing the …' He smacks his lips together. 'Anybody else thirsty? I could use a drink.'

'How did they look?' the Frenchman presses. 'You recognised them?'

Brett shakes his head. 'It was dark, and it all happened so fast. The one I saw. The one who … who did it. He was wearing a mask. You know what a catcher's mask is?'

Only Maggie nods, pale-faced. 'Baseball.'

'Right. Probably just something they had lying around. It was old, the sort of thing you'd pick up from a thrift store. Maybe it came with the bat, I don't fucking know.'

'I feel sick,' Sarah says. 'Who could do that? Who could do that to a little boy?'

'Was that the last you saw of him?' Maggie asks, reaching out and placing a small hand on Brett's arm. 'Was that the last time … the last time you saw your son?'

Brett pauses for a moment, eyes flicking between Sarah on one side and Maggie on the other; it lasts only for a second or two, this pause, but Linda notices it.

'Yeah,' he says. 'That's the last time I saw him.'

And in the dead air that follows, five o'clock arrives, and every phone in the parlour receives a message.

YOU MADE IT. CONGRATULATIONS.
YOUR WELL-EARNED REWARD IS A HINT.
THE GAME IS A LESSON IN RESPONSIBILITY.
IT'S A LESSON YOU'LL NEVER FORGET.
EACH OF YOU HAS FAILED IN YOUR BASIC DUTY
TO PROTECT ANOTHER.
TONIGHT IS YOUR CHANCE TO MAKE AMENDS.
RELAX. REGAIN YOUR STRENGTH.
THERE IS STILL SOME WAY LEFT TO GO.
ONE PLAYER HAS YET TO JOIN OUR GAME.
YOU MUST WORK AS A TEAM TO FIND PLAYER 6.
INSTRUCTIONS WILL FOLLOW.
PLAYER 6 HAS THE ANSWER YOU SEEK,
BUT IT WILL NOT BE GIVEN UP EASILY.
FIND PLAYER 6, PLAY THE GAME,
AND BY DAWN WE WILL HAVE OUR WINNER.

LEVEL THREE

LEVEL THREE

38

PREGAME

There were sixteen of them in the back of the stretch Hummer.

Streamers, influencers, cosplayers, gamers.

Creators from around the world.

The window dividing them from the conventional seats upfront was open, and a bald photographer was leaning through it, alternating between filming and photographing the raucous passengers. On one side of the photographer sat the driver. On the other was their host for the afternoon, a friendly local named Lola. It was Lola who temporarily muted the pounding music – to catcalls of playful protest – and spoke into a microphone that broadcast through the whole vehicle.

'Ladies! It is my pleasure to welcome you to beautiful Monaco.'

They all shrieked as they crossed the border.

'*Monaco, bitches!*'

'*New York represent!*'

'*I've got to post, oh my God, I've got to post!*'

The seating ran down one side of the limo beneath pink neon

lighting opposite an open bar filled with bottles of Prosecco on crushed ice, which the girls were rapidly working through. Glitch was sitting at the very back, sipping fizz and staring out through the one-way strip window at the immaculate blue of the Mediterranean. They'd been on the road for a little over half an hour, and the alcohol was already going to her head, making her thoughts slippery. She wasn't a drinker, and this was all just too surreal. Not so long ago, she'd been trudging through the mundanity of her ordinary life, wondering where she was going to go after college. Then the first invitation had come into her inbox. It had looked so dubious she'd almost deleted it.

DEAR PLAYER.
YOU ARE INVITED TO BE PART OF A PILOT FOR WHAT WILL BECOME THE MOST PRESTIGIOUS INTERNATIONAL EVENT IN THE CALENDAR.

THE GAME
THERE CAN ONLY BE ONE WINNER.
MONACO. AUGUST 9th
COME AND PLAY.

FURTHER INSTRUCTIONS TO FOLLOW

And now she was in a limousine, all expenses paid, with some of her favourite creators.

Somebody should've pinched her.

The girls – most of whom were already acquainted from various events – were all shout-talking over the music.

'They going to have mods at this thing? I didn't organise my own. How could I when I didn't know what to expect?'

'San Diego's getting too mainstream …'

'Look, I shared one post saying Master Chief would own Doomguy and I'm sick of hearing about it. Doom Slayer, though …'

'Hey, fuck him. You do that and you deserve to get cancelled.'

Amy Choe was beside Glitch, talking to a fellow American with heavy winged eyeliner – almost everybody onboard had heavy winged eyeliner – on her other side. After a few more minutes, Amy introduced her.

'Glitch, this is Lisa Mayfield from Tallahassee, Florida.' She pronounced it *Floorduh*, and Glitch adored the sound. 'You probs know her from the *Fortnite* boom.'

'Hello, Lisa.' Glitch reached for her hand. 'You're *Nurse Joy Division*, aren't you? I followed you, but …'

'I got shut down.' Lisa rolled her eyes. Her hair was the colour of a lime-flavoured ice pop, but it had, Glitch could recall, once been pink. She was wearing a leather choker around her neck. 'Turns out the name had ties to concentration camps. Obviously, I didn't know about that, I just liked the band. Now I'm just Lisa Mayfield.'

'You use your real name?' Glitch asked, surprised. 'Isn't that a bit of a nightmare?'

Lisa laughed. 'Why? Because of stalkers? Honey, I got me a lot of *big guns* at home.'

'Besides,' Amy joined, 'it's not exactly hard for them to find you, not if they really want to. I've been doxed three times now, just for having the audacity to game in a man's world. 'Course, I use a PO Box for the mail. Some of the garbage I get sent …'

Glitch gasped. 'I *love* your unboxing videos! Opening your hauls. You're so *funny!*'

'Sugar, what you see on camera, that ain't even *half* of what I get. You should see my garage, it's full to the roof. Bags. Shoes. Lego. Toys. Some guy in Russia gifted me a pair of leather stockings and a nine-thousand-dollar *Twilight Zone* pinball machine, and all he wanted in return was a photograph of me sitting on one dressed in the other. Mostly though, it's just dick pics. Hundreds and hundreds *and hundreds* of dick pics. And the occasional butt plug. I'm just waiting for a severed head.'

'Ah, dick pics.' Glitch shuddered dramatically. 'What do they think they're achieving?'

'No shit. Like we're all going to be so mesmerised, like *theirs* is the junk we've spent our lives searching for. They're proud of what they've got, I'll give 'em that. God knows why but they are. 'Course, Lisa here knows *all* about dick pics …' Amy covered her mouth with one hand. 'Miss Valentine, you are looking at a genuine, bona fide *e-slut.*'

'Oh shush,' Lisa said, applying lip gloss. 'I prefer *variety streamer.* And if some loser wants to buy me a whole new wardrobe for a video of a rubber tentacle up my ass, then more fool him.'

Glitch choked on her drink, blood rushing into her cheeks, while Amy said, 'I draw the line at nipples and holes. See?' To demonstrate, she lifted one forearm across her chest and rested her hand holding her glass between her legs. 'It's all about strategic placement. Once you post cooch, the mystery's over and you're a subreddit within the hour. Why bother with that shit anyway when my ASMR bitches will pay me two thousand bucks a month just to eat fucking Doritos by a microphone.'

'Because it's fun,' Lisa said, 'and it's easy. Besides, just because they can have a peek when I allow it, that doesn't mean they have a right to my body, or to harass me.'

'Right,' Glitch nodded. 'Only, do *they* know that?'

'They better. *Big guns*, remember?' Lisa grinned and winked. 'Hey, I bet my *ahegao* blows you bitches out the pond. Check it out, they love this shit.'

She threw back her head, crossed her eyes and stuck out her tongue, panting heavily as if in the throes of some insane cartoon orgasm. Amy snorted and did the same, turning her eyes up and mewling.

Giggling hard at their faces, Glitch dipped her fingertips into her drink, sprinkled the prosecco over her own forehead like sweat, then protruded her tongue and stared at her nose until all the brightly coloured hair in view doubled. They were still pulling these faces when the music lowered again, emphasising their exaggerated squeals of ecstasy from the back of the limo, and the three of them burst into howls of laughter.

'All right, Valentine,' Lisa cried, wiping her eyes. 'You got me. That was tight.'

Glitch beamed. She was in her element. A little woozy, but euphoric.

'OK, ladies …' This was Lola, their host with the microphone; Glitch could see that the photographer was still hanging through the hatch, only now he'd lost his camera and was instead handing a stack of white papers to the nearest girl. 'Please take one copy of the printed agreement and a pen and pass the papers along.'

Sitting at the very rear of the row, Glitch got the final clutch of papers in the bunch, and she had to hold her glass between her thighs while she examined the document. There were more than a dozen papers stapled together, and each page was absolutely smothered, front and back, in tiny, cramped text. She tried reading the first sheet, but her eyes were becoming sort of shimmery at the edges. It was warm, even with the air-con blowing, and the prosecco must have been stronger out here on the Med.

She asked Amy what the contract was about.

Amy shrugged, turning the entire stack over on her thigh and looking for the place to sign. 'Dictates what you can or can't post, stuff like that.'

'Really?' Glitch studied the paragraphs doubtfully, then began to read it to Amy in a hushed voice. '"The entrant, who has self-verified that she is above the age of consent and shall hereinafter be referred to as the 'Player', which definition shall mean and comprise the entrant herself, as well as any authorised representative that may be appointed on behalf of the Player's interests from the commencement of this agreement until perpetuity …" Doesn't that sound a little overcomplicated to you?'

Amy glanced up at her, an eyebrow raised. 'Do you actually sit and read those terms and conditions before you click Accept on your iPhone too?'

'No! No, of course not.'

'Exactly. You want to know what I think of overcomplicated?'

She signed her name on the back with a flourish, without ever reading a word.

Not wanting to look like a bore, Glitch did the same.

39

PLAYER ONE

Maggie can feel her millionth headache of this short week coming on strong.

'Another player,' she says, hearing the exhaustion and the whine in her own voice. 'I just had to cross the world to get here. What makes Player Six so special that we have to go to them?'

'I'm not going anywhere,' Sarah says, slipping her own burner phone back into her pocket. 'I was told to come here, and I came here. I'm done. I'm putting my foot down. We're going to the police, all of us, and I am getting my girl back.'

'Didn't you hear what I just told you?' Brett asks. 'What they're prepared to do? They broke his leg like it was nothing.'

'But this is what they want!' Sarah's voice rises sharply. 'It's what they *need*. Whatever they're trying to do, whatever point they want to prove to us, they can't do it unless we're afraid and divided. We report this together, and whatever sick game they're trying to play comes to an end. Don't you see that? Every minute we waste jumping through hoops, every minute we *play along*, is another minute that the police could be out there searching!'

Maggie says, 'I'm sorry, but that's off the table,' but with her hand she waves for Sarah's attention and, when she has it, puts her finger to her own lips, then points at the phones that are now out, in front of their respective owners, across the table. 'They listen,' she mouths, ending her finger up at her ear.

'I don't give a shit!' Sarah replies.

Maggie feels a flush of anger and frustration. 'Well you should, damn it, because this is my child's life on the line!'

Sarah turns desperately to the older woman beside her. 'You must *know* how this will end, Linda, if we try to … to solve this ourselves. You know what we need to do. How many abductions have you seen over the years? How many have you worked on? Aren't the first few hours the most crucial in these investigations? The hours we're wasting!'

Linda's eyes return a glance to Sarah, something Maggie would swear is almost a warning. There's a heavy pause.

It takes Maggie a moment to catch up – by the puzzled expressions on the faces of the two men, she guesses she's not the only one – and when she finally feels the penny drop, she actually laughs out loud. She laughs so hard she loses a couple of tears and bangs her hand upon the table.

'You are kidding, right?'

Across the table, Linda's face is anything but kidding.

'Oh, this is *perfect*!' Maggie says breathlessly, still giggling. 'Yesterday morning I had to run out of my apartment in my goddamn *underwear* to avoid the cops! Now I'm forced to fly across the world, only to wind up sharing a table with one!'

The French guy physically recoils, pushing his seat out a couple of inches. 'You're a fucking cop?'

'I am not a cop,' Linda says quickly, hands raised and bracing herself in his direction. 'I *was*, a long time ago, but I'm nothing now. I work at an airport, for God's sake.'

'They broke his leg,' Brett is saying, mortified. 'They broke his damn leg because of me, because I was going to talk, and you're—'

'Airport security, that's all I am! A woman who works at the airport, who is trying to get her daughter back. I'm in the same position as every single one of you. My hands are just as tied as yours.'

'This is bullshit,' the Frenchman says.

'Why?' Linda snaps, body still turned in his direction. 'Why are you so afraid of the police? Career criminal, by any chance?'

He stares right back, the two locked at the eyes, and when he reaches into his coat pocket, everybody – including Maggie and especially Linda – flinches. He fishes something out and holds it up for them all to see, almost like a police badge.

It's a lanyard designed to look like a backstage pass hanging from a guitar strap. With his free hand, he simultaneously shrugs his coat down from one shoulder, revealing the same logo embroidered in orange thread on the shirt sleeve there. The nametag hanging from the lanyard says HARD ROCK CAFÉ PARIS: NOAH.

'Not such a great detective, Madame,' he says coldly. 'I am a waiter. I was working last night when this started.'

Linda looks vaguely unimpressed.

Staring at the nametag – and in spite of her own, much more distant, journey – Maggie feels a subdued jolt of amazement. 'You were in Paris last night?'

He pockets the lanyard and fixes his coat, breaking his eyes away from Linda. 'Yes, I was in Paris.'

She gestures to Brett beside her. 'We changed flights at Charles de Gaulle. I didn't notice you on the plane.'

He actually nearly smiles, and the gesture makes him look even more exhausted and somehow so much sadder. 'There are more ways to England than your plane.'

There are, of course, and she feels a little stupid.

'I was in Salford,' Sarah joins in quietly. 'That's Greater Manchester, only an hour away from here.'

Brett is looking at Linda. 'What about you? Where'd you come here from?'

'Luton. It's down south.'

'Luton,' he says, and then he points at each of them, including himself, as he goes clockwise around the table. 'Luton. Paris. Minneapolis. New York. Manchester. Five abductions in three countries over two days. That's a logistical nightmare. How could somebody execute something like that? For all we know, we could be in the middle of some serious, next-level conspiracy shit here. We've got no idea how high this thing goes.'

'*How high this thing goes?*' Noah repeats in an awful, hammy impersonation of an American accent. 'Dang, I bet this goes all the way to the top, all the way to the White House!'

Brett stares back, looking more embarrassed than angry. 'Yo, if you've got any better ideas then you just let us know, all right?'

These last two words he pronounces '*aight*', and it's only now that Maggie realises the entire cadence of his voice has changed, either since they first entered this building together or, more likely, since *Monsieur Noah* arrived. True, Brett hadn't spoken a great deal during their shared ride here – he'd corroborated his story of a kidnapping, including almost identical text messages, with her while they'd been standing stunned at the side of the taxi, and they'd remained wary, almost silent, when sitting around the cab driver – but his voice definitely hadn't sounded so ... Brooklyn. So *street*. She's sure of that. Is it a character he's playing? An outright lie? She wonders if he's even aware he's doing it; people under stress have the weirdest defence mechanisms, and men around strange men are like animals butting heads.

'This isn't a conspiracy,' Noah says. 'Modern crime has no borders. Not with the internet. One person here sends money there. All they need is a phone.'

'He's right,' Linda says, sounding physically pained to agree. '*How* it was done isn't the most important question right now. It's *why*.'

Maggie groans, pressing at her temples with both index fingers. 'We're going in circles here. We've said it can't be for money.'

'No,' Linda agrees, 'I mean why we – specifically we five – were chosen.'

'It's random,' Sarah says. 'It has to be. Some sort of organised gang that sits there, scrolling through Facebook, and just ... chooses.'

'I don't believe that,' Linda says. 'I think there's something more. Something about the five of us that—'

'Six,' Brett says, tapping his phone with one knuckle, warily, as one might tap an injured rat to make sure it's dead. 'If this last message is legit, there's another player out there. We find them, we find our answer.'

The door to the room opens, doing so with a bang, and everybody pivots towards it.

A girl backs into the parlour, using her rear end to hold the door while she carries a large tray of drinks. 'Evening,' she says, still with her back towards the group. Her accent, like Sarah's, sounds so dense in Maggie's ears; they both sound like the northerners in *Game of Thrones*. The girl with the tray turns her big smile onto the group, only to have it falter at the edges when she finds five fatigued faces staring back at her. It's funny. Kind of.

Seeing the cold glasses, Maggie realises how parched she actually is. She hasn't paused for a drink since breakfast, which was actually served at around lunchtime, on the plane. Compared to her though, Noah looks as if he's actually salivating, and Maggie wonders – from the shaky look of him – if he has stopped for anything other than cigarettes since leaving France.

'Who ordered?' Brett asks, glancing at his fellow players.

'Oh, this is your pre-order,' the server replies, placing the tray onto the table. Under one of her arms is a clutch of A4 paper, which she also puts down, faceup; from Maggie's point of view, the top sheet looks like a printed-out email. 'OK ...' The girl leans closer to the paper, reading with a humoured expression as she selects a glass. 'Who's Number One?'

Maggie slowly raises her right hand. 'I guess that's me.'

'All right, Southern Comfort for you ...'

She places the glass in front of Maggie, and then does the same for the remaining four. Around the table, they are all staring down at their respective handout with expressions of horror.

'I'm sorry,' Brett says, looking back up from a short glass with a floating slice of orange, 'but have these been paid for?'

'All taken care of,' the girl says, 'we've never had cash come like that in the post before. It came last week with this …' From beneath the printed email she produces a plain brown sealed envelope. 'Who am I giving this to?'

Nobody claims it.

'You can just leave it there, thank you,' Linda says, sounding like the matriarch of their strange group, eyeing the envelope as if it might explode at any second. Her voice sounds very dry, and when she takes a sip of her own clear-coloured drink, her eyes widen and she makes a surprised, choking sound. 'Would it be possible to get some water for the table?'

'Of course,' the girl says, carrying the empty tray back to the door. Before leaving, she glances back. 'You lot really *do* take this seriously, don't you?'

Silence.

'I'll, um … I'll get you that water.'

In the time that it takes her to gather five glasses, fill the carafes and return, nobody else tries their drink. Nobody speaks. It's only when the girl has, once more, left them alone that Noah begins the cycle of filling his empty glass and necking the water. He does this five times without ever touching his milky cocktail.

'Old Fashioned,' Brett says miserably, swirling the fruit in his own glass. 'My favourite drink.'

'Gin and tonic,' Linda nods. 'It's what I'd order.'

'So they know what we like to drink,' Maggie says, shunning the alcohol – for the moment – and pouring herself a water. 'How long have they been watching us? Following us? Weeks? Months?'

'Maybe not,' Noah says after drying his lips on his sleeve.

'This is what they want us to think. They are trying to,' he pauses, searching for the word, 'intimidate us. They want to seem *omnipotent*.'

'Yeah,' Maggie says, 'well they're doing a good job so far.'

'You have Facebook?' Noah asks. 'Instagram? Who here hasn't posted a photograph from a party, or a night on the beach, in the last ten years? You've never posted a picture with the hashtag "*favourite drink*"? Everything they have done so far can be found on a phone from ten thousand kilometres away. They know what drink you like,' pointing across at Linda, 'and what pornography *you* watch at home,' pointing at Brett.

Brett's face moves through offended, defensive and then guilty, and he takes a massive swig of his cocktail.

'They don't know everything …' Sarah says. She is staring down at her drink with a look of confused terror unparalleled by the others. It's only now Maggie notices that, even in these modern times, the huge glass of dark, frothy beer looks quite out of place in front of the grief-stricken woman. 'This is a pint of John Smith's,' she goes on. 'I can't stand the stuff. Never have been able to.'

'OK,' Maggie says, 'so that proves that they aren't such hot shit after all. They don't know everything about you, at least. That's good.'

'Is it?' Sarah is still gazing at the drink as if it's alive and dangerous. 'My husband, Neil. This is *his* favourite drink. What do you think that means?'

Silence.

Maggie drinks her Southern Comfort in one; it's sweet and sickly, strong, but she doesn't pause for breath. She has a suspicion about what *that* means, and she thinks that everybody else must have one too: either whoever did this made a mistake choosing Sarah's drink … or they have made a mistake that is far, far worse.

Their phones rattle and beep then, each jingle or vibration a little out of sync as the various data providers from across the world receive the latest message. They all snatch for their own burner. Maggie looks at her screen, bracing herself for yet more bad news, and realises that her phone must be struggling to download the words.

'Something's wrong,' she says. 'This can't be the full message. "Leave at." That's all it says.'

'Mine's only a fragment too,' Linda agrees, 'but it isn't that. Mine says "and wait there."'

Brett says, 'They're splitting up the directions on purpose. Making sure we're working together and stopping anyone from leaving. This way, we're relying on each other. Try reading them in order, starting with Player One.'

Maggie sighs. 'Leave at.'

'Six. Walk,' Brett continues.

'Until you reach six,' Sarah grumbles.

'Black carriageways.'

'And wait there.' Linda turns her eyes across the table. 'The envelope. Somebody open it.'

'You volunteering?' Brett replies.

Maggie pockets her phone. 'I'll do it. Pass it here.'

'Carefully!' Sarah says when Noah, who is closest, moves to slide the envelope clear across the table. He gets to his feet, rolling his eyes, and carries it to Maggie.

'Whatever's in there,' Brett says, 'I don't know if I want to see it.'

Maggie studies the front, where today's date and F.A.O. The Game, Private Meeting, have been printed by computer. With one fingertip she gingerly presses down on the envelope, feeling bubble-padding and something else inside.

'It's solid,' she says.

As she turns the envelope over in her hands, and slips her thumb under the seal, her mind summons images of severed fingers and toes, and she has to pause for a second to remind herself that, according to their waitress, this arrived here a week ago. It couldn't possibly contain any part of Jackson.

She tips the contents out onto the table.

It's a key. A car key. The old-fashioned sort, just a plastic hexagon with a metal arm.

'Great,' she says. 'We have a key. Now what?'

Noah answers. 'We wait until six, and then we find what the key goes to. We do it together. We beat this thing together. Agreed?'

Around the table, they sip their drinks.

But nobody commits to anything.

40

PLAYER TWO

If these are the famous English moors, then they really are every bit as cold, desolate and depressing as popular culture had led Brett to believe. He never knew such a vast space could feel so paradoxically isolating.

Whereas the air had been still when he'd landed in England, sleet has now begun to fall, and it swallows the group in an increasingly violent vortex that can't quite decide whether it wants to soak or freeze them to death. Brett's glad it was cold enough in New York for him to have left in a coat. Only Maggie, who must be so familiar with the dangers of winter in Minnesota, isn't wearing one. She's dressed in jeans and a hoody that, until this walk began, had looked brand new. Cheap though. Several times he thinks about giving her his coat, but he never does. He has a feeling that, before the night is over, he's going to need whatever strength he can hold onto.

In spite of the freezing temperature, Maggie is leading the way, following the built-in compass on her phone. The others have their phone flashlights pointed at the ground, while Linda is using an actual torch, the small yet powerful kind that police officers carry. Whether she'd come specifically prepared, or whether she always happens to have it on her person, nobody asked.

They don't talk; it's far too cold, the wind is wild, and the moor itself, which is full of stones, shrubbery and other ankle-breaking hazards, rises and falls, taking the last of their breaths away. Whenever they get high enough, Brett sees streams of headlights moving along invisible roads in the distance, but he mostly keeps his eyes turned down. Sometimes there are clusters of trees, and Maggie has walked into a couple of them.

Sarah is, of course, at the very back of the group. From the moment he saw her, Brett knew that she would be the weakest link. Noah is skinny and impudent, but he looks at least streetwise and prepared to fight; Maggie is certainly the youngest, but she seems to have a fierceness about her; Linda is clearly as tough as nails. Sarah though … There's something so *beaten* about her, and Brett hopes, for her sake, that this won't come down to survival of the fittest.

He thinks he can hear her now, panting and wheezing, but that's surely in his head. Through this wind, he'd be lucky to hear an oncoming truck.

They've been walking for more than half an hour already, battling through the blanket of darkness and the driving ice, and several times she has asked them to stop because of aches in her knees and her legs. Brett is starting to resent her for it. She should try talking to Craig about leg pain.

Craig. There's another lie that, with a simple incoming message, could be brought to light at any time. Brett never told any of these people that he's a father. He didn't say that he's fighting for a lost child. They made an assumption, and he chose not to correct it. The problem, of course, is that the longer he leaves it, the worse their wrath may be when the truth comes out. If the truth comes out.

Will these mothers really risk sacrificing their own children to save a forty-year-old homophobe who can't even hold down a job? Of course not. They would turn on Brett in a heartbeat just for deceiving them in the first place. None of that, however, makes Craig's life any less valuable. Brett doesn't know how it feels to be a parent, but he knows what it is to love. Why should Craig be at any more risk than the others? Shouldn't these women have kept a closer watch on their children?

Besides, Brett has a feeling that he isn't the only one playing his cards close to his chest. Maggie may look far too young to have an eight-year-old son, but Brett doesn't think she's lying. If she is, she's doing a good job. The French kid, on the other hand, doesn't look much like a dad. In fact, he hasn't said a thing about the person he's looking for. Shouldn't he be getting the third degree too?

A part of Brett – what, until today, he would've always thought of as the major part of him – knows that these thoughts are unfair, almost psychopathic, and surely the result of some peculiar coping mechanism his brain has come up with to help distance himself from the others. Still, he's somehow glad that he is the largest man in the group. He'd be a lot more worried if he wasn't. Not because he plans on doing anything. It's just that desperate people do desperate things, and who knows what these people will try.

The group have stepped over a couple of fences on their trek, both of which were the stretched wire sort, and there's another coming up, captured in light from the phones. This one is immediately after a line of trees; it runs directly across their path, and it's made of two parallel steel bars.

Maggie, who is still up front, nimbly climbs over it with Noah close behind. Brett follows, swinging his legs over the metal, and his feet find hard ground on the other side.

Ahead, Maggie continues to walk forwards, her eyes on her glowing compass.

'Wait a minute,' Linda says, reaching the barrier. 'Get back on this side …'

'Why?' Maggie asks, halting and turning around. She looks up from her phone. 'What's the m—'

The car comes out of nowhere. One moment Maggie is in the dark, and then she's bathed in headlights as it rips out of the sleet from Brett's right, screaming west, and passes a little more than a foot away from Maggie's back. It's a near miss, but the rush of air drags her like an autumn leaf, and she goes spinning and then sprawling on wet tarmac. Every impulse tells Brett to go and help her, but he finds he cannot move. He sees her there, groaning in the road, and his feet won't let him go to her. It's the strangest feeling.

She isn't down for more than a second or two before she gets back onto her feet and, though she seems mostly unhurt, she is close to distraught. 'Fuck! Somebody give me some light! I need light!'

Linda obliges, climbing the barrier and casting her beam onto the surface of the road, catching more swirling sleet than anything else. Maggie starts to hurriedly collect pieces of plastic from the ground. They all watch her do it. Nobody helps. She carries the pieces back to the barrier, cupping them in her hands like a dying bird. It's her phone.

In the glare of Linda's flashlight, Maggie's face looks long and almost skeletal. 'What do I do?' she asks. 'What the fuck do I do now?'

'You could've been hit,' Sarah says, only just joining them at the barrier. 'You could've died! My heart! I don't know how much more of this I can take.'

Linda trains her light ahead. 'Six carriageways,' she says. 'A motorway.'

'The M62,' Sarah agrees. 'What do they want now? For us to get out there and play chicken?'

Sarah, it turns out, is correct. They don't have to wait long, only a couple of minutes of shivering in a huddle, before the instructions arrive. Noah and Maggie are working together, trying to piece the broken phone back together; because of this, when the messages come through, there are only four alert tones.

'If it's fragmented again,' Linda says, 'then we're going to be missing the first line.'

'It's not,' Sarah mutters.

Maggie looks impatiently between them. 'Isn't someone going to read it to me?'

Brett does. '"A lay-by roughly one mile west …"' he pauses. 'Lay-by?'

'A rest area. Go on.'

'"A lay-by roughly one mile west is your goal. It takes the average runner nine minutes to run a mile. You have a generous ten. This part of the game is called …"' He glances up at Sarah, whose face looks very white in the glow of her phone, and finishes, '"Chicken"'.

The wind howls. Maggie is already pocketing the pieces of her phone. Noah stretches his legs.

'Wait,' Sarah says. 'Everyone just hang fire for a second …'

On the screens of the phones, a new timer appears. Ten minutes begin to race downward.

'We all refuse,' Sarah goes on. 'We just say no. We just—'

But the French kid is already off, slipping into the dark like a shadow, and Brett finds himself following at a sprint.

He leaves Sarah at the barrier, begging for them to wait, but all he's thinking about is Craig.

All he ever thinks about is Craig.

41

CRAIG

Consciousness comes back to him, and with it comes the agony. This is how he knows he is awake, although he can't see anything in the blackness.

Overwhelmed by sheer pain, dazed from passing out, his body is telling him to throw up. He can't allow this to happen. If he does, with the tape still on his mouth, he knows he'll choke to death.

Stay awake. Stay calm. Breathe slowly. Focus.

Easy enough to think that way, but there are white clouds behind his eyes, and his right leg feels as if it's about to burst. The ankle is shattered. The foot too, he suspects, although it's hard to differentiate specific areas of discomfort in the overall colossal throbbing. Craig has broken bones before, and he remembers this shade of deep, nauseating ache from his childhood.

His father taught him all about it when he was six years old, followed by a refresher course when he was nine. His father taught him a lot of things, and few of them were good.

Craig's skin feels like a jacket of ice and his entire body is trembling. No, not trembling. *Quaking*. This is the shock. The break is bad then. Really bad.

How long has he been unconscious? Impossible to tell. Time is non-existent here. The room is lit only when the men are present.

They're gone now. Two of them, one black guy, one white, both junkies. They're scrawny and erratic, and for the first few hours – the first night? – they took it in turns to go and smoke meth somewhere nearby. Craig could smell it each time they returned. They were probably smoking it in their own apartment, because they couldn't be smoking it directly outside the building. Craig knows this because there is a cop station right across the street. Craig knows there's a station across the street because he is, unbearably, in the basement of his own apartment building.

What's even more depressing? He brought himself down here. He ran right into this mess.

Sunday had been tough. For the first time in years, Craig had cried like a bitch. It was partly the hangover, but mostly it wasn't. Brett was his brother, his only family, and Craig envied him like any blood sibling. Brett had a beautiful house and a goddess of a gal, and the whole thing was a dirty fucking sham. Their friendship, the only real thing Craig had ever had to hold onto, was built on a lie. Perverted. Grotesque. Reprehensible.

The emotion he couldn't name, he has since realised, was grief. He had never wanted things to change and, in a single night, everything had.

Sunday afternoon had turned into evening, and the thought of bumping into Brett at work in a matter of hours was making

Craig feel physically ill. He left the apartment only once, to pick up a pie from Tepango's Pizza and Mexican a few doors down, and then he kicked off his pants and ate in his underwear and his Rangers jersey, sipping beer and staring blankly through a *Fast and the Furious* movie. He thought about rubbing one out – anything to take him away from his own self-pity, to restore some sense of masculinity – but he only stared at his old magazines, feeling nothing.

It was coming up to eleven o'clock when he lay back on the couch, wrapped in the jersey of a team he might never love again, and slipped into a dreamless sleep.

It was around an hour later, as Craig turned forty years old, that the stranger booted his way through the front door.

Craig barely had time to sit upright before the guy was standing over him, dressed in a mask of tangled wires and swinging something heavy – a hammer – down at his face. Disorientated by sleep, Craig shifted too slowly; the hammer clipped him near the temple, sending fireworks across his eyes and blood spattering down his face. He deflected a second blow with his forearm and managed to get onto his feet. His size, he thought at the time, put the fear of God into the bastard because, the next thing Craig knew, the skinny intruder was running out of the apartment.

'Mother*fucker*!' Craig roared, clutching the wound on his head, and then he did something he would regret for the rest of his life. He surrendered to his temper, and in bare feet and boxer shorts he gave chase out into the hall and down through the tight, emergency stairwell.

When the attacker continued going downwards, following the turn of the stairs *below* street level, clattering past the basement with the central boiler, Craig had grinned in savage triumph; the dumb bastard was heading straight into the old sub-basement, a dead-end maze of padlocked rooms that are prone to flooding, each filled with maintenance equipment, rat traps and the junk left behind by former tenants. Craig never paused to wonder why the door was open, the lock having been removed with a bolt cutter.

He followed, into the darkness, and he has been down here ever since.

The ones who did this – the two who tackled and tied him up here – live in this building. They're his neighbours. He's seen them shambling around the entrance area, and even stepped over them in the downstairs hall once or twice when they've been too trashed to make it into their own apartment. The guy who kicked in his door, the white one with the tattoos and the peroxide, Slim Shady haircut, had been wearing that ratty old catcher's mask at the time, but they mostly wear scarves over their faces while they're in here, shining their torches into his eyes to dazzle him, and Craig has caught enough of their outlines and gaits to recognise them both. Two months ago, the hot Puerto Rican mom from downstairs had tried to get a petition going to have them evicted once and for all. Craig never bothered to sign it.

They got bored of babysitting pretty quickly, and soon stopped taking their absences in turns and instead began leaving Craig alone in this rotten blackness. Each time they leave, they check the tape over his mouth, take their torches with them and lock the door behind them. They must've removed the existing padlock and replaced it with one of their own. Nobody comes down here anyway.

How Brett comes into this, Craig isn't sure. Maybe these junkies have seen Brett visiting, liked the look of his designer clothes and decided to extort him. Whatever the reason, only one thing matters right now. If Craig doesn't get out of this chair, he will die down here in his own filth, mere yards from the nearest NYPD precinct.

He has emptied his bowels twice already – filled his shorts, as they used to say – and pissed more times than he can count. His right leg, he can feel, has swollen to outrageous proportions and is being choked in the zip ties; a couple on each ankle and three on each wrist hold him to the old barber's chair. Invasive thoughts of amputation come to mind. A best-case scenario, perhaps, if he ever gets out of here.

He had at first, quite naïvely, placed some hope for escape in a simple trick, something he'd seen on a YouTube video. Craig likes the sorts of videos posted by doomsday preppers, gun-nut hillbillies and former Navy SEALs. He has taught himself, without practice, to start a fire using broken sticks, and to filter undrinkable river water. One video, featuring some limey bastard from the British special forces, demonstrated how to escape a kidnapping situation. The first thing to do, the guy had said, is to clench your fists as you're being bound. Later, when you unclench, your wrists should shrink in size, loosening the restraints.

Craig had clenched – he'd still been trying to swing both fists as he was forced into the chair – and all he has to show for it now is maybe an eighth of an inch of useless slack. Another method involved using a shoelace as a kind of saw. Great. Craig's feet are bound and bare, and there's duct tape around his middle.

It's difficult to tell without light, but he feels like he's slipping again, falling into unconsciousness. If he does, he might not wake up again. He shakes his head, but this only worsens the urge to vomit. He has to get this tape off his mouth. For the hundredth time, he leans as far forwards as his body will allow, desperately pushing his face towards each hand in turn. Just as in the hours past, no matter how hard he tries, his head goes as far as maybe two inches above his fingertips.

He groans, hanging forwards, and when he sways slightly, he feels something stroke across the back of his hand. He sways again and the sensation returns, stroking along his knuckles. The realisation hits him harder than any junkie's hammer. He's still wearing his Rangers jersey. Like most hockey jerseys, it has drawstrings at the neck. A shoelace, and one that reaches his open fingers. All he needs now is a limb to pull it. His mind turns, reluctantly, to his broken bones. How shattered are they?

He lifts his right thigh, pulling the ankle up against its restraints, and the darkness turns white around him. The pain is devastating, and yet, for just a moment, he feels a deep, irregular shifting.

As he sees it, he has a simple choice: slip the zip ties or die.

He clenches his teeth, sweat already pissing into his eyes, and heaves his leg upwards as hard as he can. He screams into the tape. Screams until he is on the brink of fainting, but he doesn't stop. There is a crunching, wrenching, grinding in his ankle, and then his right knee rockets upwards, suddenly released.

His leg is free.

His motherfucking leg is free.

He brings his right foot up to meet his left hand. With his fingertips he can feel the toes, rubbery and bloated, but with his toes he feels nothing in return. The nerves are seriously damaged, and that might not be such a bad thing, considering what he has to do next. He dumps the broken ankle up on his left thigh and leans forward again, crunching his abdominal muscles and bringing his head down towards the foot. Now his chin, left hand and right foot are all more or less aligned above and below the left arm of the chair. Once again, he catches the dangling lace in his fingertips, only now he threads it down with his index and middle fingers, working it around his thumb, towards his wrist. It takes a long time, twisting and writhing his hand around in the almost negligible muscle-space he'd created for himself, and he keeps losing his grip.

On perhaps the fiftieth attempt, he manages to thread the end of the lace through the minuscule gap between the skin of his wrist and the zip ties. Stuck where he is, with his head bent way forwards and the lace now threaded down through the restraints, he lifts his mangled foot up off his thigh and begins to sway it around in the area beneath the hand. It doesn't take long for him to feel the slightest movement at his collar and, using the foot, he brings the end of the lace back to his fingertips. He pants through his nose, jaw locked against the tearing in his overworked muscles, leg screaming. Using his fingers, he ties the end of the lace around his big toe, so that the string now goes from his collar on one end, through the zip ties and onto his foot. When he lowers his foot, his collar and chest is pulled down, and when he straightens his back, the leg is – agonisingly – lifted.

He shrieks into the tape, hot tears of triumph and desperation burning tracks across his face, and then he begins to move, bobbing up and down as if fellating himself, heaving his leg upwards and downwards with every motion, faster and faster and just praying that the lace won't snap, that the jersey won't rip in two. In theory, this movement creates friction, turning the lace into a saw. He only half believes this, and in the split-second after his leg starts to fall, he is sure that the lace has broken; even when his neck is snapped suddenly forwards by the dropping weight, he doesn't allow himself to believe that they're still connected.

But they are. The lace has burned through the bondages. His left wrist is free, and he catches his falling leg before it breaks his neck or hangs him. His hand is out. He peels the duct tape from his mouth and laughs deliriously. His next impulse is to scream for help, but he bites his tongue. If *they* hear him first, then he is only advertising his improved situation. His right wrist is easier to free, holding the lace between his left hand and his teeth, and his remaining ankle takes only seconds with both hands at work.

He lowers himself out of the chair and drags himself in the rough direction of the door. Along the way his elbow lands painfully on something wooden, cylindrical, rolling, and he takes it along with him as he feels for the exit.

He waits by the door on his knees. He doesn't wait long.

Footsteps and the click of a padlock.

Craig never pauses to see which of his kidnappers has drawn the short straw. He never asks why. The door opens, torchlight falls onto the empty chair, and Craig swings the Louisville Slugger with everything he has left, which turns out to be enough. When the guy hits the floor, Craig swings again and again, bringing the bat down in devastating arcs.

Then he climbs, dragging his shattered limb up over riser after riser, moving with the grace of an eel on land.

As he approaches the ground floor – five minutes later? Ten? – he can hear distant sirens and hissing ducts, the sounds of the city at night.

Craig Wilson has done it. He is free.

It is a little after one o'clock on Tuesday morning, and Brett is somewhere over the Atlantic, on his way to England.

42

PLAYER THREE

'Please,' Sarah says to Linda. 'I can't physically do this.'

The others are already running, and Linda is over the barrier. 'You can,' she replies. 'You can do this. You have to.'

'Can't you just take my phone with you? Please? You could take it in your pocket, the GPS would think it's moving, and then I could just catch up. I wouldn't have to—'

'I'm sorry. I daren't. You can do it. It's only a mile.'

Then, after a final apologetic look, Linda is gone too, and Sarah is alone at the roadside.

'Only a mile,' she tells herself. 'Only a mile for Hannah. Only a mile.'

She pockets the phone, another infuriating ticking clock, and breathes. The barrier is only waist-high, but she has to cling onto the freezing steel to maintain her balance as she gets one leg over – carefully saddling it – and then the other.

'Only a mile,' she repeats. 'One mile.'

She tests the surface of the road. It's gritted, which is one small blessing because the sleet is coming down harder now, the temperature dropping fast, and she thanks the salt-crunch beneath her feet as she starts to move. There are slippery patches, but she thinks she can manage. Through the dark she can make out the other runners in the near distance. Already so far away.

When was the last time she ran? Properly ran. She doesn't remember, but she would've been many years younger and several stones lighter.

She repeats Linda's final words in her head like a mantra, a song, a broken record:

Only a mile, it's only a mile. Only a mile, it's only a mile. Only a mile, it's ...

It almost helps keep the images away, pushing out pictures of baseball bats and Hannah's tiny limbs ... but not quite.

Only a mile. It's only a mile.

Falling ice fills her eyes, and she blinks it away as she moves. Coins jangle in her coat pocket.

She hasn't gone far, fifteen yards or so, when the road around her brightens; she's already running out of breath, and her knees and hips have started to sing their miserable tune, so she doesn't notice the change in light until it becomes more pronounced, etching the shapeless chunks of falling white into higher definition. Then she hears the horn.

She stumbles left onto the hard shoulder as the car goes screaming past, its brake lights burning panic-red and its wheels spinning noisily on the wet road. Sharp grit and rank slush pepper the side of her body, making her gasp in pain and surprise. Looking ahead, she sees the other runners go scrambling out of the lanes they had blindly run into, tripping over themselves to regain the left-hand barrier as the car approaches. She's grateful this slows them down; she's terrified of being left here alone.

She prays that the car will stop and offer her a lift. She half hopes it's a police car – an act of God, not cheating – but it's already off in the distance, regaining speed, still blaring its horn.

Shit.

She holds both hands over her chest, squeezing her startled heart back down to normal rhythm, and then starts to move again. It's only moments before another car passes on her right, and then another, each tearing out of the increasing downpour from behind her, both sending harsh slaps of shrapnel across the right side of her face.

'I can't do this!' she shouts, slowing to a shuffle as she wipes stinging road salt from her eyes. 'I can't fucking do this!'

She turns for the safety barrier, hands on flaking steel, and lifts one leg over. She will simply run through the bushes and the trees. It's not ideal, but at least she won't end up beneath the wheels of a car going at ninety.

Saddling the barrier once more, still palming at her eyes, she lowers her foot on the opposite side … and finds nothing. No ground. Her weight slips, and she has to grip onto the barrier tightly to stop herself from plummeting. Blinking down, she sees only a void beneath her dangling foot. Somewhere down there, the surface of a reservoir is a blank sheet lost in swirling ice.

'Fuck!'

The motorway is suspended. The clock is ticking. Back on the hard shoulder, she runs.

Blinding lights from both directions now. Each moment of respite from the rear encourages those driving over on the oncoming side to switch to full beams. Sarah wants to cry. Every new metre tightens her muscles. Her lungs shrink. Engines race by, ever closer. She's suffocating. She curses her weight, her grotesque lack of fitness; she thinks of all the fats, the carbs, the laziness, and how she can't protect her own child. She hates herself. She thinks, not for the first time today, of Sam, her ex-fiancé. The lost babies. How he'd lost his children too. How *he* must have been feeling. How she'd taken Neil into Sam's bed and—

'Stop!' she screeches at herself. 'Just stop!'

Her mind says, *you deserve this*.

Still running – hobbling, really – she fumbles for the phone in her pocket. Checks the screen. Half of her time has disappeared, and she still sees no lay-by in the distance. She can see the others though, pounding ahead. They're making it look so easy. Another car. It occurs to her that, being at the back, she'll be the first to die. She's wheezing like a pig, tasting blood, falling further behind, knees threatening to buckle. She'll never make it. This is hell.

More white light comes burning up from behind, projecting her shadow down the lane ahead, her silhouette elongating as the engine gets closer. This time the horn is deep, the vehicle huge, and though it steers away in time, the eighteen wheels are taller than Sarah, and the next thing she knows she's swept off the ground, flying, being inhaled like plankton by a mechanical blue whale.

The sensation is brief; gravity brings her back to the road quickly enough, and she lands in the centre lane hard, crashing down on her kneecaps. Adrenaline doesn't do much to dull the impact. She screams the last air out of her lungs.

Her vision clears and she tries to stand. Can't.

Wheezing, reaching out a hand as if she might catch the distant runners by the coattails. 'Help me! Please!'

They don't hear her, of course, though she tells herself they're choosing not to. More lights from behind. She's in the middle of the road now, a lump in black slush, invisible. She has to move.

She crawls a couple of metres to the left, agony driving up through her lower half, and glances back along the first lane. Another lorry. The driver swerves, frantically flashing his headlights and pounding his horn, and this time she simply balls up like a trembling hedgehog waiting for the wheels.

Another near miss. Once it's passed, she chances a look up.

What happens next happens fast, in no more than three or four seconds, but Sarah sees it all occur in hideous slow motion.

The latest lorry has passed, taking the light with it, leaving her on all fours in the dark. Her vision is blurred, and the sleet is heavy, but she looks up in time to see the others now caught in its headlights; the driver is still flashing from high beam to low, casting the backs of the four figures in a frenzied strobe, and then the headlights clear the runners, leaving them in shadows alongside the wheels.

This is when one of the four makes a sudden, strange movement.

It's impossible to tell who it is, just a dark shape shifting in black, but he or she throws their weight clear across the lane, arms outstretched, and tries to *shove* the next runner in line beneath the passing wheels. They miss the runner by inches, and the victim never notices how close they come to dying.

Sarah watches this in disbelief, trapped here on the motorway.

At least one of them, she realises, is playing this for keeps.

43

PLAYER FOUR

Noah regrets every cigarette he has ever smoked, and his cheap black waiter shoes feel as if they're going to burst into pieces at any second.

He is beyond drained. Running not just on empty, but on a severe calorie deficit. His head is swimming, his chest burning.

He sees a sign for the tiny rest area, maybe thirty yards ahead, reflected in the headlights of another passing lorry. He's past the empty drop on his left-hand side now, clear of the plummet, and there's once again land bordering the motorway.

His mind goes to the stolen Mercedes he left in the car park of the pub; how fast those wheels could've cleared this mile; how pointless this all is.

The lay-by is in a cluster of trees. He can actually see it now, and this is enough to push him into a flat-out sprint. He slips into the driving lane to overtake the other runners. He keeps one hand on his coat pocket, holding it steady, worried that a particularly harsh jolt might cause the revolver to blast a hole right through his abdomen. When he finally gets to the lay-by and hurls himself out of the road, he's neck and neck with Maggie.

He skids to a halt, then drops to his haunches with his head between his knees, gulping oxygen, covered in freezing grime. Another meaningless task completed. He checks the timer. Ninety seconds remain. His mouth tastes like an old fuse.

Brett comes third, grasping a stitch in his side, followed by Linda who is somehow still wearing her coat zipped up to her neck.

Crouched, Noah looks down the length of the hard shoulder behind them. He doesn't see Sarah. Not at all. The muscles in his abdomen contract.

The others are panting around him, regaining their equilibrium, and Linda has collapsed onto her backside in a patch of grass; she's staring at her phone, hammering the screen.

'How do we – let them – know?' she gasps.

'GPS,' Maggie says, livelier than her elders. 'Got to be. They've been watching us this far.'

Yet another lorry is barrelling up the first lane, headlights flashing, and that's how Noah sees Sarah shambling along in the distance like a wounded animal. Sixty seconds left now.

'She won't make it,' he mutters.

Linda cranes her neck. 'What?'

'Shit,' Maggie says, following his gaze.

Noah stands fully upright for a better look. Now that he has seen her once, he can track her movement. Something's wrong. She's no longer coming straight towards them but listing sidewards, further and further into the road. She's moving like a blind woman trying to navigate a swamp.

'She's fucked,' Brett says quietly.

Sit down, Noah thinks to himself. *She's not your responsibility. Just sit down.*

Two years old, his mind responds. *Her daughter's two years old.*

More traffic in the distance now, picking out her silhouette in scattered pinholes of light. Still she careens across the lanes.

'*Merde*.' He takes a step forwards and finds himself snagged. He looks down. There's a hand on his coat, gripping his sleeve, holding him back. Brett.

Noah opens his mouth to ask what he's doing, but in Brett's face he sees something that chills him more than the grit on his skin or the sleet in his hair. Brett's expression is pained and apologetic, but his eyes are distant. Solemn. Dead.

'You sure about this?' Brett asks.

'What?'

Brett doesn't remove his hand. 'One winner. Only one.'

Noah's mouth is very dry. He glances off to the road, and then back into Brett's empty stare. All at once, in a bright wave of inner-senses, he sees Sofia lying on her belly, her naked rear catching lamplight; he smells her hair, and he hears her voice; he imagines their wedding day, lifting a veil and looking into her beautiful face, knowing what he'd done, what he'd allowed to happen, to get there. Perhaps the others could live with that.

Forty-five seconds. He snatches his arm out of Brett's grip, and then he begins to run.

This, he knows, is the stupidest thing he has ever done. He's now pelting headfirst towards the growing line of oncoming traffic, with a loaded handgun flying around in his pocket.

To his surprise, however, he isn't alone. Pounding footsteps match his own and, when he glances to his right, he sees the American girl sprinting alongside him.

They don't speak. They only run.

By the time they reach her, Sarah is hobbling directly up the centre lane. They tackle her beneath the arms, one apiece, and with no time to get her back to the hard shoulder before the nearest lorry arrives, they have no choice but to haul her straight down the middle of the motorway.

Traffic engulfs them. Noah isn't sure who's screaming. Maybe all three of them.

The centre lane is now the eye of a steel hurricane, and they run along it heaving dead weight between them in a cacophony of squealing brakes, bellowing horns and flashing lights. Vehicles moving faster than eighty swerve around them. Slipstreams from both the left and right fight for purchase and Noah is certain that, if there were any fewer than the three of them, he'd be dragged straight under rending, churning wheels.

It seems to go on forever, dragging her along the road like this, waiting for the impact that will shatter their spines.

But the whole thing lasts just forty-one seconds.

Forty-one seconds.

He knows this for a fact because, by the time they drop Sarah into the lay-by and he checks his phone, there are still three seconds remaining on his timer.

44

PLAYER FIVE

Linda is, quite frankly, astounded.

She would never have seen that coming, especially from the French one – *the drug dealer*, her brain insists – and for a moment, as she stands up off the wet ground, she feels as if all her prejudices are being laid out bare before her. She feels as if she's being interrogated by her own conscience.

Has she been wrong about him? How could she have just sat here, watching it happen? Was she honestly ready to let an innocent woman die, cause a fatal motorway pile-up, or see a two-year-old girl *killed*? What would Alyssa think?

The American one didn't go either, she reminds herself. *He tried to stop them from intervening. Isn't that worse?*

She decides that it is. Linda, after all, is practically an old lady compared to the rest of them. She ran her mile.

She watches Brett now. He's walking around the perimeter of the rest area looking shellshocked. Maggie is still desperately trying to get her phone working – 'Come on, you piece of shit!' – while Noah shines light into her hands. Sarah is sitting on the freezing ground, as drenched as the rest of them, massaging legs that look swollen through sodden jeans.

Linda doesn't like being here. Not one bit. Any number of those drivers should have called the police by now; if they haven't, then it's only a matter of time before a passing traffic officer notices them congregated here in the lay-by without a vehicle. She wants this to be over quickly.

'Yes!' A second glow has appeared from inside Maggie's hands, this one shining up into her face. 'Fricking A!'

Brett, who is peering through the hedgerow that marks the back of this small tarmac landing strip, croaks, 'Yo ... I – I think this is our ride.'

Linda turns to Sarah, the last one on the ground. 'Can you walk? We ought to clear the area.'

'Yeah. I just needed a minute ...' Sarah doesn't move though. 'We could've come around the reservoir, do you realise that? We walked up from the south, circling the water, just to run directly over it. We could've walked right here. We could've *driven* here, as a matter of fact. What's the point in all this?'

'No point,' Noah says, cupping his burning cigarette from the weather. 'Just to fuck us.'

'Fuck *with* us,' Maggie says.

Noah shrugs. 'You have the key?'

Maggie's eyes momentarily widen as she checks her jean pocket, then she blows air in relief. 'Still got it.'

Linda offers her hand down to Sarah. For a second, she doesn't take it.

'I thought ...' Sarah says quietly. 'I thought I saw something ...'

'What, Sarah? What did you see?'

Sarah considers it, gazing into nothing, and then she shakes her head very slowly. 'Doesn't matter.' She takes Linda's hand and heaves herself upright, but for a moment – just a moment – she fixes Linda with a look that is strangely penetrating and, Linda would swear it, almost suspicious. 'I guess we'll find out before the night's over.'

Linda doesn't like that look at all.

As the others make their way towards Brett, he groans. 'There's no way this thing's going to run.'

Linda clicks her torch into life and casts its beam over the vehicle that has been unceremoniously dumped in the overgrowth. It's a Vauxhall Corsa with a terminal case of rust, a poky little hatchback from the late nineties with three doors including the boot. Linda's light penetrates the windows and moves over mouldy seats with dull springs pushing up through the foam. Maggie goes to slide the key into the driver's door and Brett catches her arm.

'Wait! It could be, you know … boobytrapped.'

'*Boobytrapped?*'

'He might be right,' Sarah says. 'I wouldn't put anything past these people.'

Linda snatches the key from Maggie's hand and opens the door before they have a chance to stop her. Nothing goes bang. 'It's fine,' she says. 'Now there must be some instructions in here. A map. Help me look.'

The others shine the lights from their phones inside the car. Noah goes around to the passenger side and, once Linda has reached across to open the locked door for him, he leans in and searches the glovebox. 'Here.' He pulls out a screen and a tangle of wire.

'Satnav? Pass it over.'

It's an early model, and it burrs a little in Linda's hand as it comes to life. 'There are coordinates,' she mutters, studying the screen. 'Longitude and latitude.'

'How far?' Sarah asks.

'Far. Almost five hours.'

Sarah makes a small, despondent squeaking sound. 'Who's driving?'

Noah circles back to their side of the car, flicking his filter off into slush. 'Not you. Not with these legs.' He holds out his hand for the key, catching sleet on his palm. 'I can drive.'

Linda almost laughs. 'In these conditions? I don't think so.'

'She's got a point,' Brett says. 'Do you even have a licence?'

Noah scowls. 'OK then. Why don't you take the wheel, hero?'

Brett's mouth opens – an ashamed, hurt expression on his face – and then he peers into the car and shakes his head. 'I can't drive a stick.'

'Stick?'

'Standard transmission,' Maggie answers. 'Neither can I.'

'Right,' Linda says impatiently. 'Looks like I'm it then.'

There's a quick succession of vibrations, and everyone reaches for their phones. Three, however, remain blank. Only the ones belonging to Maggie and Noah have messages.

'I'm not getting anything,' Brett says, holding his burner higher for signal.

'Me neither!' Sarah frets. 'What is it? What do they say?'

Maggie and Noah exchange an awkward glance, and Maggie reads from her shattered screen. '"*Well done, Players One and Four, for being the joint winners of the previous round. You have both received a prize …*"' She looks up, eyes wide in the dark. 'That's it.'

'*Oui.* Mine too.'

'What prize?' Brett asks. 'What the hell?'

Maggie licks her lips. 'I have no idea.'

Sarah falls against the car, breathing hard again. 'If you win something for being first, do I lose something for being last?'

'Nah,' Brett says. 'This ain't fair! They left the endzone, which means I was first, and if anybody's getting out of this shit then it should be me!' He holds his phone close to his mouth, yelling into it like a tin cup on a string. 'You hear me? They *left* the area! That's a fucking forfeit!'

Sarah is staring at her own phone as if it's about to blow up in her hand. 'What do I lose? What do I *lose*? Oh God.'

Before anybody can answer, both Maggie and Noah's respective phones do something incredible, and silence falls. They begin to ring.

'It's a video call,' Maggie breathes. 'What do I do?'

'Answer it,' Linda says, stomach tightening.

Noah has already answered his; he's stumbling away from the group, into the black grass, and what follows is thirty seconds of dizzying chaos.

'Sofia? Sofia!'

Behind him: 'Jackson! Oh my God, Jackson!'

'*Noah?*' A woman's voice from Noah's phone, dazed, sounding through the loudspeaker as if she's speaking from inside a glass bottle.

From Linda's right, a boy's voice, small and scared enough that it could be mistaken for a girl's. '*Maggie, is that you?*'

Noah's words are choked English. 'Who has you, Sofia? Have they hurt you? Where are you? Do you recognise anything? What's happening?'

Linda's eyes bounce back and forth between them, the two youngest of their quintet, and she is overcome with a rising sickness; it's the stabbing, rending sickness of utter envy. This should be her, talking to Alyssa, and right now she'd hurt every one of these people for a single conversation with her daughter. This, she knows, is the point of this reward: give them hope, break them with carrot-on-a-stick kindness – good doggies get treats, after all – but she doesn't care. She'd do anything to have Alyssa's voice coming out of her blank, silent phone, and she can see the same agony on Brett and Sarah's faces.

'I'm coming, little man,' Maggie is saying firmly. 'It's going to be all right!'

'*Noah,*' from the phone to the left, '*they have guns. They haven't hurt me yet, but they say … They say they'll kill me if you don't … if you don't … I'm so scared.*'

'Nobody is going to kill you! You just hang on, OK? We are going to be married, and this will all be behind—'

A lorry passes, spraying more wet across the lay-by.

'*I'm sorry,*' the little boy, Jackson, is saying. '*I had an accident. I didn't mean to*—'

'Oh, Jackson, don't be silly. You just do whatever they say, and I'm coming, I'll—'

Babbling from the phone on the left now, Eastern European slurring into nonsense.

'Sofia? Stay with me, Sofia!' The call ends, and Noah bellows her name one more time.

Maggie's conversation lasts a moment or two longer, and they can do nothing but stand around listening to the little boy weep on the other side of the world. '*Maggie. Please. I want to go home.*'

'I know you do, little man. I know, and you're going to be home very soon.'

'*Where are my mom and dad? I want Mom and Dad. Please, I just want Mom and—*'

Maggie's phone goes silent in a click, and darkness returns to the roadside.

45

PLAYER ONE

With more than two hundred miles left to go, the atmosphere in the car is thunderous.

Sarah is sitting up front because of cramps in her legs, while Noah, Brett and Maggie are crammed in the back. Maggie isn't thrilled about this, but at least she has the benefit of shared body heat; the passengers are wet, the car's heaters don't work, and the damp interior is freezing. It stinks in here, like green bread or toadstools under rotting wood, and bare springs are digging into her thighs.

They are almost an hour into the drive, and the tension, increased tenfold by physical discomfort, is unbearable. Maggie can't take it anymore. 'Look, if anybody has something they'd like to say to me, then they'd better get it off their chests.'

She thinks they aren't going to answer. To her surprise, it's Sarah who does.

'You've been lying,' she says without turning to face her. 'We all heard the phone call. *Him*,' she means Noah, 'I'm hardly surprised by. He's never said much one way or the other. But *you* … You've been making out as if you know what we're going through. As if you know what it's like to have your child taken, but you don't. I just think it's a shit thing to do, that's all.'

Whatever annoyance Maggie had been feeling flash boils into rage. 'Jackson is my son. I carried him for nine months, and I gave birth to him. He's mine!'

'We don't know that,' Brett says. 'We all heard what he said back there. He asked for his mom and dad.'

Maggie moves as if to round on him, but she's squeezed in between his right shoulder and the door and she can't do anything except growl at the side of his head. 'You don't know a goddamn thing about me! Any of you! How dare you judge me?'

'Nobody's judging you,' Linda says, 'but you've got to admit, from where we're sitting, it doesn't look as if you've been straight. Is Jackson your son, or isn't he?'

'I don't have to explain shit to you,' Maggie says, and they return to silence.

It should've been obvious that Jackson would want his adoptive parents, his immediate family, at a time like this … but hearing him say it, after all she has been through, cut Maggie like a broken bottle and the pain goes deep. She rests her right temple on the cold, vibrating glass of the window and looks out into the dark.

'I was sixteen when I got pregnant,' she says quietly. 'They couldn't have kids. Shaun and Caroline. Jackson's … parents. I don't know how long they'd been trying for, but they'd already gone through the whole adoption process at least once, and that had reached full term before the birth mom changed her mind. They'd had all the kit waiting when they found out. Can you imagine what that must have been like?'

'Yeah,' Sarah says. 'I can imagine.'

'It wasn't long after I'd fallen pregnant that I was forced to drop out of high school,' Maggie continues. 'My pregnancy was …' A deep, squirming shudder. 'Let's just say it was public knowledge. I got so much abuse I had to delete my social media. Messages calling me a slut, a whore, telling me to kill myself. Dad kicked me out. For a long time, my family wouldn't acknowledge my existence. I met Shaun and Caroline through an agency, and they covered my living expenses as part of the adoption agreement. I moved into this shitty one-room apartment in downtown Saint Paul, our neighbouring city. No friends. No one to talk to.'

'Maggie.' This is Noah, and she realises it's the first time she's heard her name in his accent, and it sounds beautiful. 'You don't owe us anything.'

She goes on, wiping her eye with the heel of one hand. 'A lot of women will tell you that pregnancy is the happiest time of their life or whatever, and maybe you ladies felt that way, but I've got to tell you, mine was gross. I spent most of it throwing up, dizzy. My hands swelled up so bad I had dreams about them bursting like gloves. I didn't know what the hell I was doing.

'My mom never showed up when I went into labour. Shaun and Caroline, these strangers I'd chosen from a brochure, were there in the room with me. Took eighteen hours for him to arrive. By the end I was on my hands and knees, and I would've sworn that my intestines were being unravelled with a hook. Seriously, I've never been all that religious, but I remember thinking of God – that wrathful, pissy, Old Testament God, you know – and how I was being punished for the way I'd gotten myself there. It was so fucking surreal. I had Caroline holding my left hand and her husband holding my right, squeezing them like you'd expect the baby's dad to do …'

She smiles, shaking her head with a strange, sad mixture of happiness and rue.

'They sobbed when they first held him. I still could've called it off, but I couldn't do it. Even if I wanted to.'

'Did you?' Sarah asks. 'Did you want to call it off?'

'I don't know. Seeing them like that, holding him, I saw everything he would grow up to have, everything he could turn out to be. They were the parents he deserved. They sent me photos for the first couple of years, but I didn't know what to do with them. I was in a bad place. Wasn't until last year I started to come out the other side and felt well enough to be in his life. I told myself I could be a positive influence on him but that was obviously bullshit. It was the other way around. I thought he could help me. Now this …'

'I don't understand,' Noah says. 'Why are you here and not these parents?'

Maggie laughs, feeling no humour. '*That* is the million-dollar question. Maybe I just deserve it more.'

They're quiet again for a minute. The windscreen wiper bats sleet off into the night.

'We talked about adopting,' Sarah says. 'We'd been trying for years. Not my husband. My ex and I. What you did for those people … You found yourself in a bad situation and you turned it into something positive. You gave somebody a child, and that's the greatest gift you can imagine.'

Guilt gnaws at Maggie – she has omitted the withdrawal of some fifty thousand dollars from the Taylors' bank account – and she briskly moves past it. 'But your girl wasn't adopted?'

'No.' Sarah turns to face her with an expression of ghostly pride; it's the closest thing to a smile Maggie has seen on her face, and she's much prettier with it. 'Hannah's all mine. You should see her; she has this flaming ginger hair like I used to have. I wish I had a photograph.'

'But you were thinking of adopting …?'

'I had three miscarriages in my twenties,' Sarah clarifies quite calmly, a woman who has either long since come to terms with these horrors, or who's simply too beaten down and exhausted to be anything less than candid.

'Jesus,' Maggie says, almost tasting the foot in her mouth. 'I'm sorry.'

'It's OK. They called it *unexplained infertility*. Maybe we just weren't a match, Sam and me. I think about that sometimes, the pointless cruelty of it. We could've been so happy. We *were* so happy, but nature just didn't want us to have a family. No reason, no rhyme, nothing they could find with any test. We tried fertility treatment, and my fourth pregnancy, our little girl, went to full term.'

'This was Hannah?' Linda asks.

'No.' Sarah turns back to face the front. 'No, our fourth pregnancy … she was stillborn.'

Maggie closes her eyes, skin flushing. 'Fuck.'

'My God,' Linda says. 'Sarah, I am so sorry. I didn't realise …'

'Why would you? One in four women have miscarriages. One in four. They told me that at the hospital, and all I kept thinking was, well, how come I feel so alone?

'The first, we found out during our twelve-week scan. We were devastated, but there was something else, something I never told Sam. I was sort of … revolted by it. My baby had

294

been dead inside me for about a week. I didn't know whether something the size of a plum could really be called a *corpse*, but that's how it felt. Like I'd been carrying a corpse inside me. I could either wait for the body to miscarriage naturally or have it removed, and honestly, I just wanted it out. That's something they don't talk about in the brochures, or on the chat shows. Maybe I'm the only woman who ever felt like that, but I doubt it. Anyway, you don't have a funeral after three months.'

'I don't think you should feel guilty for how you felt then,' Maggie says. 'You have nothing to feel weird about.'

Sarah shrugs. 'Anyway, I met Neil, and I fell pregnant after, you know, the first time. That was Hannah, my little miracle. We got married while I was pregnant, all within half a year of leaving Sam, and then we had Archie, our youngest. Neil's nothing like my ex. I don't think you could find a more opposite kind of man, but he loves his kids. God knows what he's going through ...' She quickly shakes her head. 'What about you, Linda? You have any others?'

'Just Alyssa. She was born on a Wednesday. Caesarean.' She wipes a tear of her own now, the first Maggie has seen, now she thinks about it. 'She was a gorgeous baby. And she turned out to be so polite, so gentle, never any trouble ...'

'We'll get her back,' Maggie says, placing a hand on Linda's shoulder from behind, feeling the collarbone. 'We'll get them all back.'

Linda sighs. 'God, listen to us. Some mothers' meeting.'

'I know,' Sarah agrees. 'What about you, Brett? Any words from a father's point of view? You going to tell us all how easy it is from the other side?'

But Brett doesn't answer. His breathing has turned heavy, and he is sleeping soundly between them all.

Or, Maggie thinks, perhaps he is only pretending.

46

PLAYER TWO

Brett has never believed in love at first sight. Attraction, yes, and basic lust, but never love. That, he thinks, takes something more than a cursory glance across a crowded room.

Case in point: he had seen Craig Wilson countless times before they ever shared a spoken word, and he'd felt no attraction whatsoever. Of course he hadn't. Brett was your average, all-American, heterosexual boy.

OK, so some of his old-fashioned countrymen might have contested his status as the archetypal *all-American* boy, and he probably had fewer close friends than the average kid; he'd never had a girlfriend, and his rare juvenile experiments with pornography had made him feel about as enthralled as he did during church, but he was as straight as an arrow, despite what the other kids called him. He just wasn't interested in *anybody* like that.

He was straight. He believed that then. Some days, he believes it still.

Craig was supposed to be crazy, just like his old man. Rumour had it that Officer Donny Wilson, a legend in the

NYPD, liked to shoot unarmed black boys on the weekends, and in a public school where less than a tenth of all pupils were white, this should have singled Craig out for a severe, if not fatal, reprisal. It didn't though. Even the hoods seemed to be afraid of Donny Wilson, the untouchable bogeyman of Brooklyn, and they were, by proxy, wary of Craig.

Brett doesn't remember the first time he saw Craig – they must have passed one another in the halls every day for a year – but he remembers the first time they spoke. It wasn't the sort of day somebody forgets.

Their long friendship can be traced back to one vindictive shit heel named Roland Washington. It's a familiar chestnut: Roland had taken an inexplicable interest in Brett – specifically in the art of making his life miserable – and every day for three straight weeks, this kid waited somewhere beyond the school gates to inflict some kind of pointless torture. This soon inspired Brett to seek out new, unnecessarily extensive routes home, and that's how he found Craig Wilson, hidden in the alleyway behind Joe's Convenience with his right hand buried in Rosie Bryant's panties.

For three reasons this caused Brett to halt in his tracks: firstly, he had never seen anybody exploring the contents of a girl's pants before because, at this age, their classmates had barely begun to sprout breasts; secondly, because Rosie Bryant was two years *older* than the boy, which was surely unheard of, and she was black, and wasn't this the son of some psychotic racist? Mostly though, Brett froze because, compared to Roland Washington, this Wilson kid was supposed to be deadly.

Craig had his back turned to Brett, busying himself as he was, but the Bryant girl opened her eyes, returning abruptly from whatever happy place she'd been soaring, and saw the voyeur blinking at her through huge, jam-jar glasses. She cleared her throat, whispered something, and Craig glanced back irritably; he never removed his hand.

'What you looking at, dipshit?' he asked.

Brett didn't answer. In truth, he almost pissed his pants before bolting back the way he'd come.

Emerging from the alleyway, preoccupied with his own shock, he ran straight into Roland and his pals.

'Nice try, fag,' was all Brett heard before he was on the ground, head ringing, and then he was being dragged across rough pavement by the bag on his back. His shoes fell off. He still remembers that clearly.

'Over here!' one of the boys – maybe Roland, maybe not – was squealing excitedly. 'Over here! Check it out!'

Brett managed to look around just far enough to see that he was being hauled backwards towards the trashcan outside the convenience store. He was thrown up against it, pinned in place by his rucksack, as Roland reached into the trash and fished out a knotted plastic baggie; it looked heavy and full.

'Open it up,' Roland giggled, tossing it to one of his play-mates. 'Open it up!'

'No way! It's full of dog shit!'

'Don't be a pussy, just rip it a little.'

'Why?' the kid – Brett doesn't remember his name – asked, and it seemed like a good question from down on the ground.

'Fags eat assholes, don't they?' Roland was practically screaming now. 'We gon' give his scrawny ass a decent meal for once.'

Laughter everywhere. Animal howls. Panic. Brett tried to

scramble away, but he was too frantic, too damn terrified to simply slip his arms out of his bag's straps.

He has never forgotten the smell. To this day, if he accidentally steps in some dog's mess on the sidewalk, he is overwhelmed by humiliation, haunted by the scars of a child, a little boy, who had done nothing wrong, and who wanted to die.

The bag was brought down in an almighty slap, held in whichever sadist's palm like a fastball pitch without the release, and cold, dense shit smashed over Brett's nose, chin, lips, teeth. What he heard in that moment – as his eyes burned, and his vision exploded into white, and the vomit rushed up into his mouth – was something else that has always stuck with him: it was one of the boys, yelling in disgust:

'Ah, gross! You got it on my leg!'

And the one who had done it saying, so goddamn sincerely, 'Oh man, I'm sorry,' right before wiping his own palm clean in Brett's fuzzy hair.

They ran after that, leaving Brett spitting and sobbing by the trashcan.

That's when he decided to kill himself.

He would throw himself off the bridge, just wash all the shit away in the waters of the East River. It wasn't just an empty threat. It really was going to happen.

Then he heard another voice.

'What the fuck, dipshit? Those other fucking spades do this to you?'

Brett froze, halfway through smearing excrement, vomit and the nosebleed onto his sleeve. The Wilson kid was standing over him. He was big for his age, already growing handsome, in spite of his long hair and grungy clothes, in that tough kid way that would soon turn the heads of older, occasionally married, women.

'Come on,' he said. 'Get up.'

Craig guided him back into the cover of the alleyway and told him to wait. The girl was gone. Brett, sure that this was some kind of cruel joke, was about to get up and leave when Craig returned from inside the store carrying bottled water and kitchen towels.

'It's all I could fit up my shirt,' he told him honestly.

Craig smoked while Brett cleaned himself up as well as he could in silent shame.

'They give you a lot of shit, huh?' Craig asked, exhaling smoke, and then he grinned. 'What am I saying? 'Course they do, you're covered in it.'

Brett only blinked, bewildered, still fairly certain that any moment now this big dumb racist was going to flip out, mug him and leave him for dead in the alleyway.

Instead, Craig walked Brett the six blocks home to his mother. The following morning, to Brett's astonishment, Craig was there waiting outside Brett's front door, and after their final period was over that day, he was waiting at the school gates. Roland Washington never so much as glanced at him again.

For the first few days, as far as Brett can recall, they didn't even speak; that might be a trick of the memory – they must've said *something* on those walks – but that's how he remembers it. Just two quiet kids, sharing their loneliness. On the third or fourth day, Craig asked him what he thought about the Rangers, and Brett went home and learned everything he could about hockey.

By the end of the month, Craig had introduced Brett to

Soundgarden, Mudhoney and Pearl Jam. In return, Brett offered – without success – to loan him his Michael Jackson records.

Brett took Craig with him to Four Quarters, the best arcade in Brooklyn, and schooled him in *Street Fighter II* and *Lethal Enforcers*.

When Craig lost his virginity two years later, he wasted no time telling Brett about it with all the detailed vulgarity a teenage boy can manage. Brett laughed, called him a bad motherfucker, and then went home and cried himself to sleep. He had no idea why.

Craig's father was gunned down by a crackhead in '97. That was also the year that Craig stopped showing up at Brett's house with black eyes, bruises and cigarette burns. Craig went to live with his aunt in Queens, an hour away, and soon dropped out of school. When Brett eventually went off to college, they kept in touch on the phone. When Brett returned, they picked up right where they left off, a rarity among adults. Craig's inner-city connections even helped to get Brett his first ill-fated editing job.

Almost thirty years. A hell of a friendship.

Brett thinks about all of this while the women talk babies, as women like to do. He retraces the beats of their lives, his and Craig's, forever intertwined.

He thinks about all this to distract himself from what happened at the roadside. The feeling it brings into his stomach is horribly familiar, like the stench of dog shit he has never really scrubbed away, but he can't ignore it entirely. Sooner or later, he knows, he is going to have to make a decision. It is going to come down to a simple choice.

These four strangers, and the children he has never met, or the man who was the boy who saved his life.

Brett has never believed in love at first sight.

But he knows for certain, from simply being here and doing the things he has done, that he has always loved Craig Wilson.

47

PLAYER THREE

Ten o'clock.

This is the longest, and the latest, Sarah has ever been away from her children. No city breaks, no cottage weekends. Even on her honeymoon, Hannah was there in utero.

There's no radio in the car. Conversation is staggered. There's only the squeaking of the ragged, flailing windscreen wiper. And her own thoughts.

She's thinking about those sleepless nights, the ones that followed the birth of each baby. Not because either child was unusually restless. On the contrary, Sarah's nights were wakeful because her infants were *too* quiet. She would listen for hours, trying to assure herself that Hannah was still breathing. She'd sit by Archie's Moses basket, unable to trust his fate to the night.

After this, how will that paranoia ever pass?

It's with her now, of course; it's the hairs on her neck, refusing to settle; it's the voice in her ear, telling her that the others are keeping her around because she's weak and they might need a sacrifice; it's the belief, the innate surety, that she is sitting in a car full of liars.

Since their motherly conversation, however, Sarah has been finding her own misgivings about the others difficult to trust. She's no longer sure about what she thought she saw on the motorway. Did somebody try to throw another player beneath a passing lorry? Why would they? To cut the numbers and increase their chance of winning? Winning what?

Besides, Noah and Maggie came back for her. That surely rules them out. Doesn't it?

There's something about Brett though. He seems to have changed since the motorway, and she doesn't know what it is. As if there needs to be any more reason than this life-or-death stress. She tries to imagine Neil in Brett's situation, and she can't see him sitting down at any table for a conversation. She can't imagine anything close to rational.

Poor Neil. She tracks his day in her mind.

He checks his phone late afternoon and finds dozens of missed calls and voicemails from his wife, which must have sounded terrifying, though Sarah doesn't quite remember what she said. He tries to call back and finds her phone off. Around this time, his mother-in-law gets in touch to say that Archie is with her, Duke is dead, and Sarah has taken Hannah … somewhere. He asks Ann how Sarah had seemed, and she tells him that she'd been in an awful rush, itching as if there was a gun at her back. Had Ann actually *seen* Hannah in the car? No, strangely enough, she never saw her.

And now it's late at night, and there's been no word from his wife, no sign of his daughter, just a murdered dog in the back garden. Will he ring the police? If he recognises that Duke's death was no accident then yes, and what will they suspect? Duke may have been adored, but he was only a dog as far as the law is concerned, a piece of damaged property. Sarah, though … How often has Neil questioned his wife's mental health? In how many arguments has he called her unstable?

Has he already wondered, just for a second or two, if she has finally snapped?

Killed their dog and driven their firstborn down to the water?

No! Because of this, as much as anything else, she has to get a signal to him. Just one short message like a wink across a crowded room. She should've left a clue behind, and she feels so stupid for not doing so. All she'd been thinking about was technology, the phone and cameras, and it never occurred to her to just leave a single scrap of paper behind. It had all happened so fast. That, of course, was the point. Headless chickens don't stop to think things through.

Now that she's thinking rationally, more ideas come. Steve at number twelve has a video doorbell installed. Might the police knock on the surrounding doors, questioning about Duke's death – a suspected attempted burglary – and ask to check the footage? What would they see, she wonders; not merely a dog killer, but some stranger emerging from the Mulligan house carrying Hannah? Would they see *the car*?

Sarah's heart, which had finally, mercifully steadied, begins to pick up its pace again. Only this time it's not just fear. It's adrenaline. It's a chance.

She feels closer to the people in this car, but nowhere near close enough to share this stream of consciousness, and she buries it deep inside like a winning hand. She even slides her left hand into her coat pocket, squeezing the damn burner phone, wrapping her hand around it as if the microphone might be picking these treacherous thoughts right out of her head. It's infuriating having a phone on her, knowing Neil's number by heart, but being unable to use it. If she could only get one message out, a code perhaps, something so fast that it leaps past whatever spyware is monitoring her actions.

But it's impossible. The phone is a non-starter. She can't risk it.

With her hand still in her pocket, she moves away from the phone and begins passing cold metal objects back and forth between her fingers. She rubs the smoothed, sore tip of her ring finger against them, feeling the milling in the metal. The burner is unusable, but there has to be another way. Something simple.

She does this for a good thirty seconds or more, moving the pieces of metal through her hand, before she realises what's in her grasp, and her breath halts in her throat.

Bingo.

Her skin turns incredibly hot, and she slowly, casually, turns her face to the passenger window to stop anybody from noticing.

What had her mum said?

'*Let me give you some pennies to give to her …*'

'*Mam, honestly, I really need to be—*'

'*I won't be one minute, Sarah. Am I not allowed to give my own granddaughter a little bit of pocket money on a day like this …?*'

Sarah's pulse has increased to palpitations.

How much, she wonders, have we come to rely on our mobile phones?

How often do we miss the answer because it's too basic, too old-fashioned, too *obvious*?

In those first hours after Hannah was taken, Sarah had been so lost to utter shock, so terrified for her daughter's wellbeing, that not only had it never occurred to her to leave a message behind, but it also never crossed her mind to simply pull over on the journey to the postcode, leave her bugged mobile in the car and use a public payphone to call for help. Likewise, once she'd actually arrived at the inn, she didn't consider finding a phone on the premises because she was too damn afraid of who might be involved, and too conscious of who could be watching.

She doesn't think any of the others in this car would have considered such a blindingly obvious solution either. Hadn't Noah, after all, hit the nail on the head while they'd all been sitting in that firelit parlour?

'*This is what they want us to think. They are trying to intimidate us. They want to seem omnipotent.*'

She slides her fingers through the coins, counting softly, careful not to make clinking sounds. Such a paltry sum, but it could turn this situation around. Instead of the nine grand she'd originally expected to pay, this palmful of pocket money could change her daughter's fate.

Sarah's second lucky break – her second miracle, one could call it – comes only a few moments later; it's as if Linda has read her mind, mother to mother.

The headlamps pick up a sign beside the road, and Linda clicks her tongue.

SERVICES 2 MILES

'Bad news,' Linda says. 'If we're going to make it, then we're going to have to stop to fill the tank.'

'Good,' Sarah replies, and she quickly changes her tone. 'I'm dying for the loo.'

The three in the back agree that they too could use a break.

'I don't know if that's a good idea,' Linda says. 'It'll draw too much attention. If you all need the bathroom, I'll pull over at the next treeline and—'

'Forget that,' Brett groggily says. 'My guts have been liquid since the changeover in Paris. If you think I'm going to drop my pants in some ditch, then you've got another think coming.'

Linda sighs through her nose, but she doesn't touch the indicator. There seems to be some internal battle raging behind her strangely blank face. The exit is coming up fast and Sarah can see from here that the red petrol light is glowing.

'Linda,' she says softly, heart hammering in her throat, palm sweating on the coins in her pocket. 'If the car runs out of fuel then you'll never get to Alyssa.'

Linda fixes her with a flat, sideways stare ... then flicks the indicator to the left.

As they pull up to the pump, Sarah does her best to memorise their destination's longitude and latitude, which are still displayed in the corner of the satnav's screen, but the numbers are too long and she has to get out of the car first to allow those in the back to disembark. She holds her seat forward for them. Then, when everybody is out, and because she is still conscious of its microphone, she discreetly drops her burner under her seat and closes the door.

There's not even time to memorise the licence plate without looking suspicious. She feels like it's written all over her face.

The toilets are on the far side of the service station. The public payphone is outside them. The group divides by gender, and Sarah chooses the end cubicle in the ladies, walking a little slowly – but not *noticeably slowly* – to make sure that

309

Linda and Maggie choose a cubicle each. They do. Sarah walks into her own cubicle and locks the door. Further along the row, she hears two more locks go sliding into place. Silently, she opens her door and races back out of the bathroom.

999 would be free to dial, but there's no time to waste with an operator, not enough answers for their inevitable questions.

She drops Hannah's pocket money into the slot and punches in her husband's number. She squeezes the receiver so tightly it hurts.

One ring. Two rings. Three. Four. He doesn't answer. He'll see the unknown area code and assume it's a telemarketer. She wastes twenty precious seconds before replacing the handset; she does it slowly, resisting the urge to slam it and cry out in frustration. She winces as the coins rattle noisily down to the returns tray. She reinserts them into the slot. Again, she presses the square buttons.

This time, on the fourth ring, Neil answers. 'Whatever you're selling, mate, you've chosen the worst possible—'

'Shut your mouth and listen to me.' She has never spoken to him like this before.

'Sarah!'

Trying not to break down at the sound of his voice, she whispers the following at a verbal sprint.

'I have thirty seconds, maybe less, so shut the fuck up and listen. Somebody has abducted Hannah. They killed Duke, came into our house this afternoon and took her. I don't know who. I don't know why. They call themselves The Game, and they've been blackmailing me using text messages. There are four more people in the same position. We're in an old Corsa heading north. I'm not sure where. You have this phone number now, so work it out. Call the police, but this is crucial: the police *cannot* intercept us until Hannah is found. They *cannot* try to contact me. If whoever has Hannah finds out that I've spoken to you, or that I've tried to contact the police, then they *will kill her*, Neil. They'll kill our little girl. Our Qashqai is parked close to a bed and breakfast called the Gamekeeper's Inn, north of Saddleworth Moor. That's the *Gamekeeper's Inn*. We were told to meet there. My phone's still in the car. The pin number is 0903, Hannah's birthday, but the phone is bugged. If you turn it on, they may know, but there are messages on there. For all I know, your phone's bugged too. If it is, then this could be over already. I had to try though. I have to go. Don't call this number back. Find her. Find our daughter.'

And that's it.

She returns the phone and once again cringes when the pocket money clatters down, this time deep into the machinery. After a second thought, she repositions the phone slightly off its cradle, leaving it off the hook. Neil will automatically try to call back, despite what she told him. She knows he will. She'd do the same thing.

After a noiseless sprint back into the restroom, she slips into the last cubicle, heaves huge, silent breaths until she's no longer panting, and then walks out as calmly as she can. As she approaches the sinks, Maggie and Linda emerge from their respective stalls.

The three women stand in a line there, washing their hands, and when their eyes meet in the mirrors, Sarah can almost see the neon GUILTY sign on her forehead.

'Yeah,' Maggie says. 'I know.'

Sarah's jaw tightens.

Linda raises an eyebrow. 'Know what?'

'I look like shit,' Maggie says. 'You don't have to say anything.'

They don't. This is as far as the conversation goes.

When they return to the car, Sarah fishes her burner from beneath her seat. As far as she can tell, nobody notices a thing.

48

HANNAH

Hannah has slept a lot this afternoon. Now she feels sleepy again, but she doesn't want to sleep here.

She's curled up against the headboard of an unfamiliar bed. It's very dark outside, though the curtains are closed. She wants to be at home.

'Bed-byes,' she says, talking around the tip of one thumb. 'Time go bed-byes.'

'Yeah,' the woman sitting on the neighbouring bed replies without turning to face her. 'It's late. You go sleep now, sweetheart.'

Hannah sucks her thumb harder. Her skin tastes sweet from the white chocolate buttons she ate for supper; the empty foil pouches are still scattered around her on the bedspread. 'Bed-byes with Joot,' she says. 'Joot smuggles.'

Sighing, the woman breaks her gaze from the screen of the television and looks over at Hannah. 'I can't understand what you're saying. Take your thumb out your mouth and try again.'

Reluctantly, Hannah does. 'Joot smuggles. Bed-bye smuggles. Joot kisses.'

The woman squints, thinks about it, shakes her head. 'Nope. Don't know what you mean.' She looks instead to the quiet man standing by the window. 'Don't they learn kids to speak proper these days?'

'She's saying Duke,' the man says. 'She's talking about the dog.'

Hannah nods. 'Every night bed-byes, Joot smuggles.'

'Oh.' The woman smiles. 'Soon, darl. If you're a good girl.' She turns back to the television, and Hannah replaces her thumb between her lips.

The woman is older than Mummy, but not quite as old as Nan. She's bony and she smells vaguely unpleasant. Some of her teeth are missing. The man is round, and his hair is thin. There are green drawings all over his hands.

The woman had woken Hannah from her afternoon nap. The man had been waiting in the car outside. They told Hannah this was a sort of game, a funny trick to play on Mummy and Daddy, but it doesn't feel funny anymore. The man isn't smiling; he walks around a lot, whenever he isn't standing with his head buried in the curtains looking out over the car park. They talk between themselves and, just as they find it difficult to understand her, Hannah struggles to follow what they're saying.

'We shouldn't have come here,' the man says from within the curtains. 'This was a bad idea. We must be mad.'

The woman sniffs, eyes on the TV. 'What, you reckon we should've driven about all night instead? No one comes out here except prozzies.'

'No shit. A hotel full of whores, plus one toddler. We stick out like a sore bollock.'

'And keeping your face pressed up against the glass like that's going to help, is it?'

He steps back, snapping the curtains closed. 'We should've camped. Got a tent in the woods.'

'Tenting out in no-degrees. That wouldn't have looked dodgy.'

He paces, shoes dragging over scuffed, grotty carpet. 'This was meant to be easy money. That's what you said. Easy money.'

The woman gestures over her own body, her unfurled, malnourished-feline posture, with gnarled hands. 'This *is* easy money, darl.'

'You reckon so?' He shakes his head, then turns to Hannah. 'It's late. Try shutting your eyes.'

'Wh—'

'No arguing,' he snaps. 'Now go on, roll over and face that way.'

She does it quietly, without arguing, because she's starting to feel something inside; she's starting to feel the way she does in a very dark room, even though the TV is on in here, glowing like a nightlight; she's starting to get scared. She closes her eyes tightly, so the man and woman whisper, and their whispers sound like snakes.

'You shouldn't have done it,' the man says. 'The dog. You shouldn't have done it.'

'Oh, here we go again. I don't remember you rushing to get into the garden with it.'

'We had a plan, that's why. I boost you up onto the fence, you drop down with the meat. They were decent bangers. It would've taken them right out your hands. You unbolt the gate from inside, I get the dog into the alley and it stays there, out the way.'

'Sausages? It wasn't a cartoon, Daz, it was a fucking Alsatian. I wasn't putting my hand anywhere near it. Besides, it *knew*.'

'It didn't know shit.'

'It knew,' she repeats. 'As soon as it saw me on the fence, it knew what we was after. They sense these things.'

'Right. So you stuck it.'

'Yeah,' she says. 'Like a pig. Get over it already. You reckon that's as messy as this is going to get? You know how this ends. You knew what this was.'

'Easy money, that's what you said, like the York job. Only, we haven't heard shit for hours now. No instructions or nothing. We don't know this cunt from Adam. He says jump and we're supposed to say how high? Well, what if we've been left holding the bag? What if we've been stitched up? What if—'

'All right!' she bites. 'I get it, but what do we do about it now?'

'I say we just dump her outside a petty station, let them deal with her.'

'And lose the cash? No chance. It's gone too far for that. We give it two more hours, how about that? Two more hours.'

'And then what?'

Whether she wants to or not, Hannah can feel herself slipping, the room warping into an infant's dreamscape around her, and she's almost fully asleep when the woman next speaks her name.

'Hannah?' She's talking softly, closer now, and Hannah can smell her breath coming from over her shoulder; it smells bad. 'Can you swim, honey?'

Half-asleep, Hannah grumbles. 'No. I go splash.'

'That's great,' the woman whispers. 'Brilliant. You shush

now, sweetie. Get some sleep. In a couple of hours, maybe we'll take you down to the water.'

'Water,' Hannah repeats dreamily. 'Go splash.'

'That's right, Hannah … Two more hours. Then you go splash.'

49

PLAYER FOUR

No one in the car has said anything for a long time.

Just like it had in the bottom of that trailer last night, it feels wrong to sleep, unthinkable to be hungry, taboo to be human in such horrible circumstances … but Noah is all of those things and more, and the others must be too, because they doze in turn and their stomachs rumble around him. All except Linda, who looks increasingly wired behind the wheel.

Travelling. This endless, monotonous travelling. From Paris to Calais to Dover to Manchester to Scotland. Where will it end?

To lose a loved one, and then be forced only to move further and further away from them in never-ending increments; what could be the point of this torture? Maybe, Noah thinks, there'll be another map at the end of this drive, another countdown, and then another, and another, until they are forced right off the edge of the earth. Journeying to nowhere but their own nervous breakdowns. Maybe *that's* the game. Torture for the sake of torture. Noah is starting to believe it might be.

As he considers this, with his head against the rear side

window of the car, a memory comes out of some distant corner. Six or seven years old, he happens across a pretty little girl sitting by herself on the banks of the Seine. She's playing some kind of game with a broken stick, so he goes over to see what she's doing. The girl, he discovers, has used the stick to dig a long groove into the earth. Through this groove, she is herding ants by the hundreds, maybe the thousands, from their hill, along a spiralling course, and finally into the river to drown. Noah watches them march for a minute or two, transfixed, before he asks why she's doing this. 'Why not?' the girl replies with a bored little shrug.

Why not?

He stares out through glass into grey. There's a light blinking in the far distance; a helicopter, he presumes, braving the bad weather. There are vehicles on the road. Not an enormous amount, but some. From here they seem like window dressing, as genuine as those reels of busy roads they used to roll behind actors in stationary cars in Hitchcock movies. Noah finds it hard to believe there's still an ordinary world out there.

For more than four hours he has been crammed in here, and he's feeling increasingly self-conscious about his own hygiene. It should be the least of his concerns, but he can't help it. His mouth tastes foul, and he can actually smell himself.

I need to shower, Sofia had said to him last night. *I'm beginning to smell like a Frenchman.*

Sacré bleu! he'd replied, and then he'd told her to wash and said he'd call her after work. Those were the last things they had said to one another face to face. How sad.

Desperate to get out of his own head, he turns his face to

the front of the car. 'How are you, Linda? This is a long time to drive. You want me to take over?'

Her eyes flick to him in the mirror; their whites are red in the glow of the satnav's screen, the skin around them dark, but the pupils still have that keyed-up look, almost as if she has been dipping into one of his stashes.

'No. I'm fine.'

'A lot of lights over there,' Sarah says, pointing to the right. 'A city?'

'Glasgow,' Linda says. 'We started passing it a few miles ago.'

'Is that where it's taking us, you think?'

'If it isn't, it'll be close. We're less than an hour away now.'

The wave of discomfort this evokes through the car is palpable.

'Can't wait,' Maggie says. 'I wonder what's waiting for us next.'

Against Noah's right shoulder, Brett stirs slightly and speaks through a huge yawn. 'Maybe they're going to make us blow up a hospital ... Steal a truck and drive it into an elementary school.' He smacks his lips together.

'That isn't funny,' Sarah says. 'Don't say that.'

'I wasn't joking.' He rubs his eyes and cracks his neck. 'Anybody see that movie where this bunch of strangers are forced to go through some gigantic maze, and the rooms are full of laser traps and shit?'

'*Saw*,' Maggie says. 'Second one, maybe. Isn't that the one with the house?'

'No, not *Saw*, it's older than that. Has a one-word title, I think. It might be set in outer space or something.'

'*Saw*'s old,' she reasons. 'One-word title. You're thinking of *Saw*.'

'It's not *Saw*, goddamn it! Didn't I just say that? You got something wrong with your ears?'

'OK! Jeez!'

'Come on,' Sarah intervenes timidly, maternally, 'let's stay civil. We're all exhausted and stressed out, but—'

'Ah, cram it,' Brett grumbles, cutting her off.

Noah glances at the man beside him, and he doesn't like what he sees. Brett might dress like he belongs in front of a computer, or behind the desk in a library, but that doesn't mean he isn't a different kind of dangerous altogether.

Had he really been willing to let Sarah's daughter die?

'*Cube*,' Noah says, still eyeing the man beside him.

'What?' Sarah asks.

'*Cube*. This is the film.'

'*Cube* …' Brett says. 'Hey, you might be right.' Instead of being gratified, he fixes Noah with a suspicious sidewards glance. 'Favourite of yours?'

'*Nom de Dieu*, no. But I know films. When I was a boy, we had one videocassette machine in our building, and we would come together to watch the tapes we could get. This was our, um …' He rolls his eyes, his brain tired of English. '*Treat?*'

'In Paris?' Maggie says doubtfully. 'You were born in one of the most desirable cities in the world, I'm sure you could've found plenty to do.'

This momentarily astonishes and then angers him. 'You know *Department 93? Quatre-vingt-treize?* This is a *banlieue*, the poorest area in not just Paris, but *all* of France. You know nothing about me. None of you.'

'Yeah yeah,' Brett says, 'we've all had it tough. I was raised in Brownsville, Brooklyn, in a twenty-two-storey housing project.

My mom worked three jobs to keep the clothes on our backs, and we slept to the sound of gunshots. That's no joke. By the time I was ten, I'd been to more kids' funerals than birthday parties. I had to fight to get my scholarship to college, and I made some hard dollars, did things I wasn't proud of, but that's just life. That doesn't mean I deserve to be stuck in this piece of shit car with you. Life's tough all over, kid.'

A pause, then Linda asks, 'What things?'

'What?'

'You said you've done things you aren't proud of,' she says frostily. 'What things?'

'It's just a figure of speech. Nothing criminal, Officer.'

Noah sees a flicker of something on Brett's face, but he doesn't push him on the subject because he wishes he could say the same.

Soon they clear Glasgow's limits, and the land on either side of the road begins to rise into sheer faces marking the start of the Scottish Highlands. Noah thinks of those ants, the ones following that chasm towards their pointless doom, and a shiver runs down his spine.

The car skates through brief flurries of heavy snow up here and, even from the backseat, Noah can feel the surface of the road becoming slicker. Linda seems tenser than ever, if that's at all possible, her knuckles glowing white on the steering wheel.

It isn't long before the elevated land to the right of the car suddenly opens up, simply dropping away, and there are no more cities over there, no silhouettes or landmarks; there is only a seemingly infinite stretch of solid, impossible blackness.

Noah leans his head around the back of Sarah's seat – pressing uncomfortably against Brett to do so – and sees that the black outside is represented as a massive expanse of blue on the screen of the satnav.

'We're at the sea?' he asks.

'No,' Linda says. 'It's a loch.'

'Oh.' Noah turns his face back to the blackness, and to him it looks like the edge of the world. The edge of the world, and they're going to drive right off it.

Why not?

50

PLAYER FIVE

With just fifteen miles to go, the satnav instructs Linda to leave the main road for one last time.

She turns onto a treacherous single-width carriageway that winds and turns, rising and falling at lethal pitches, so that she has no choice but to drop down to second gear and crawl.

The engine moans, and there's a furious ticking noise inside. Only now does it really hit home that, even if she can somehow manage to keep the tyres from skidding off the narrow, icy road, the engine simply might not make it.

Astoundingly the vehicle endures, but Linda's vision is foggy at the edges and filled with small, shuddering black stars that frequently dart across her eyes. She has driven from Luton to beyond Glasgow with only a hike and a sprint through freezing temperatures to break up the day. She could have let one of the others drive, probably should have, but it felt safer to be in charge of the vehicle. Running along the motorway was another reckless move that could've got them arrested already; she didn't want to press her luck by allowing one of the others to go racing through a speed trap.

Just nine miles to go. The faces of her strange passengers crowd the electric map over the dashboard like tribesmen around the first fire.

Eight. Seven.

'This is freaking me out,' Sarah says quietly. 'The closer we get, the less there is.'

Linda couldn't have put it better herself. Out here there is no light, no civilisation beyond the cracked tarmac under headlamps, and soon even the tarmac is gone and there's only compacted dirt. Winter foliage, skeletal and clawlike, reaches at them from both sides.

Four miles. Three.

The satnav, blue-white in the car's interior, beckons them onwards with the humorous malevolence of a will-o'-the-wisp.

Two miles. One.

The final stretch is on a slight decline, so Linda kills the rattling motor and allows the car to roll the last hundred yards in neutral. She lowers her window and listens hard for any signs of life, but all she can hear is thin ice cracking under tyres and the sound of her own heartbeat, as if blood is being shotgun-blasted around her veins.

She switches the headlights for the dimmer sidelights and closes her eyes, just for a second, to listen harder.

It's calm behind her eyelids. Peaceful, even with the racket of her own pulse. It seems like a long time since she has had any sort of peace, either outside or in here.

'Whoa!' Sarah's voice.

Linda comes back with a start, and it takes her another moment to see that, about twenty yards ahead, the ground abruptly disappears. They're rolling towards a plummet. She slams on the brake pedal, and the car keeps sliding. Beyond the horizon there is only night and another loch waiting greedily below them, and Linda is overcome by a strange, terrifying certainty that this will be the conclusion: lungs full of water, body floating, grey flesh stripped by lampreys and eels.

Panic causes her to freeze – it may be for the first time in her life – and it's Sarah, of all people, who reaches over and spins the wheel through Linda's clammy hands, aiming for a tree that might stop the car before the drop, a net of branches to catch them. When the front-left tyre dips into a depression in the earth, and the vehicle shunts to a halt, all the passengers exhale at once.

Linda kills the sidelights. 'I don't think I've ever … I mean, I couldn't … I didn't … The water …'

'It's OK.' Sarah places her hand on Linda's arm and squeezes. 'You did it. You got us here. We made it.'

Linda stares at the hand, fascinated, until the satnav dings, announcing their arrival, and she quickly shuts it off, casting the car into total dark.

They sit this way for a few seconds; it feels like a very long time. Lazy snowflakes drift down in singles, one at a time, to melt and cover nothing.

'I don't see anything,' Brett whispers. 'Anybody else?'

'No,' Maggie replies. 'We should get out and look.'

'Yeah? After you.'

'Thanks.'

They step out into the night, this peculiar quintet, and Linda hears their sharp gasps as the bitter air spikes their lungs. When they close their car doors, they do so softly, only just allowing the latches to click home.

It must be well below freezing up here. Through all her layers, through her very flesh, Linda feels the cold seize her skeleton with needle fingers. It makes her feel old. Much too old for this. While the other players silently bounce on the spot, pivoting cramped shoulders and stretching numb legs, Linda finds herself drawn slowly to the precipice ahead. Her sense of dread is deep and ultimately inescapable, but she also feels hypnotised as she shuffles forwards, a passenger lost in the zone.

She swallows a breath of ice, as crisp and unpleasant as the air in a mortuary, and looks down.

There is a drop. It's not quite as high as she'd imagined, nor is it positioned directly over black water. There's a stretch of shoreline below. On the shoreline stands a small, solitary building. Nothing else down there. Just this private cove.

Linda's heart is beating so hard now that she can feel it in her temples, and it hurts.

The building is a fishing cottage, and in the absolute darkness it looks practically primeval. Ivy clings to exposed, weather-battered stone. Frost clings to the ivy. The windows are timber. The walls lean.

By day, it might be pretty. Quaint. Charming.

By night, though …

'Dear God.' Sarah is here now, whispering. 'Do you think … Linda, are our girls inside?'

Linda only stares at the building, sending out her own will like exploratory fingers. For a moment, just a fraction of a second, she believes she really can feel Alyssa trapped inside there.

'Whether your girls are or not,' Maggie says quietly, joining them. 'Jackson isn't. He can't be, can he?'

'Sofia too,' Noah says. 'But Player Six? The end of this fucking game? Maybe.'

'Player Six has the answer,' Sarah breathes. 'That's what the message said.'

'I don't like it,' Brett says. 'I know I come from a city, but it's so … *quiet*. It's like having your head underwater.'

This sends a tremor through Linda, and again it's water she's thinking of, water in her lungs, an old nightmare of being submerged. She's never seen a loch before, and she never expected one to be so bowl-like, so enormous on every side. She's trapped in the bottom of a well. She's trapped here, listening to four people who don't care one bit for her daughter. Listening to their jaws vibrate, their teeth chatter, their frightened whispers as their breaths go up in white clouds. Rage gathers inside her, swelling up, a star ready to go supernova. She is mother, and she's close now. Close, but still too far.

'It's got to be deserted,' Brett goes on. 'What'd I tell you? This *is* The Game. This is the funhouse. We go in there, we die. The whole place is wired with traps.'

'*Oui*, I see Macaulay Culkin in there now, putting Micro Machines on the floor.'

'Oh, you'll be first, pal, then we'll see if you're laughing.'

'You're wrong,' Maggie says. 'Don't you smell the smoke? There's a glow in the downstairs windows too. Somebody's home.'

This jolts Linda like an exposed wire. 'Where? I can't see anything.'

'It's faint. Embers, maybe. There's a boat on the water too. See it?'

Linda does, but only once Maggie has physically pointed.

From here it's just a white shape, floating like a rock in space or a ghost in a void. Linda's fists tremble and clench.

'So far out,' Noah says. 'Somebody is onboard?'

'Probably not,' Maggie admits, 'but it could explain how they got here. I'm surprised it hasn't been winterised and shored. Must be anchored out where the water is deeper, and then the sailor rows to shore. There's a tarp down there. That'll be the rowboat.'

'What are you? In the navy?'

'Minnesotan, Brett. Land of ten thousand lakes.'

Even as they watch the boat, it moves slightly, and there's a huge cracking sound that makes them all jump.

'Ice on the surface,' Maggie mutters, but she doesn't sound so sure.

'How do we get down?' Linda asks, fighting the urge to simply go off at a run.

'Over here ...' Maggie breaks off a little way to their left. 'Here's a path.'

It slopes thirty feet down to the shore, not wide enough for any car; it's the only way down, and the only way up again. Maggie takes a slow lead, cautiously navigating a route to the bottom, and the rest follow in a tight huddle.

'Wait!' Sarah stops, halting the procession, to state the obvious. 'It's late. Proper late, and we're in the middle of nowhere. What are we meant to do? Knock on the front door and say we've broken down?'

'British manners,' Noah says, shaking his head. 'We should break the window. Go in with force.'

'OK,' Sarah replies. 'And what if it's just another person like us, somebody looking for their child or their partner? It could be a frightened mum and her baby, or an elderly lady.'

'Could be,' Maggie agrees. ''Course, it could also be a guy with six of his buddies packing hunting rifles.'

'All the more reason not to rush this,' Sarah says. 'We should take some time to plan our next move.'

Linda peels her eyes away from the cottage long enough to study Sarah, who is now rubbing her own upper arms in a desperate grab for warmth. She looks a little different, somehow. There's still worry in her face, of course, but there's something else too. Is it courage? Cunning? That makes no sense. For all Sarah knows, Hannah could be inside this building ... So why does Linda get the impression that the mother is willingly stalling?

Moving mechanically, Linda unzips her coat, revealing the stab vest underneath. She takes the set of handcuffs from her kit belt. 'I have these.'

Noah recoils. 'You carry these around all the time, or did you bring them for us?'

'For whoever took my daughter.'

'This is crazy,' Sarah groans. 'You look like you're ready for a riot! Has it occurred to any of you that they might be trying to turn *us* into the monsters? If we burst in there now and restrain whoever's in there, then we're only repeating what's already been done to us.'

'So we take it slow,' Maggie says. 'Linda, you know cop-speak. Maybe you could get them to open up and let us inside.'

Not only does she know *cop-speak*, Linda is still carrying her expired ID, and though every bit of her internal processing is demanding she go in now, go in hard, she's willing to let the others help make this decision. It's important that they all play their part. Except, perhaps, for Sarah. Linda's mind goes back to the pint of beer that had been left behind, untouched, in the Gamekeeper's Inn – the drink that Sarah said she never liked – and what that could mean.

'I think it's worth mentioning,' Sarah says, 'that panicked people do irrational things, and if we start putting in windows and kicking through doors then this could blow way out of hand.'

'*Oui*, but if this *is* a criminal, and you cry "police", it could also go badly.'

'Maggie should go,' Brett says firmly. 'If there's somebody in there, they're more likely to open the door to a skinny white girl.'

'What?' Maggie chokes. 'No fucking way!'

'Nobody should go down there on their own,' Sarah says. 'As to whether we do this with manners or not, either the front door or … another way … I reckon we vote.'

'OK.' Noah holds out both fists and opens them one at a time, palms up, as if they hold physical choices. 'Polite. Not polite. Choose.'

Sarah and Maggie opt for the civil approach. Both men do the opposite.

All four look to Linda.

All she wants is Alyssa. The answers are near now, but everything – *everything* – may hang on this decision. It could be life or death. Pressure strangles her organs.

'All right,' Linda says. 'OK.'

She takes another incredibly cold breath, and with it she casts the deciding vote to meet Player Six, and end this once and for all.

51

PLAYER SIX

In the mornings he fries himself breakfast in the compact kitchen that constitutes a galley.

On open water, in the middle of December, hot food is a wise investment. He's gaining weight from the oils, which is a good thing; he feels better for it.

He starts his days by scouting the horizon to make sure he hasn't blown into a shipping lane overnight, and then he eats in either the wheelhouse, dressed in a sweatshirt, or out on the deck, dressed in two sweatshirts, a parka and a hat. Outside, he has to eat his breakfast wearing gloves. If he didn't, he might lose his hands to the cold. He has grown a beard; it's thick, rusty and all his own. His hair used to grow fast, and then he had no hair, and now it grows fast again.

He crosses the English Channel and berths overnight in Devon, where he picks up more food, kerosene for the heater, a bumper book of puzzles and a Clancy paperback. Until this year, he'd never read a novel. The hobby was recommended by his doctor, and he must admit that he finds it relaxing; he only wishes he'd started doing it sooner. He's forty-two years old. His twenty-nine-foot boat is the same age. That's why he named her Kismet.

From Devon, it's almost six hundred nautical miles home, and the British coastline is practically deserted this close to Christmas.

He steers under sail, cruising at around five or six knots, and sometimes hours pass without him seeing another vessel. When the sun breaks through the clouds the days are bright, beautiful and crisp. For one memorable stretch of the west coast he's joined by a group of mischievous seals – that night he reads in a textbook that their collective noun is a *bob*, which makes him laugh – and they play with one another like puppies, chasing, splashing and barking; he never would've believed this if he hadn't seen it for himself. It's stunning.

On the shortest day of the year, he reaches Scotland.

He anchors up in the loch, drains the onboard taps and freshwater tank, turns off the seacocks and removes all the fabrics he can; he's only planning on staying for a few weeks, but Scottish temperatures can fluctuate spectacularly, and these are the most aggressive weeks of the year for doing so. He unloads the dinghy and oars the rest of the way to the shore. His shore. His own private stretch.

As usual, Malcolm and Mhàiri, the local caretaker and his wife, have done a good job of scrubbing up the cottage ahead of his return, and they've stocked it with enough food and firewood to last him the better part of a month. They've managed to air the worst of the damp out of the place, and they've distributed jars of scented oils and reed diffusers to mask the lingering odour, but it never goes away. Not entirely. The ancient walls are porous stone and the windows are timber-framed and single-paned – all except for the recently installed floor-to-ceiling bifolds overlooking the water from the kitchen end – so the place is susceptible to draughts, mice and creeping patches of black mould. Malcolm and Mhàiri have also, he discovers, erected a Christmas tree for him. It's simple enough, dressed in a single string of lights and a dozen red baubles, but it makes him smile. He wishes he'd sent them a card and makes a mental note to leave a bigger tip behind next time he leaves.

On Christmas Day, he defrosts Mhàiri's homecooked turkey dinner and video calls his mother at the care home in New Jersey; four times she refers to him by the name of the long dead father he never knew. On New Year's Day he drinks port by the roaring fire and watches *The Great Escape* on his projector; he's too young to have seen it at the cinema, but his home system is close enough. For most of the festive period, he charts his upcoming course.

He's owned the cottage for almost two years, ever since emigrating across the Atlantic, and has used it as a base from which to sail a considerable slice of the Western world. Still, he hasn't yet explored the most northern reaches of his newly adopted home nation. As soon as the weather improves, he intends to rectify this.

He posts a semi-regular video diary online, chronicling his adventures, and tells his followers that – unless the weather turns fantastic before then and he simply cannot wait – he plans on setting off on the first day of February.

He consults fellow sailors on message boards, using his boat's name as a handle. He studies maps of shipping lanes and trade winds, easterlies and westerlies, and he plots a course north to the Outer Hebrides, around to Stornoway, and then on to the higher latitudes: the Faroes, Orkney and the Shetlands; whale country. It'll be difficult going – Scotland sits in the track of Atlantic weather systems that range from dank to deadly, and its waters can turn treacherous even in the finer seasons – but he can't afford to wait for summer. He doesn't have forever.

He does consider leaving in the first week of January, ignoring both his own plans and the warnings on the message boards, but wakes up to find himself snowed in. The following week, he's fogbound. So he watches films and reads. He works out until he gets tired, which doesn't take long, and then meditates. He takes his clubs up onto the rockface behind the cottage and whacks golf balls into oblivion. It's a quiet, solitary life. Peaceful. He hasn't quite *found Jesus*, not by a long shot, but he keeps to himself, and he tries not to be a bother. Life is good, but life is short.

*

Either very late on a Tuesday or very early on a Wednesday in the latter half of the month, he is woken by the security lights outside the huge bifolds. Deer occasionally trip the sensors, and he often sleeps by the fireplace downstairs, in the warmest area of the cottage. He doesn't care if this leaves him on show; the water is usually empty, the closest neighbour is a mile away, and it's a little late in his life for shyness.

He rolls over on the sofa, pulling the goose-down duvet higher over his face.

Then, as he's drifting off again, there comes a sound no deer has ever produced.

At first, he thinks he must be dreaming. But he isn't.

It's the middle of a cold night in January, and somebody is out here, in the middle of nowhere, knocking on his front door.

ENDGAME

ENDGAME

52

PREGAME

Princess Grace! Casino de Monte-Carlo! Supercars, super-yachts, super-everything!

This was Monaco, and it was beautiful. Beyond beautiful. Glitch was in love with the place. She felt like her chest was about to burst.

They were gathered on the world-famous marina, waiting for a smaller powerboat to taxi them out to their destination on the sparkling blue, where yachts boasted helipads and swimming pools on decks the length of small streets. Lola, their host, announced that she would soon be leaving the girls, and everybody groaned; they were all beyond tipsy by then.

'I'm sorry!' Lola said, showing her bottom lip, then she read from a prepared script filled with bullet-pointed information. 'Before you go, I must first explain some of the rules of The Game. Since this is an exclusive pilot for a future project ... what you ladies might know better as a *beta test*,' – some brief hollers – 'there are stipulations on what you should be sharing. This is going to become the biggest social media event of the year, a defining moment for the online scenes you are helping to build, but it all comes down to you guys. You are the marketing. Everything you share, you should be tagging The Game, OK? Hashtagging The Game. We want luxury, but this should not include the use of drugs. On camera.'

Something about that momentary pause, what on paper might've been nothing but a full stop, caught Glitch's attention. Lola went on.

'From the moment you arrive on the boat, you will be streamed almost constantly. Your every move is being monitored. What you are selling to your followers is a dream. *The dream.*' With a wave of her hand, she gestured to the scenes around them.

'But ...' This was LOL-eater, two million followers on TikTok. 'What *is* The Game?'

Lola paused. Her face turned into something Glitch would return to in her mind throughout the following hours; it was something between a frown and a total blank, like an actor who has forgotten her lines on opening night at the National Theatre.

'It's the biggest social media event of the year,' she said, returning to her trusty script. 'It's the dream.'

'No, I get that. But what *is* The Game? What will it consist of?'

The following pause lasted longer. Apparently, their host didn't know.

53

PLAYER ONE

Security lamps burst into light, bathing the approaching intruders – Linda, flanked by Noah and Brett – in dazzling white. The three of them halt, looking from a distance like jailbreak convicts beneath a roaming searchlight, and then Linda mumbles something to her escorts and they continue towards the door, feet crunching over shingles.

Maggie is watching from what she guesses is the boundary of the cottage's grounds on this stretch of beach. The beams of the security lamps don't quite reach her, so she's probably more or less correct. Sarah is standing with her. Brett had, naturally, wanted to stay back here, but it was unanimously agreed that, out of the entire group, he looked the most like a plain-clothes cop and he soon relented. Linda had really seemed to want the two men at her side. Maggie doesn't blame her. She's a tough customer, old Linda, but she's clearly getting on in years.

Their vague plan, which they'd thrown together in approximately half a minute, is for Linda to use whatever cop-wiles she still possesses to gain peaceful access to the property. Then, when the situation has been deemed civil and secure, they will calmly ask Maggie and Sarah to join them. Then they'll get their answers. If it's some kind of trap, Noah had said, then it's best for a couple of their group to remain at a safe distance. Hence the two ladies watching from the beach. It's only now though, as the first rally of formal knocks lands upon the door, that Maggie realises two of these three trespassers had actually voted for the more violent approach. She's suddenly glad that Linda is with the boys, lest they try to turn this into some raiding party.

Out here the knocking is loud. As far as Maggie can see there's nothing else around, although beneath the glare of the modern floodlamps the cottage at least looks less dilapidated than it had without light. It's still creepy, but more eccentric-wealthy-loner-creepy than inbred-wilderness-cannibal-creepy. Plus, it's so damn *cold* here. It isn't like the dry freezes of her home, which reach much, much lower temperatures, but rather a wet, soggy chill that penetrates the organs.

The loch frightens her too. She has always seen the fabled Nessie as something comical – *two big old humps and then you never see him again, LOL* – and this expanse of water might not be the Ness itself, but right now a monster lurking in that primordial tar doesn't seem very amusing at all … It doesn't seem so unbelievable, either.

'Who's there?'

A man's voice. It comes through a speaker, another surprisingly contemporary touch, installed in the external doorframe of the cottage. The voice is wary. Gravelly, but not Scottish. It's American. Something about it makes Maggie's toes curl in her sneakers, her thighs involuntarily clamp together, and distant alarm bells begin to ring inside her head.

Far away, Linda talks. 'Good evening. My name is Detective Inspector Malone, Major Crimes. I'm sorry to bother you at this time, but we're investigating a serious assault in the area and I wondered if we could ask you a few questions, Mr ...?'

A good performance, Maggie thinks, and surely anybody would open their door for it.

Except the man doesn't. 'You're not in uniform.'

'At Major Crimes we aren't required to wear the standard kit, sir.'

A pause. A long one.

'There's a camera embedded in the doorbell you didn't use. Hold your identification up to it please.'

Maggie watches, alarm bells loudening, as Linda holds something up to the lens.

A few seconds pass, and just when Maggie is sure that the locks won't turn, they do, and the door opens slightly. It doesn't open far enough for Maggie to see inside the building, not clearly, not with the trio hunched together on the doorstep, but what she *does* see reflecting the white of the security lamps is the golf club in the homeowner's hands.

What she sees next, and somehow senses, even from here, is the physical transformation of Linda. The woman's shoulders tense up and her feet shift slightly, widening into a fighter's offensive stance, and she expertly butts the top half of her body into wood and the door bursts inwards, revealing the figure of a man standing in those shadows the security lights don't touch. Noah reaches into his own coat as if about to pull a weapon, but there's a hideous *thwack*, followed by a deadweight thump, and he's suddenly on the ground inside

343

the cottage's entrance and Maggie is somehow pelting, without thinking, towards the chaos.

When she gets close enough, she sees with a sickening lurch that Noah isn't moving; the bearded man in the doorway is standing over him, still an indistinct outline, looking like a deranged samurai; he's arching his golf club for another swing, silk dressing gown billowing around him like a kimono. This is when Linda goes nuclear. The ID is gone from her hand, and she's now armed with one of those retractable police batons, the sort that can easily reduce a breezeblock to dust, and she's using it to whale on the stranger in a frenzy. By the time Maggie gets to the cottage, leaping over Noah in the entrance, the golf club has already gone spinning across the floor and the now-unarmed bearded man is lying huddled, foetal, with Brett's shoes and Linda's truncheon raining down upon him.

The scene is berserk, the man screaming.

'What are you *doing*?' Maggie cries, trying in vain to shove Brett aside before he inadvertently stomps the man to death, not daring to get too close to Linda's reckless animal swings. They don't know this person. For all they know, Player Six really *has* lost somebody close to him, and yet they're tearing him to pieces. They're going to kill him. Maggie looks at her fellow players, and she sees only savage, broken monsters. If the allocation of numbers had been different, if *Maggie* had been Player Six instead of One, would she have opened her door to this same treatment?

She thinks of Jackson; imagines him watching this scene …

The battering stops just long enough for Linda to roughly plant one knee into the man's lower back, causing him to cry

344

out again, and she cuffs his left wrist. Looking up, her eyes wide and hectic, Linda screams, 'Over there! Get him to the staircase!'

Maggie turns. 'Where?'

'The stairs, you stupid cow!'

Even through everything, this stings Maggie. She reaches out, palming the nearest light switch, and it illuminates wall lamps in an open-plan living space with exposed timber beams. The staircase is cast iron; it spirals down to land about eighteen feet away, and Brett is already helping Linda slide the man towards it across his own varnished floorboards.

Feeling disorientated, Maggie spins around to find that Sarah has entered the building. She's staring down at Noah, and her face is deathly white. There's a pool of blood around Noah's black hair, and the pool is spreading.

Sarah utters two words, 'Oh no,' and faints, unconscious, against the wall.

Maggie pulls at her own hair with both hands – 'Fuck!' – and closes the front door, shutting them all inside; it's all she can think to do. When she turns back, she sees that the homeowner has been thrown against his staircase, on his knees now with his arms raised over his head, and Brett is pinning him in place while Linda cuffs him to the iron balustrade. Once he's secure, Linda tells Brett to go upstairs and make sure there's no one else in the building. Without bothering to check on Noah or Sarah, Brett arms himself with the man's dropped club and begins to ascend the stairs.

Maggie looks desperately around her for any sign, any clue, any *hint* of The Game. She sees a gigantic pair of stag's antlers mounted on red brick above embers in a log stove. A table papered with fishing charts, a paperback novel and a book on whale spotting. There's a pile of Blu-Rays by a projector, which faces a screen that's currently rolled up and fixed tastelessly to one of the overhead beams. An untidy but stylishly restored kitchen area, complete with range cooker, on the other side of the open-plan space.

No collection of burner phones though. No hi-tech monitors. Crucially, no children.

Maggie is still searching when something catches her right ear, bringing with it a hot flash of pain, and she's astounded to discover that Linda has actually clipped her with the precision of a scolding grandmother. She clutches her ear, wincing. 'What the hell?'

'Pass me a pillowcase!'

Maggie shakily grabs the closest cushion from a mismatched scattering on the sofa – wondering just when, why and how this situation descended into Linda's dictatorship – and slips off the white cotton cover.

'Quickly,' Linda snaps, 'over his head!'

The man has been mostly groggy since his beating, but as Maggie approaches, he begins to thrash his head from side to side, desperate to avoid the cotton sack. 'No! No, wait! Don't do it!'

'*Do it!*' Linda roars.

'No, please!'

Maggie spreads the open end wide above his head. 'I'm … I'm sorry.'

He looks up at her before the darkness engulfs him. He's hanging like Jesus Christ in a silk Hugh Heffner robe, confused, angry and in so much pain. 'Please.'

Maggie starts to lower the hood, wincing, and then a realisation hits her like a wrecking ball, and her body seizes up. For an impossible time, she stares into the man's bulging eyeballs.

She wants to scream. She *needs* to scream. But she can't. Her chest has locked up.

Her hands finish the job for her. They pull the hood down over his face, swallowing his features, and then Maggie's feet carry her backwards until she bumps into the sofa and falls onto the duvet laid out there.

She stares at the man with her jaw unhinged. She stares because she knows him.

She stares because the man handcuffed to the banister with his arms above his head, hanging like a pagan sacrifice ready for burning, is Jackson Taylor's biological father.

54

PLAYER TWO

Brett pads along the upstairs landing with the nine iron hooked over his right shoulder.

Linda told him to look for anyone else who might be in the cottage. She didn't say what he should do if he happens to find someone. And just when did she start running the show, anyway?

Of course, if there are more people in the building then they would've heard the commotion downstairs, and Brett will hardly have the jump on them now. Quite the opposite. He starts to tell himself, as he reaches the first door, that there could be somebody with a cocked shotgun waiting on the other side … but he doesn't really believe that. Perhaps for the first time in his life, he isn't afraid. It's liberating. Exhilarating. Overdue.

And what if I find a kid hiding in a closet?

He weighs the golf club in his hands. Best not to think about it.

His adrenaline is still pumping, his limbs quivering with it. He's aching and he might have pulled a muscle, but it doesn't hurt in the ordinary way. He reflects on his actions at the front door and feels a shiver around his testicles.

He's binged most of those drawn-out documentaries on Netflix, all the overhyped murder mysteries, and they always include at least one of the following hackneyed lines:

I saw red.

I just snapped.

I lost my mind.

Well, Brett can now empathise with those basic sentiments, because – in the seconds surrounding Linda's first blows – something really had come rushing over him. He was furious about what they'd done to Craig, sure, but it went further than that. If Brett's entire history was stored up in a bottle, then the bottle had just shattered. It had shattered in somebody's face, and the genie inside turned out to be wrathful.

He doesn't even feel guilty. He only has to remind himself that he wouldn't be here if he hadn't been forced. Violence begets more violence, as his preacher used to say.

The rooms upstairs are nice – certainly nicer than he would've guessed when he was looking at the cottage from a distance in the dark – but it's obvious that this is no family home. The master bedroom is neat enough, but masculine. No wife. Probably no ex-wife either. The second bedroom has been turned into your basic home gym. And the *third* …

As he flicks on the ceiling light, a peculiar sense of recognition comes over Brett. He *knows* this room. Not exactly, not literally, but there are elements here of a world he understands. A desk with three computer monitors. Shelves stacked with top-of-the-line recording, lighting and editing equipment. It's the home office version of his own workspace, and thousands of other workstations like it.

No games though.

No cartridges for Atari, Sega or Nintendo. No pool table or chess set. Not even a board game in sight.

As far as The Game is concerned, this is obviously a dead-end.

As Brett kills the light behind him, and continues along the landing towards the bathroom, he hums under his breath.

He keeps on humming until he walks into the bathroom, an area where perhaps the stone walls aren't quite so thick, and there's enough phone reception here for him to receive The Game's final instructions.

55

PLAYER THREE

As she comes back to the world, swimming through grey fog, Sarah thinks she can see Hannah leaning over her like she had in their kitchen on Monday afternoon, a lifetime ago.

Mummy poorly?

Then her vision clears enough for her to make out Maggie's features, and her heart sinks. Still here, then. Still in this awful mess.

Maggie, at least, looks relieved. 'Can you hear me, Sarah? Are you OK?'

'I'm all right.' She sits upright, running clammy hands over her own even clammier face. 'It's blood. I have a – a sort of phobia.'

'You scared me pretty badly.'

She clearly means it, because in the short time since Sarah fainted, Maggie's face has turned several shades paler and she looks, even by tonight's standards, like the victim of some inconceivable trauma. Sarah remembers the ugly scenes at the doorway, and she understands how she must be feeling.

'How long was I …?'

'Couple of minutes. You always faint?'

'Started after the first … The first time we lost … You know … You lose a lot of blood.'

'PTSD.' This is Linda, who's standing some distance behind Maggie. 'You'd be surprised by the ways it can affect you.'

Sarah laughs coldly. 'Yeah? After this, I think we're all going to be …' She stops talking. She has only just looked past Linda and seen the shape, handcuffed and groaning, at the foot of the spiral staircase. 'Oh no. What have we done?'

Maggie avoids her eye, colour mounting in her pallid cheeks like faint sunburn on a corpse. 'We need answers,' she whispers, not very convincingly. 'Jackson's life is at stake. Hannah's too.'

Sarah looks at Linda, whose face has returned to that absolute blank from earlier in the evening. 'Innocent until proven guilty. Isn't that what you used to live by?'

Linda simply turns her back on her. As if she's nothing. As if she isn't grieving too. As if her say in the matter is now void. This turning around – which is such a simple, rude gesture – tells Sarah that, as far as Linda is concerned, the time for compassion, and for sanity, is coming to an end. And this scares the living shit out of her.

'We need to move Noah,' Maggie says quietly. 'There's a position, isn't there? Semi-prone or something?'

'The recovery position, but I don't know if it's any good for head injuries.'

Maggie hesitates, biting her lower lip. 'There's blood but, do you think you could … I mean, can you help?'

Sarah inhales, huge and slow. 'Maybe. I'm usually better the second time. It's the shock that hits me hardest.'

'Will it help if I get you some water?'

'It might.'

Maggie nods, places a reassuring hand on Sarah's shoulder, then crosses the room towards the kitchen area, choosing a path on the opposite side of the sofa to where Linda is looming over the shackled man, who's now alternating between coughing and moaning incoherently.

Sarah begins to turn towards Noah, bracing herself, and hears a cruel, scornful voice coming from behind her, not in physical space but in time.

'*For Christ's sake, Sarah, you're thirty-seven years old. What if something happened to one of the kids? Would you fall on your arse then?*'

She cringes and is overcome by an overwhelming urge to burst into tears.

Because she had, hadn't she. She'd opened the back door, and she'd seen the blood around Duke, her first adopted dependant, and she'd fallen on her fat arse. Just as predicted.

'*Mummy just needs to be more careful, doesn't she?*' Neil had said. '*Tell her she's a naughty mummy.*'

That had hurt at the time, after she'd fainted over a mere scratch, and it all but kills her now. Neil may have been proven correct, but that doesn't make him right.

She wonders where he is now. Hours have passed since her phone call from the service station. Greater Manchester Police should be combing the entire city. There might be a team at the Gamekeeper's Inn, studying surveillance footage and questioning the staff. Linda and Noah's vehicles, which Sarah recalls being left in the car park, may have already been traced. Motorway cameras could have tracked the Corsa's route after leaving the service station.

Tracked it north. But how far?

Unless Neil didn't hear. Phones are a nightmare. Signal drops. Voices dip. Sometimes audio cuts out completely.

She can't allow herself to believe that.

She isn't going to win this game. She knows that now. What happened at the front door, and what is still happening all around her, is proof enough of that. Her only chance now lies with the authorities, and with her husband; if they can get to Hannah first, then they disarm The Game. What happens to Sarah after that is inconsequential. Hannah must be found before The Game is over.

The problem is that no one knows when or how it will end. Nobody really knows what The Game is. All that Sarah can do is try to buy time, slow things down and stop this from going even further off the rails.

Because there's a smell in the air. It's sort of like the thick, copper musk of a menstrual flow, only it's not really here at all. Perhaps it's more of a feeling than an odour. Whatever it is, the ancient, animal part of Sarah recognises it. It's bloodlust, and it's getting stronger.

She drinks the water Maggie brings her, and then she places the glass onto the floorboards and turns to the French heap beside her. If Maggie is pasty, then Noah is close to transparent. His eyes are eerily open, but only the whites are visible. The wound behind his left temple has started to coagulate, giving his hair a sticky, matted look, but the spilled blood is still enough to bring the water rushing back up Sarah's throat and it takes all her willpower to keep from throwing it straight back up. With a huge effort, she helps to roll him off his back – feeling the incredible, unsettling chill of his body – and then she leaves Maggie tending to him while she staggers for the sofa opposite the prisoner to regain her composure.

As she takes her seat, Brett comes down the staircase holding a golf club in one hand and his phone in the other. He looks expectantly from woman to woman, then shakes his phone pointedly. 'Well? What's it supposed to mean?'

'Shit.' Linda clicks first and gets out her own phone. 'I haven't got signal here.'

Neither, it turns out, have Sarah or Maggie.

'Wi-Fi,' Sarah says, panicking now, feeling as if she's had her ability to see or hear suddenly stolen away from her. 'Is there Wi-Fi?'

'There's a router by the projector,' Linda says, marching for it.

'And what's the message say?' Sarah asks.

Brett laughs hollowly and shrugs. '*Play The Game*.'

'And?'

'And nothing. That's all there is. Play The Game.'

Sarah shakes her head. 'There has to be more. That can't b—'

'*Who are you people?*'

Sarah gags on her own last word, slamming her hands over her mouth, and shrinks back in her seat. The words came from inside the cushion case. That rasping American voice.

Brett flicks a lizard tongue over his lips. 'Who are *you*?'

The man coughs, speckling his makeshift hood with red dots. 'You cocksuckers come to my home in the middle of the night. You beat the fuck out of me. Chain me up like some dog. And you're asking who I am?'

Linda, who had been copying something into her phone

from the underside of the internet router, turns her blank eyes on Brett. 'Use the club. The joints work best. Knees and elbows.'

Sarah cries out, '*What!*' but Brett is already drawing back the club, taking aim. '*Don't!*'

He does. Only, at the last second, he alters his swing to instead clang it off the iron banister with a reverberation so piercing that the man yelps, 'Paul! Paul Benishek! Fuck!'

Brett freezes. His shoulders slacken and he almost drops the club. Sarah, who had herself been cringing, sees it as clear as day: the dawning horror on Brett's face; the unmistakable look of recognition.

He knows him. He didn't recognise him in the dark of the doorway, but he knows him.

She opens her mouth to say so, but she never gets the chance.

'Guys …' Maggie's voice, very hushed, from across the room. 'Guys!'

'What?' Linda snaps, her eyes also trained on Brett's face.

But Sarah knows what. As soon as she turns to look at the young American girl, she knows. The expression on Maggie's face is one she has seen time and time again. She had first seen it on the sonographer who had gone on to haunt her dreams, the one who never found a heartbeat. It's an expression that makes Sarah's muscles go loose.

'It's Noah,' Maggie whispers, looking down at the congealed blood on her own hands as she inexpertly presses two fingers to the side of his neck. 'Noah's dead.'

56

SOFIA

Sofia pictures her perfect wedding, while she is waiting to be raped.

This, she decided many hours ago, is the inevitable conclusion.

Not her wedding. Her sexual assault. Her rape.

These men she doesn't know, men she has never bore an ounce of ill sentiment towards, are going to hurt her in the vilest way imaginable. And then they may kill her. Put an end to her whole universe. She will die more than one thousand five hundred miles away from her family in Estonia, and she doesn't know why. Hasn't a clue. But life, or rather death, is cruel sometimes. Cruel and senseless. Twenty-five years have been enough for her to have learned that much already.

For the first many hours – impossible to know just how many in here – she had been unable to keep her imagination in check. She wondered how they would do it. Whether they'd cut her. Beat her. How creative they might be. The first time they'd entered the room, which must've been around dawn, Sofia's bladder had given out. One of the men had laughed. It was an honest laugh, the sort you might hear from a kid after a loud fart, and it had made her cry with shame.

They're West Africans, she thinks. Ghanaian or Liberian maybe. There are three of them. They speak in their native language, they dress in the sort of ragged hand-me-downs Sofia sees on the refugees who tent in the city centre, and there's a sense of desperation about them. They never cover their scarred faces though, and that quietly terrifies her. It's as if they're already confident that she won't ever get the chance to describe them. It's like there'll never be an *after this*. Not for her.

The first time she slept in this place, she'd dreamed of the rat-catcher.

Back in Tallinn, their building had been full of rodents, but it wasn't the rats Sofia had been afraid of; it was the rat-catcher. He was a fat man with dirty overalls and wandering, hungry eyes. He put down poison, and he put down traps. Sometimes the mice would survive the snap, and Sofia would find them in the morning, pinned to the board but still wriggling, mewling with their backs broken and their insides hanging out in purple spools. Because of this, Sofia invested in a more humane live trap, essentially a plastic tunnel that she loaded with peanuts. When the mouse went inside, the door would close gently behind it so it could be released far away the following morning.

The design worked perfectly, and the mice were physically unharmed … but they were dead every time. There was no damage Sofia could see, no trauma. Eventually, after this had happened six or seven times, she got up enough courage to ask the rat-catcher what was going wrong.

'What you are doing is cruel,' he told her. 'Trapped mice die of fear.'

This is what he'd returned to tell her in her dream. *Trapped mice die of fear.*

She has slept a lot since then. Now when she sleeps, she dreams of Noah.

The men have involved him in this. She doesn't know why, and she doesn't know how they got to him, but she heard his voice tonight. Heard it through a loudspeaker. He sounded so afraid. So broken. She'd do anything to take that pain away from him. She's locked in a filthy apartment, waiting to be assaulted, but she still can't stand the thought of him being in danger. Whatever they're putting him through, she prays that he is safe.

She pictures their wedding. Only there's no Eiffel Tower. No terrace. No guests.

There is Noah, and the rest is unimportant.

He will come, she tells herself. *Noah will come for me.*

And as the hours pass, she tries her hardest to believe that.

57

PLAYER FIVE

Linda's head is really starting to hurt. This is all going wrong.

The French kid is dead. Sarah and Maggie are shellshocked, both of them now sitting on the sofa and about as useful as tits on a bull, while Brett is trying to get answers out of the illustrious Player Six.

They have all connected their phones to the Wi-Fi, hijacking it via the default password stickered on the router, and they've all received that same three-word message.

Play The Game.

Paul Benishek obviously isn't well, but he's surprisingly stubborn. Or just stupid. Whenever he coughs, which is more and more often, blood spatters onto the inside of his cotton hood. The result is a grim, burgundy Rorschach test that gets steadily more complicated. *What does this bloodstain look like to you, Ms Malone?*

'You've murdered a guy,' Brett says to Benishek. 'Split his head open with your golf club.'

'Self-defence, asshole. You broke in here. That shit ain't going to … to work on me.' Another hacking cough. More blood-spit. 'If it's cash you're after, then you're shit out of luck.'

'It isn't cash.'

'So who are you? What do you want from me?'

Brett takes a moment to consider, swinging the golf club like a pendulum at his side. 'We're strangers. Five strangers from across the world. We met for the first time today. We were sent a message to come here, to this cottage, tonight. We were told to come and find you, Paul.'

Benishek groans. 'Ah shit. Is this a religious thing? I don't know what peyote you morons have been eating, but there ain't no messiah here.' He coughs again, or perhaps it's a hoarse laugh, then moans at the pain it causes him. 'Only visitors I've had up here since I bought the place, and it turns out to be the fucking Manson family.'

Foolish, Linda thinks, for a man who is not just defenceless but crucified. His silk robe has opened further now, and his body is swelling and turning black with remarkable speed; she can actually see the bruises forming in real time as vessels bleed beneath his skin. The muscles of his chest and abdomen have a wasted, struggling look, as if they were once three times more defined but have shrivelled in a microwave. His white Calvin Klein briefs are visible, and the sight makes Linda feel bilious. When Brett looks to her and shrugs, she returns a stern nod.

Thus endorsed, Brett takes a deep breath and swings Benishek's own golf club into his elevated elbow, causing him

361

to bellow for a long, long time. The two women on the sofa bury their faces further into their hands. Linda feels nothing.

Brett cocks his head, adrenal sweat dripping from his hairline onto the lenses of his glasses. 'How do we play The Game, Paul?'

'What … *game*?'

'The Game! The Game! The reason we're here! How do we play it?'

'I don't … know what … you're talking about. How can I … possibly tell you how to play something … if you won't tell me … what the game *is*?'

Brett clangs the nine iron off the banister again, inches from the hooded skull, and Benishek cowers further.

'But you have the answer! We know you do, so why don't you stop playing—' Brett pauses, an abnormal, feverish expression on his face, and laughs. 'Why don't you stop *playing games*?'

Benishek's head flops forwards, the pillowcase turning from side to side as his breathing worsens; he's starting to sound like a toddler with croup.

Alyssa had several terrifying bouts of croup, Linda recalls flatly. Twice she ended up in hospital.

'I don't … I don't … know what …'

Brett doesn't even bother waiting for him to finish. 'Fine.' He bowls the club overarm into the staircase, then storms into the kitchen area. When he comes back, Linda's own adrenaline cranks up yet another notch, taking her further into dizzying heights she didn't know existed. Brett is carrying a very chic block of knives.

Sarah has looked up from her hands. Her face is all dismay. 'What's this?'

'Simple,' Brett replies, crouching to place the block of blades on the floorboards between them. 'Since Paul here doesn't know what we're talking about, we're going to have to invent our own game. This game is called … Everybody Take a Piece of Player Six. We all pick a knife each, drawing them out the block like we would straws, see?'

He flexes his fingers dramatically and then chooses a handle at random and slides it out, revealing a twelve-inch carver.

'Shit, maybe I've found my sport after all. So we each choose a knife blind, then we set ourselves a timer, because we're all used to timers by now. How long shall we say? Ten seconds each?'

Maggie is shaking her head. 'This isn't the way. This can't be the way.' She looks at Linda to intervene. Linda holds her gaze. A whisper from somewhere inside asks when she's going to step in and put a stop to this – the wheels are well and truly off now – but she only shoves it down deeper.

Either way, Brett doesn't have to go any further. The gambit pays off without a drop of blood being shed.

'*Wait!* I – I think I know what you want.'

Silently, the surrounding players share glances that are simultaneously relieved, bemused and afraid.

Maggie says, 'You do?'

'The p-pantry in the kitchen. Pull on the bottom shelf, pull hard, and the whole back wall will come away. There's a safe in there. 8008, that's the code. The Game's inside.'

'It's inside a safe?' Brett asks slowly. 'The Game?'

'I swear to God … You can play it on … the projector … if that's what you want. Just let me go … Please … I can't fucking breathe with this on my head.'

Linda doesn't move. She has no intention of releasing him

363

yet. 'This safe. It wouldn't be the kind with a false code that alerts the police, would it?'

'Christ, I … wish it was.'

She eyes him for a moment, weighing her distrust, then turns to Maggie and Sarah. 'One of you make yourself useful. Go and have a look.'

The expressions she gets back are ones of resentment, but Maggie goes to the pantry. Brett follows, carelessly dropping the knife into his coat pocket on the way. Linda looks at the block sitting upright on the floorboards, five assorted handles left sticking out of the top like that old Pop-up Pirate game Alyssa had loved when she was little.

From inside the small pantry, the sound of falling packets and rolling cans. Linda's mind goes back to the robbery at the Express Food and Wine, her local shop in Luton.

'Come on,' Benishek wheezes. 'Let me go … You don't understand … I'm sick … I'm fucking dying.'

Sarah glances desperately to Linda. Linda shakes her head.

From the kitchen area there come five distinct beeps, followed by a click.

Almost time now. Linda can feel it, and the feeling is a contradiction of relief and dread; it's like finally reaching a feather bed after an exhausting journey, knowing that sleep will bring nightmares beyond comprehension.

She joins Brett and Maggie at the pantry. Sarah follows.

The four of them stare into the safe, which is as tall as Linda. Sarah's voice, barely a squeak, breaks the quiet. 'What is this?'

At the very top of the safe is a satchel filled with money. 'No cash,' Linda grunts, and she tosses it aside so that it spills paper notes over the floor of the kitchen area.

The safe is otherwise filled with dozens, perhaps hundreds, of videotapes, DVDs and memory sticks. They all share a home-made look; plain black cases catalogued by silver marker pen on the spines.

A long, pitiful whimpering noise comes out of Brett's throat. He reaches into the safe and, with slow, shaking hands, slides a rectangle of sleek black plastic out from the stacks. It's smaller than the DVD cases, and it has a single umbilical cord of cable that ends in a USB.

'External hard drive,' he utters, holding it up so they can all read the two words written across it.

THE GAME.

'Play it,' Sarah whispers, sounding numb. 'It's what they've been telling us to do since the very first message. *To save them, you must play The Game.*'

'The projector,' Linda agrees. 'Can you get it to work?'

Brett nods, leading Sarah away. Maggie, however, remains in her place. She reaches into the pile and chooses a single DVD. Then she just holds it tightly in both hands, staring at it as if it's the missing piece of a puzzle she doesn't want to ever see completed.

Over her shoulder, Linda gets a look at the case.

Silver handwriting: KAREN, MN.

It's dated, and the date is around nine years ago.

'What is it?' Linda asks.

'It's nothing,' Maggie says, but she slips the DVD into the front pocket of her hoody when she walks away.

She does this because, clearly, she is lying.

58

PLAYER ONE

'Do you think I could model?'

Maggie had returned to the front passenger seat and dropped the sun visor. She was studying herself in the vanity mirror, raking errant strands of blonde that were stuck to the sweat on her face. Her cheeks were rosy pink, and she liked it. She was indifferent about the sex itself, but she always liked that flushed look. That was probably how rouge was invented.

Zack was still on the backseat with his jeans around his ankles. He lit a pre-rolled joint, held the first chestful of smoke for a while, then exhaled. 'Uh-huh.'

Maggie pouted, cocking her face to the left and then the right. 'An agency messaged me on Instagram, you know.'

'No shit?' Zack passed her the joint.

'Yep. They tour the States looking for models, and they'll be in Minneapolis next weekend. It's good money for a one-off shoot. What do you think?'

Zack arched his back to pull up his pants and fasten his belt. 'What do I think about what?'

She blew smoke out the window. 'Should I try it?'

'Oh. I don't know, Dawson. You're smoking hot and all, but a model? Those bitches are bare tall. I mean, pornos, maybe,' he reached from the backseat and squeezed her right breast, '*if* you had a bigger rack.'

She smacked his hand away and slammed the sun visor shut. 'Fuck you!'

'I'm being serious, I think they have like a height limit or something.'

'So *porn?*'

He shrugged, grinning, but there was something in his eyes. He waited two seconds before he answered. Time enough to know what he was saying. Long enough to make it sting. 'Anyone with Instagram can call themselves a model, but real, *paid* models are sort of… classy, right? Glamorous. I'm not saying you're poor or nothing, your mom and dad have got that sweet lake house, but it's the way you carry yourself. Shit, Dawson, no offence, but compared to legit models, you're about half a step away from being white trash.'

Hurt, humiliated, furious, the next thing she knew she was slamming the car door.

'Ah, come on! I was only kidding! What are you going to do, walk home?'

She took several steps, her midriff tight with rage, then went back and threw the joint in through the open window.

'Hey, what the fuck! You burned my mom's seat!'

She thundered away without looking back. It was a sweltering July in Minneapolis, and Maggie was sixteen years old.

*

The name of the agency was Roar Talent Casting. They put Maggie in touch with a former client who video called her the following Friday. It was a good company to work for, the gorgeous girl from Nebraska told her. Above board. The real deal.

'They'll most likely hire a penthouse apartment,' Miss Nebraska said, filing her nails onscreen, 'that's what they did for me. The place was the bomb. You'll be paid two thousand dollars for a one-hour photoshoot.'

'I'm sorry.' Maggie moved closer to the camera. 'Did you say two *thousand* dollars?'

Nebraska laughed. 'That's what I said, honey. Cash.'

A thousand bucks an hour. How was that for legit? Glamorous enough for baby-dick Zack Peterson, maybe?

'Oh,' Nebraska said, 'obviously you'll need your ID to prove you're over eighteen. Don't forget that.'

In the corner of the video call, Maggie saw her own face drop. There was a moment of near silence in which she could hear groaning from the next room. Her sister Karen, home sick from college.

'You still there, hon? I think the connection's dropping.'

'I'm still here,' Maggie said slowly, listening to her sister through the wall. And then the idea came to her. 'I'll have my ID. Don't worry about it. No sweat.'

'Super!'

The next day, dolled up and dressed in her tallest heels, Maggie took a taxi to a hotel downtown. She met the director of the shoot, who told her that the penthouse suite was unfortunately booked out, but he'd managed to get a room. This, Maggie later thought, should've stirred the first disquiet inside her. A hotel room, after all, is just a bedroom.

The director introduced himself as Andy. Years later, Maggie would learn his actual name through court documents. Paul Benishek was in his thirties then, fairly handsome with the sort of muscles that come from two daily hours at the gym. He was dressed in a pristine white shirt, blue jeans and moccasins without socks, and he smelled strongly of cologne. He didn't have a beard. He was very polite, and he had a smile too perfect to be anything but veneers.

He led Maggie into the double room on the fourth floor with the Do Not Disturb sign hanging outside. The first thing she saw was the pile of cash on the bedside table. The second was the video camera. The third, which altered the whole mood, was the cocaine. Was coke a glamorous drug? She couldn't say, but when she heard the door click behind her, it sounded much too loud.

Andy – Benishek – gave a cursory glance over the ID card she'd brought along, then handed it back and smiled. 'Get comfortable, Karen. Help yourself to a line.'

There was only one armchair, and he sat in it. The coke was already racked up beside a rolled-up note on a small mirror. Rather chic. Not white trash whatsoever.

'Gee,' Maggie said, perching on the edge – the absolute limit – of the bed. 'A few puffs of weed, that's usually my limit.'

'Try it,' his smile was still there, but his eyes were fox-like. 'I've been shooting for years now, and I've found it really helps our models get into the zone.'

Her eyes moved briefly to the door, but she never went. Her body seemed unusually heavy, anchored, weighted to the spot. Unsure of what else to do, uneasy in the silence, she inexpertly snorted a line, shooting a blast of ice up into the space beneath her right eye, and immediately registered a cold numbness that was not unpleasant spreading over the lower half of her face. She gestured to the camera. 'It's a photoshoot, right? Two grand?'

'It's two thousand per photoshoot,' he agreed. '*Unfortunately*, Karen, I just don't see much room for another photoshoot in our portfolio right now. We're stocked up after Nebraska. Overstocked, if anything. We are, however, looking to expand our advanced shoots. These are a little more selective, but they pay four thousand dollars.' He squared up his index fingers and thumbs as if they were a viewfinder and studied her through them with one eye. 'I think you might be good looking enough to be considered.'

She rubbed a hand across her increasingly anesthetised lips. 'Four thousand dollars. What does that consist of?'

'First things first. It is *not* pornography. I can't stress that enough. It's erotica, and there's a big difference. Porn is the smut you see spread all over the web, but what we do is work with private collectors who are interested in a certain class of woman. Our material is never released in the United States, that's contractual, and the DVDs are digitally watermarked so they can't be uploaded onto the internet or screenshared.'

She looked at the money and it didn't look so tempting. The door, on the other hand, seemed much more appealing. So why did she feel like she couldn't walk out of there? Was she more afraid to get up and leave than she was to stay? Somehow it felt as if, even in a few short minutes, things had come too far to back out now.

She cleared her throat, aiming for a mature tone that would put her back in control of the situation. She was suddenly glad she'd done the coke; she suspected it was the only thing stopping her hands from shaking.

'What *exactly* would it consist of?'

'First, I'll offer you the money on camera, that's important. It's part of the narrative we're telling. You'll introduce yourself, following a sort of script we'll come up with together. Again, that's an important part of it.'

'And then?'

'And then we'll just keep the camera rolling and see what happens.'

Ten minutes and another four lines later, Maggie was gazing into the black hole of the camera's lens. She could see her reflection in there, but it was very far away. The cocaine had filled her head with electricity, and she felt like she could do anything. Almost anything. She felt alive. She felt like a million dollars. She felt classy.

'What's your name and where are you from, baby?'

'My name's Karen, and I'm from Minneapolis.'

'Minneapolis. Does that mean you're going to show us some of that Minnesota Nice today?'

She forced a smile, just like he'd told her to. 'I guess I am.'

*

She left with a thousand dollars cash. The rest, he told her, would be figured out once he'd subtracted the coke, the price of the room and the cost of editing time.

By then she barely cared. She hobbled out of the hotel with her face on fire, feeling the snide gazes of every clerk.

When she got home, she found her sister on the couch with

a microwavable heat pack clutched against her abdomen. Maggie got a heat pack of her own and held it tight against the unbearable aching below her belly. Sitting like that, side by side, watching old episodes of *Friends*. It was to be the last time Maggie ever sat in the same room as her big sister.

The video was online by the end of the month.

Zack Peterson played his part in spreading it through school but, in the grand scheme of things, those were comparatively small numbers.

Within twelve weeks Jackson's conception had racked up more than a million views across the globe.

59

PLAYER TWO

It was sunny outside, but it was gloomy in O'Brien's. It was always gloomy in O'Brien's. On the flatscreen TV, mounted high up in one corner, it was the seventh-inning stretch. The fans were singing 'Take Me Out to the Ballgame', but the atmosphere at Yankee Stadium looked a long way from upbeat. There was losing, and then there was losing to the Red Sox at home.

Craig sighed, slapping his Yankees cap onto the bar. 'Christ's cunt, what a shitshow.' The feed cut to a Burger King commercial, and Craig drank half of his beer in two large gulps. He belched. 'You take a look at this Benishek's work yet?'

From the neighbouring stool, Brett flashed Craig a glance, eyebrows raised in a *boy-oh-boy* expression, while he sipped his own drink. 'Oh yeah. I took a look all right.'

'And?' Craig scooped up a palmful of peanuts from the bowl and shoved them into his mouth. He spoke around them. 'What's the problem?'

'The problem?' Brett lowered his voice. 'It's fucking *porn*, Craig! I don't want to work in porn!'

Craig burst into laughter, showering the bar in his own brand of masticated peanut butter. He choked the peanuts down and continued to roar until he wept.

'They're not asking you to get your four-incher out on camera, dipshit!' Everybody in the bar looked over then, and Brett cringed. 'Besides, it's hardly *porn*-porn. This is the entertainment industry, pal. You've been bitching about getting your foot in the door since you graduated, right? I give you the open door, and you can't see past the bouncing titties.'

Keeping his voice lowered for the both of them, Brett said, 'How do you even know this guy?'

Craig shrugged. 'I know everybody worth knowing. Met him while you were off at college. Benishek, I'm telling you, he's going places. He's like a, whatchamacallit, intrepun …?'

'Entrepreneur.'

'Exactly. Guy's like Willy Wonka, everything he touches turns to gold. He's going to invent the next Myspace or some shit, just you wait.'

'The next Myspace, huh? From what I saw online, all his big ideas seem to involve women taking off their clothes.'

'And you don't want to work on that because …?' Craig shook his head at Brett, then rapped his considerable fist on the mahogany. 'Two more over here, Charlie!'

Brett finished his Bud. 'Did he actually tell you what the job consists of?'

'Sure! This titty game, that's just a stepping stone. No one's interested in that California, silicone shit no more. Benishek's seen a gap in the market on the East Coast, and he's going to exploit it for a while. He's already got a dozen domain names registered to some fucking island in the South Pacific, and a list of investors lined up from Montreal to Monaco. He tells me he wants an editor onboard to airbrush the material. Same as they do on these *Vogue* shoots or whatever. He says these chicks, you know, they do a lot of yakking on camera. A lot of bitching. I says I know how that goes. It'd be your job to edit that shit out. You'll never be on set. Working from home, no more fucking cube farms. And most importantly, you'll be in the game from the ground up. As far as I see it, there's only one major drawback to the deal.'

'Yeah? What's that?'

'You're going to have to learn to work with a raging boner.'

*

Brett had worked, without boner, for Benishek's fledgling company for a year. This was a decade ago, and he quit when the shower would no longer run hot enough to make him feel clean without scalding. Soon after that, he met Kelly, and he never saw those films again.

Not until he saw them at the bottom of the stack in a safe on the other side of the world.

As Brett loads the external hard drive onto the projector, he's overcome by a sense of understanding that's every bit as liberating as it is nauseating. That shitty job is the reason he's here in this cottage tonight. It's why Craig was taken. It might even be why the other four players were brought here, though he doesn't yet see the connection.

His head is spinning, and he's worried that his concept

of reason, and of what constitutes reasonable behaviour, is being eroded by stress. He keeps thinking about that very first message, the one he'd read on the subway to Manhattan.

There can only be one winner. And if you lose, your loved one will die.

He thinks he's beginning to understand. He knows what's contained in the safe, whereas none of the others do, and this might actually give him an advantage. He could win this thing ... If he has the balls, but he has to be certain.

Linda crosses the room to kill the wall lamps. Now it's only the white light of the projector illuminating the room, and everybody can see the single video file contained in the external hard drive.

Benishek is still wheezing, so Linda – to the noticeable surprise and fear of everyone else in the room – removes his bloody hood. Maggie and Sarah both stiffen, turning their faces away.

Linda returns to sitting on the bottom step of the stairs, behind Benishek, and when she speaks her voice is tense, teeth gritted, as if she's readying herself for a blow. 'Play it.'

Brett does.

The film is of a bunch of people on a boat. Tropical waters, possibly the Med. The deck is almost exclusively populated by what Brett thinks of, through his knowledge of the industry, as *e-girls*. Lots of brightly coloured hair and cutesy outfits.

A minute in, Sarah is shaking her head. 'I don't get it. What's th—'

Then a voice on the film, a voice they all now know – Benishek's voice – yells through the surround sound. '*What are you here to play?*'

And everybody onscreen yells in response, and when he hears it like that, with such jubilance, Brett can't help but shudder.

'*The Game!*'

60

PREGAME

The day is scorching, and the music is loud, but it doesn't really begin until one of the men yells into his microphone, 'What are you here to play?'

And everybody screams, '*The Game!*' and confetti cannons blast the air with colours that fall into the perfect water.

There are two men among the sixteen girls, filming and hosting on the deck, breaking off to occasionally edit the live stream from a bank of computers in the shade.

The main man – that's how Glitch thinks of him, because he seems to be in control – is relatively handsome with a perfect smile. Designer shades, designer clothes, an all-round designer man.

'The winner today,' he says, 'will go home with five thousand dollars cash!'

They all cheer.

'That's right, but there can only be one winner! Now, to make things easier for the fans at home, we're going to assign you numbers. Your name is the number I give you, OK?'

He points at random, assigning numbers as he lands.

'Player One! Player Two! Player Three …' Glitch is Player Seven. 'Lucky number seven,' he adds, giving her a cool smile before moving onto number eight.

By the time he gets to Player Sixteen, Glitch has lost interest in the numbering and she's dancing, the world around her a riot of movement and bright, shimmering colours. She feels as if she dances for hours, and maybe she does, because by the time she flops onto something comfortable she's thirstier than she's ever been in her life. She turns to the girl beside her on the seating and grins, delighted.

'Amy Choe!' she yells, then in a deep, serious voice, '*Infinitear.*'

Amy lowers her round shades to give her a wink, and her eyes are very black, as if the pupils are taking over.

'Hey, Valentine. What's cooking?'

'Your legs are. Bet the prize money your legs are!'

Amy looks momentarily puzzled, then gazes down in amazement. 'Man, I knew I was hot! Need to get out of these fucking stickly, prickly cacti legs.' She rubs her hands over own neck, collecting sweat from the tattoos there. 'I need a shower. Or a swim. You think there's sharks in the water?'

Overhearing this, a passing girl – *Fyrestarter* – joins her palms as if in prayer, raises them above her head like a dorsal fin then swims away singing the theme from *Jaws*. Amy and Glitch burst into wails of laughter.

When she has finally caught her breath, Glitch leans confidentially into Amy. 'I don't know about sharks, but you know what I *do* think?'

'What d'you think?'

'I don't think there *is* a game!'

'Whaaat?'

'I think they just wanted to create a buzz. I mean, that's all social media is, isn't it? We don't sell … anything!' She opens and closes her hands to show how empty they are, and the movement feels good through her muscles. 'There's no product. Nothing actually exists. *We* don't exist! *Infinitear* doesn't exist! *Glitch Valentine* doesn't exist! I think they got so wrapped up in the hype of The Game, they forgot to come up with The Game! What do you think of *that*?'

Amy stares at her, jaw slightly open and moving from side to side. 'I … think … that there's something wrong with the drinks on this—'

For Glitch, time does a peculiar thing then.

It skips, like a needle missing the groove on an old record player.

Like a sudden leap forward after a lag in a bad stream.

Like one of those things in a video game. A glitch.

And the next thing she knows, she is sitting on the edge of the boat, looking down into the water, and the water looks good.

Behind her, all around her, the man's voice through the microphone again. 'All right, Players! Let's have ourselves a bit of a warm-up. This part of the game is called Chicken, only it's not precisely Chicken as you know it. I'm going to assign you Players into pairs, and the *Chickens* are the first to stop making out!' He pauses, then adds. 'Oh, and extra points if we get to see some titties!'

Glitch sees two girls kissing with tongues. One, she sees with dismay, is Amy.

Another leap through time, and she's on her knees in

a strange little bathroom. It's sweltering in here and she needs a drink badly, but all the cocktails on deck aren't helping to quench her thirst. The drinks are somehow like the seawater in that old poem. *Water, water, everywhere* … The more she drinks, the thirstier she gets. She hasn't eaten all day, but her body is desperate to purge. The thought of food right now is somehow revolting.

And there must be a corridor outside, because fuzzy voices are coming through the door.

'What are you trying to pull up there?' the man, *the main man*, is asking.

'What?' A woman caught by surprise. Followed? Southern accent, but not Amy. 'I … I …'

'You're making an ass out of me!' The man's tone is very *off-camera*. 'You take your clothes off for money, but you're going to cry about showing some skin on *my* platform? Do you know how much money my investors have put into getting you here from that fucking swamp Tallahassee? I thought you were a professional.'

Tallahassee … Something clicks through the fog in Glitch's head. *Floorduh! Lisa … Simpson? No, stupid. Mayflower? Lisa Mayflower?*

'You're making me uncomfortable,' Lisa says quietly. 'I need to use the restroom.'

'You do that, and you have a think about why you're here. If you still don't want to participate, then that's fine. We'll settle up the money you owe us for the flights and accommodation, plus the limo and the drinks, then you can leave the boat and make your own way back home.'

'But … We're on the water …'

'You can swim, can't you?'

A pause. Around Glitch, the bathroom continues its relentless spin.

The man laughs hard. 'Hey, I'm joking! Lighten up. It's just a game.'

Another lag in time, and she's back on the deck. Something's happening. Something big.

The man is on his microphone. 'It's time to announce our first winner of the evening! Your fans have had a couple of hours to get to know you, and to place their bids, and it's my pleasure to announce the first winner of The Game!'

Glitch thinks this should be exciting, but somehow it isn't.

'Our first winner, with a bid of *five thousand euros*, is ... Player Twelve! Stand up, Player Twelve!'

Player Twelve is Infinitear. Amy Choe. She tries to stand up to receive her prize, but she can't quite do it on her own.

61

PLAYER THREE

Sarah doesn't like this.

Everybody in the film is having the best time. And yet, some-how, it feels like nobody is having a good time at all. There's something below the surface, or just beyond the perimeter of the lens, which you can *almost* see. It's like dipping bare feet into warm water and feeling the cold, slimy movement of a passing eel. Something's wrong here. It's in the girls' enlarged pupils and their sloppy, stumbling movements.

Time passes and the party goes on. Sarah feels unbearably uncomfortable watching, and she's obviously not the only one. Beside her, Maggie is peering out from between splayed fingers like a kid at a horror film. Looking back, Sarah sees that Brett is biting at his thumbnail and even Benishek, the star of the show, has a hollow, haunted expression on his rapidly bruising face. In front of him is the knife block that Brett, thankfully, never got a chance to utilise. Sarah's gaze lingers on it for a second or two, lying there on its side with four assorted handles emerging from it like toppled birthday candles.

Behind Benishek, sitting on the bottom step, Linda is silently crying. Sarah knows why. If this onscreen really *is* The Game, then what's Alyssa, Linda's own teenage daughter, being made to do right now? What's Hannah being made to do? Sarah's stomach rolls.

Onscreen, Benishek is the embodiment of grotesque sleaze. But there's no law against sleaze. Is there? The women don't appear to be kidnapped.

Then again, Sarah reminds herself, *you don't need a rope to hold somebody hostage.*

'Turn it off,' Maggie says. 'We've seen enough.'

'No,' Linda replies. 'Brett, skip ahead a while. Twenty minutes.'

Brett, once again, does as he's told. When the footage recommences, Benishek is holding the wrist of a tattooed and incredibly striking woman of Asian heritage. She has neon pink hair with a close undercut, and when Benishek asks her to give the camera a twirl, presenting her as if he's one of those seedy, old-fashioned pageant hosts, she almost trips over herself. Laughing at her instability, he says, '*Let's show your sponsor what his donation has bought him!*'

Sarah can only watch as, without warning, Benishek whips the woman's leggings down to her ankles. He immediately begins to jeer. The camera turns, revealing his face in close-up, his tongue pushed out in an exaggerated retching, and when it wheels back around it's focused directly on the girl's confused attempt to shield her panties, and the menstrual blood that has run onto her inner thighs.

Sarah feels herself being torn in two. One half is desperately trying to calm her rising blood pressure, fearful of succumbing to uncontrollable violence like the others, while her other half wants to snatch up the golf club and get to work on the joints Brett missed. 'OK,' she hears herself say. 'Maggie's right. Turn this filth off.'

Brett ignores her. He's looking to Linda, waiting on the alpha, and when the alpha says nothing the film keeps rolling.

'*Due to technical errors*,' Benishek of the past says through the speakers, '*we're going to have to go to our runner-up … And wouldn't you know it, it's Lucky Number Seven!*'

'Did you hear me, Brett?' Sarah asks. 'Turn it off!'

'*Player Seven,*' Benishek goes on, '*with a bid of four thousand euros from our regular, Mr Neil B-Four Me in Greater Manchester, England!*'

Everything. Stops.

Sarah forgets how to breathe as she turns slowly back around to face the show.

Onscreen, the winning player is being brought forwards. Benishek asks, '*What's your name and where are you from, baby?*'

Something about these words triggers Maggie to jump up out of her seat and practically scream, 'That's enough!'

The way she's standing, casting her silhouette over the white rolldown screen, the film projects over her entire body. It almost looks as if Maggie is in the film.

A voice slurs through the speakers. '*My name is … Glitch Valentine.*'

A gross. Dirty. Chuckle. '*Are you going to be our valentine, Glitch?*'

Maggie moves for the projector, freeing up the light's path to the screen, revealing a girl with cobalt-blue hair and a white T-shirt that says PWN ME. She doesn't look eighteen. And, of course, that's because she was never really eighteen at all.

They say blood freezes, and Sarah feels it happen. It's the girl's face. From somewhere in the recent whirlwind of her life, Sarah knows that face. She saw it only hours ago. She saw it in a photograph.

'No,' she hears herself heave. 'No.'

Onscreen, the girl is helped out of her T-shirt, and Sarah turns to face the back of the room.

That's where she sees Linda, holding one of Benishek's kitchen knives to her own throat, tears rolling down the blade.

'Yes,' Linda says. 'Yes. It's my daughter.'

62

PLAYER FIVE

'Alyssa! Come down here! You won't believe what just happened!'

Linda went to pour herself a glass of wine – white, since in the last hour she'd shattered her first bottle of red over a thief at the local shop – and noticed that the sink was empty of dishes. This worried her. It seemed as if Alyssa was eating less at the minute, and had been for a while. In Linda's motherly opinion, the girl was just one missed meal away from a disorder.

'Alyssa? Have you eaten today?'

No response. Linda told herself it was probably the headphones – Alyssa was always wearing that headset, always playing her games – but as she climbed the stairs, she couldn't shake the feeling that something was wrong here. Almost … frightening.

'Alyssa?'

By the time she threw open her daughter's bedroom door, a little harder than she meant to, and flicked on the ceiling light, the first teeth of panic had bitten.

Alyssa wasn't there. Her phone was.

There was also an envelope containing a short letter, hand-written in Alyssa's usual comic book block capitals. Linda read it twice before phoning her ex-husband.

Half-awake, a quarter attentive: 'Linda?'

'Richard, please tell me Alyssa's at your house.'

She wasn't.

*

Hadn't Linda's own subconscious been recording changes in her daughter's behaviour for weeks now? The loss of appetite. The uncharacteristic quietness from her room. The streaming, which was her daughter's life, and which always made the house sound so full, had all but silenced.

'Since when?' Richard asked later that night. He was driving with Linda in the backseat of his Audi. Becky, his thirty-year-old girlfriend, had come along too. She was sitting in the passenger seat with a look on her face that said she was worried, that she was a part of the family too, that she had a right to be there. 'I don't understand. Why would she stop doing her streaming?'

'I don't know,' Linda replied defensively. 'She went to that convention … That was late July or early August, and she hasn't really been into it since then.'

'What convention?'

Linda squinched her eyes closed. 'I told you this, Richard. It was for her games. London. She went with her friends.'

'Which friends? Have you met them?'

'You know how they are nowadays, they're all online. America. Australia.'

388

'Linda?' This is Becky, whose phone is lighting up the front-left portion of the car's interior.

'What?'

'When did Alyssa delete her social media?'

*

Before morning, Linda had Facebook messaged every one of Alyssa's friends she could remember from nursery through to college. She did it sitting on her daughter's bed, a place from which she would one day compose a very different series of messages for strangers, messages that were simple and authoritative, in a future she would at that moment have never been able to dream of.

She glanced around the room, fighting exhaustion. Alyssa's bedroom didn't look much like Linda's had at seventeen. Alyssa was, in so many ways, still a child. There were figurines, some she recognised as Pokémon, as well as posters of other bizarre Japanese cartoon characters. There was the stuffed dragon she'd adored as a child. The headset for when she was recording, and the enormous armchair she sat in to use it.

'So, these people just watch you play the game?' Linda had asked when helping her erect that chair. 'They don't actually play the game. They just watch *you* play. And they pay you money to do it.'

'Yes, Mum.'

Linda lifted the chair's back onto its seat, speaking around an Allen key that hung out from her mouth like a cigarette. 'And you don't ... I mean, if these people are sending you money ... you aren't ... You know, taking off your clothes, or ...'

389

'Jesus, Mum, I am *not* having this conversation with you.'

'Well, you've got to be careful, because there are a lot of weird people out there on the internet. Trust me, I've seen things—'

'Mum, please. I don't need a lecture from a woman who started using dial-up in her forties.'

That must have been one of the last times she'd had her natural hair colour.

The computer was gone now. Linda had personally handed Alyssa's devices directly to Sally Maitland's team of forensic analysts; they were the best Linda had worked with. Digital forensics usually took weeks. They'd be able to study everything from search history to app usage. Nothing digital was ever truly deleted.

After sending her messages, Linda went out again. She never slept that night.

She checked parks. She trudged through woodlands and wastelands and all the awful, secret places she knew from her police days. The places Richard would never think, or want, to search.

Sometime after the sun had risen, Linda returned home to see if Alyssa had come back yet. The house was as empty and agonising as she'd left it. She brushed her teeth in a daze.

When the police officer knocked at her front door, she almost fainted.

It was Chris Hudson, the constable who'd attended the robbery at the shop the previous night.

'It's not about her,' he blurted as soon as the door was opened. 'I'm sorry, Ma'am, but I'm not here about your girl. I haven't heard any news. Can I come in?'

'I need to get back out there,' she said, impatiently showing him through to the living room. 'I'm assuming every officer in Luton knows by now.'

'Every officer in Luton is out looking for her, I can tell you that much. I don't think there's one who wasn't back in the parade room by midnight, paid or unpaid. We don't forget, Ma'am.'

She nodded, turning her face away. 'Is that why you're here? To pass on your best?'

'No. I hate to do this to you now, considering, but ... It's the suspect from the robbery. He went into a coma overnight. They're trying to save one of his eyes, but chances are he'll lose both. The glass went deep.'

Linda collapsed onto her sofa. 'Alyssa is missing, Hudson. Why in God's name would you—'

She shut up fast and got straight back onto her feet. Her phone was ringing. Sally from forensics.

'Tell me you found something. Please. Anything.'

Sally's voice sounded dull, nothing like Linda had ever heard in the duration of their working together. 'Your daughter's gone to serious efforts to delete a lot of content, Linda. She's tried to wipe everything. And I mean *everything*.'

'Why?'

A terrible, lingering quiet. 'We're going to need you to come in. There's a ... video. Online. It could be significant.'

Linda could hear her own heart now. She fished in her pocket and took out the letter her daughter had left behind. With the phone against her ear, she read through it once more.

It didn't take thirty years of policing to recognise it for what it was.

It was an ending. It was a last. It was a note.

YOU'LL LEARN THINGS ABOUT ME.
UNFORGIVEABLE THINGS.
THINGS THAT WILL CHANGE YOUR OPINION OF ME
FOREVER.
I'M SORRY FOR THE DAMAGE THEY'LL CAUSE.
I'M SORRY FOR EVERYTHING.

UNDERSTAND THAT I NEVER WANTED TO WIN,
BECAUSE WINNING MEANT LOSING EVERYTHING.
FOR ONCE, I JUST WANTED A CHANCE TO PLAY.

63

ALYSSA

Her suicide is twofold. She dies in two halves.

Glitch goes first. She's already half-dead by then anyway; finished, cancelled, inboxed with hate from suicide-baiters across the world. Murdered.

Everything Alyssa has worked towards, everything earned, exists in Valentine's accounts. Her followers. Her feeds. Her entire life history. It's all in lines of code, and then, with the click of a button, it simply isn't. It's as if she never existed, and of course she never did.

Except for the video. The video remains, the ghost she leaves behind.

Alyssa Malone goes second.

She does it in the water. Ever since the boat, the water has been calling.

Water baptises. Water cleans.

She sits on the edge of a bridge and binds her feet tightly, then her wrists, pulling at the knot with her teeth. It's evening, and her final breath is a cold one.

She's falling when the panic comes. It's not a big enough drop to scream.

As she swallows dirty water, and the water swallows her, she begins to struggle, kicking her legs and wanting nothing except to live.

But the knots are strong, and this final regret, this ultimate terror, is something she takes with her, a secret her mother will forever suspect, but no one will ever know for sure.

64

PLAYER ONE

'Anyone moves,' Linda says, 'I'll push this blade through my jugular and your loved ones will be dead in twenty minutes. Try to hold onto that thought before you make any rash decisions.'

The flesh of Linda's throat looks very soft, but she hardly needs to emphasise her threat; Maggie is too winded to do anything close to rash. She feels as if she's been punched in her chest. 'You did this?'

Linda's eyes are still reflecting images from the projector screen, and hideous grunting sounds continue through the speakers.

'Mute the footage but leave it running,' she tells Brett. 'I'll move because I wouldn't want you to miss anything. Unfortunately, I already know how it ends.' She gets up and walks very slowly across the room, still holding the blade steady, and settles on the floorboards with her back to the screen, facing the others, low enough to keep from being blinded by the projector. With her free hand she takes out her burner and places it on the floor in front of her crossed legs. Above and behind her, the rape of her daughter continues in monstrous high definition. Brett mercifully silences the audio.

'We've seen enough,' Maggie mutters.

'No,' Linda says coldly. 'You haven't. You people won't turn a blind eye to this anymore.'

'Alyssa,' Sarah utters in a low voice. 'Where is she, really?'

'Drowned. Fourteen months ago. I have photographs from when they dragged her out of the water, if you'd like to see them. Not pleasant, but I look at them from time to time. They've given me the strength I needed to do this. And I had to do this. Because you took her from me. You're all culpable.'

'No,' Maggie says. 'That's not true.'

'No?' Linda shows her teeth. 'How long did your pay off last, Maggie? How about you, Brett?'

'Pay off?' Sarah says quietly. 'I don't understand.'

'Six years ago,' Linda says, 'a civil suit was filed against Benishek by five women who'd been coerced to appear in his films. What their attorney needed was two key witnesses. One was the editor of Benishek's early work, the other a former high school student. With their testimonies, the class-action would've led to a federal indictment for sex trafficking by force, fraud and coercion, and producing child pornography of a sixteen-year-old girl. Paul Benishek would be nearly halfway through his custodial sentence by now, and my daughter would be at university.'

Maggie looks into Linda's eyes, searching through the frightening blackness for compassion within, finding none. 'I was eighteen years old when that suit came about. Living alone, scared out of my mind. You think I should've faced him across a courtroom? Had my sexual history torn apart by some defence attorney? I was isolated, full of self-blame, trying to get my life back on track.'

'But you took his money. You and Brett both did. His people came to you first and offered you cash. Five thousand each, and you didn't hesitate.'

'So that's what this is about?' Maggie says, feeling delirious. 'Victim blaming? Punishment?'

'Responsibility. Your actions have consequences, whether you're the witness too cowardly to stand up in court, or the part-time drug dealer who sells to pornographers and doesn't consider the consequences.'

'And me?' Sarah asks.

'I think you know by now.'

Sarah shakes her head slowly, running her hands through her hair. 'He said he lost it in stocks. Four thousand pounds. I believed him. Is that why you've taken my girl from me? Is that why you've brought me here? Because I was foolish enough to believe my husband?'

'Not exactly.' Linda looks momentarily awkward and apologetic; with a knife against her throat, it's a peculiar sight. 'If you want something doing right, do it yourself. This is what happens when you're forced to hire the dregs of society. Rely on timers and set up automated messages. It's a mess. Your phone contract is under your husband's name, I suppose?'

'My contract? What does that have to do with ...' Sarah falls quiet. She closes her eyes. 'Oh no.'

Maggie catches up, and she feels close to hysterics. 'You bugged the wrong phone, didn't you? Blackmailed the wrong spouse. It was supposed to be her husband all along.'

'It wasn't *supposed* to be like this at all,' Linda admits, more to herself than the room. 'The lesson was simple. You people didn't act on your responsibilities, and because of that

I lost the one I loved most in the world. Tonight, you had to act or else you'd lose the one *you* loved most. It was a chance to right your wrongs.'

At the back of the room, Brett is mumbling. 'Have to act. Right our wrongs ...'

'There was only ever supposed to be one winner,' Linda goes on. 'Whoever took this opportunity to ensure that this could never happen again, whoever ended this, would be free to go, and the rest ... you'd learn what it means to lose everything.' She sighs, looking utterly exhausted, and for a horrible second Maggie thinks she might simply pass out onto the blade. 'But you weren't what I expected. You're just ... people.'

'Yes,' Sarah says softly, coming back to the conversation. 'And you need help. I know loss. I've been there, and the brain gets sick very easily. We're fragile creatures. If I'd had somebody to blame for all the loss, then maybe I would've been the same. If *this*' – she gestures to the screen in disgust – 'had happened to my child, then I'd want the world to pay too. But can't you see how irrational it is? How can you honour your daughter's memory by killing my baby girl? Even if there is blame in this room, our sons, daughters and fiancées don't deserve this. It has to end.'

'It can't,' Linda replies. 'Not yet.'

'Why?' Maggie asks. 'Why did this have to happen now? Why tonight?'

'The night Alyssa ...' Linda takes a long, slow breath. 'The night she passed, I intervened in a robbery. Right place, right time; that's what I would've said then, anyway. The thief had a knife, and I hurt him. Hurt him a lot. He spent a year in a coma, only to die two months ago. Bad luck. In three weeks,

I'll be in court for manslaughter, and I'll be sent down. It's inevitable, and I can't allow that to happen. Paul Benishek, meanwhile, is working on his terminal bucket list. He left his legal troubles in the States, and he keeps a video diary online, charting his adventures. He doesn't deserve to die fulfilled. So I used police forums to find the sorts of people who could find you. Some of it was easy. Most of it wasn't. I needed to get here, to get on his Wi-Fi, and who better to help me than the people responsible. *This*' – she's referring to the film behind her – 'can never be deleted, there are copies all over the internet, but Benishek's online world can be razed. All I have to do is use my phone, and the same malware that brought you here will erase any device connected to this network, and any online accounts ever accessed through it. A pornographic empire will crumble in minutes.'

'Excuse me.' This, to everybody's surprise, is Paul himself. 'It wasn't just me, OK? It's a fucking business. One billion people consume internet porn every day. That's a fifth of the planet! If it wasn't me, it'd be somebody else. It's just a job, that's all. Supply and demand.'

Maggie shivers. Supply and demand. Maggie was looking to sell, and the Taylors were looking to buy. She gets up off the sofa slowly and crouches in front of Benishek so that he can get a good look at her.

'You really don't recognise me, do you?'

He stares at her, the cock on the projector reflected in his eyes, and says nothing.

For once, even the delirious giggles won't come to her. She is momentarily speechless. 'You're unreal,' she manages. 'Have you been listening? You fucking raped me. Nine years ago, on camera, in a Minneapolis hotel room. I was sixteen years old. You manipulated me, you fucked me, and then you uploaded the video online. You ruined my life! You raped me, you piece of shit, and you don't even remember!'

Brett, meanwhile, has recommenced his unnerving muttering. 'Only one winner … There can only be one winner … Right our wrongs …'

Benishek shakes his head, at a total loss, but he never apologises.

Maggie turns back to Linda. 'And you think I'm to blame? I lost my family. My home. My education. He raped me, I was left pregnant and alone, and you think I need a lesson in responsibility? What the fuck is wrong with you? The mistakes I made were exactly the same as your daughter's, but you're punishing me for it?'

'Wait …' Benishek wheezes. 'Wait …'

He's frowning now, thinking hard, and when his eyes suddenly widen, Maggie sees something that will haunt her for the rest of her life.

The man has Jackson's eyes.

He opens his mouth to speak, but whether he remembers her or not, she never finds out.

Because before he manages a word, Brett buries the entire blade of a kitchen knife into Benishek's right ear.

65

PLAYER TWO

They scream. Everybody but Benishek. The noise is high drill-ing mayhem that nearly makes Brett want to skewer his own damned ear.

The blade went in straight enough, but it doesn't want to come back out. At first, it's stuck tight, clenched in brain, and then it reluctantly looses into Brett's hand with a sound like shucking oysters. Benishek starts convulsing, face slack, his entire body rattling as he hangs from his wrists. He reminds Brett of a marionette. A puppet on a string.

There's a lot of fluid inside a man. This is something Brett learns over the next minute or so. When it's finally done, he turns to the rest of the players.

Sarah has slid down off the couch onto the floor and she's doubled over – no surprise there – with her entire head cra-dled as if for an emergency landing. Maggie is on her knees near Noah's body to Brett's right, hands flat on her cheeks in a parody of Munch's *The Scream*. Linda is watching from between the two of them, an expression on her face that is both shaken and sadly satisfied.

Towering over them all, Brett whispers, 'I did it,' and then shrieks, '*I did it!*'

'You did it,' Linda agrees. 'You did what I couldn't.'

He places his empty hand over his own mouth, considering what this means.

'I win.' A wave of elation – of *winner's elation* – crashes over Brett, the lifelong loser. He stamps one foot, splashing Benishek's blood, and fist pumps the air. 'I'm the winner! There can be only one, and I'm the fucking *Highlander*!'

Linda says nothing.

Still surfing his winning wave, Brett aims the wet knife at Linda. 'You'll let him go? Craig. Let him go now!'

She only fixes him with that same infuriating solemnness, sitting on the floor like she's some high and mighty monk in a stab-proof vest. 'I can't do that.'

The wave breaks, dropping him a mile. 'What?'

'I can't do it. I'm sorry, I really am, but Craig is—'

'You'll do it.' Distantly, he can feel his own face folding into an insane grimace of fury. His knees pull him towards her in a lunge, but halfway there the crazy bitch pushes her own knife a little way into her neck, bringing forth a trickle of blood, and Brett has no choice but to halt.

'Think about what you're doing,' Linda says. 'Sit down and listen to what I have to say, and then you'll get the winnings you deserve.'

'*No!* No more talking! No more bullshit! Let Craig go!'

She shakes her head again, gallingly calm. 'I can't.'

He brings his face down to his own knees, the image of Benishek's writhing body burned into his eyes, and screeches. Then he staggers to his left and snatches Sarah, the whining

402

one, by her hair from behind. He knows he has made the right choice too, by the wonderful reaction on Linda's face. The bitch is afraid.

'Let's try again,' Brett says. 'You can either let Craig go right now, or I'll kill both of these cunts starting with your favourite. You want another couple of deaths for your daughter's legacy? A baby boy with no sister *and* no mummy tomorrow morning, and it's all precious Alyssa's fault?'

Sarah is shaking in his grip, so he tugs her hair harder.

'Don't do this,' Linda says. 'Just let her go, and—'

'No! No more games! You can cut your own throat, Linda, but you can go to hell knowing what you did!' He reaches around Sarah from behind, lining the blade up over her chest, and looks Linda in the eyes. 'This is on you!'

Almost serenely, Sarah says one more thing –

'It's OK. Just let her go, Linda. Please. Just let her g—'

– as Brett swings the blade down towards the centre of her chest.

66

PLAYER THREE

Sarah closes her eyes, and the last thing she thinks, before the blood showers over her face, is that she loves her kids. All of them. The ones who lived. And the ones who didn't.

They're waiting for her somewhere, small children now. Sam's children. She's finally going to hold them.

The blood is hot. There's no pain, only a sense of an explosion that leaves her ears ringing, then a change in pressure as Brett relaxes his grip. She looks to her chest, expecting to see the handle of the knife, but there's nothing there. She turns her face to the right and, instead, sees something her brain takes a moment to decipher.

Noah is on his knees. He's alive. Awake. And aiming a revolver at a place slightly behind Sarah's head. He squeezes off another shot, and another. By the third, Sarah is mostly deaf in her right ear.

Brett collapses somewhere on her left, and she doesn't need to look to know he's sporting three new breathing holes. The room is full of blue smoke. Maggie, who had been beside Noah, is covering her ears. Linda is still sitting upright beneath the projector screen, watching this French revenant warily.

He pushes himself up and wavers on the spot for a moment, holding the gun by his side. His eyes are black holes in a face painted with blood. 'It was you,' he says.

'Yes,' Linda replies.

He nods. Coughs. 'Sofia?'

Linda considers him carefully. Then, with the hand that isn't holding the knife, now slackly, against her own throat, she picks up her phone. Her eyes leave Noah only to type in short bursts. When she's done, she places the phone back onto the floor.

They stare at one another in silence. There's a vibration inside Noah's pocket. He reaches in, takes out his phone, looks at it.

'Congratulations,' Linda says. 'You saved a life. Sofia will be released, unharmed, outside your apartment building in fifteen minutes. You have my word.'

'Your word,' he mutters. He pockets his phone and lifts the revolver. Sarah can only watch in stunned terror as he aims it at Linda's head and thumbs back the hammer. Then his eyes flicker up to the projector screen, where the party in hell is still ongoing. He lowers the revolver.

There's an overturned coat stand by the door. The three women watch as Noah helps himself to thermals, gloves and one of those earflap hats. Then he takes the goose-down duvet from the sofa, dragging it along the ground behind him. On his way, he spots the satchel of Benishek's secret cash on the kitchen floor and, naturally, takes that too. He opens the front door and walks out the cottage without looking back. It's the last Sarah ever sees of him.

Maggie dazedly sniffs at the smoke on the air, her face a portrait of shock, and says quietly, 'I love that smell.' Then she walks over to the projector and yanks out the hard drive, finally cutting off *The Game* and showing an empty finder window on the screen. 'Is that it?' she asks, turning back to Linda. 'Is it over?'

Blood is still trickling from Linda's neck. When she drops her knife onto the floorboards, she looks exhausted. 'I suppose it is.'

'Then by all means,' Maggie says, 'if it's not too much bother, can you let our children go?'

Linda picks up her phone, types something in, and this time there is a text on Maggie's burner. She drops onto the sofa, slumping back, and sighs.

Sarah's throat is painfully dry. 'Now me,' she says. 'Now Hannah. Let her—'

From her left, a choking sound.

Brett.

Sarah turns to face him, stomach roiling, and waits for the blessed grey-out, but it doesn't come. She focuses on his staring eyes, ignoring the rest. His glasses have blown off his face, and this isn't surprising because there's a piece of his skull missing somewhere above. The other two bullets are in his chest. This much she knows.

'I need ... to see him.' His voice sounds like a puncture. 'I need ... see ... before ...'

Sarah can't help but feel sympathy for him, and she turns to Linda. 'Can't you ...?'

Linda shakes her head. 'I can't.'

Brett gags. 'Wh ... Why?'

'Why not?' Sarah asks. 'It's over.'

Linda sniffs, adopting her police voice. 'Around twenty-four hours ago now, Craig Wilson managed to escape his confines. He killed one of his captors, which may bring some comfort to you.'

Brett makes a horrible sound; it may be a laugh, or at least a smile. 'Thas ... Creg.'

'Unfortunately, he was found in the lobby of his building by his other captor. I don't know exactly what happened next. I can only suppose that the man was unhappy about his partner, because he put a bullet through the back of your friend's head and was arrested within minutes. I had instructed them not to take Craig's life ... But that's what you get when you hire druggies.'

Sarah gapes, unbelieving, at Linda.

'L ... Liar.'

'No, Brett. I'm not lying. Craig was dead, and your game was over, before you ever touched down in England.'

Brett grasps out blindly, finding Sarah and pulling her towards him without strength. He croaks as if imparting some great secret, what might legally be known as his dying declaration, in her left ear. 'I ... only ... ever ... loved him.'

Then his hands drop away, and he falls still forever.

Sarah shakes her head, frowning. 'Why? Why did you have to tell him that? Why be so cruel?'

'Somebody had to go ...' Linda holds up her phone. 'Would you have preferred it to be Hannah?'

Sarah stares at the phone hungrily, hypnotised, and feels sweat on her cheeks. 'Send the message. Please.'

Linda nods, somehow satisfied, and begins to type with her thumbs. Only a couple of seconds in, however, she stops. Her face comes up slowly, eyes darkening.

'Is that what I think it is?' She looks hard at Sarah, then Maggie, and moves decisively back to Sarah. 'It was you, wasn't it?'

Sarah opens her mouth to tell her she doesn't know what she's talking about ... but all that comes out is an empty cracked sound. Because she has heard it too. It just took her a moment longer because her right ear is still ringing so badly.

There's a helicopter over the building. A helicopter, and it's getting lower. Sarah throws herself onto her feet and looks over the kitchen area, out through the bifolds at the far end of the cottage. The water is no longer black; it's strobing blue. The sirens reflected on the loch are silent, but they are surrounding the cottage.

There's no sense of relief. Terror seizes Sarah's belly.

Wasn't she clear that Hannah's life is on the line? That the police should only show themselves once this is over?

Once this is over.

And now they are here.

Either Hannah has been found alive.

Or Hannah has been found dead.

'How did you do it, Sarah?' Linda asks with a tone of motherly disappointment.

'Service station,' she breathes, wheeling around. 'Linda, please. Is she ...? You know, don't you? Is she ...?'

Linda clicks her tongue. 'Cheating, Sarah. And I thought so much better of you.'

Sarah glances back, heart racing. There are men beyond the bifolds now. A dozen men with automatic weapons. Back to Linda, who is typing something on her phone. She hits return, drops the phone and sighs. Her eyes go to the kitchen knife on the floorboards.

'Sod it,' she says, then picks up the blade and plunges it into her own throat.

'*No!*' Sarah flies through the air, arms outstretched, and catches Linda by the neck. She presses her hands firmly against the wound. Blood is gushing through her fingers, but she barely notices. '*No! No! No!*'

Over her shoulder, Maggie is screaming for help.

'*Don't you dare die!*' Sarah yells in Linda's face, her palms slipping in blood. '*Is she alive or dead? Tell me! Give me a sign! Is Hannah alive or dead?*'

She's still asking this when the bifolds shatter and the officers flood the building.

She's still asking when the phones vibrate, and every device connected to Benishek's Wi-Fi, every account he has ever owned, and every piece of hardware connected to The Game are wiped clean forever.

67

PLAYER FOUR

Noah sees the flashing lights from almost a mile away. The low cliff face above the cottage must be covered in vehicles.

He stops to watch those lights for a moment, as he had watched the fireworks every Bastille Day as a poor, grubby child, and then he continues to heave the oars through that bottomless abyss. The boat pulls him further and further away from the cottage, breaking apart sheets of thin ice on the water.

The tarpaulin that was covering the rowboat is now wrapped around him, yet another layer around the duvet. His head is throbbing, the pain radiating from the top of his skull down through his neck, but he is alive. He's alive, and Sofia is free. She's out there somewhere, confused and afraid.

Maybe she'll go into their shitty apartment, looking for him. He'd give anything to be there waiting for her, starfished on the bed they share and touching every wall at once. More likely she will be with the police, and that's the right place to be.

He whispers into the night, 'Stay safe, *mon amour*. Wherever you are, I will find you.'

His burner phone vibrates then, and it takes him a few

seconds to dig it out through his layers. He gets one last look at the light on the screen, and then it goes out forever. He tries to turn it back on and nothing happens. If he is to call Sofia, or anybody else for that matter, then it will not be from this phone. He scrubs every part of it with Benishek's gloves, then drops it overboard. He does the same with the revolver. Whatever happens next in his life will have to happen without the gun.

Time passes. The oars squeal. The boat creaks. The water softly sloshes. He considers taking the yacht, but he wouldn't know how to get it moving. Perhaps Maggie would have, but he is alone in the tiny rowboat.

His breath still plumes upwards to join the occasional snowflake, but the temperature's not so bad in his nest of fabrics, and the tarpaulin keeps any splashing water away. The effort of rowing generates warmth, and the layers are keeping it in. What concerns him more is the amount of battery power he has left. He wonders if he could row all the way to France. It'd probably be some kind of record for mankind, even if he wasn't setting off exhausted and almost mortally wounded. For now, he will just keep rowing and see where it takes him. There is a case of money at his feet, and that's a start.

He looks around. It's so empty. Like floating through outer space. On any other night of his life this might have frightened him. Now it's a relief.

He doesn't know what will happen when the police catch up to him. In a best-case scenario, he'll be kept in a migrant camp, unable to contact the outside world, until his identity is confirmed. Either that or he'll end up in a British prison, and is there really any difference between the two?

While he rows, he dreams of his perfect wedding. Sofia is

there, and she is smiling. All of the rest, the whole universe around her, is unimportant. The venue, the false grandeur, the lies he has told and the image he tries to project … None of those things seem important anymore.

He'll do anything for her, and he'll do anything to keep her safe.

Anything.

Even if that means letting her go. Whatever she wants to feel secure. Whatever she needs to be happy.

The helicopter has landed on the distant shore now. A few minutes later it takes off again, and it races away through the night.

To a hospital? A jail cell? Noah can only wonder.

Whoever's left will probably warn the police about him. He hopes they don't. They know what he wants – just a fighting chance to get back to Sofia – but will they break the law to give it to him? He isn't sure. He has realised that there is a gulf between what people deserve and what they actually get, and the gulf is vast.

If Maggie, Sarah or Linda alert the police to Noah's escape, then boats will apprehend him before he ever makes it out of this loch.

All he can do is keep rowing. Stay warm. And wait to see if the survivors turn him in.

Wait to see if the sirens advance. If the police come for him tonight.

They never do.

POSTGAME

POSTGAME

68

MAGGIE DAWSON

It's early evening on Jackson's ninth birthday. Orange sunlight pours in through a window that's newer than every other pane in her apartment.

The room is mostly empty now. The bed gone.

Maggie pauses in the doorway, as she so often does when she walks in here, and for a beat she sees the scene from that morning. Then she blinks and the image is gone. She crosses the room. Double-checks the lock on the window. Lowers the shade.

She sold his bed on Craigslist. She couldn't bear to look at it perpetually empty. For now, there are boxes against the skirting boards, but she's thinking of turning this room into a sort of study space. An office, like the one she visited in her sister's house the only time she ever went there. She could use a desk, because she has enrolled in adult diploma classes at the Hubbs Centre for Lifelong Learning in Saint Paul. She's trying to earn her GED, or General Equivalency Development certificate, a diploma for high school dropouts. She'd like to be a counsellor; isn't that a real side-splitter? Either way, the classes keep her busy between shifts at Taco Bell and waiting for the lawyer to call.

It's all going to end up in a courtroom. That, she thinks, is pretty ironic, although she's never been certain on the definition of irony. She often wonders, usually at night, how many lives could've been saved if she'd only gone to court in the first place. But she isn't to blame for what happened. It took the worst horror of her life for her to realise what she had been all along: she was a victim, but she's stronger than she ever thought possible.

The legal case is *endless*. The lawyer tells her that she could, at the very least, be facing a felony charge for passport fraud, which carries up to a decade in prison and a $250,000 fine. The outcome will depend on whether it can be proved she was acting under duress. Proving that is a case involving multiple bureaucracies on both sides of the Atlantic, and it could take years for any prosecutor to track down witnesses spread out across the States, the United Kingdom, France and Monaco. The silver Mercedes alone, which had been discovered abandoned in the car park of that Yorkshire inn, had turned out to have connections to an organised crime syndicate involved in some ongoing investigation into people smuggling. Maggie had drawn a genuine blank on that one. She can only assume that it was a part of Noah's tale, but she's never told the investigators Noah's name, and she doesn't think Sarah has either. Linda's final act – uploading the virus that had corrupted every branch of Benishek's online businesses – had probably added at least another two years' worth of issues for the prosecution. All Maggie can do for now is try to live in the present and get on with her life; it's all a person ever can do.

She feels more serious though. When she looks in the mirror, she sees somebody older staring back at her. She's paler, but it has nothing to do with physical pigments. These feelings do soften. They did once before, the last time her life was derailed, and she thinks they will again. It just takes time. Clichéd but true.

Would time have cured Linda Malone if she'd simply waited a few years? Maybe not.

Maybe something like that never really leaves you. It only ferments. Festers. Poisons.

She feels sorry for Linda. Even after everything that happened, she feels sorry for her. The world can be cruel, and its cruelty is usually pointless. Maggie thought she'd learned all about that when she was sixteen years old, but this lesson was even harsher.

She feels sorry for Brett too. She thinks about how quickly, under the right stresses, a life can spiral out of control. How fast it can end. When the five of them had been sitting in that strange parlour, Brett had introduced himself and invited them to look him up on Facebook. Later, weeks after she'd seen his head blown apart, Maggie did just that. His account was still there, a museum exhibit of a life stopped. He'd asked for recommendations for a good Chinese takeaway. He'd uploaded photographs of meals in restaurants. Just before he died, he'd posted from a hockey game at Madison Square Garden. He'd had a girlfriend. Pretty woman. Another person for Maggie's midnight sympathies.

And, of course, there's Sarah Mulligan. As much as Maggie loves Jackson, the fact is she'd had a baby without trying. Sarah, on the other hand, had lost child after child after child.

Where's the sense in what happened to her? The pain of such things must be unbearable.

Maggie misses Jackson though. She thinks about him every day. The life she created, and the life she saved. The boy she gave away.

The visits are over. The courts see Maggie as a danger to Jackson, and she doesn't have much room to argue. Her lawyer thinks this will be overturned when the case is over, but that won't make much difference. What the courts don't enforce, the Taylors surely will. At least Maggie trusts them with Jackson. She did when she handed him over nine years ago tonight, and she still does now. They're the parents he deserves.

Will he be forever scarred? Will he remember everything that happened? His memories will be bad, but hopefully nothing like Maggie's. She doesn't know what it means for his future. In just another nine years he will be an adult, old enough to make up his own mind about how much he wants Maggie in his life.

Maggie is on her way to bed, running through these same old exhausting thoughts, when she gets the text message from Caroline. It isn't long, but it takes her a while to read.

The birthday boy. He's sleeping better. Happier every day. Kids are resilient. He misses you. Understands what you did for him. So do I. Be safe Mags.

Maggie flops onto the edge of her bed, staring at the message in disbelief, and she begins to cry. There's a photograph attached. The sense of déjà vu makes her shiver. She moves her thumb to download the image … and hesitates.

It has been three months since she last saw Jackson. Only three months, but children grow quickly. He probably looks more like him now. The dead man hanging from the banister.

This thought stays her thumbs. Will Jackson grow to be like him? Nature versus nurture.

Will the boy have the face of the man who raped his mother?

The man Maggie helped to murder.

She does open the picture, and all she sees is her own son, blowing out nine candles.

She smiles, smudges a tear from one cheek, and kisses the screen.

'Happy birthday, little man.'

Because she'll always love him.

69

SARAH MULLIGAN

She's seated on the sofa, waiting for Neil to arrive home from work.

The house is immaculate, and she doesn't like the way that feels. She misses the smell of dog in the carpets. She misses the dog a lot, especially now that she takes longer walks. She has lost sixteen pounds, and her legs are getting stronger; you never know when you'll need to run; never know when you might have to be strong.

Also, she misses the chaos. The sense of a full home. A family. She pines for the way things were and the things she has lost.

She doesn't miss the bingo though. Unsurprisingly, her taste for games has diminished.

She runs a hand through her hair and checks the time. It's almost half past five. Not long now. He'll be on his way, and this afternoon she'll face him down. Three months have passed in a heartbeat, and she finds it harder and harder to look him in the eye.

He hadn't meant to hurt anybody. About that she's sure. He'd broken down when he'd found out what had happened to Linda Malone's only daughter, and Sarah believes that his guilt was, and still is, genuine. He's a father, after all. He's just a man.

Glitch Valentine, as Neil would have known her, was a streamer who'd caught his eye months before the horror at Monaco. Some men, he'd clumsily tried to explain to Sarah, like to have a drink and ring up the old-fashioned sex lines. Neil – whom Sarah's mother had always called a *proper bloke*, unlike the last one – got his kicks from watching young women dress up as Japanese cartoon characters or play computer games. It sounds funnier than it is. Sarah will never understand why, just as she'll never understand what compelled him to spend hundreds of pounds every month – behind her back – on paid subscriptions to these girls' softcore social media feeds.

But she understands that everybody has their own vices and addictions. Everybody has their secrets.

When Neil heard about *The Game*, he must've thought he'd died and gone to camgirl heaven. Benishek's livestream probably promised the exclusive that nobody else could: the biggest upcoming streamers and influencers in the world, willing to bare it all to the highest bidders. Social media meets smut; the clash of the internet titans. Or maybe that wasn't quite right. Not in the beginning. Perhaps Benishek really had wanted to move into more legitimate social media, to be the man who created the next big thing, but when the day was hot and the drugs were flowing, he'd gone back to what he knew best. He'd given his fans what they wanted. Supply and demand, as he'd said.

As far as Neil had been concerned, most likely sitting there with his laptop open and his dick in his hand, Miss Valentine had just been another consenting adult along for the ride. His excitement had got the better of him.

Sarah has since wondered how many people – not just men but women too – have failed in what Linda once called the *basic duty to protect another*; how many choose to stay ignorant to the impact of their own vices; how many consume pornography without questioning the ethics, or choose not to see the look of discomfort in the actor's eye; how many sell drugs on the side, or indulge in an occasional dabble without considering the lives destroyed. The problem, Sarah has discovered, is that these questions stem from a philosophical black hole that's hellbent on swallowing every hour of her sleep. Once it starts, where does it stop? Is your average voter responsible if the government sells arms used on Yemen infants? Is your choice of coffee the cause of a bloodbath in Colombia?

Is your husband culpable for the rape of a teenage girl?

Supply and demand.

Neil has changed since finding out about Alyssa, that much is true. He has changed since the day Hannah was taken from them. But no matter how much he changes, that doesn't alter the way Sarah feels about him. She can't help it. When he's in bed beside her, they're miles apart. They haven't had sex since it happened, and she knows – or, at least, she believes in her heart – that they probably never will again. When she thinks about him climbing on top of her, it's a projector screen she sees in her mind, and a girl with cobalt-blue hair.

This is why she's leaving him.

This isn't the first day she has sat here, waiting to have the conversation. It isn't even the first time this week. She has been practising for months.

Today, though, is the day.

The media circus has finally blown over, and she has her bingo winnings withdrawn. She will have to rent, and the money will help to keep her on her feet for the first few months, but she will eventually have to find a job. The thought of that makes her incredibly anxious, but it's just another problem she'll have to face down when she reaches it.

Of course, leaving creates the issue of custody.

To leave is to take Neil's fatherhood away from him, or at least diminish it.

To leave, Sarah thinks, would be to kidnap from her husband.

Whatever Neil has done, he's a good father. Better than Sarah's had been. Can she take that away from him, even for five nights out of every week? And what about those other nights when he has custody, and she's alone, unable to check on her children, unable to hold?

And if Neil fights for full custody, what then? Sarah had, after all, been gambling in a bathroom when Duke had been killed. She'd been unconscious when Hannah was stolen. She could lose custody altogether, and is that a risk she's willing to take?

She hears his van coming to a stop outside the front gate.

Stay or go. She has to decide. Stay or go.

She sits up a little straighter, moving carefully because her children are sleeping against her. Archie on her left. Hannah, the first miracle, on her right.

She looks down at her daughter, strokes the red curls behind her tiny ear.

What do you dream about? What will you remember?

The key turns, and the front door opens. Stay or go.

It's now or never …

Only, that isn't really true.

If she doesn't do it today, she knows there's always tomorrow.

70

LINDA MALONE

Everyone who grieves must flirt – at least once, even if they aren't thinking in these exact terms – with the idea of parallel dimensions. The theory that a branch of reality exists for every decision, a plane of existence for each choice made and its outcomes. For all its science fiction claptrap, it must be an idea as old as human consciousness, a fantasy begat from regret, fear of irrevocable consequences, and the concept of *if only*.

If only, instead of erasing the evidence, Brett Palmer had chosen to report his concerns over Benishek's tapes to the police; if only he'd testified in court.

If only Alyssa Malone had decided to delete her ill-fated invitation.

If only Paul Benishek had opted to drive home after some long ago night on the town and been burned alive in his overturned vehicle; if only his mother had chosen the abortion.

One choice, one outcome, one reality. That's all a person gets.

Revenge may go some way towards balancing the books,

but it doesn't alter the fact that, in the end, it could never be changed, and there's still one person left for her to blame. One player her game could never fix.

If only I'd been there when my daughter needed me most.

This was why Linda had decided to end her own life at the climax of her game.

If only it had worked.

*

'Eleven o'clock, Malone. Time for exercise.'

Lukasz, the enormous orderly, makes this same joke every day before rolling her down to physical therapy in her wheelchair. Along the way, voices blabber and jeer at her from behind closed doors. She hates it.

Afterwards, when Linda has managed the exhausting feat of wiggling one big toe in an hour, Lukasz parks her up in her usual spot by the caged windows in the Blue Room. They've called it the Blue Room, she's been told, since it was painted a relaxing shade of cornflower in the eighties; it's all white now, but the name remains.

'What today?' Lukasz asks her. 'Chicken or tomato?'

'*Chi … ck—*' She winces, instinctively bringing a hand up to the latest dressing around her neck, then chooses the A4 whiteboard off her lap instead. There's a red drywipe marker attached to the board, which she uses to draw a rudimentary bird's skull: O>

Lukasz raises his eyebrows and cups one massive mitt around his ear. 'Let me hear.'

Linda glares up at him. He smiles patiently. Every day they

go through this. It makes her want to try ripping the staples out of her neck. Again.

She closes her eyes, fighting pain and humiliation, and croaks, '*Ch ... kin.*'

'Good choice.'

He leaves her alone by the windows, and that's all right; the rest of the women in the Blue Room keep to themselves. They're incapable of posing much of a threat to anybody anymore. Linda watches them stare into empty space. Watches them gape back at whatever horrors brought them here.

If only their lives had been kinder. If only their choices had been better.

If only they hadn't been caught.

If only, if only, if only.

While Lukasz is off fetching soup, the woman Linda has been waiting for is wheeled into the room in her own chair. Linda knows this woman, despite never having met her in the real world. It took her a few weeks to recognise the face because the face has grown so gaunt, its features permanently catatonic. The woman's name is Primrose Madison; it's not the easiest name to forget, though it's her crime Linda remembers best from her own tenure with Bedfordshire Police.

Twelve years ago, there'd been a nationwide hunt for the young Primrose Madison, a former student of the illustrious Wilkes Girls School in nearby Oxford and a suspect in the killing of a former tutor. Except, killing is an understatement. As the police closed in and her capture was imminent, Madison uploaded a now infamous post online describing years of systematic abuse at the hands of the Wilkes staff. She named them all. Nine of them in total. Then she hanged herself.

She survived, medically speaking, but by the time the officers cut her down, her brain had been starved of enough oxygen to leave her speechless, and she'd suffered a complete cervical spinal cord injury. Those teachers never even went to trial.

If only.

Linda scrubs out the bird's head on her whiteboard and, in honour of Primrose Madison, doodles simple gallows as if she's playing hangman.

The doctors tell Linda she's lucky to be moving her arms at all. They tell her she's lucky to be alive.

She wipes off the gallows and writes *GOOD LUCK* then alters it to *BAD LUCK*.

This becomes *WIN* then *LOSE*.

Primrose Madison, drooling in her chair. If only she'd died. Linda can empathise.

She's still planning on ending her own life just as soon as she gets the chance. She doesn't believe in heaven or hell, so she doesn't expect to see Alyssa again, but she knows she doesn't want to stay on this planet without her. She'll probably be ashes by her own trial. Hopefully. Until then, she'll just have to find a way to get through this nightmare. A way to pass the time.

Still staring at Primrose Madison, she begins to think of that teacher, the one whose balls Primrose fed to his own terriers. There were eight more names on that list. Men and women. The list will still be online somewhere, of course. Nothing digital is ever truly deleted. Once unleashed, it can't be taken back. The internet is irrevocable.

It's only when Linda hears the faint squeaking of her marker pen that she realises she has been writing. There are three words scrawled in red across the surface of the whiteboard.

MAKE THEM PAY

Linda stares at these words for a moment, frowning. It's only when she makes a slight adjustment, adding one long vertical line straight through the sentence, that she feels something unfolding across her own face. It hurts at first, pulling at the wound below her chin, but it's not entirely unpleasant. It's a smile.

She wheels herself forwards a couple of feet, until she's perfectly aligned with Primrose Madison's vacant stare, and holds the whiteboard up for her to see. She holds it like a scorecard.

Whether Primrose acknowledges the message or not, Linda isn't sure. It doesn't matter anyway; it's just a game to pass the time.

MAKE THEM P|AY

GAME OVER

ONE PLACE. MANY STORIES

Bold, innovative and
empowering publishing.

FOLLOW US ON:

@HQStories